THEIR VIRGIN HOSTAGE

THEIR VIRGIN HOSTAGE
Masters of Ménage, Book 5
Shayla Black and Lexi Blake

Published by Shayla Black and Lexi Blake

Edited by Chloe Vale and Shayla Black
Print ISBN: 978-1-939673-02-2

THEIR VIRGIN HOSTAGE

Masters of Ménage
Book 5

Shayla Black and Lexi Blake

Bonus material and excerpts at the conclusion of this book.

Chapter One

Kinley Kohl looked at herself in her custom Pnina Tornai white wedding dress with its sweetheart neckline and lacy, glittery bodice…and she wanted something more. More emotion. More excitement. Just more. But she didn't know what.

Her dress was gorgeous. The elegant hotel, all decorated in wedding regalia, looked stunning. No doubt, her groom-to-be had dressed impeccably for the occasion. The sky above Manhattan was a cloudless, perfect blue. Five hundred of the country's wealthiest and most influential people waited to see her walk down the aisle in the Plaza's grand ballroom. It was a dream wedding, but the encroaching panic made it feel more like her nightmare.

Was it too late to run screaming down Fifth Avenue?

"Are you sure you want to wear that dress?" Becks asked, standing behind her and eyeing her critically.

Kinley sighed. It was a good thing her father hadn't remarried and brought a wicked stepmother into her life. She hardly needed a hypercritical parent when she had her sister. "What's wrong with it?"

There was always something wrong, according to Beckin Kohl Abernathy. Admittedly, her sister was one of the most prominent fashion plates in New York. Society looked to Becks for style advice, while those same women, along with the tabloids, mostly called Kinley unpleasantly plump.

"Oh, don't get me wrong, hon. The dress is fabulous." Becks gave her a little half hug, careful not to crush or ruffle her perfectly coiffed platinum hair. It was longer in the front than the back and had an asymmetry that accentuated her high cheekbones and drew attention to her well-glossed lips.

"It just seems a little…snug." Becks gave a delicate wince. "Did you and Greg decide to start your family early?"

Kinley turned on her sister, feeling her face flush with humiliation. "I'm not pregnant."

In fact, what Becks suggested was impossible. She and Greg had never shared a bed. Actually, Kinley had never had sex with anyone. And now, she was about to become a virgin sacrifice to help the family she loved. Of course, it would be easier to feel good about this whole choice if her sister wasn't quite so judgmental.

"Well, I guess stress eating with such a big wedding is understandable." Becks sent her a tight smile of sympathy. "But unadvisable. Don't frown. I'm only saying that for your own good. The press is already unkind to you."

Tears filled Kinley's eyes. She had eaten only protein shakes, brown rice, and fish for three weeks. She'd lost thirteen pounds so she could fit perfectly into this dress. She thought it had worked…until now. "I want to be alone, Becks."

Her sister sighed, brushing imaginary lint from the sleek gray sheath she'd selected for the bridesmaids. Kinley had wanted a soft pink, but Becks had insisted that her choice was much more elegant. Her older sister had a way of getting what she wanted.

"I didn't mean to upset you on your wedding day when I know you're already nervous. I'm sorry, Kinley. I'm being a bitch. Don't mind me. I'm sure Greg will think you look lovely."

But now she couldn't look at herself and not see the slight curve of her stomach that no amount of dieting ever eradicated. She wasn't a size six. Hell, she wasn't even a ten. The dress had been custom made because it didn't come in her size. She sniffled a little.

"Don't cry, Kin." Becks grabbed a tissue and handed it to

her. "This is your wedding day, and you're marrying the richest guy we know. What could you possibly have to cry about?"

"I don't love him." There she'd said it. She was shocked everyone hadn't guessed. Her father kind of knew, but he was ignoring it. Becks couldn't possibly think she loved Greg. They had nothing in common, but each had something the other needed.

Becks rolled her eyes and crossed the room to reach for the champagne sitting by her bouquet. "Is that all? No woman I know loves her husband, at least no one in our world."

That stunned Kinley. She'd always wondered, but… "Not even you?"

"Please…" With a surprisingly unladylike snort, her sister rolled her eyes. "After Brian and I got married, I tossed out my birth control. The key to my future was in spitting out a couple of kids and tying him up legally. Even if he starts thinking with his pecker and tries to trade me in for a younger model, he's going to pay handsomely for the privilege."

"Becks, how could you think like that?" Children weren't to be used for a payday.

Then Kinley started imagining her own children. Panic engulfed her again. She couldn't imagine being pregnant by Greg. She couldn't even imagine sleeping with him, like married people were supposed to do. And by sleeping, she was sure that Greg expected something more active than snoring.

Kinley gulped back her nerves. He was good-looking, but she wasn't attracted. Did that make any sense? How could she have babies with someone she had no interest in touching intimately?

Becks gave her a dazzling grin. "It was hell for a few years, but the nanny certainly helped. My personal trainer whipped my body back into shape, and it was bye-bye pregnancy pounds. Then when the kids turned six, I shipped them off to boarding school. Now, life is grand again. My two angels are practically my retirement fund." She chuckled. "If

Brian wants a divorce, he'll have to pay through the nose before he sees his kids again. That's how I've kept my hand wrapped firmly around his balls. Oh, his dick probably runs around on me, but as long as I have his testicles, he's not going anywhere. You should take a page out of my book."

"No." That parody of marriage wasn't at all what Kinley had in mind. Shouldn't "'til death do us part" be about commitment and devotion? "That's you, Becks. Mom loved Dad."

Kinley wished her mother were still here. Mom would never have allowed either of her daughters to marry someone they couldn't give their hearts to. Her father was a wonderful man, but...he was weak. Though the situation wasn't entirely his fault, he'd put her in a position that basically forced her to marry Greg. If she didn't, they would all be ruined.

"Not in the beginning," Becks said. "You have this silly, white-lace ideal of their marriage, but Daddy married Mom because Granddaddy told him that if he didn't, Daddy was getting cut off. Aunt Mayrene gave me the whole story. Daddy ran off to become an artist and ran right back three weeks later and proposed. He liked the art part, but apparently he didn't love the starving."

"Neil and Sharon Landry are in love." They were the sweetest couple she knew. They sent out the loveliest Christmas cards with all four of their kids dressed in red sweaters while Neil and Sharon held up mistletoe and kissed. She'd looked at that last card and wondered if she would ever be so in love.

"He's fucking his barely legal nurse, Kins," Becks said, wrinkling her nose. "How did you not hear about that? It's all over town. And for a highly respected obstetrician, I've heard he's rough on that girl's vagina, if you know what I mean. You would think since he's got his hands shoved up them all day that he would be a little more tender."

But Neil and Sharon had looked so happy. Blinking mutely, Kinley gaped at her sister, trying to process this ugly underside to marriage. "That's horrible."

Becks held her glass of champagne up in an ironic toast. "That's life, sister. The love thing is for people without money. Two nobodies without a cent to rub between them are perfectly free to fall in love and get married and have a cluster of children because nothing is at stake."

Kinley turned slowly because her dress was still a teensy bit tight and grabbed her phone like a comfort object. "Hello, Ms. Hypocrite. I'm a nobody without any money now. Or have you forgotten?"

Their father had lost everything in a Ponzi scheme. For two hundred years, the Kohls had acquired money, property, and political power. Her father had lost it all in the blink of an eye. Then he'd gotten sick, and the need for money had become critical.

"No, you are not." Becks wagged a finger at her. "You're an heiress. You inherited a majestic and vastly respected name that's valuable to a man like Greg. Because of you, the doors to every old-money house on the East Coast will be open to him."

Her name was all she had, and she was basically selling it. "I don't have to do this. I could get a job."

"Doing what? You have a degree in art history."

It had seemed like a good idea at the time, but then she'd never thought she would need an actual job. "I could work for a nonprofit. I've run our charities ever since Mom died."

And now that money was running out rapidly. The economy had gone south, and demand for assistance among the poor had grown. Greg said he'd endow the charity her mother had started with fifty million dollars after their honeymoon. He'd already started making business connections for her, including several manufacturers willing to donate clothes for the organization at cost. He had also instituted some changes in the way the charity ran that he swore would make them more efficient so she could get more aid to the people who needed it. And he was willing to pay for her father's medical treatment and support her whole family. All she had to do was marry him and become his smiling hostess.

Fifty million dollars bought a lot of clothes and coats for inner-city and rural kids. People were counting on her, and all this wanting "more" and pining for love was hopelessly selfish.

"It's a sweet thought," Becks said. "But working at a nonprofit wouldn't pay enough. This is the only way. I'd help if I could, but since I'm already married, walking down the aisle with a really rich, handsome guy falls to you. Poor Kins." She winked. "Brian's business does okay, and you know I'll kick in what I can, but…times are tough all around. You understand, don't you?"

Becks had a point. Kinley just didn't like it. She sighed and forced herself to face reality. "Sure."

"Good. For a minute there, I thought you were going to be unreasonable." Becks sipped her champagne. "Are you waiting on a call?"

She glanced down at her phone again, just like she did every couple of minutes. "No. It's just habit."

Becks's eyebrow rose. "Really? Who's Michael?"

Someone I've been wishing I could talk to all morning.

"He's a business contact." Becks didn't have to say anything. Kinley felt herself withering under her sister's judgmental stare. "I'm telling the truth. I've never even met the man. How do you know his name?"

"Because I saw it on your phone earlier. He's sent you a lot of texts. And he's either called you or you've called him at least once a day for the last week. This sounds like more than business. How do you think it would make Greg feel to know his fiancée is consorting with another man?"

"You spied on me?"

"I'm your sister. When, in all of the years you've known me, have I ever respected things like privacy? It's a sister's right to snoop." She grinned. "So are you fucking him?"

"No! Like I said, I've never actually met him. He's

starting a charity on the West Coast. He contacted me for some advice, and we started talking. He's a nice guy. That's it."

No way was she going to admit that she thought about Mike from California way too much. And yes, she'd been looking down at her phone, hoping he would call. Hearing his voice had become something she looked forward to everyday because it made her smile. God, she was pathetic.

Becks shook her head. "Don't screw up the chance to be rich again for some guy you've never met. You know how much Daddy is depending on you."

And that was why she still stood here instead of giving into the impulse to fly out to California and meet Mike. Everyone was counting on her. She couldn't abandon the future she had planned for a man she'd only known a week. Mike seemed wonderfully down-to-earth, and Kinley enjoyed talking to him—but that had to be it. Somehow, she had to stop hearing his gravelly, rough-and-tumble voice in her dreams. Heck, she didn't even know what the man looked like, but she got a little giddy every time he called. Mike always put her at ease. With him, she felt interesting—and oddly cared for. Their relationship didn't mean anything and it was fleeting. Once his charity was up and running, she would have no more reason to talk to him.

She wasn't looking forward to that day.

"I know. I'm not screwing anything up."

"Well, that's good to hear. Keep it that way."

A knock sounded on the door adjoining her suite with the one next door.

Becks ignored it. "I'm going to call the caterers and make sure the cake is ready. Is that all your luggage? It needs to be ready since you're not coming back here after the ceremony."

"Yes. I've got it." Kinley made her way across the suite in her heavy wedding gown and opened the adjoining door.

Her best friend Annabelle, who had stayed next door last night, walked in—or tried. She was wearing the sheath Becks had selected, too. While the gray looked lovely against her café au lait skin, unfortunately Annabelle possessed curves like Kinley's. The dress didn't camouflage a thing.

"Hi. How are you holding up?" Her friend's pretty round face, framed by dark curls, softened with an encouraging smile.

"Hey. I'm..." *Having really cold feet and wishing my sister would shut the hell up.* "Fine." Kinley forced herself to grin back.

No sense in dragging Belle into her misery. Besides, her friend would only pounce on it.

Kinley glanced back at the Louis Vuitton vintage luggage that had been a gift from her fiancé. It was beautiful, and she'd gasped and teared up a little when he'd first given her the two trunks, two roller bags, and a brand new oversized shoulder bag that had a name, the Metis. She'd liked the jeans and blouses he'd sent along with them, although it wasn't what she normally wore. Someone with an ass her size didn't need to draw attention to it with a bunch of bling all over the back pockets. But her trunks and cases were all packed up and lined in a row. The Metis had a little stowaway in it, too.

"Yes, everything's packed and ready to go," Kinley answered dutifully. She'd spent an enormous amount of time packing. Greg had left her a list and then there was Gigi to think about. Gigi had a very sensitive stomach. She wasn't about to hope a tropical island had the food her dog was used to. If Gigi missed a meal, the world knew it.

"And you're taking everything Greg asked about?" Becks asked with a frown. "You don't want to disappoint him on your honeymoon."

Her husband-to-be had given her a list of essentials that he expected her to pack. "I've got everything. I'm a good girl."

"Yes, you are. Ta-ta, sister." With a jaunty little wave, Becks slipped out and closed the door behind her.

"You know I call her Skeletor behind her back," Belle said with a grimace.

Repugnance shone in her dark eyes, hidden behind

chunky librarian glasses. She tucked back a strand of her raven black hair. "I would say it to her face, but I tend to avert my stare. I've heard some Medusa-like stories about looking into your sister's eyes."

"You are so bad, Belle." She held her hands out, and Belle took them immediately. Becks might be her sister by blood, but Belle was the sister of her heart. Since they'd been little girls, Belle had stood beside her. Even though Kinley's family had been Belle's mother's employer, class hadn't meant anything to either one of them.

"She's the mean one, Kinley. You're just too good to see it." She stood back and shook her head. "You look so beautiful. If your mama could see you now, she would have cried."

Kinley had really needed to hear that today. "Thank you. I have to admit, I'm going to be really happy when this whole wedding thing is all over."

"I would be happier if we left and headed for Vegas right now. Come on. Let's *Thelma & Louise* this sucker."

"And drive off the side of the Grand Canyon?" The thought horrified Kinley.

"It would be better than marrying Greg Jansen. Before you do this, I really wish you would just meet with the private investigator—"

"No! I'm getting married in less than an hour. Don't bring this up again. I'm marrying Greg." She had to.

Belle sighed. "Has Mike called lately?"

She should never have told Belle about him. "He's just a work peer. Sort of."

"You talked to him for three hours one night, and I doubt it was all about tax exempt status and donation channels. I think you like him."

She did. "But that's no reason to call off the wedding, Belle. Come on…"

Her rapport with Mike had started out all business with a few calls. She'd talked about how her mom had set up Hope

House and what it had meant to her to help her mother with a cause so meaningful. Before long, Mike told her about his military service and his desire to start a charity with his brothers for wounded soldiers and their families. After a couple of talks that strayed more into the personal, she'd begun looking forward to hearing his voice over the line.

One night she'd spent three hours on the phone with him, rapt and fascinated. He'd admitted that he wasn't married or even dating now because what he really wanted was a woman to share with his brothers.

Kinley had been shocked. And utterly intrigued.

And she couldn't even think about this again. She had to marry Greg. Her father's chemo bills were stacking up, and he didn't need the added stress of wondering where the money was going to come from. He was so embarrassed by his weakness and distressed about it all that he wouldn't even allow her to go with him to his therapy sessions. And with her charity about to go belly up, Kinley needed the money, too. She couldn't allow years of her mother's good work to end.

So she had to sacrifice and do what thousands of women had done before her. She had to keep her chin up and make the best of things. "I love Greg."

She couldn't tell Belle that she was basically prostituting herself. Besides, if she said it enough, maybe she could make it true. Kinley was a great believer in affirmations. If that didn't work…maybe Becks was right, and no one was really happy in marriage. Maybe all a woman could do was put on a smile the same way she affixed her makeup.

"Sure you do." Belle rolled her eyes, then looked around the room. "Where's Gigi?"

Her little Yorkie baby had shown her deep disdain for the proceedings by crawling into Kinley's Louis Vuitton bag and settling down for a nap. Gigi had taken an almost instant dislike to Greg and everyone on his side of the wedding party. At first, Kinley had thought it would be fun to include her little dog in the ceremony, but Gigi had refused to go anywhere near her fiancé. "She's asleep. She had a rough night."

"Yes, she did. She growled at Greg all through the rehearsal dinner. Your dog is very smart."

Kinley wanted to cry. She was utterly and completely alone, and arguing with her best friend in the world sent her into a tailspin. "I wish you could accept that Greg is going to be a part of my life."

Belle leaned in. "Are you doing this because you need a man? I can get you one. If you're not interested in California Mike, I can find you the hottest man who will rock your world. Then you will forget you ever heard the name Greg Jansen. As a matter of fact, I could find you two or three amazing guys. I could get them here really fast, too."

She wondered what Mike and his brothers looked like and wished she could see them just once and indulge in a moment of fantasy before she had to face reality again.

Kinley turned back to the mirror because she couldn't stand to look at Belle when she was lying through her teeth. "I only want Greg."

Two or three hot guys might light up her world for a night, but all her responsibilities would still be waiting the next day. She just had to accept that sexual desire wasn't in the cards for her.

"Kinley, I don't understand. When we were kids and we were planning out our weddings, I ask you to describe your groom. Do you remember that?"

"I remember that you wanted to marry Leonardo DiCaprio." They had watched *Titanic* about a hundred times that year and she'd cried every single time. What would have happened to Rose and Jack if he'd lived? Would she have regretted leaving the money behind? Would Rose have been able to live with the ruin it would have brought her family?

Or would she have been happy to have lived with her soul mate?

There were tears in Belle's eyes as she forced Kinley to turn. "Yes, I was very picky back then. But you weren't. You only had one requirement. Do you remember?"

"I said it didn't matter how he looked or how much money he had as long as he was a good man." Which just showed how young she was. Naïve. God, she wanted to be that little girl again.

"Greg Jansen is not a good man, Kinley." She whispered the words as though they had some kind of power, as though she prayed they would make their way into Kinley's heart.

She couldn't let them in.

Kinley broke away and turned back to the mirror, forcing down the need to cry. She didn't want to lose Belle, but it looked like she might. "The feds cleared Greg of all charges. And I don't care about how good he is. He's going to be my husband. Have you seen all the gifts he's already given me?"

A long sigh came from Belle and her oldest friend hugged her from behind. "I'm not stupid." She put her head on Kinley's shoulder. "I wish I was more than a secretary so I could bail you out of this mess."

Relief swept over her. Maybe she didn't have to tell Belle a thing. "You understand?"

Her best friend's face softened. "I know you feel like you have to marry him. I think it's wrong and you deserve better."

"Then why are you here?" She sniffled a little. It would be horrible if Belle walked out.

Belle took her hand, giving it a hearty squeeze. "Because we made a promise. I will love you forever. You are my best friend and that will never change. I will forgive you for the stupid things you do and I will be there to help you hide the bodies. God, Kin, call me when you need to bury Greg. I will come with a shovel and a bottle of tequila."

She laughed a little but shook her head. Once she said "I do," she was in it for life. No matter what Becks or Belle said, Kinley was going to make her marriage work. Even if she worried that her husband was a major douchebag.

Belle peered closer at her. "You look pale. You're not eating, are you?"

"I had a light breakfast." Of course it was almost three o'clock now, and all she'd had today was a grapefruit. With a little bit of sugar, and she'd felt guilty about that.

"I speak Kinley so I know what that means. You had next to nothing. I'm calling room service." Belle moved toward the phone.

"Don't. I'm getting married in an hour. I can't eat."

"Eating is normal. You have to do it or you're going to pass out."

She did feel a little faint, but... "I will after the ceremony. It's just…Becks said the dress looks too tight. I don't want to be the fat bride."

"You're not. Becks planted that idea in your head because she's a heinous bitch. You're perfect the way you are. Seriously, you have a whole ceremony and pictures to get through. It could be hours before you get to eat again, so I'm going to make sure you do it now."

"Belle, I—"

"Damn it. I'm your best friend. I'm going to watch out for you." She picked up the phone. "Yes, we're in suite 2010. That's right the Presidential Suite. We need a couple of burgers."

"A salad." If she ate a burger, she would split her dress open. But a burger sounded so good. "No dressing."

Belle rolled her eyes. "A salad with grilled chicken and vinaigrette on the side. And a burger, medium with fries, and two Diet Cokes." She hung up. "I will get some of those fries down your throat." She stopped for a moment. "You know I love you, right?"

"I know." She counted on it. Sometimes the only thing in the world she could count on was Belle's friendship. "Please understand that we all have to do what we feel is best."

Her lips turned down in an almost sad expression. "That's true. I just need you to know that I want only the best for you."

Belle's cell trilled.

"You should answer that," Kinley said. Belle called

herself "just a secretary," but Kinley knew that she valued her job—and the three lawyers she worked for. She ran their office like clockwork and had for the last year.

"It's Kellan," Belle said apologetically. "I'm sorry. We're working on a big murder case. Do you mind? I'll probably have to run back to my room because my files are there."

"Go." She was glad Belle had a career she loved.

The door closed behind her best friend. Someday one of those three lawyers she worked for was going to wake up and see what a huge catch Belle was. She'd met Kellan, Eric, and Tate. They were gorgeous and smart, and any one of them would be a great husband for Belle.

Or all three.

Kinley let her head fall back. She had to let that notion go, but the idea of those three hot lawyers just played in her head. It wasn't that she thought they were right for her—they had their eyes on Belle—but the idea of being surrounded by strong men just did it for Kinley.

She loved her dad. She really did, but she'd watched her mom have to be the strong one all her life. Certainly, it wasn't wrong to wish for something more…

Was Greg capable of loving and protecting her? She worried about that…

Staring at the woman in the mirror, Kinley acknowledged that she was his entrée into old-money society, a second chance for Greg Jansen. His first wife had been a model. Carrie Anthony had been beautiful and successful. As far as Kinley could tell, she'd become a star. Then mental illness had tragically cut her life short.

Two months after their marriage, she'd killed herself.

But Kinley wasn't that girl. She was strong. She didn't run away from her responsibilities. Once she said "I do," she would be there forever.

Kinley turned back to the mirror and straightened her dress. It was almost time to start the rest of her life. Nothing could save her from it now.

* * * *

Through the hidden cameras they'd planted in the suite the night before, Dominic Anthony stared at the blonde in the wedding dress on the screen. After a few minutes of surveillance, he knew that the gorgeous bride had a pretty heart-shaped face and a juicy hourglass figure. Too bad she was a money-grubbing whore.

"There. I think I fixed the audio. Is the sound in the suite back on?" Riley asked, looking up from his computer, already dressed in the black and white uniform of room service staff.

"I think so." Dom nodded.

"Good. Shitty that it crapped out through that whole conversation with her sister," Riley groused.

Dominic didn't care. He'd doubted they'd missed much. Everything was in place now. Years of planning was finally coming together. So why did he have a deep pit in his stomach, a feeling of gnawing anxiety as he listened.

"Oh, the audio is definitely working again. She's talking about how much she loves the creep." And Dominic couldn't stand it. Somehow hearing her say she loved a hardened criminal made his skin crawl.

He almost wished Riley wasn't so good at his job. To be honest, he'd enjoyed just watching the blonde. She was so freaking beautiful. Her seeming innocence made her look like a girl who would appreciate a man's—or men's—comfort and protection. But the second Riley had restored the sound, the words that had come out of the bride's mouth proved the image was all false.

I don't care about how good he is. He's going to be my husband. Have you seen all the gifts he's already given me?

And to think he'd mooned over her for even a second. He was a stupid ass. He'd seen Kinley Kohl's picture and half fallen in love with her sweet face and banging body on the spot. Blonde curls and caramel brown eyes, and that husky voice that went straight to his cock.

But she couldn't wait to jump into bed with Satan, so she was pretty much on the "no touch" list.

Still, he was going to do what he must in order to save her life. She wasn't going to die like his baby sister had. Greg Jansen was going to pay for his crimes—and Kinley Kohl was the key.

Law Anders stepped up and looked at the screen. He was wearing the same starched uniform as his brother. It was almost go time. "Does that mean she's stopped talking about how fat she is?"

"What?" Dominic scowled.

"Yeah, just before all that crap about loving Jansen." Law made gagging sounds. "I heard everything she said to both her sister and Annabelle. I don't get it. She's gorgeous. How can anyone think she's fat? I swear, my hand is itching."

Law liked to spank women, especially pretty women who mouthed off about how unattractive they were. Kinley Kohl was practically his perfect woman. Fuck, she was practically all of their perfect woman, if only her heart was half as sweet as her looks. But no. She was willing to marry a violent killer because he bought her some luggage.

"Focus, man," Dominic barked. "She's talked a lot about how much shit Jansen's bought her."

Law frowned, his eyes never leaving the screen. "I'm telling you, it's an act. She's scared. She needs us."

"You're insane, Law. Delusional."

He stared at his friend. Law Anders was supposed to be the surly one. He mostly communicated in growls and snarls, but ever since Dominic had put him on the surveillance of Kinley Kohl, he'd been all complete sentences and smiles. Oh, his lips didn't curl up much, and he looked a little like he was in pain, but for Law, that was a brilliant grin.

Riley stared at his older brother. "This isn't like you, Law. You know who she is."

So they'd had conversations. Dominic had wondered

about that. Riley and Law Anders were the closest thing he had to a family because he'd more or less grown up with the brothers.

He'd helped Riley get into Harvard and they'd attended the Ivy League institution together for a time. When patriotic duty had called, Dominic had gone off to the military. Law had joined up, too. Before it was all over, Law had taken an IED and lost function of his legs, so Dominic had left the service to come home and help the men he considered his brothers. Law was a tough son of a bitch. Even after the doctors had told him he would never walk again, he was up and running eighteen months later. Now Anthony Anders was one of the premier investigative firms in the country. They worked for law firms and police departments.

But this case was personal.

"She's the target," Dominic said in no uncertain terms. "She's the woman who's going to give us all the ammunition we need to finally prove what kind of a man Greg Jansen is."

The kind willing to kill a woman for money, Dominic thought in a rage. Even a woman as sweet as his sister.

The time had come to avenge Carrie by beating Jansen at his own game. And Kinley Kohl was his sledgehammer. He had everything he needed with the singular exception of a witness. After today, problem solved. He'd do whatever it took to make Kinley spill everything she knew until she practically sang. What he didn't need was Law falling in lust with her.

Even though it would be a really easy thing to do.

"You guys haven't been watching and talking to her the way I have." Law's eyes never left the screen. "She has little tells. She smiles a little too brightly when she's lying."

"She has different smiles?" Riley asked with a frown.

"Yep," Law replied. "And she's using her fake smile now. Watch the difference between the one she uses on our little Benedict Arnold and her sister."

"Hey, she's trying to help Kinley." Dominic wasn't going to let Law throw Annabelle Wright under the bus. She was a hell of a woman, choosing to do something brave and save her friend's life. "If Annabelle hadn't agreed to intervene, do you really think Kinley would have come back from her honeymoon alive?"

"I'm not saying we should let her marry the fucker," Law replied. "I just wish you would let me talk to her instead of carrying through with this crazy plan. She's a smart woman. She'll listen."

Dominic seriously doubted that. "Like she's been listening to Annabelle all this time? She's a socialite who takes lunches and goes to charity balls. How fucking intellectual can she be?"

"She's raised millions of dollars for the homeless. And those lunches she takes are usually about her charity."

He hated to burst Law's bubble because the guy so rarely had a positive outlook on anything, but he had to do it. "Her charity is on the brink of ruin."

"Because of her father." Law could also be a little like a pit bull with a nice hunk of meat when he decided something. He never fucking let go.

But Dominic needed Law on his side. "Her gambling father who's run the whole family into the ground. Yeah, and she just keeps feeding him money. She's giving him funds earmarked for warm coats and shoes for poor children. She's probably hoarding some herself for shopping sprees."

"You've got her all wrong." Law's jaw squared, and Dominic just knew he wasn't going to like what his best friend was about to say. "I think she's the one for us."

"Fuck." Riley put a hand to his head, shaking it as though he couldn't believe what his brother had just said.

Dominic felt his blood pressure tick up. "Are you fucking crazy?"

Law held out his hands in defense. "Just listen to me. She's not what you think she is. I don't know why she's marrying him."

"For his money," Dominic shot back.

Law ran a frustrated hand on top of the dark stubble of his buzz cut. "Yeah, but the money isn't for her. I think she's trying to save her family. You should know something about that."

"I never spread my legs to save my sister." What he didn't say was that he would have. He would have done anything to save Carrie. "This isn't the same thing at all. She's marrying for money because her father gambled everything away. You are willfully misjudging her because you want to fuck her. Do I need to take you off this case? You're either with me or against me, brother."

He wasn't sure what he would do without Law. Riley was the computer genius, but Law was really smart muscle. He'd come to rely on the man's instincts, his training, his sheer tenacity. His friendship.

But he owed it to Carrie to succeed. He couldn't allow Law's obvious attraction to Kinley Kohl to stand in the way of justice.

He could still hear his sister's whispers on his voice mail.

Dom, I need to talk to you as soon as possible. Please call me back. It's all going wrong. I'm leaving Greg. I think he's...I have to go. He's here. Call me.

He'd been off with Riley and Law, screwing some brunette he'd met at a bar while his sister was being murdered.

Law's face cleared, becoming a polite blank. "Of course not. I know how much this means to you. I'll do whatever it takes."

He turned away from the monitors, all excitement gone. Law was a predator again, cold and unfeeling. Exactly what Dominic needed. So why did he feel like he'd just taken something precious from his friend?

Riley leaned in. "He's fine, man. We're both here for you. She's just his type, that's all."

Pretty, blonde, and stacked was just about every man's type, but he'd never seen Law react so fiercely to a woman. What had he learned about her that Dominic hadn't?

It didn't matter. Getting her isolated and making her talk did.

"We've got movement. Annabelle just rang for room service. That's our cue. She'll make sure Kinley is alone in that suite for the next fifteen minutes." Riley turned back to him. "Who's ready to roofie a blonde? This guy. Come on, Law, you can stare at her boobs up close."

Law sent his brother his happy middle finger. "Let's get this done."

Dominic put a hand on Law's shoulder. "We're not going to hurt her. We're saving her." She might not thank him for it, but… "You know that."

Law nodded, but Dominic wasn't convinced. "Sure. We need to go. See you at the extraction point."

Sometimes Law sounded like he was still in the military. He and Riley walked out.

Dominic turned back to the screen. Kinley was a gorgeous woman, and he had a wistful, fleeting thought that it would have been nice if she had been the one woman who could love all three of them. The woman who could become the center of their world.

She turned, her face so sad, so beautiful that he nearly reached out and touched the screen.

He growled a little as he turned away and started wiping the room clean. He didn't have time for bullshit. He had a killer to catch.

And a hostage to nab.

Chapter Two

"I deserve to find happiness." Kinley forced herself to take a deep breath as she paced the floor in her white, four-inch Manolo Blahniks. "Greg will be my happiness and my joy."

The room responded with an echo of utter silence. Yeah, no one believed that, not even the walls.

Was this how she would spend the rest of her life? Would she wake every morning and try to convince herself that she was happy and fulfilled? Since she was a kid, she and Annabelle had a ritual before big events like Christmas, birthdays, and big dates. They would get together and hold hands and wish out loud for their dreams to come true.

Tears threatened as she remembered the last time they had done it. It had been at her mother's bedside. Annabelle had flown home from Chicago. She'd beaten Becks to the hospital, despite the fact that her sister lived only a few miles away at the time. It was a silly ritual, a daydream between young girls. It hadn't saved her mother's life, and it wasn't going to work today. But when Annabelle had taken her hand, she'd wanted so desperately to believe that magic could work.

Kinley sighed at herself. Wishing for happiness and joy and love was futile now. It was time to grow up.

A brisk knock on the door startled her out of her thoughts. "Room service."

That was quick. Still, how could she possibly eat now? She could barely move in this dress. All these sad thoughts were killing her appetite… But it would be rude to send the food away when Annabelle had gone to the trouble of ordering it.

She made her way across the suite. It was very likely a long way here from the kitchens.

Tip. He would want a tip. Oh, she hoped she had some cash.

Why hadn't Annabelle come back? Must be a long phone call with Kellan.

Kinley opened the door, ready to graciously thank the worker, accept the food, and send him away. But the sight that greeted her stunned her mute.

The two most gorgeous men she'd ever laid eyes on stood in the hallway, a large cart between them. Something was off about that cart, but she couldn't stop staring at the men long enough to figure it out.

Tall, with broad shoulders ready to burst out of their white jackets. The one closest to her had to be six and a half feet tall. He had a military cut of pitch-black hair and the most arresting blue eyes she'd ever seen. She wouldn't really describe his face as beautiful. He was far too masculine for that. There was something savage about him that belied his formal tuxedo-like uniform.

"Miss Kohl? May we come in?" Though the words were spoken more like a growl and a rumble, they were so very polite.

And for some insane reason, that voice felt like a caress to her skin. He could make love to a woman with that voice—and if she wasn't about to walk down the aisle to meet Greg, she'd probably let him.

"Yeah." Her own words came out in a breathy little puff. She forced herself to look at Hottie Number Two.

He was an inch shorter than big brother—and there was no question they were brothers. It was in the set of their eyes and the identical coloring, but after that, they differed. The shorter one looked slightly younger, as though the world hadn't weighed him down as heavily as his brother. There was the beginning of a truly gorgeous smile on his face.

"Miss? It's hard for us to move into your room when you're standing in the doorway." Hottie Number Two couldn't help but laugh a little. "You don't want your food to get cold, do you?"

How could anything possibly get cold when they were around? She actually felt a stifling heat. Except for her feet. Her feet were ice cold—at least metaphorically. Not only did she not want to meet Greg at the end of the aisle, but she'd rather find herself in between these two men in a totally inappropriate position.

She flushed and stepped back, allowing them into the room. Her runaway thoughts were all Annabelle's fault. She joked about being in love with three guys and refusing to choose. She'd told Kinley that she would have them all or they simply wouldn't have her.

She'd been joking, surely. But Belle had planted an interesting notion in Kinley's head…

"Where do you want it, sweetheart?" Hottie Two asked.

She could think of several places that she wanted it, each more inappropriate than the last. But that probably wasn't what they meant. Even so, Kinley got totally flustered because all she could think about was the man's lips. They were full and sensual, and she couldn't help but wonder how he would kiss.

"The tray. I meant the tray." Those lips were curved up in a knowing smile.

Embarrassment flooded her. If they could read her thoughts, she'd die. "By the window, please."

She needed to pull her damn self together and stop being an idiot. And her heels were already killing her. She stepped gingerly around the couch and reached for her purse. She pulled out a ten.

"This light must be bothering you." Hottie One was standing at the windows. The view was spectacular, but he made quick work of the first set of blinds, closing them and blocking out the afternoon light.

"Not at all." She liked the view.

The man slid the second set of drapes closed. "I think you'll like it better if you know prying eyes can't see in."

"Prying eyes?" Kinley asked. "Why would anyone want to look at me?"

Hottie One turned and pinned her with his stare. He was so much more serious than his brother. She could tell it by the set of his mouth. This was a man who almost never found anything to smile about. "Because you're lovely."

Tears threatened. They perched right there, making the world watery. She wasn't lovely. She was too fat and her eyes were a muddy brown instead of Becks's spectacular green. Even though she was only twenty-five, her breasts probably sagged a little. Nothing about her face was remarkable.

But when the man told her she was lovely in that low rumble, she almost believed him.

Greg never said a thing about her beyond the fact that she would be a good business asset to him. He would never find her lovely.

"Are you all right, Miss Kohl?" Hottie Two asked, his expression graver than before.

Yes, she was rapidly making a complete fool of herself. She gave them her brightest smile, the one she used on the snootiest society ladies and men who thought she didn't have a brain in her head. "Of course. Here. Thank you so much."

She held out the ten-dollar bill. As she did, her stare fixed on the cart they'd pushed in. It was far larger than normal. At least twice as large and three times as tall. There were two silver trays on top, but no glasses and no silverware.

"Miss Kohl," the one with the unsmiling eyes began.

A little thrill of fear spiked up her spine. Something was wrong. "That's not a delivery tray."

What they had rolled in was made of canvas. She could see it plainly now.

"No. It's not," the second man agreed. He took a step toward her.

Kinley backed up. "That's a laundry hamper."

It was the industrial kind used in hotels. Why had they brought her food on a laundry hamper? Except there wasn't actually any food because that would have come with silverware and glassware, not two silver covers that she could now see weren't actually covering anything at all.

"Don't scream, sweetheart. We're not here to hurt you." The second man was inching his way toward her.

Holy crap! Then what were they going to do?

Kinley wasn't about to obey them. She opened her mouth and let out a long shout as she turned on her heels and sprinted for the door.

At least she meant to sprint for the door. Unfortunately, she tripped on the stupidly long train of her dress and fell to her knees. She scrambled, her heart pounding. *Get up!* She had to. Kinley had no idea what these men wanted, but she wasn't about to give it to them.

An arm wound around her waist, and she was pulled back against a hard body. She screamed again, but this time a hand clapped over her mouth.

Did they mean to rob her? Rape her? Kill her? God, was this really happening? Tears overflowed.

The first man, the really big one, stepped in front of her. "It's all right, Kinley. We're going to take care of you."

Yes. It looked like they were going to take care of her—by burying her somewhere or tying her feet to cinder blocks and dropping her in the ocean. She'd watched enough ID TV to know what came next.

She tried to sink her teeth into the hand that covered her mouth. He cursed, and she managed to gain a tiny bit of purchase, but otherwise, he held tight.

"She's fucking biting me, Law," he hissed.

A smile crept across the face of the one called Law. It looked rusty from disuse, but when he smiled, his eyes lit up. "Good for her, Ry. I told you she was stronger than you thought. Baby, you have to stop fighting us or I'll have to do something I'd rather not. I want to talk to you. I want to explain everything."

He wanted to explain how he was going to rape and murder her? She bit down harder. The arm around her waist tightened, but the hand never moved.

"Goddamn it, Law. She's about to take a fucking piece out of my hand. She's got two of the fingers I type with," he snarled. "Take her out or I will."

Law stepped up, and she noticed the needle he was carrying. Nothing scared her more than that. She stopped biting the hand over her mouth and tried to scramble away. She couldn't be unconscious. She couldn't be at their mercy.

Kinley kicked back, desperate to escape their hold.

The mass of muscle behind her didn't move an inch.

Law looked down at her, those blue eyes of his filled with some unnamed emotion. He reached out for her with an odd tenderness as he smoothed back her hair. "I will take care of you, baby."

She shook her head frantically, but that needle hit her arm anyway. It went right through her silk gown and sank into her flesh.

"Go to sleep now," he whispered.

Almost immediately, the world began to turn hazy, her vision fading from the periphery in. Her muscles went soft, her knees weakening. But she didn't hit the floor. Ry picked her up, lifting her into his arms as he started across the room.

"Gently," Law said as he pulled the top off the laundry cart and shoved it to the side. "I don't want to hurt her."

No matter how hard Kinley tried to stay alert, she couldn't fight the drug anymore. Her whole body went limp, held up only by Ry's strong arms. As her mind floated, she had the vague thought that it was nice. She'd never been held like this before. She was too big. She would probably kill his back. She opened her mouth to protest, but nothing would come out. Her eyes slid shut.

"I'll take care of her," Ry promised, holding her close.

He lowered her down as the world went dark.

* * * *

Law looked down at the woman in the cart and felt a blazing sense of satisfaction. Kinley Kohl was safe, and he intended to make sure she stayed that way. Two months of surveillance, then adopting a cover to watch her a bit closer for the past week had convinced him that Dominic was completely wrong about her.

And, if his instincts were right, she was also a virgin—and a submissive one at that.

Yeah, that got his cock hard. He'd always been a raging pervert, but Kinley Kohl had turned him into an obsessed freak. The moment he'd seen her, he'd known he wanted her. She was gorgeous and had the kind of soft body that made him hard all over. If he'd just wanted to bang the fuck out of her, he would have been all right. Then…he'd seen her with a bunch of homeless kids at a charity event, and his damn stupid heart had engaged for the first time.

He had to protect her. Yeah, from Dominic, but mostly from her dickwad fiancé.

Riley walked out of the bathroom, shaking his right hand. "Well, we know she has all her teeth. Fuck that hurt."

"Don't be a pussy," Law barked, still staring at her.

He was proud that she'd fought back, especially since she tended to be submissive to the stronger personalities around her, like Greg and her bitch of a sister. More than once, he'd seen them take advantage of her sweet nature. Law had been a little worried that when he and Ry abducted her, she would just cry and beg. He wouldn't have been able to handle that. Instead, she'd bitten the shit out of his brother.

"I'm serious," Riley screeched.

"You're lucky she had her back turned to you or she would have kneed the holy fuck out of your cock."

"Do you know how crazy you look right now?" Ry's

question dripped sarcasm. "You are the very picture of a psycho stalker. Do I need to grab a camera for you so you can capture the moment?"

Law needed to be honest with his brother. "I care about her."

A long sigh filled the room. "It's a mistake, man."

"She isn't who you think she is." Riley and Dominic hadn't watched her for months. They weren't looking past the façade.

Riley slapped a hand on his back. "Even if she's the sweetest thing in the world, I would tell you this is a mistake. She won't be able to handle the lifestyle you want. How the hell would all her society ladies react if she showed up at the charity gala with her three husbands, two of whom came from the wrong side of the tracks?"

"We have money now." He could take care of her.

"Yeah, and we got it the hard way by dealing with criminals and lowlifes. None of us is a poster child for the country club set. Even though Dominic comes from money, he looks like a gangster. Despite this buff body, I'm a computer nerd. And dude, you talk to your guns."

Only occasionally. "Everyone has their quirks."

"She won't do it, Law."

"She's not Simone." He was so sick of this argument. The one woman they had thought for half a second about marrying had turned out to be more concerned about other people's opinions than love, so Riley had given up trying.

"They're all Simone in the end, brother. If we try this long-term thing with someone, it's damn near impossible to hide. What woman in her right mind wants to be thought of as a whore? You remember what it was like for Mom to even go to the grocery store."

"It's not like we'd pimp our wife out."

"It doesn't matter. That's how everyone would see it, especially among Kinley's old-money circle. It won't work."

"I think you're wrong."

Riley sighed. "I think we have to get her out of here before someone wonders where the bride is. This ceremony is supposed to start in less than thirty minutes." He grabbed the heavy canvas cover they had brought along to hide the fact that they weren't pushing the laundry around.

Law shook his head. "Don't cover her yet. We have to get her luggage."

Riley rolled his eyes. "We are not bringing the princess's luggage."

His brother wasn't thinking. "She can't run around in her wedding dress the whole time. We don't know how long she's going to be with us."

Riley picked up his cell and started texting. "Then you're in luck. She can run around naked. Actually, I wouldn't mind seeing her naked. She is fucking gorgeous. Too bad she's in the habit of banging a douchelord. What the fuck does she see in him except a whole lot of zeroes in his bank account?"

"She doesn't sleep with Jansen. They don't spend the night at each other's places. When they travel they have separate rooms. And we're taking her luggage. She could have medication packed that she needs."

She didn't. She didn't take anything more than a couple of vitamins a day, but his brother didn't have to know that. Having her belongings around Kinley would comfort her.

God, when had he turned into a guardian angel? Law wasn't suited for the role. He was pure muscle, good at killing scumbags or making them wish they were dead. He didn't know a damn thing about taking care of a woman. Riley was probably right. She was too sweet to want what they needed. Even the suggestion would probably shock her down to her painted pink toes.

So he'd have to settle for watching over her in Alaska.

Grumbling, Ry grabbed the first of her suitcases. There was room in the cart…if they mashed down the shit ton of puffy fabric in her dress.

Gently, Riley laid the first piece next to her. Law helped

him with the next three bags. He guessed she'd gotten them all secondhand because they were embossed with someone else's initials. Someone really fucking liked themselves. There were little gold Ls and Vs all over the luggage. If Kinley was his woman, he would make sure everything had *her* sweet name on it.

"Dominic is having trouble finding a parking spot. We have to hold tight for a few minutes. Damn New York traffic." Riley cursed at his phone, then lifted the drape to peek out the window as though he could see where Dominic was circling the building. This high up, there was no way. Everyone looked like ants from this height.

He tucked the last of the four cases around her. She moaned a little, and the sound made him goddamn hard. Why did he have to ache for *this* woman?

"Why the fuck does it have to be her?" Riley asked. Sometimes Law thought his brother could read his mind.

He shrugged. "It doesn't. It won't. You're right. She won't want me."

Again those eyes rolled. His brother needed a better form of communication than sarcasm. "Oh, she'll probably want you. I just don't think she's going to keep you. Or any of us. Women like a ménage for sex, but no one wants to put up with three dudes for life. The laundry alone would choke her."

Law didn't think that was funny. "I can do my own. All of us can."

"Look at this from her point of view. If by some miracle, Kinley could handle a relationship with all three of us, would the pressure from her family or the tabloids be too much for her? How long would it take her to want to leave? Maybe you should try to win her on your own."

And leave his brother and best friend behind? "No."

He wanted what the James brothers had. He wanted a family. He'd spent too many years needing someone watching his back to go it alone. Maybe it was his perverse nature, maybe it was something he'd learned, but he didn't even want to try making this a solo act with Kinley.

And there was a little voice inside that worried what would happen to her if he died. He couldn't leave his wife alone the way his own mother had been. He couldn't stand the thought of her turning to a terrible life on her back just to feed herself and her kids.

"Nah. I just like her, okay? I'll get over it. I don't particularly love the idea of going into the kidnapping business, and she'll want nothing to do with me after this, most likely."

God knew he'd been forced to play the bad guy most of his fucking life. One more time shouldn't matter. He just couldn't stand the idea that she would be afraid of him.

"We're saving her life. Eventually, she'll understand." Annabelle slipped into the room through the adjoining door, her voice low. "Is she all right?"

The curvy secretary approached the laundry cart and looked inside.

"She's fine. She'll sleep it off on the plane."

As soon as he grabbed her handbag, they were out of here. But when he lifted it, Law frowned. It felt heavier than it looked. What was she carrying? Not that it mattered. He laid it in the cart beside her with the rest.

"How is it coming from your end?" Ry asked.

The law firm of Baxter, Cohen, and Kent was working on their side—to bring Jansen to justice and to try to keep their asses out of jail. Law wasn't sure which would prove to be the harder job.

"I brought Eric with me. He's waylaid her sister. She was probably coming back in to snip at Kinley one more time. Good, you got her luggage. She'll be calmer if she can keep her things around her." Tears were threatening to spill down her cheeks. "Am I doing the right thing?"

He'd pondered the same question every day since they'd decided on the assignment. "You tried to tell her the truth, and she wasn't accepting it."

Annabelle shook her head. "I know. Kinley is so loyal and wants to believe the best about everyone. If I'd pushed too much more, she would have gone straight to Greg and demanded explanations. You know how he would have taken care of the situation."

"We'll make sure she's safe," Law assured.

Riley stepped up. He was always the one to handle the ladies. Being somewhat civilized, he didn't tend to scare the crap out of them the way Law did.

His brother gave her his surest smile. "She's in good hands, Annabelle. I went to college with Kellan. He's talked to you about me, right?"

She nodded, relaxing a little. "He said you were a good guy."

"If you trust him, then trust me. I'll be good to her. And Law here is already half in love with her, so there's no worry."

Law felt his jaw drop. "You motherfucker."

Riley shrugged. "Hey, I tell it like it is."

Annabelle went silent, her dark eyes staring through him. Damn it. Riley's sense of humor was going to get him gutted one day. Now Annabelle would be afraid to let Kinley go with him. The secretary could cause real trouble.

"I'm not going to…" Law struggled. How did one politely tell someone that he wasn't going to molest her friend? "Touch her. I swear."

"Oh, I sincerely hope you do." Annabelle stepped up and smoothed down his tie. "You charm her and seduce her and you make her very happy in bed. That's practically an order."

He hadn't heard that right. "What?"

She stepped back, wearing a mysterious smile. "I love that woman. She's my sister and she deserves someone who can make her feel good. You've been watching her. I see the look in your eyes. You seem like a smart man, Law Anders. I know Dominic Anthony is. No truly smart man is going to be able to resist my best friend." Her eyes narrowed as she studied Riley. "I don't know about you. You might be dumb."

"I graduated top of my class at Harvard." Riley seemed slightly put off.

"Then you'll get with the program because she'll need the security and affection all of you can provide. Just remember…if you taste that particular icing, you've bought the whole cake. If you try to get out of taking the cake home and enjoying every bite, I will come after your asses. And you have not seen fury until you've seen it from this girl. Are we understood?"

They both nodded dutifully. Law was pretty sure that Riley had been struck as mute as him.

Annabelle took one last look at her friend, then stepped to the door. "I'm going to make sure the coast stays clear. You two think about what I said. And take care of Gigi. She can be a handful."

Annabelle disappeared, leaving Law with one final question.

"Who the fuck is Gigi?"

Riley shrugged. "I don't know. I think that girl might be crazy. Are you thinking of trying Kinley's cake?"

"Well, I couldn't just eat the frosting and then not take a bite of the cake, if you know what I mean. Hell, I'm not sure what I mean. I'm confused."

Damn, he didn't understand women half the time. Shaking it off, he looked down at Kinley, who appeared to be sleeping so peacefully, despite her awkward position. She was really the most fucking gorgeous thing he'd ever seen. And what had he done? He'd shot her full of tranquilizer, stuffed her into a laundry bin, and dumped her luggage inside.

Very smooth.

"I really want to try the frosting," Riley admitted. "But Annabelle will take our balls off if we do and then don't eat the cake." He frowned. "Is that what she's saying?"

"Dumbass." Sometimes he wondered if Harvard was all it was cracked up to be. "She was saying she approved."

"I kind of thought so. She shouldn't." Riley stood beside

him staring down, too. His brother's face softened. "We'd only get hurt if we started something with her. She really is quite lovely when she's not biting my hand."

His phone buzzed, and Riley's whole body went on alert. "We're a go."

Law grabbed the canvas and covered the bin. "Sleep well, princess. When you wake up, you'll be in a whole new kingdom."

And he would very likely be in hell.

Chapter Three

Riley stared down the long hallway just outside Kinley's suite and wondered what jail would be like. If he and Law were caught, they'd probably be sent to a maximum-security prison for violent offenders. He hoped he wouldn't be popular there, but he worried. Because deep down, he knew there was no fucking way they got away with kidnapping and transporting a debutante across state lines. Hell, with the amount of Louis Vuitton luggage Kinley Kohl had, they would probably get nabbed for grand theft baggage, too.

He was going to end up living out the rest of his days as some thug's girlfriend, being traded for cigarettes and sexual favors. It wasn't really how he'd expected his life to play out, but he couldn't back out of this assignment. A man didn't have much if he didn't have any loyalty.

"We're clear to the elevator." His brother was cool as a cucumber. Not a single line on his face revealed a hint of anxiety. He wasn't thinking up ten different ways he could be shanked in prison. No. Law Anders was steady.

It was the way he'd been all their lives. Nothing fazed his big brother…but for a few minutes, Law had warmed up while staring down at the woman who would likely cost them twenty-five to life. Just for a moment, there had been something like hope in Law's normally barren expression.

If they weren't careful, Kinley Kohl might cost them more than their freedom.

Riley pushed the laundry cart forward, keeping his expression carefully blank. *Nothing to see here, folks. Just a couple of average Joes doing their job, kidnapping a blonde with nice tits. Happens every day.*

Actually, Kinley's tits weren't just nice. From what he could see, they were gorgeous. Round and full… At first, he'd suspected they were cosmetically augmented, but then he'd held her close and she'd been so fucking soft against him. His cock had gotten hard as a rock. Then she'd bitten the holy shit out of him.

And he'd gotten even harder.

Riley wondered what she would look like when he tied her up, when he had so much of his rope around her that she couldn't move. He could imagine the pattern on her fair skin, a tortoiseshell that would mold her curves and wrap around those breasts, making them thrust out proudly. He would dress her in silk rope and nothing else. Well, next to nothing else. Those ridiculous heels she was wearing would look awfully good wrapped around his neck while he shoved his cock into what was likely a very tight pussy.

"Is there a problem, brother?"

Riley nearly groaned. He was in the middle of a criminal endeavor, and he was hard as hell, thinking about all the ways he could violate his pretty little hostage.

He wasn't just going to prison. He was going to hell in a hand basket. Well, a laundry cart, at least.

"I'm coming."

But he wouldn't be, not in the way he wanted to. Nope, there was going to be no coming around Kinley Kohl at all. He pushed the cart again and swore to all of the mystical beings of the universe that he wasn't going to molest their prisoner. No way. He was keeping his hands to himself. The only way he'd be coming in the near future was by the power of his own fist or with a properly paid for hooker. And he wasn't above either method.

The elevator door was open at the end of the hall, not the pretty one the guests used, but the hefty, industrial-sized one meant to keep the workers out of sight of the hotel's posh clientele.

On his left, he caught sight of one of the CCTV cameras that dotted the hallways. He kept his head down. All anyone watching the feeds would see was a tall man with dark hair pushing a laundry cart along the hallway. There would be nothing to distinguish him.

Just a few more steps and then they would be safely in the elevator.

"Hey!"

To his horror, the canvas started to move and a perfectly manicured hand appeared.

Law rushed across the hall, his feet making not a single sound against the carpet.

"Hafta getta way." Kinley was trying to haul herself out of the laundry cart. One fist came up. "Won't let you. Won't."

Riley peered down at her. How did she make that look so fucking adorable? She was a mess of white tulle, and all he could think about was wrapping himself around her.

"Baby, it's all right." Law reached for her hand, his voice softer than Riley could ever remember hearing it. Law was rough and tumble, but he got so tender around this one bit of blonde fluff. "What the hell. I thought I emptied the fucking syringe in her arm. We need the chloroform, Riley."

Yes, it was their last resort. It wouldn't keep Kinley out for very long, but they had to keep her out long enough to escape this damn hotel.

"Don't want to get married. Want the beach. Happy there." They weren't taking her to the beach, but at least Law seemed to be calming her down. Then she turned those kick-him-in-the-gonads brown eyes his way. "So pretty. Wanna get married?"

Just then, he almost did because she was so sweet with her ridiculously sensual bow of a mouth and honey blonde hair. In that moment, he could picture her at the center of their world. It was perverse. He fucking knew it, but he couldn't shake the image of the three of them loving her—their queen, their beating heart—as she loved them in return.

He had to stop indulging in ridiculous fantasy. Sure, she was soft right now, but she wouldn't be when the drugs wore off. Besides, they couldn't abduct her on her wedding day, then imagine she'd be receptive to romance with him…and Law…and Dominic. The pretty blonde would likely cut them cold for trying to steal so much as a kiss. If they were dumb enough to bring up marriage to all three of them, she'd probably laugh her ass off. If she was crazy enough to try it and stay, she'd end up leaving.

Even so, he couldn't bring himself to say anything beyond, "Sure, honey."

"Really?" A brilliant, if loopy smile crossed her face. God, she was gorgeous. His freaking heart nearly stopped. "You'll be good to me?"

She asked as if it was the gravest of concerns. Maybe she knew her fiancé better than he thought.

"Every single day." He grabbed the rag from his pants pocket and held it up. She didn't even flinch, just kept smiling at him as he placed the cloth over her mouth. His heart sank a little as the light left her eyes and she slid back down into the laundry bin.

Law caught her, helping to ease her down. He smoothed back her hair. For just a moment, a primal growl started in Riley's throat. He craved the chance to soothe her. It was stupid. When she came to, she'd want nothing to do with them, yet he couldn't stop imagining how nice it would be to put his arms around her and hold her while she slept off the drugs they'd just fed her. Then making love to her when she awoke.

Yeah, he was going to do well in prison.

After Law settled her, his head came up. Right into the line of the cameras.

"Dude, look down. Now!" What the hell was his brother thinking? Law never fucked up an op. Law was the be-all, end-all of operatives. He was ice cold, but it looked like Kinley Kohl was getting his brother too hot to think. Damn!

Law jerked his head down. "Shit! Sorry. Let's get her out

of here. Dominic is probably freaking out by now."

He jogged down the hall and pushed the elevator button again. Luckily, it hadn't gone anywhere. Riley started pushing the cart in, his thoughts racing.

Okay, maybe Law hadn't fucked up all that badly. Maybe the cameras hadn't been pointed in their direction. Or maybe no one was watching them. In that case, they'd be gone before anyone noticed Kinley was missing. And with any luck, the cameras hadn't been recording. No one would know anything about her disappearance then, at least until Dominic had the proof he needed. What they'd do with her when it came time to release her and how they'd keep her from running to the police… Well, none of them had figured that out yet.

"Hey, hold up!"

Fuck. As fast as he could shove the cart in, a man in a badly tailored suit was right behind him, crowding into the elevator.

"Sir, the guest elevator is down the hall." Law's voice was perfectly steady as he held the door open for the man to exit.

Not just any man. *Fuck times two.* Vincent Dargo, Greg Jansen's heavy. There was no way to mistake the man. He looked like something a pit bull had chewed up and spit out before someone decided to shove him into a suit.

"Nah, I hate those fucking snooty elevators. I hate places like this in general. Will this get me to the ballroom floor?"

Riley wondered if there was any chloroform left. Law shook his head slightly and removed his arm from the doorway. The doors closed with a little thud, and Law hit the buttons for the ballroom floor and the street level.

"Of course, sir. We'll get you there," Riley forced himself to say.

This was a man who, by all accounts, did Greg Jansen's dirty work—and had for years. Being this close to the asshole who probably had more than a thing or two to do with Carrie's murder made Riley want to strangle him.

"You two working this fucking sham of a wedding?"

Out of the corner of his eye, he saw his brother tense slightly, but Law's eyes stayed on the doors as the elevator descended. "Nah. We're dropping this set off for cleaning, then we're done for the day."

Vincent frowned. "I thought you had maids to cart that shit around. You two aren't dressed for laundry."

It was Riley's turn. He'd had a lot of experience with being friendly and non-threatening. He'd spent much of his life making up for the fact that Law acted like a Rottweiler on steroids. "Normally, we wouldn't have anything to do with the laundry, man, but there's this girl…"

Vincent nodded and sent him a knowing wink. "Hey, you gotta give a little to get some. Well, some of us do."

"She's a cute little thing. I don't know that she'll last long in the job, though. She's skittish about some of the nasty stuff we have to send out for cleaning." Riley shrugged. "When you work in a hotel for as long as I have, you see just about everything."

"Doesn't the hotel have its own laundry?" Dargo scowled.

"Sure, but some couple got freaky on one of our thousand thread count sheets. Can't just throw those out. You know how it is. Some stains are harder to remove and need a professional."

Vincent Dargo was a stain that Riley would dearly love to remove, but Dargo's boss was more important. "Well, you won't have that problem in the bridal suite tonight. God, I'll be surprised if they fuck at all. That girl is so bangable, but she's cold. Society women. You think you have a rough job. Try having a boss who tells you to go out and find him a wife with society connections and a fat ass. Oh, but she has to be pretty. Lucky me, I found one, but it was hard. I had to find a go between, if you know what I mean."

Riley didn't. Thankfully, the door dinged and opened to the ballroom level because Riley could practically see his brother vibrating with the need for violence.

Down the long hall, Riley caught sight of Jansen in his

immaculate tuxedo. For all that Dargo looked like a thug, Jansen fit into society perfectly, a shark masked by designer wear.

He spoke to a man Riley recognized as a senator from Georgia. They were having an intense conversation. Chamber music flooded the halls. It sounded like the wedding was getting ready to start. Someone would start looking for Kinley soon.

"Gotta go." Dargo rushed out to meet his boss.

Riley reached out and very calmly pressed the button to close the doors.

"I'm going to kill him," Law said under his breath.

"I'm sure that would make you feel better." Sometimes he thought snuffing the breath out of lowlifes like Dargo was one of Law's ways to relax. Today, Riley understood. "When the time comes, make him suffer."

"What do you think he meant?"

Riley had already reviewed the conversation in his head. He was pretty sure he knew what was bugging his brother. "You mean, why was he concerned with her ass?" He'd seen her pictures. Kinley Kohl had a luscious backside that she tried to camouflage with her clothing. He shrugged. "Maybe he's an ass man."

"His other girlfriends have all been model types, very thin. So thin that I've wanted to feed them a cheeseburger," Law muttered. "Even Carrie was that way."

Carrie Anthony had been beautiful, but neither Riley nor Law had ever been tempted by her. She'd been like their little sister, too. Beyond that, she hadn't been anywhere close to their type. Sometimes Riley wished they didn't have a type, but it was true.

Over time, he'd fallen into sharing women with his brother and Dominic. It was just the way he preferred things. Oh, it wasn't that he couldn't have sex on his own. He could totally do that, enjoy it even, but he didn't picture picket fences and forever without backup.

Life in a trailer park, watching his mom pay for their food by whoring herself out, had taught him to always have a contingency, other resources. But finding someone who wanted to be involved with him and his backup had been next to impossible.

So if Jansen wasn't attracted to juicy asses, why had he insisted on one?

The doors opened, and suddenly that was a problem for another day. It was time to get a move on. Workers rushed around them as they strode down the hallway toward the loading docks.

"About time," Dominic said. He was dressed in coveralls emblazoned with the name of a local specialty cleaner. "Is that everything we need?"

He was holding a clipboard that likely contained a crossword puzzle and nothing else. It was all just a part of the ruse.

"This should do it." Riley pushed the cart into the back of the truck.

Just before he was about to close it, Law jumped in. "I'll ride back here, make sure the merchandise doesn't get damaged in transit."

He slammed the door shut.

"Don't be a pervert."

Now that they were about to escape the hotel, the worry that Law's face had been captured by that hallway camera returned. Riley was right back to wondering how he would look in an orange jumpsuit. His guess? Not so great.

But some part of him was more fixated on the moment, was the tiniest bit jealous that Law had Kinley all to himself. He would very likely pick her up because it wouldn't be nice to leave her in a laundry cart. He would cradle her to make sure she was safe. He would have that very fine ass sitting right on his lap.

Maybe Law wasn't the only pervert.

"Can we go now?" Dominic asked. "Or do you want to

ride in the back, too?"

His longtime best friend was so obviously not amused. "I'm good to go."

He jogged around the truck and hopped in.

As they lost themselves in the Manhattan traffic, Riley's thoughts stuck on the woman in the back of the truck.

* * * *

Dominic couldn't quite take his eyes off the woman reclining in the seat of the private jet he'd chartered to take them to the James's landing strip in River Run, Alaska. They'd been in the air for over an hour and she hadn't moved yet.

She didn't look anything like Carrie. He'd known it from the pictures he'd studied, but somehow he'd thought that when he got into the same space as Kinley Kohl, he'd see something that reminded him of his sister.

After all, they had both fallen for the same man—a cold-blooded killer who had offed Carrie and intended to do the same to Kinley.

Riley sank into the seat next to him. "Law says we'll be flying all night."

It was somewhere around ten hours from New York to Alaska. Dominic had a long night to ruminate on the task he had to complete tomorrow.

He had to break Kinley Kohl.

"Can we get her out of that ridiculous dress?" Dominic asked, eyeing her all wrapped in white silk and satin. He couldn't contemplate playing hardball with her when she looked that damn innocent.

When Law had passed her to him from the truck, she'd nestled down into his arms like a trusting child. Or a lover. But she could never be his lover. Or Law's—no matter what he imagined.

"I think Law would be happy to undress her," Riley said. "You want me to take his place in the cockpit?"

Riley wasn't half the pilot his brother was, but he would be able to keep them in flight.

"No." He didn't want to tempt Law any further. "She can change when we arrive and she comes to. She won't wake up during the flight, will she?"

Riley shrugged. "She hasn't gotten much sleep lately. At least that's what Annabelle said. But she had a weird reaction to the sedative. She came out of it for a minute in the hall. Law held her then and stroked her hair. She went back to sleep."

Dominic bet that little episode had done nothing to dampen Law's infatuation. That man had a deep-seated need to protect. Kinley looked fragile right now, but surely when the interrogation started tomorrow, she would show her true colors.

"Gigi." She started to mutter in her sleep. "Where…Gigi?"

Dominic frowned. "Who's Gigi?"

"Annabelle mentioned her. Then she gave us that half smile women often do, the one that looks a little evil and makes you wait for things to start falling. You know what I'm talking about?"

Annabelle could be a bit mysterious, but he had other problems now. "Did you check through her luggage? I don't want to find a cell phone."

Cell phones had GPS. GPS meant they were up shit creek and all his careful planning had been for nothing.

"I left it sitting on the table in the living area of the suite."

Not good enough. There had been a ton of people going through that bridal suite all day long. "How do you know it was hers?"

"Have you looked at her? Look, man, it was in her room and it was pink and blinged within an inch of its life. She seems to like little fake diamonds on everything. I don't get it."

He was going to have Law's head. It had been a sloppy operation. Law should have made damn sure that was her phone. He could forgive Riley, who was usually behind the scenes, but Law knew damn well how to run an op. Now Dominic had to check through the luggage to make sure they weren't going to be met by feds when they landed in River Run.

"Why did Law decide to bring a half ton of designer luggage with us?"

Dominic knew he shouldn't, but he stared across the aisle. Her blonde hair was the color of honey. The pictures didn't capture its natural beauty. Lighter shades threaded through the darker ones, forming a gorgeous honey and amber color that contrasted beautifully with her skin.

Porcelain. Her skin was like porcelain, perfect and creamy white.

He needed to remember that porcelain, while beautiful, was also cold.

"He was worried she might need something in there," Riley answered with a touch of disbelief, as if he, too, thought his brother had gone mental.

"So he wanted to be the guy who brought all her clothes along. He's going to kill me over this." He pulled the first bag free and slid the zipper around. The top popped open as though deeply happy at being free. She'd stuffed the bag to the hilt. "Holy shit. How many pairs of jeans does one woman need?"

There were at least a dozen pairs of jeans in the case, each with more and more elaborately placed rhinestones across the pockets that would hug her ass. It was like Las Vegas had taken over her luggage. Every eye in the world would go straight to her ass because there was no way anyone could miss it.

"There seems to be a theme here. She likes shiny objects. Maybe if we get some jewelry we can distract her enough so she'll just give us all the intel we need," Dominic offered.

There were several shirts but they were blousy and draped, rather modest by modern standards. Her bras and panties were utilitarian, all white cotton. Nothing lacy and pretty to show off her stunning body on her honeymoon. That was a riddle. Dominic would have bet that Kinley used that sexy body to get everything she wanted, but her underwear told a different story.

There was a makeup bag with bright pink trim and black polka dots. In fact, nothing was plain about anything Kinley owned—except her underwear.

He opened the makeup case. Nothing was sacred now. He needed to know everything about her, understand her better before he began his interrogation.

Her makeup was drugstore. Cheap. That surprised him. The luggage was wretchedly expensive, but she got by with crappy makeup and inexpensive moisturizer.

He was sure she would be wearing Chanel right before Jansen killed her.

Dominic took a long breath and repacked her bag, using the little gold lock to run the zipper back around the edge.

"This one is full of shoes." Riley held up a pair that he would expect a stripper to wear. They were fucking hot. "She has twelve pairs of shoes for a five-day trip. Why does she need all those shoes?"

To make a man crazy. To make her legs look a million miles long. To wrap them around his back and press into his flesh. Her shoes were everything her undies weren't. They were hot sex on stilettos.

He had to turn away because he was getting agonizingly hard just thinking about her in those heels.

The bag to his left began to shake. And bark.

Well, now he could guess who Gigi was. He unzipped the travel bag and a puffball leapt out.

"What the fuck is that?" Riley asked, frowning down at the little thing. Kinley had tied a pink bow in its fur, and there was a rhinestone-studded collar around its tiny throat.

"I think it's supposed to be a dog." It started to yip, a deeply annoying sound. The little thing started to bark and run in circles as though trying to communicate.

"It looks more like a rat. Why would she put bows on a rat?" Riley leaned down and held out a hand. "Here, girl. Let's get you back in the bag. That's your home, right? Don't you want to go back home and stop that infernal sound you're making? I can't call it a bark. Real dogs bark."

But the little rat thing proved it could bite. The minute Riley reached for it, it nipped him.

Riley popped back up, shaking his hand, then staring at it. "Damn it. I'm going to go wash my hand and hope that thing doesn't have rabies."

He stalked back toward the bathroom.

Riley didn't seem to understand that all creatures needed to know their place in the pecking order, whether person or dog or weirdly dressed rat thing. Dominic knew who was in charge—him.

He picked up Gigi by the scruff of her neck, lifting her high in the air, and bringing her up to meet his eyes. Gigi made an odd sound in the back of her throat that Dominic thought might pass for a snarl in rat-dog world.

Dominic spoke in a language the animal could understand. He gave her a real snarl.

Gigi whimpered and tried to rear back into a protective ball.

Now, they understood each other. He set the dog thing back down. It immediately ran to hide in Kinley's skirts, apparently not caring that its mistress was unconscious.

Dominic sighed and sat back in his chair.

Riley plopped down beside him. "It didn't break the skin. Maybe its teeth aren't sharp enough. Have you thought about the fact that Butch is going to eat that thing?"

His bulldog was already in Alaska. River Run and the compound there had become their base of operations for this particular mission. One of their largest clients, Black Oak Oil, had offered to let them use the large house they kept outside their center in Alaska. When Dominic had asked about it, Gavin James had simply handed over the keys and the security codes, insisting that he didn't want to know a damn thing else.

Gavin knew him fairly well, but their connections in public were almost purely professional. If Kinley's kidnapping got tied back to him, it would be a while before the feds got around to questioning Gavin. "Butch will be a perfect gentleman."

He hoped. Kinley probably wouldn't be too helpful if his dog swallowed hers whole and burped up those pink bows.

With great effort, she lifted her head and sighed. "Find Gigi…"

The words were slurred like she was totally trashed. It was a reasonable reaction to the sedatives, though they should have just knocked her out for at least eight to ten hours. She was certainly stronger physically than he'd imagined.

"Gigi is hiding in your skirts," he explained in a soft voice.

She smiled, and his heart actually skipped a beat. What the hell was that about? Those plump lips curled up, and she flushed a little. He could imagine that exact expression on her face when he pressed his cock deep and found that perfect place deep inside her.

Had Jansen ever given her a screaming orgasm? The thought of his sister's killer fucking Kinley deflated his dick in a second. He wasn't going to have sex with Jansen's leftovers. No fucking way. No matter how much he wanted her.

She lurched up on wobbly feet and immediately stumbled, landing right in his lap.

"Go to sleep, Kinley." He tried making it an order. Maybe Kinley was a little like her rat-dog thing and just needed a firm hand.

"Kay," she slurred and nuzzled her face in the crook of his neck where he could feel her breath on his skin.

Yeah, his cock was hard again. She settled her ass against it, and Dominic thought he might come in his slacks. Damn it. "In your own seat, Kinley."

"Kay." But she just snuggled closer and sighed as though

she'd found right where she wanted to be.

"She seems very affectionate when she's incapacitated." Riley had the faintest smile on his face. "You probably shouldn't move her. She might sleep better like that."

"Then get Law out here to hold her." He couldn't just sit here with her all pressed up against him for hours. Even as he thought it, the plane hit an air pocket. With the momentary turbulence, his arm wound around her waist, tugging her more firmly into his lap. She would fall if he didn't, and he couldn't have her injured at this junction. That was the only reason he did it.

"Unfortunately, Law is flying the plane," Riley pointed out, then turned quiet for a moment. "She seems sweet actually. She's not totally what I thought she was."

Fuck. Riley drank her in with that same glazed, lustful expression Law did. This could spell trouble.

Kinley's breathing evened out as she went utterly limp. Knowing he was stuck with her indefinitely, Dominic held in a curse. "Pull your head out of your pants. She's exactly what we thought. She's just better at manipulating men than I gave her credit for. She even does it in her damn sleep."

Riley snorted. "We gave her the equivalent of a horse tranquilizer, and she's managed to worry more about that little hairy thing than herself."

It was time to remind his partner of some hard truths. "She's marrying for money."

Riley sat back, sighing a little. "Is that really the worst crime you can think of?"

He could think of worse. Murder, for instance. But once Jansen had the money his sister had earned modeling and entrée into her glitzy New York social world, Jansen hadn't needed her anymore. So he'd killed her. Carrie had married the bastard because she thought she loved him.

"She's going to spread her legs for money," Dominic reminded. "You know what we called that back home?"

Riley's face flushed angrily. "Yeah, I'm sure you called

those women whores. Of course I called her mom. I think I'll go sit with Law for a while."

Dominic's stomach dropped.

"I wasn't talking about your mother," he said, trying to come back from the precipice of a really nasty fight. God, he wasn't thinking these days.

Riley didn't bother to turn around. "Yeah, you were. I just think you should stop for five minutes and consider that the world isn't always fair. Some people get dealt a shitty hand."

"You think I don't know that?"

"Do you? The world isn't black and white." Riley gritted his teeth. "Good people can sometimes do bad things for the right reasons. The fact that I have to say that to you is ridiculous. We just kidnapped a woman, and you're planning on making her life a living hell until she gives you the information you need. In light of that, ask yourself if whoring really seems that bad. I'll see you when we touch down."

"Riley," he called out, but the other man ignored him and disappeared behind the cockpit door.

Kinley didn't move, just laid there trustingly in his arms.

He heard a little whimper and looked down at the floor. Somehow Gigi had managed to work free of the endless yards of freaking fabric that made up Kinley's skirt. And now the little thing was looking up longingly at its mistress. It whined and turned those bug eyes on him.

God, he was the wicked witch in this scenario. He was taking out Dorothy and her little dog, too.

"All right, then. Come on."

Dominic reached down and scooped up the little dog with one hand. As soon as he set it in Kinley's lap, it curled against its mistress and immediately went to sleep.

Which left him holding his beautiful hostage, who would likely hate him come morning, and her dog thing. It really couldn't get worse.

He would make it up to Riley and Law. He had zero intentions of really hurting the girl in a long-term way. But in the short term, she would likely be…uncomfortable. At least she would be alive.

He wasn't the fucking bad guy here.

"So warm." She rubbed her head against his neck and her hand petted the dog.

He had a sudden vision of that soft hand stroking his cock. That quickly, he was the uncomfortable one.

Dominic closed his eyes and tried to not think about how close his rigid dick was to her silken pussy and her lush ass. He could withhold her orgasm until she told him exactly what he needed to know. God, that would be a sweet bit of torture.

And then he would walk away and never think about her again.

Yeah, he was a real fucking good guy.

So he wouldn't touch the girl sexually. Good thing he had other methods to break her down.

He was just about to doze off when the dog started snoring.

It was going to be a long flight.

Chapter Four

Law looked through the windows in the great room, over the lawn—not that the wilderness around the compound could be called that. The River Run, Alaska, facility sat in the middle of endless miles of pristine beauty toward the southeastern end of the state. There was a small town a few miles away, but everyone who lived there was on the James's payroll. They wouldn't be calling the cops. He doubted anyone even knew they were here with the exception of the man who tended the grounds and had been dog sitting Butch while they'd been in New York. An hour before they'd arrived, they'd called to let the man know they'd care for Butch from here on out. No sense in putting Gavin's employee in the sticky position of being an accessory to a crime.

Morning in Alaska this time of year came mighty early, but it was something to see. Fog around the mountains and brilliant colors lighting the sky.

Right now, Kinley probably didn't really give a damn about the view.

Down the hall, the banging on the door began again. She'd been awake for half an hour, but he didn't think she had complied with his very reasonable request.

"Have you changed your clothes yet?" he called, striding to her door.

"Go to hell. I'm not getting naked with you around, criminal!" Kinley's voice got higher with each syllable and carried quite well. The doorknob jiggled before the banging began again. "Let me out of here!"

He leaned against the wall with a sigh. She'd been

screaming since the minute she'd awakened. With the exception of a few delirious interruptions, she'd slept for almost fourteen full hours. He'd gotten worried about her and had started looking up the names of doctors in the area, but once she'd opened those pretty brown eyes, she'd started fighting. He'd left, hoping that she would comply. And calm down. No such luck.

"Baby, you can't run around in that wedding dress. Isn't it uncomfortable? And you can't eat in it. You've got to be hungry, so why don't you take a nice long shower and change into the jeans and shirt I left for you. Then you can eat some breakfast. I'll fix it for you."

He'd start out civilized, try not to scare her too much.

"I'm not doing anything you say! I'll fight to the end. I'll—"

"I know you're scared, but we're not trying to hurt you." He closed his eyes briefly. "Think about it for just a second. I'm trying to give you a little privacy so you can change and be more comfortable. If I was a violent rapist, would I give you clothes? If I was a crazed killer, wouldn't I have at least tied you up or something?"

That last phrase flashed lightning to his cock. When he tied her up, he wanted it to be totally consensual, with their mutual pleasure in mind.

God, he had to stop thinking that way.

"Maybe you're trying to lull me into a false sense of security before you kill me because you like to play with your victims' minds," she shot back.

The only thing he wanted to play with was her boobs. Hell, that wasn't the total truth. He wanted to play with her mouth, pussy, and ass, too. He could even think of some fun things to do with her feet. "I promise, I'm not trying to mind fuck you."

That was Dominic's job.

Riley joined him in the hall, a single eyebrow arched quizzically. "No luck getting Sleeping Beauty to give up the white gown?"

Since she'd awakened, only Law had dealt with her. He hoped maybe his brother could sway her with some smoother logic.

"Who is that? How many of you are there?" Kinley whispered the question through the door as though she was terrified of the answer.

"It's just me and my brother right now, baby. Neither one of us is going to hurt you. We're here to help you."

Maybe it was time to let her out. She was scared. If he let her have her way this once, she might see that they could be reasonable. Hopefully, they could start building some trust so she wouldn't be terrified out of her mind.

Trying to play Prince Charming? You kidnapped her, dumbass. She's not going to buy that. Sometimes the voice in his head was annoyingly honest.

Dragging in a deep breath, he shoved the key in the lock and opened the door. He spilled into the bedroom as though she'd yanked it open. When she tried to run out and slam the door behind her, Riley kicked it open and blocked her path, catching her between the two of them.

Kinley stopped dead in her tracks, letting loose a breathy gasp. Law wasn't surprised that she was star struck by his younger brother's Hollywood good looks. It was a typical female reaction, but it hit Law squarely in the chest. Women preferred his brother, and he'd never cared much until now.

As Law leaned around her for a peek, he saw her simply stare at Riley. His gut clenched.

His brother frowned down at her. "Are you going to bite me again?"

She gasped a little and scrambled back—into his arms. She turned on Law. "You two! I remember. You came into my suite and pretended to deliver food. You drugged me."

Kinley stared at him as well. She probably only saw a monster who'd kidnapped her from her wedding—a rough-and-tumble ex-soldier who was better at killing than talking.

Still, he had to try to reach her. "It's okay. Deep breath. No one is going to harm you here."

His reassurances didn't make her look any less terrified. "M-my fiancé is wealthy. He'll pay you a big ransom for my return. Anything you want."

Jansen probably would, but Law didn't give a shit. "We're not interested in money. Are you hungry? Do you want breakfast?"

She shook her head, her face paling beneath her smudged makeup. Her hair was a complete mess and every inch of her dress looked wrinkled and worn. And he both felt bad for Kinley and found her adorable.

"So you can poison me after you drugged me? I'll pass. If you let me go right now, I won't call the police. How late is it? I need to get back to the hotel. I need to get married today," she said with a grim look of determination. There was no desperate pleading for her love, just a simple statement of duty.

In his gut, Law knew he was right about her. It made him very patient.

"It's Sunday now, baby. You were supposed to get married Saturday afternoon, so it's all right for you to take a shower, change your clothes, and eat some breakfast. I'll make some eggs and toast." It was all he could cook.

Her hands shook a little. She put one to her head as though trying to clear it. "It's Sunday? How long was I out? Why did you bring me here? What do you want?"

Law wanted to reach out a hand to steady her so badly, but knew the tactic would be counterproductive just now. "We'll explain everything once you're dressed and fed."

"No! I have to get out of here now. I have to find Greg. How am I going to explain this to him?"

Riley's eyes narrowed, and Law knew whatever came out of his mouth was going to be nasty. He was obviously taking on the bad-cop role. Because he'd been listening to Dominic again. Because he wanted her and he didn't know how to not imagine that she wasn't Simone all over again. Riley hated being confused. It brought out his worst. Law sighed.

"You miss your sugar daddy?" Riley glared.

Kinley whirled back to his brother and her voice shook. "He's my fiancé."

It was obvious to Law that she hadn't enjoyed the accusation.

Unfortunately, it wasn't obvious to Riley. "Really? You had a very quick engagement. You went out with him for a month and decided you were in love?"

Her eyes slid to the floor. "It's none of your business. I'm not talking until you tell me why I'm here. If you don't want money…"

"You see, I think you don't love Jansen any more than he loves you. I think he bought you."

"That's utterly ridiculous," she shot back. "I don't have to listen to this. Move out of my way. I'm leaving."

"No, you're not." Riley didn't budge, just crossed his arms over his chest and blocked the narrow hallway. Then he invaded her space, backing her up into Law. "I think Jansen wanted your social connections. They would be very helpful to a man like him."

"A man like him?"

Riley sent her an ugly laugh. "Like you don't know everything about Jansen. I have no doubt that you know exactly what he does for a living and you just don't care."

"He's an importer," she replied hesitantly, nervously, trying to stand her ground. "He imports merchandise, then he sells it. He also helps foreign companies make connections in the States."

Kinley sounded like she was repeating something she'd forced herself to memorize.

"Baby, no." Law kept his voice low because he was pretty sure she was going to be hurt by the fact that Jansen had been lying to her. "He's a criminal."

"You're wrong. I've been to his offices. His business is

legitimate. Your accusations are preposterous, and I'm not talking to you. Stop calling me baby."

Riley pressed his advantage, towering over her, backing her up again until her ass rubbed his cock. "His business is a front. He's in bed with more than one mafia group. He's making a name for himself in the cleaning biz."

Law gripped her hips to keep her from backing into his granite-stiff erection. "It's true, swee… My brother isn't lying."

"Greg doesn't own Laundromats," she argued.

Riley's eyes rolled. "Going to play the dumb blonde, huh? He launders money, cupcake. But I suspect you knew that. How many people died so you could have that ridiculously expensive luggage or wear that overdone bling all over the ass of your jeans? You think you're just selling him your social connections and that pretty, tight pussy of yours, but he's Satan and you sold him your soul."

A loud smack cracked the air around them as Kinley slapped Riley's cheek. She didn't back down an inch now. She tilted her head up and glared at him. "Don't talk to me that way! I might be here against my will, but I won't have it. I'm still a lady."

Riley stepped back. "Sure you are, cupcake. The sort who sells herself to gangsters."

Law sighed. His brother was fucking this up. "Enough, bro. Let her shower and eat and take a fucking breath."

Kinley ignored him. "I don't know what your game is or what you want, but I don't deserve this. If you're some enemy of Greg's, then take up your problems with him. Why involve me, especially by taking me from my wedding?"

Tears streaked down her face, ruining what was left of her makeup, and Law couldn't stand it a second longer. "Kinley, we're not going to hurt you. I promise. We really are here to help you. You don't know Jansen or what's going on behind the scenes. If you'll calm down, I'll explain it to you."

"Go to he—"

"Did you realize that your fiancé took out a life insurance policy on you two weeks ago?" Riley butted in.

Her eyes widened. That got her attention… Then her body slumped, shoulders curling in as though she was protecting herself from a blow. "No."

"He did," Riley confirmed. "I have copies of the policy, Kinley. In the event of your death, he's the sole beneficiary."

She took a deep breath and seemed to rally. "So? Married people take out policies on one another. They protect their future, just in case. I'm sure he took one out on himself, too. He probably meant to tell me, but life has been so chaotic. All we've been able to talk about lately is the wedding. After the ceremony, he would have told me."

"No, he wouldn't. And he didn't buy a policy that would protect you in the event of his death. He only made sure that he'd pocket money if you died." Law hated stripping away her illusions. She might not love Greg Jansen, but she'd certainly thought well enough of him to marry him and trust her future with him. His guess? Kinley felt guilty for not loving her fiancé.

"That doesn't prove anything. I'm sure after our honeymoon, he would have talked to me about taking out a policy on him. You're acting like insurance is a crime. I'm sure he just…wanted to feel secure."

"And he needed a ten-million-dollar policy to do it?"

"What?" She half gasped, half choked the question. "Ten million dollars? Why would he need that much money if I died? He's already rich."

Now she was finally listening. "That's a good question, one we've been asking since we discovered the policy." Law nudged Riley out of the way and led her to the great room. "I know this is a lot to think about. Sit down and I'll get you some coffee, baby."

She put a hand up to stop him. "No. I'm not going to sit down and have a civilized conversation with the men who drugged me and took me to…god knows where. Just because

Greg did something that doesn't make sense to you, you're casting him in the worst possible light. There must be some reasonable explanation. If I asked him to explain it, I have little doubt it would be perfectly logical. Why are you even telling me this? You're criminals, men who kidnap innocent women. And I told you to stop calling me baby."

Riley was right back to his interrogation. "Use your head, Kinley. We know why you're marrying Jansen, and it has absolutely nothing to do with love."

"How would you know that?"

Riley shrugged a little as though he didn't really give a shit. "It's the way women like you work."

Her perfectly plucked brows rose. "Women like me? What do you mean by that?"

"Beautiful women."

"You think I'm beautiful?" She frowned, then shook off the question. "Never mind. It doesn't matter."

Riley's stare slid off her, his fist clenching. "Yeah. Gorgeous society women like you don't give a shit what a man is really like. You only care about how much money he has or how he can enhance your public image."

His brother was never going to get over Simone. One lousy woman, one lame relationship, and she'd ruined Riley for all time. God, Law wished he'd never fucking met her.

"Give Kinley a break," he told his brother.

Once again, she seemed intent on defending herself. Law was actually a little proud of her.

"You have no idea who I am," she insisted through clenched teeth. "None. And I don't want breakfast. I want to go back to the hotel. Greg must be waiting to hear from me and is terribly worried. You ruined my wedding, you bastards. I'm supposed to be on my honeymoon now."

"Are you fucking kidding me?" Riley got right in her face. His voice was low and grave.

"Ry, tread lightly." He felt the same way, but there was no reason to piss her off. It was obvious she didn't understand what was going on.

Kinley didn't even look at him, preferring to stare at Riley. Hands on her hips, she rose to her tiptoes, but she still couldn't even reach his chin. "No. I'm not kidding, and please watch your language. You have a horrible potty mouth."

Riley's whole face turned red. He wasn't used to women doing anything but falling at his feet. Law had to admit, it was kind of cool to watch his usually unflappable brother fucking up right and left with a woman. "You are either insane or stupid."

"And you are rude!" Kinley screamed right back at him.

Not only was Riley rude, he also looked hard. His brother's erection was practically poking her in the belly. If his damn jeans weren't so tight, his cock would very likely be knocking on Kinley's stomach right that second.

He might be acting like the bad cop, but Riley was obviously the horny cop. And that probably pissed him off. He didn't want to want Kinley.

Slowly, her body softened. Her lips flushed and parted. She was responding. To his brother.

"I'm going to speak really slowly so you can understand." Sarcasm dripped from Riley's mouth. "I'll bet you don't know why Jansen asked you to marry him, but I do. Ten million dollars, cupcake. He was going to kill you on your honeymoon and collect the insurance money."

"I am going to use very small words so you can understand. Fuck off." She slapped her right hand over her mouth. "You made me curse!"

Riley growled and rolled his eyes.

She turned to Law, her shoulders squaring. "You can't prove any of this and you're wrong. Let me go."

"Eventually, we will—but not until it's safe. But you need to listen to us. We do have evidence and we're going to prove our case to you."

All that blonde hair ruffled around her shoulders as she shook her head stubbornly. "It's impossible to prove that Greg is a criminal because he's not."

"If you're so sure, then it won't hurt to listen. But you can't listen without eating, sweet…I'm sorry. Kinley." Law remembered that she didn't want endearments from him. And it pissed him off. "That's final."

She sighed in annoyance. "I can't eat."

"You don't like eggs? I'll get you something else."

She bit her lip and hesitated, clearly not wanting to admit the reason. "I can't eat when my dress is so tight. And I can't get out of it by myself. I tried. I can't unbutton the back without help."

Oh shit. He had to undress her. His fantasy and his nightmare rolled into one. "Turn around."

She hesitated.

"I promise not to touch you. I'll be careful. I don't mean to make you uncomfortable."

She slowly turned around, as if she wasn't really sure this was a good idea. But if she wanted out of the dress, what were her more appealing options?

Finally, she showed him the elaborate back. The bodice was snug in a good way, and he couldn't help but notice how it exaggerated the curve of her waist, the way her skin glowed against the lace, looking creamy and so damn soft. He wanted nothing more than to run his hand down every patch as he exposed it, but he couldn't. His hands were callused. They didn't belong touching anything so fine as her flesh.

Riley sat down on the sofa, shaking his head in an exasperated fashion. "We don't have to torture her. That dress already does it. We should leave her in the sucker until she tells us what we need to know."

"We're not going to do that." Law sent Riley a nasty glare as he stared at the buttons. Would the calluses on his hands snag the silk?

"Can you not undo it? Is it too tight? Oh, god. Are you going to have to cut me out?" She sounded horrified. "It really is too small for me. Becks was right; I shouldn't have picked this dress."

Becks was full of shit. The dress was perfect. "It's lovely on you. And it fits just fine. It's supposed to hug your curves, baby." Damn it. "Sorry."

Kinley looked over her shoulder at him. "Apology accepted. I usually like endearments. Just not from my kidnapper."

She should have someone in her life who adored her, who called her baby or sweetheart every day of her life.

He reached for the top button, his hand shaking slightly. "Is it all right if I move your hair so I can reach the buttons?"

The soft honey strands were everywhere, long tresses of blonde silk that made him want to fist it as he fucked her deep. Law swallowed against his lust.

"Please. I would do it myself, but my arms are sore. I think I slept on them wrong."

He brushed the curtain of golden tresses to the side and stared at her graceful neck and feminine shoulders. God, he was the horny cop now. What was he doing? Staring at her back and thinking about all the things he wanted to do to her once he got her undressed.

With a curse, Law forced himself to move. He began to unbutton the dress. "I'm sorry about your arms. We tried to make you comfortable."

"Hell, most of the time you were being held like a baby," Riley interjected.

"What?" She sounded scandalized by the thought they'd been anywhere near her in her sleep.

"Would you shut it?" Law snapped. "Now she thinks we're perverts. We have a purpose. Convincing her that Jansen is a creep. Let's not stray."

And as soon as they were alone, he was going to have a long talk with his brother. Especially since Kinley had been softening again, responding to his attempts to be gentle. It worked—except Riley kept pissing her off.

"I'm terrible when I'm under the influence of anything.

God, please tell me I didn't do something I'll regret."

How the hell could Riley or Dominic think she was a manipulative bitch? Here she was being held hostage by three men she didn't know and she was worried that *she* had done something wrong.

Kinley wasn't a gold digger. She was the perfect sub, sweet and soft. Yet there was a core of strength to her. The people around her took advantage of her kind nature, her desire to please others. She, no doubt, had a hard time saying no. She needed a strong Dominant partner to lift her up and lend his strength.

But it wouldn't be him. He just had to make sure Dominic didn't tear her up while he sought his pound of flesh.

"You were very sweet," he said.

"You asked me to marry you," Riley said with the hint of a grin.

Her shoulders squared again. "Well, that was obviously the drugs talking. When I wasn't on a cocktail of god knows what, I showed you how I really felt. I bit you. And I'll do it again if you try to touch me."

Law had half the buttons undone, but now he saw another problem. She was wearing a delicate, lacy white garment with metal boning. Corset. She was corseted and she was lovely. Fuck, she would look so gorgeous walking around his club wearing nothing but that corset, a tiny white thong, and stilettos. And his collar, of course. But he would never leave her in a corset for this long. Never. "Can you even breathe?"

"Is that a corset I see?" Riley loved them on a woman, and he sounded choked that Kinley might be wearing one.

Her skin flushed everywhere. She wouldn't be able to lie effectively. The pink of her skin would always give her away. Law counted that as a plus.

"It was the only way I could fit in the dress. I think I need to sit down. I'm very dizzy." She fell back into his arms, her whole body going limp.

Damn it. She'd starved herself trying to get into that dress, then they had fed her sedatives and failed to remove a device that restricted her breathing. Fucking brilliant. "Give me a knife. I'm getting her out of this thing."

"Here." Riley was at his side, handing him his pocketknife and finally looking like he gave a damn. "Should I get her some water?"

Her eyes fluttered back open. "Did I pass out? Was I dreaming? Please let me be back in New York. I'll click my heels three times and everything."

"I'm sorry, baby. This isn't a dream, and you aren't in New York. There's no help for the dress. You need to breathe." He sliced through the buttons and then made short work of the lacy ties of the corset.

She breathed a deep sigh of relief. "Oh, my god, that feels so good."

The corset had left deep grooves in her skin, a map of where it had held her in. He touched one, unable to stop himself, and felt her shiver.

With distaste? With desire?

It didn't matter because they were no longer alone. Dominic stormed into the room.

"Do you have any idea what you two have done?" He was in full-on angry commander mode and the soldier who had never quite left Law responded.

"Sir, no, sir."

Kinley held the front of her dress to her chest and tried to scramble away, but she was caught in her skirts. She blinked up, her eyes wide and focused on Dominic.

"What the fuck is going on in here? Why isn't she dressed and ready to talk? Law, I swear to god, if you fucked her, I'm going to beat the shit out of you. She is the hostage, not your girlfriend."

"I'm no one's hostage. Let me go!" Kinley demanded, obviously realizing that Dominic held some power over that situation.

Dominic scowled. "No. You're going to be our guest here

until we get the information we need. That was the plan, but now we have to step it up because of something your careless suitor did."

"Me?" Law's head shook. "Crap. The cameras in the hallway of the hotel?"

"Ding, ding, ding. Get the man a prize." Dominic flicked on the television and quickly found one of the national cable news shows. Within five seconds, Law felt his eyes widen as a clip of grainy CCTV footage came over the television.

"Heiress Kinley Kohl was kidnapped yesterday afternoon from her hotel room in New York City. She was preparing for her four o'clock wedding to controversial tycoon, Greg Jansen…"

The news anchor went on, but Law barely heard her because he was far too busy watching the scene play out.

"That's me," Kinley said, watching the screen intently. "Oh, I look horrible. Is that when I asked you to marry me? No wonder you said no."

Riley snorted. "Actually, I had a moment of insanity and said yes. Oh, here it comes." On the screen, Law turned his face up and was captured right there for everyone in the world to see. "That's the twenty-five-to-life shot, big brother."

Fuck, how had he done something that sloppy? He hadn't been thinking at all. He'd been worried about Kinley and forgotten about the cameras. Now he'd screwed everything up. "We're on a clock."

It could have taken the police days to realize Kinley Kohl wasn't a runaway bride. He, Dom, and Riley should have had up to a week to really talk to her, to bring her to their side and win her help. With that one image, they were out of time.

Dominic kept his eyes on the screen. "Yep, and it started the minute you looked up at that camera. So we're not going to play games anymore." He turned to Kinley. "You will get up. You will dress yourself or I will do it for you. And you won't like what I pick out for you. Are we clear?"

She moved to Law, reaching for him. "I want to go

home."

He let her take his hand. Just because he'd screwed up didn't mean Dominic should take it out on her. "It's going to be okay, Kinley. He's not going to hurt you, either. Can you trust me?"

"I shouldn't."

"I promise you, I'll keep you safe, baby. Just go get dressed. Then we'll sit down and eat and have a perfectly nice talk. I know I look scary, but I won't hurt you. Ever."

She stepped back, and he felt the loss of her warmth. Just for a moment, she'd been looking up at him with softness in those eyes. "A-all right. Please excuse me. And you don't look scary. You're quite handsome, but I suspect you know that."

Dominic stepped up, towering over Kinley. "Don't try to run. The whole place is secure and you'll only get hurt if you run."

Her chin came up in a stubborn pout. "I think you would be surprised what I can do. Where are we? Upstate New York? We can't have traveled too far. Somehow I think I could find my way to a road, Mr. Whatever your name is."

"It's Dominic Anthony, and this isn't New York, honey. Welcome to Alaska."

For the second time that morning, Kinley fainted, dropping into Law's arms. He hoisted her up and held her to his chest before turning to Dominic. "I hope you're fucking happy. She was starting to trust me. You just ruined all of that. I'm going to make sure she gets something to eat. She can't give you information if she's passed out or dead."

Law carried her out, wondering why he'd ever agreed to this scheme in the first place.

* * * *

Dominic walked into the kitchen, well aware that he was completely unwanted there. Law had taken his damn time. An hour had passed since he'd carried her out like a fainting

Southern belle's gallant beau.

"Wow, he's serious," Riley had said, then gone thoughtfully silent as they both waited.

Well, Dominic was serious, too, and it was long past time that he got Law firmly on the same page as him and Riley.

He stopped as he caught sight of her. She was sitting in front of the big bay windows, staring out at the expanse of trees and grass and mountains in the distance.

"That's a whole lot of nature. Like way too much nature." She shook her head. "Do you think there are animals out there?"

Law laughed, the sound of a deeply amused man. "Absolutely. You wouldn't believe how many, baby."

He needed to rein this thing in. She was beautiful and seemed fragile, but he knew something Law didn't. "Tell him about your charity, Kinley. Tell him about the checks you've been writing."

She turned, a startled expression settling on her face. "What? You can't have abducted me to talk about Hope House."

Luckily, he had everything laid out. He opened the folder in his hand and set the documents Riley had dug up on the table in front of her. "Is that your handwriting?"

She set her coffee mug down, then picked up one of the copies of the checks. Her face flushed. "Yes. That looks like my signature. But why is it made out to '*Cash*'? I never need cash for the charity. Everything comes through vendors and we use our Tax ID to get exemption. These are the private checks, but they're just for backup. I've never used one."

So she was going to play dumb. "Over the last six weeks, you've drained almost fifty thousand dollars out of that charity."

She put her hand to her mouth. "No, I haven't. You're lying!"

And now Riley came in handy. He had his laptop open and ready. "This is your bank account for the charity. As you can see, over the last six weeks, there have been five checks written for cash, each for nine thousand nine hundred ninety-nine dollars and ninety-nine cents. One penny more and you would have been required to fill out forms. Someone knows their banking regulations. You're down to almost nothing in that account."

He saw Law's face fall as he looked down at the evidence in front of him. Damn, Dominic knew he was to blame for this mistake. He'd allowed Law to focus fully on surveillance and hadn't brought him into the loop during the investigative portion. All Law needed was firm proof that his honey was involved in Jansen's organization, and he would stop thinking with his dick and be ready to roll on the mission again.

Law took a step back from Kinley. "When did the money start disappearing? What date? What time was the check cashed?"

Riley ran his hands across the computer screen. "The first date was May tenth and the time stamp on the check is two thirty-five pm."

Law held up a hand. "Give me a minute."

Kinley sank into her chair. "I don't understand. I knew the balance was bad, but I had no idea the account was so close to empty. Greg promised he would write a check for a hundred thousand as a wedding present to me."

"As a wedding present or to cover your tracks?" Dominic paced as he talked.

"What? No! It wasn't to cover up anything. It was the first part of the fifty million he promised to endow the charity with."

"All right. Did he ask you to take out the funds?"

There was a time and a place to be the good cop. He'd be the best cop ever if she could help him pin illegal activities on Jansen.

"Greg never mentioned anything about it. I know this looks bad."

"This looks criminal," Riley pointed out.

"But I didn't have anything to do with this."

Was she telling the truth? Dominic sat across from her. Sometimes he thought he'd become far too cynical because he saw lies everywhere. Still, he had those checks. She'd signed them. She'd taken the money. Maybe she'd had virtuous reasons. Maybe not.

Dominic felt a little wave of peace flow over him. He was in control again. This was right where he needed to be. She didn't know it yet, but he was her best bet to avoid both jail time and her own murder. "Then don't make me use this. Work with me. Let's talk about your fiancé."

"I already tried, man," Riley said.

He ignored his friend. "The feds haven't been able to catch your fiancé, but I'm going to."

Her eyes came up, narrowing as she looked him over. "What did you say your name was?"

"I'm Dominic Anthony." There was no reason to lie to her. At the end of the day, she would be grateful he'd helped her. And if her gratitude didn't keep them out of the pen, then he would blackmail her with the information she was looking at.

"Are you any relation to Carrie Anthony?"

His gut turned a little. Had that fucker been talking about her? "Yes. She was my younger sister."

Those brown eyes turned sympathetic. "I'm so sorry about her death. She was far too young to go."

"Yes, she was." He let a moment of silence pass. "Especially since Greg killed her."

She should fully understand why he had chosen this path.

"Is that what this is all about?" She stared at him. "Mr. Anthony, I am truly sorry about your sister. Greg says she was a wonderful woman. He has a portrait of her that he keeps in the house. She was so beautiful."

Rage threatened to choke him at the thought of Jansen staring at a picture of his sister and remembering how easy it had been to take her money and her life.

Kinley leaned forward, her hand almost touching his. "But she was sick. It wasn't Greg's fault. He tried to get her into rehab."

Dominic practically saw red. Before he knew what he was doing, he flipped the table over, sending everything crashing to the ground. He was not going to listen to Jansen's latest piece of ass tell him his sister had been a fucking drug addict. "She never took a drug in her life. He's a greedy, murdering prick. Are you really this stupid?"

She raised her chin. "You're obviously very upset. I'm sure you don't want to believe—"

"He took out a two-million-dollar policy on my sister. Do you know what he bought with the money he got for killing her? A fucking condo. And two weeks later, he moved his mistress in."

She leaned back in her chair as though needing to put space between them. "He didn't kill her. He couldn't do that."

Dominic refused to allow the distance she sought. He stood and hovered over her. "Why would you say that? Because you can't stand the thought that you fucked a murderer? Or because you've known all along what he's capable of and you hate being caught?"

"Dom?" Riley ventured, his voice tense. "Down, boy. I think you're scaring her."

"I don't think she's scared enough."

"I'm pretty scared, but you should know that I won't let you break me. I might look silly and you can call me stupid all you like, but I won't allow you to use me against the people I care for. So if this is your best shot, Mr. Anthony, you should know you've failed. I believe you dummied up those records. Or you stole the money yourself. You're a grieving man, and I am so sorry that your sister is dead, but I won't allow your need for revenge to ruin my life. Make a decision. Let me go or you should just take the revenge you so obviously need and make it fast."

He stopped. "What?"

She was shaking, but she stared up at him with steady eyes. "I mean, I would prefer that you kill me quickly. You obviously can't let me go, and this would be a great way to get back at Greg if he loved me. You know he doesn't, though. I think he likes me all right, but he's marrying me to help his business. I'm quite a good hostess and I can help him in high society. He'll likely be upset, but I doubt he'll mourn me for long."

Kinley thought he was going to kill her? She actually believed he would take the life of a woman to avenge his sister. Suddenly, he couldn't think of a single reason why she shouldn't think he was a killer.

Dominic stepped back, nausea threatening. "I'm not going to kill you."

"Then let me go home."

He couldn't do that. He'd put them all in this situation and there was nothing to do except go through with his plans. He had to prove Jansen's guilt to her. He had to break her down. "No. You'll rest for a while. Then we're going to talk. I know you won't believe me, but this is for your own good."

"You can't keep me here forever."

He turned and started to walk out. He needed to ready the big guns. He'd hoped to spare her the worst of the knowledge, but she needed to understand exactly who she was trying to protect.

It made him a bastard, but he had to destroy all of her illusions. He wondered, just for the briefest of moments, if he was really saving her. If she was as innocent as she seemed, what he was about to show her might break her heart.

Well, he was proof positive that a person could live without one.

"Watch me."

Chapter Five

Kinley looked around her rather nicely appointed prison with Egyptian cotton sheets, solid wood furniture, and a stunning spa-like bathroom. She'd assumed that when Dominic said they could hold her here forever, he'd been exaggerating. Now, she wasn't so sure. Her "cell" and everything she'd seen of the place certainly looked self-contained enough to make that possible.

She'd tried all the doors and the windows, even to the point of attempting to break one. But someone had installed ridiculously thick glass. Her puny attempts to break through it had resulted in nothing except sore arms and frustration.

She'd finally given up and showered, then slipped on clean clothes. It was practically heaven to be out of that tight dress. Kinley had eschewed her jeans for a cotton skirt and long sleeved T-shirt. They didn't have any plan to rape her, it seemed. They'd had ample opportunity while she'd been passed out and hadn't taken advantage of it. Since her skirt wouldn't be making her ravishment easier for them, why not be comfortable?

When she'd awakened in her posh prison, she'd been surprised to find all her luggage and then some, including the cases of island wear she'd packed for her honeymoon in the Caymans. With all the sandals, swimsuits, and sundresses, she wasn't packed for Alaska—and Kinley suspected that's where she might actually be. She didn't hear the hum of a fan or air conditioner. If she'd been in upstate New York in summer, wouldn't they need some cool air by midday?

The other bit of evidence? The warm clothing the guys

had bought her. Law? He seemed like the concerned one. She was struck by the fact that none of the garments were as utilitarian as she would have expected a man to buy. The sweaters were all soft and cheerful, in colors she would have bought for herself because they complemented her complexion. The sweatpants were adorable and stylish with bling running down the pant legs. Even the socks were pink and fuzzy. It was as though someone had shopped with her taste in mind. Why would they care if the clothes they bought pleased her?

They were unusual kidnappers who apparently didn't watch TV to see how bad guys should really behave. She should probably be as scared as she'd been when she'd first awakened and realized they had locked her in the unfamiliar bedroom. But that level of fear was hard to maintain when her abductors had done little but feed and clothe her. Someone had even charged her iPad so she wouldn't be bored. If they were going to give her a diversion, Kinley didn't imagine they were going to waterboard her or stick bamboo shoots under her nails.

What they hadn't done was give her a sense of time. The sun was still up—and didn't it stay up forever in Alaska in the summer?—but she had no idea how many hours had gone by. They'd taken all the clocks. Without Internet, her tablet wouldn't tell the time in her current time zone. And she'd never gotten a cellular data plan for it. The rest of the room was bare with the exception of a plush queen bed, an elegant nightstand, one chair, and a lamp that hadn't proven to be as sturdy as the locked window. One blow and it was broken.

Maybe not her best move. When night fell would she be left alone in the dark?

She gazed out the window at the mountains in the distance, heavily covered by green everywhere—trees, bushes, soft grass, dotted with a few fledging flowers, all surrounding a lake. The views were sweeping, incredible. She'd only been to upstate New York once, so she certainly hadn't seen all of it, but the bit she recalled hadn't looked this majestic. Still, she had to hold out hope that she wasn't too far from civilization to escape, that home wasn't over four thousand miles away…

A brief knock sounded on the door before it opened too quickly for her to barricade it.

The biggest one walked in carrying the one thing guaranteed to make her feel better.

"I thought you might want her." He held Gigi in his big, callused hands that had been so gentle when he'd gotten her out of that god-awful corset. He was Law. The name suited him.

Her sweet Yorkie looked no worse for the wear. Gigi's little body shook, and she yipped and barked with joy.

With tears of relief, Kinley grabbed her sweet little puppy and held her close, filled with a guilty sense of happiness. She hated that Gigi and been nabbed and wondered how she'd been enduring captivity so far. But she was so relieved to have her puppy—one of her most beloved comforts—here with her.

"They brought you here? Oh, baby girl. Are you okay? Were you scared?"

Gigi just licked her nose, rubbing their faces together.

"She might have been scared, but she fought back." A lopsided grin bent Law's lips. God, when he smiled, her heart tended to stutter in a way it shouldn't about a man who had kidnapped and drugged her. A criminal shouldn't have a smile like that. "She had the good sense to bite the shit out of my brother. He struck out with both the Kohl females."

Silently, Kinley cheered on her dog. "Gigi is the sweetest little thing to me. Not so much to others. And she can bark like crazy when she doesn't get her food on time. She's used to being fed twice a day and she knows when it's dinner time."

"Ah, that explains a lot. She's been a little high strung." He sobered as he looked at the lamp on the floor. "Did you try to break the windows or was the lamp just particularly offensive?"

"You can't expect me to not try to escape." She turned

away. Maybe if she ignored him, he would leave. Being alone was preferable to being with criminals.

Was Greg a criminal?

"The windows are hurricane glass. A couple of years back, the owners had some trouble with hunters and stray bullets. They have kids and a whole lot of money, so they changed all the windows in the house. They're very heavy and almost impossible to shatter. The house has a top-of-the-line security system in place as well. We'd know if you somehow managed to even crack a window and we'd be on you very quickly." His voice softened. "You can't get away, Kinley, and you wouldn't be very happy if you did. We're miles away from anything you'd call civilization. There really are bears out there. You could get hurt."

She clutched her dog. "If you're so worried about me, why did you kidnap me from a beautiful bridal suite in Manhattan and bring me to this wilderness?"

He sat down on the bed, his big frame incongruous against the flowery comforter. He was a masculine beast in feminine surroundings. "You won't believe me, but we're trying to protect you, bab…Kinley."

Yeah, she was buying that. "This is about the big guy's revenge. How did you get wrapped up in this?"

"Dominic and I stick together through thick and thin. Always have, always will."

So she guessed the idea of trying to divide and conquer them wouldn't get her anywhere. If Law was willing to risk prison time to help Dominic, that said something serious about their bond. The only person she'd do that for was Annabelle, so she knew they must be thick.

"Look, I'm sorry about his sister. But I don't think I can do anything to give him the…closure he's looking for."

Kinley really was sorry. She couldn't imagine losing her sister. Becks might not be the most thoughtful sibling on the planet, but she was blood, family. Whatever his faults—and she'd bet there were plenty—Dominic had really loved his sister and grieved her now. Losing her to an overdose must have been terrible.

"Carrie never took drugs," Law said softly. "I grew up with her. I was in the same grade as Dominic, but we came from different sides of the tracks, to say the least."

"He came from money." She could tell. He had an air of authority that she'd seen emanate from the wealthiest of men. It came from the world being at their feet.

"A lot of it. And Ry and I…didn't."

"So how did you two meet Dominic?" Usually kids with such divergent upbringings didn't meet. She and Annabelle were the exception more than the rule.

Law shrugged, not like he didn't know, but like he was uncomfortable. "My dad ran off when Ry and I were kids. Mom…well, she did everything she could to keep us clothed and fed. I was out hustling kids out of their money at the movie theater one day. Cards, dice, whatever game of chance I could rig. I didn't beat anyone up for it, but some of the other little pukes did. They started picking on Dominic because he was rich and hadn't gone through puberty yet, so he was small. I thought three teenagers against a twelve-year-old was crappy and unfair. I was a few months older and had already started my growth spurt…and I liked fights, so I jumped in. Ry helped. Dominic became our best friend after that. Since Carrie was younger than him, I kind of watched her grow up. She didn't do drugs. Not ever."

Had Law been in love with her? She knew she shouldn't care, but he was being so gentle now, it was easy to imagine that he'd bestowed that tenderness on Carrie in the years he had known her before she'd died. Yet... Kinley hated to admit that Law being in love with Dominic's late sister bothered her.

"Maybe not as a teenager," she argued. "But she was a model. That world is very fast. You can't know what she did, then. Unless you were with her in New York."

He shook his head. "Oh no. We were getting our asses shot off in Afghanistan."

"You and Riley?"

"No, me and Dominic."

Why would the rich guy go into a warzone? "Did he go to one of the academies?"

"We were nineteen when 9-11 happened. Dominic said he couldn't sit in a classroom when his country was in danger. He left Harvard to join up. I followed him." Law shrugged. "I couldn't let him go alone."

Her sister wouldn't even go to the bathroom with her. Only Annabelle had ever been that kind of friend. She knew the deep connection it had taken for Law to follow his friend into battle. Kinley even had to give Dominic some grudging respect. What kind of courage had it taken for him to leave his wealth and privilege behind to serve his country on the other side of the world?

Of course, Law could be lying, too, to win her goodwill or sympathy or whatever. Kidnappers were criminals who didn't normally do good things. "I don't need to know your history."

She just wanted to escape. Maybe she and Greg could rearrange the wedding quickly with the same understanding in place. Certainly, she could convince him to pay for her father's procedure until they could schedule the ceremony again. The first payment to the hospital was due in a week. Her fiancé wouldn't punish her father by making him skip his treatment because she'd been kidnapped…would he?

"Yeah, you need to know this part. We had finished up our third tour of duty. We were back here in the States for training. Carrie had married Greg while we were gone. By then, we'd moved onto Special Forces and our missions were a matter of national security. We didn't go to the wedding, but Riley did. He told Dominic and I both that he had serious concerns about how Greg treated Carrie. One night a couple of months later, Dominic got a phone call from her. She left a voicemail because, well, we had the night off and we were taking advantage of it."

He flushed just a little, letting her know that they hadn't

exactly been playing charades. Kinley frowned. Had they been taking advantage of someone together? No. Oh. Oh. Were they gay? That was a horrible thought. It was kind of an insult to women everywhere that those two amazing hunks of masculinity would be interested in each other. She would have never guess it, but…

Why did her hot kidnappers have to be gay?

Irrelevant. She forced herself off that mental track. "What did her message say?"

Greg had explained that his first wife had suffered bouts of depression. He'd cared for her greatly, but in the end he hadn't been able to love her enough to save her.

"She sounded scared." Law stared at her, as if willing her to understand. "She said that she was leaving Greg and needed Dominic to call her. She was perfectly lucid and totally scared. She wasn't taking drugs."

"But—"

"The police found her dead twelve hours later, and I know Greg damn well killed her. Carrie was like a sister to me. He's my best friend. I can't just let it lie."

"Greg was in San Francisco when she died. He couldn't have killed her." Dominic's grief was clouding his logic. Kinley might not love Greg Jansen, but she certainly didn't picture him actually killing his wife.

So why was the tiniest part of her relieved that she wasn't going on her honeymoon today?

"What do you know about a man named Vincent Dargo?"

Kinley shivered. He was Greg's head of security. She couldn't stand how he looked at every woman who walked by like she was a piece of meat he couldn't wait to tear into. Brutally. Viciously. "I don't have much to do with him."

"I believe in my heart that he force-fed Carrie drugs that night under the orders of his boss, Greg Jansen."

Law's words painted a brutal picture that made Kinley shudder and wrap her arms around herself. Unfortunately, she didn't have to stretch her imagination to think Dargo capable of that. But Greg ordering him to do it? "Why? Why should I believe you? And why should you care what happens to me?"

He stood up and seemed to fill all the space in the room. "I'm not a gentleman, Kinley, but I'm going to be very honest with you because too many people in your life haven't." He sucked out a harsh breath. "I've been watching you for months."

She took a step back. "You've been stalking me."

"I suppose you'll probably use that word in court. I had to figure out who you are. I had to know if you were going into this marriage as Jansen's partner or his victim. And I figured something out about you."

"Really? I'm sure this is going to be impressive. You don't know me at all. Taking some pictures from a safe distance can't tell you anything about who I really am."

"Talking to you for the last week certainly has."

She froze. What was he saying? Not what she feared he was. Please, no. "I've never talked to you in my life before yesterday."

"Yes, you have." He stared down at her. His voice changed completely, becoming a bit higher and more nasally, the accent flattening out. "You know it. And it wasn't all a lie, Kinley."

Tears of complete humiliation flooded her eyes. "You're Mike."

"It's my middle name, if that helps." The voice was Law's again. All hint of "Mike" was gone.

"It doesn't." She turned away and paced, unable to look at him. "Wow, I'm a complete idiot."

But he'd spoken in a different voice, damn it. And why would she have expected California Mike to be in New York City?

Regardless, she should have known he was too good to be true, but she'd wanted so badly to believe that someone could like her for her. To escape to a fantasyland were a decent guy just wanted to spend time with her, regardless of her name or lineage.

"You are not an idiot! Trusting, yes. But not stupid. And once this whole thing is through, we're going to talk about your bad habit of insulting yourself. I won't have it." His low voice had taken on a sexy growl.

"You must have laughed at me, at how much I told you about myself, the feelings I shared…"

"No, if I laughed at anything, it was the fact that I never talk much. I especially never open up. To anyone. It's why they felt safe having me talk to you."

"They? Oh, you mean the other guys."

"I was supposed to get in, ask a couple of questions, figure you out, and be done. I was not supposed to talk to you for hours, but I couldn't help myself. God, Kinley, when I heard you laugh for the first time, it was like…I could see color in the world. That sounds dumb. Forget it. I'm not fucking good at this. Riley's supposed to handle this part."

She wasn't sure what he meant. She was still reeling from her own complete naïveté. "I made this snatch and grab so easy for you. I told you about the wedding and what suite I would be in."

"You told me how scared you were and how much you wished your mother was still around to give you advice. You told me I shouldn't be ashamed of what I wanted in life, even though I knew I'd shocked the hell out of you when I explained I wanted to find a woman to share with my brothers."

He'd talked about how he'd grown up so poor. How, after his father had left the family, his mother had turned to prostitution to feed them. He'd claimed that he knew what it was like to wear faded, secondhand clothes to school because that was all he and his brother had. She'd cried for him. She'd hung up the phone and cried because she'd felt so much pain for the little boy he had been. "How could you lie like that?"

"None of it was a lie, baby. I told you all about my life. My mother died when I was barely eighteen. I worked two jobs so Riley could finish high school, then I followed Dominic into the Army. I only had to work two jobs because Dominic fed us any cash he could. So the three of us have been family for a really long time." Law put his hands on his hips and blew out a deep breath. "And I'm going to go for broke and lay it out there, Kinley. I think you could be the woman to complete our family because you showed 'Mike' just how sweet and real you are. God, Kinley. You can't listen to your sister or the tabloids. You're smart. You're loyal. You're…damn it, you're just good. And I know that this whole situation is completely fucked up, but I want you—and not just for a few nights. I think I would be a better man with you in my life. In fact, I think you would make us all better."

A million thoughts crashed through her head. Law was Mike, and Mike could act. Such a pretty speech…but what if he'd been sent to win her trust and cajole information from her again. Dominic obviously thought she knew something and wanted the information, but… Was he too angry to ask her the questions himself? Maybe they all just thought she was pathetic enough to fall for the same act twice. Or maybe—

Law leaned over and brushed his lips against hers, cutting off all thought. And breathing.

Her heart pounded. Her skin flared with instant heat. What the devil was that?

He cupped the sides of her face so tenderly, looking at her like she was the key to solving all the mysteries of his universe, so perfect and precious. Kinley found herself standing there in half horror and half anticipation as he took her mouth.

Soft. She hadn't expected his lips to be so soft. Or for time to stand still for one amazing moment. She'd been kissed before, sloppy stolen embraces that had done nothing but make her wonder what all the fuss was about. Even her fiancé's kisses were casual. A peck here. A peck there. He claimed he wanted her to feel securely married when they first had real intimacy, but she'd known the truth. He didn't really want her like that.

The thing was…she'd never cared or thought sex mattered.

Law was making her rethink that. He treated her like she was a sweet to be savored. Like she was something rich, and he was a man who had never tasted anything so good and might never again. Law held her like she was priceless.

She couldn't help but close her eyes and catalogue the moment—the way his nose nestled against hers, his lips nibbling along her lower lip, making her shiver in delight. She took in every gentle brush of his tongue and the fact that each stroke had some electric connection to her nipples. He smelled good, all clean and minty. He'd brushed his teeth before he'd come in because he'd wanted this to happen. He'd wanted to kiss her.

Of course, he'd also duped her, abducted her.

God, she was kissing her kidnapper.

She jerked away, her lips still tingling. "Don't."

Law stared at her, his jaw firming stubbornly. "Kinley, I know none of this makes sense to you now, baby, but it will. I swear. I've been thinking that I'm too rough for you, but I see now that you need a man like me."

"Leave me alone. I don't need a criminal." She backed away, but with every step, her body protested and wanted to run back to him.

"You need all three of us," he insisted. "We're going to take care of you. I won't let anything bad happen to you. I'm crazy about you, Kinley. We're going to make sure Jansen can't hurt you like he did Carrie. Once he's behind bars, if you want to leave, I'll let you go. But I'm going to do everything I can to make you want to stay with us."

"Law? If you're done here, we need you in the office."

She gasped and turned. Riley stood in the doorway. She hadn't heard him come in, but then she'd been the stupid girl kissing her abductor. And enjoying it. Not to mention wondering what it would be like to kiss him back. She'd missed her chance, and suddenly her lips ached at the loss.

She turned away, refusing to meet Riley's stare, and clutched Gigi close. She hadn't been able to press her body against Law's because Gigi had been in the way. What if she hadn't been holding the puppy to her chest? Would Law have pulled her close? Would she have felt his erection pressed against her belly? Or not because it was all an act.

She felt his big hands cover her shoulders. "I'll be back, Kinley. Be good. And Gigi, don't bite Riley again."

Her first reaction was to ask him to stay, but she bit it back. He was playing her again. He'd committed a criminal act. She shouldn't feel safe with him. He was simply a smart, gorgeous man who would use any weapon at his disposal to keep her compliant.

She had to remember that. Greg—the man who'd sworn to help both her charity and her father—was her future.

No matter what her heart wanted to believe.

* * * *

Riley locked the door behind him before rushing to catch up with his brother. "What the hell was that about?"

He'd stood there watching them together, his brother more tender than he'd ever seen with a woman. It was like watching a different human being altogether. Law was…fuck. He'd seemed almost happy.

His brother turned to him. "I was just talking to her. I returned her dog before Butch could eat it. We don't have to scare her into helping us. She'll be a much better ally if she's happy. I can make her trust me."

"I walked in on more than a friendly chat. You were kissing her."

A little smile tugged at Law's lips. "Yeah."

Riley felt his jaw drop. "You understand that you sound like a fucking prepubescent boy making out for the first time."

Law shrugged, looking almost euphoric. "Maybe that's

how I feel. With her, it's like…everything is new."

"She is up to her neck in this shit, Law," he snarled. "You know that better than anyone."

"I know that she needs saving. Jansen is using her. I have proof that she isn't the one cashing those checks. You and Dominic think you were investigating her, but I found some surveillance photos of her when the first check was being cashed. Neither of you asked me before you accused her of stealing from her charity, but she was twelve fucking blocks away. Someone is forging her signature. I've got three guesses who it is, and the last two don't count."

If what Law said was true, then Riley had a pretty good guess who'd forged Kinley's signature, too. And if she was innocent…she would soon be devastated. Of course when she inevitably broke Law's heart, he would be the one devastated. Even if she'd never so much as spoken a cross word to anyone in her life, the girl came from money. She wasn't going to marry a whore's son, much less two of them, and take on a third husband for kicks. Her friends and family would be shocked. Their opinions would mean a lot to a girl like Kinley.

"Do yourself a fucking favor and don't kiss her again."

"Why shouldn't I? I'm not forcing her. I'm being gentle. If she tells me to stop, I will. But she didn't tell me to stop and she didn't move away."

"Dude, for starters, you kidnapped her. You've still got her under lock and key. Don't you get it? She's terrified of you."

Law paled a little. "You think so?"

His brother had lost his damn mind. "I know so. You outweigh her by at least a hundred pounds. Twenty bucks says that if you'd tried to lay her out, she would have let you because she doesn't want to piss off the badass. Think about this for two seconds. You're trying to…I don't know, ask her on a date. She's just trying to survive the day."

"I told her I wouldn't hurt her." Law seemed to stumble over the words.

"You also told her that you were Mike. Did you really vomit up all that shit about Mom?"

Riley had never told a soul, and now he felt a bit betrayed. He'd left their town and found new friends who didn't know that he was the son of the town whore. Friends who didn't know that his mother had died in a car accident with one of her johns.

Law shrugged like it was no big deal. "She's easy to talk to."

"It won't feel so easy when she stabs you in the back with that tale of woe and walks away from you. Think, man. A debutante and a prostitute's boy? Yeah, she's really going to show you off at all her fancy society parties. I mean, she might take Dominic because he's got some polish, but the whispers that we all share women are attached to him. People will talk. She won't be able to take it. And she'll break your fucking heart then. Don't say I didn't tell you so."

"Kinley isn't like that. When I told her our past, she didn't judge me, you, or Mom. She said Mom amazed her because a woman had to really love her kids to do something like that."

"What?" That didn't make any sense. Socialites didn't feel for prostitutes.

"I'm telling you. You have to get to know her for yourself. You're thinking that she's as snotty as Simone and she's not, man. Not even close. She's devoted her whole life to helping others."

God, this girl had Law so twisted in knots and thinking unclearly that it terrified Riley. "Pull your head out of your ass. You wanting this girl to be the one isn't going to make it true. Goddamn it!"

"Forget I said anything." Law's face closed up.

Riley had gotten what he wanted, but for some damn reason, he felt like a bastard. But it was better to point out certain truths now. "C'mon, bro. You have to back off. Otherwise, we don't get out of this without a criminal record. Do you want us all to go to jail because you couldn't stay out of her designer jeans?"

Kinley Kohl was gorgeous and soft, and she was going to bring them all down.

Law sighed. "No."

"We have to work through this the way we would any other mission. What is our goal?"

Law frowned, but Riley watched as his game face slid into place. An icy coldness overtook his features. "To gather the information we need to prove that Greg Jansen is laundering money for the mafia. Once we do that, the FBI can take over and toss the fucker in jail."

Dominic stepped out of the office. His face was grave. He looked them over as if he'd heard what had gone on and wasn't particularly happy about it. "She's the key, Law. You've always known that. Kinley knows something. She might not know she knows it, but it's in there. We need her to talk. I'm sorry you feel something for her."

Law turned, his face a bitter mask. "Yeah? You don't feel anything for her? Neither one of you? If you're trying to sell me that shit, you should do a better job of hiding your hard-ons."

Riley sighed. "Fine, I wouldn't mind taking her to bed. If she's what she seems to be, then she's kind of sweet. At least when she's not biting me. But man, I'm not going to touch that. She'll never be what we need. And after we've kidnapped her, she won't ever get past it to be what even one of us needs. There won't be any dating or romance so we can win her trust or woo her slowly."

Dominic put a hand on Law's shoulder. "I will admit to being attracted to her, but it can't go further than that. This is for her own good, Law. She's in bed with a man who has already killed one wife. Let's focus on keeping her from being victim number two by sitting her down and seeing how fast we can close this case. Then we can all move on with our lives."

Law nodded. "Fine. I'll set up the interrogation room."

"It's just a dining room. We don't have to be dramatic,"

Riley said with a sigh.

"I like to call things the way they are." His brother turned and disappeared down the hall.

Riley looked at Dominic. "I think we're doing the right thing."

Dominic suddenly looked a decade older. "For Carrie, yes. Is it really the right thing for Law? He's in love with that girl. Damn it."

"She can't possibly want him."

Dominic stared down the hall. "Can't she? Sometimes, the sweetest, softest females can prove to have the strongest minds and wills. I wonder what that woman could be if she had a sturdy man behind her, encouraging her."

"Don't you mean strong men?"

"I don't know. You don't seem interested in that life anymore, Riley. When this is over, I think I'm going to try to settle down for a while. Date a little. Look for the right woman, someone who can handle me and Law. I can't leave him behind. He'll never be comfortable on his own. Even with financial security, he would always worry about what would happen to his wife if he died. If we leave him alone, he'll wither. I can't do that to him. I owe him too much."

"You think I don't owe him, too?" He was painfully aware of how much he owed Law. When they didn't have enough food, his brother had gone without so Riley would have a full belly. Law had been the one to sit up all night with a baseball bat in his hand when their mother brought clients home.

"If you want a different life now, it's okay. You need to be free to pursue it. We've talked about this since we were kids, but dreams change. Law and I will be fine on our own."

"It's not that I don't want that life anymore." Frustration welled. "I just don't think it's possible. And I sure as hell don't think a socialite who spends all her time lunching is going to be 'the one.'"

"Maybe. Maybe not. Law gave me a lecture on the rituals and habits of our little blonde bombshell. Neither of us has paid any attention to her except as a potential witness for the feds to nail Jansen. Law has really gotten to know her. I have to concede… she didn't cash those checks. He has the proof. She works. Apparently she works really hard. Fuck. I don't know." He raked a hand through his hair. "I see your side. I see his side. She's got me confused, and I can't afford to be."

"I hear that, man. We just need to do the job. The rest will sort itself out."

It had to.

"You're right about one thing," Dominic said as he stared at the files in his hand.

"What's that?"

"Law never stood a chance with her. If he's wrong about her, then what I'm about to do won't mean a thing to Kinley, but it will shatter all of Law's illusions."

"And if he's right?"

Dominic grew grim. "Then I'm about to tear her down and rip her world apart. And after this evening, she'll never forgive any of us."

Chapter Six

Kinley kind of wondered why they didn't just bring in a spotlight and shine it directly into her eyes. The evening had become surreal, like she'd been dumped on the set of *Law and Order: Kitchen Edition.* In contrast to the sleek, modern room, the three big, alpha men who occupied the space were all displeasure and brute strength.

"I don't know what you're talking about," she swore. "My charity gives clothes to the homeless. I do not work for the mafia. Unless they could wear husky boys jeans. Then I could likely help them out."

She was getting a headache. Worse, Gigi was getting antsy, probably because Dominic had brought in his hulking bulldog, who sat by his master's feet as though he was a physical extension of the big guy's bad mood. And the dog growled up at Gigi like she was dessert. Kinley sighed.

How long had she been in this interrogation? It felt like days, and Dominic just kept asking the same questions over and over again, with occasional help from Riley. Law barely looked at her. It might be ridiculous, but his indifference hurt. When she'd been brought into the room, she'd tried to smile at him. He'd returned a blank expression, his gaze sliding over her like she wasn't there at all. He hadn't said a word since Riley escorted her from the bedroom that functioned as her cell, into the kitchen, then sat her down in front of a ream of deeply boring accounting reports.

Then the rapid-fire questions had begun.

What do you know about account 433629? Account 775410?

Tell me about invoice 35249. When was it paid out? Who received the funds?

What were you doing on May 15th?

And she'd answered the same way every time.

"Kohl, Kinley. Bride-to-be. 4325510996."

Her name, rank, and serial number. Well, her Neiman Marcus credit card number. It was the only number she knew by heart. If they wanted to steal it and buy high-end shoes…well, they were in for a shock because she was at her limit after buying wedding clothes.

She wasn't going to give them anything else, especially answers to questions she didn't know.

"Are you even going to look at the files?" Dominic asked. He stood over her, placing his hands flat on the table. He was a gorgeous man, even when he frowned, though now that she thought about it, she'd never seen him smile. In fact, no one was smiling now.

"There's no point. I don't know what you think is going on, but someone took funds out of my charity. They didn't use it to launder money. My accountant would have alerted me to that or any abnormalities." But why hadn't Steve told her about all the missing funds…unless he had something to do with it. Come to think of it, he'd been quiet lately. God, none of this made sense, but she wasn't going to look at these reports when they'd only try to use them to hang her.

"Then why is all that money missing? And when did you get in bed with Third World manufacturers?"

She thought about answering, but when she couldn't tell them what they wanted to know, then what? They kept claiming that they didn't intend to hurt her, and some hopeful part of her wanted to believe that. They'd probably sent Law/Mike in earlier to butter her up. But she wasn't falling for it. When it became apparent that she couldn't fill in the gaps in their information, would they kill her? Or would they extract everything out of her they could, no matter how minute, then off her? Either way, her best shot was to say nothing.

"Kohl, Kinley. Bride-to-be. 43255—"

"Do you know what RICO means?" Riley asked.

"Racketeer Influenced and Corrupt Organizations Act. And the grand jury cleared him." Greg had explained that there were corrupt people in the government trying to help his competition. After her kidnappers' accusations that Greg was a criminal, she might at least think it over. Or not. Greg was a pillar of the financial community. The men who kidnapped her were…well, kidnappers. Yes, Greg had been hauled in front of a grand jury, but there wasn't an indictment. Even more compelling, one of the prosecutors who had tried to indict Greg had been found guilty of fraud himself not a year later.

Dominic shook his head. "No, the grand jury doesn't clear anyone. They simply didn't have enough evidence to move to trial. Do you know why?"

"Because he's not guilty." From what she understood, the grand jury had convened two years before and had found nothing since. The FBI had given up because there was nothing to find.

"Because the prosecution's primary witness against him was brutally murdered three days before he was scheduled to appear. The man was an accountant. He had three kids. They all died in a house fire. Arson."

A chill went through her, but she tried to maintain her logic. "I'm sorry for that family, but timing alone doesn't prove that Greg set their house on fire. It could have been anyone, a pyromaniac out looking for a kick. In the months I've known Greg, he's never been less than a gentleman. I've seen no evidence that he's done any of what you claim. I know you want to take him down because you think that will avenge your sister, but this seems like a witch-hunt. Honestly…" she teared up. "I wish I could bring Carrie back for you. But I can't."

Dominic slapped a hand down on the table, making the whole surface shake. Gigi whimpered and huddled on her lap. "I didn't want to do this. I wanted to keep everything to business and leave your personal connections out of this, but apparently you don't give a shit who your fiancé kills or if he robs your charity blind."

"He's not a murderer," she insisted, trying to calm down her dog.

"Is charity work just something that rich women do to fill the long, dull hours between Botox treatments?" Riley growled.

It was harder to look at them now that she knew Mike was really Law. He'd probably told the other men the stories she'd told him in confidence—some of her innermost secrets. But he'd also told her stories about his brothers. Dominic was obviously the idealist. Dominic fought for what was right, even when it cost him. The younger brother, Riley, he'd characterized as the brilliant prankster.

Law had humanized them, given her a basic knowledge of them. So while they fumed and paced, snarled and clenched their fists, she wasn't quite as afraid as she'd been this morning. Kinley knew that Dominic loved justice, that Riley worried they would never find a woman who wanted them all because they'd had bad luck before.

Unless it had all been a lie, like "Mike" himself had been. She was so confused. The only way to not fall into their traps was to refuse to engage them. She kept her mouth shut, concentrating on her dog. It didn't matter what they thought of her. It just didn't. They were the ones who had spied on her, taken her from her life, played with her head.

"I'm not answering your questions. If this was a legitimate investigation, I would be sitting in a police station or an FBI field office. Real law enforcement officials would be asking me questions. You three should think about that. Pretty soon, you'll be the ones answering the questions, probably from behind bars."

Dominic practically stared a hole through her. "So you don't care about Jansen's criminal activity. Maybe you give a shit who he's sleeping with."

He slapped a picture down in front of her. It wasn't one of those grainy images, taken with a cheap telephoto lens. She didn't have any trouble at all discerning the focus of the picture. Oh, no. Someone had expertise with a camera and had spent money on superior equipment and photo processing.

Kinley stared, blinking a few times, as if that would right her eyes somehow and clear the terrible image in front of her. It didn't work. Every time she opened her eyes, the awful truth was still waiting. No mistaking what the two people in the picture were doing. No way could she fool herself into believing that Greg was just giving the woman in the photo a friendly hug. They were naked, and he was clearly touching her all over, especially inside. Greg had bent the blonde he screwed into what appeared to be a lounge chair by his pool. Kinley had laid in that very chair the last time Greg had invited her family over for a barbecue.

Nausea threatened to overtake her as she stared down at the damning photo because not only could she clearly see Greg's face, the woman's identity was impossible to miss.

Becks was sleeping with her fiancé.

She looked up at Law. He wasn't shocked. Instead, he looked grim and closed off, with his arms crossed over his chest. Had he known the whole time he had followed and talked to her that she was being wretchedly deceived by two of the most important people in her life?

Tears welled up. Not for Greg's betrayal. She wasn't even sure she was crying about Becks's. The truth was, she couldn't stop berating herself. How stupid and naïve Law must think she was. In fact, all of them must think that. How had she not even suspected?

"How long?"

Law didn't pretend to misunderstand, and she appreciated that. "As far as I can tell they were lovers about six months before he met you."

"She introduced us." Kinley hadn't meant to admit that out loud. It probably made her sound even more naïve. But she supposed she was. She certainly felt that way.

Law's right shoulder shrugged up in a negligent gesture. "Sounds about right. I believe they've been colluding together for a while."

I have the perfect man for you, Kin. Don't screw this up. This is important. This could be your future.

She'd been so insistent. Becks hadn't taken no for an answer when Kinley had tried to get out of the date. Nope. Becks had come over to her apartment and helped style her hair and picked out her clothes. It had been nice for her sister to pay attention to her. She'd liked the thought they might grow closer. Becks had said she wanted that, too.

It had all been a lie.

"Your sister recently bought a multimillion-dollar life insurance policy on her husband." Riley placed a photocopy of the paperwork in front of her. No disputing the evidence. Becks had taken out a three-million-dollar policy on her husband, naming herself the sole beneficiary. She would absolutely benefit from his death, just the way Greg would have benefitted from hers once they'd been married.

Kinley took a long breath, wishing this nasty position she found herself in—deceived by her sister and fiancé, and used in a vendetta by the three men around her—wasn't real. But obviously, she'd been discounting the truth too often lately.

"Who would run Hope House if you die?" Dominic asked, his voice completely steady as though he wasn't shattering her world.

She suspected they damn well knew the answer, but told them anyway. "Becks."

"I'd bet every last dime I have that she's already dipping into your funds. I have no doubt she's the one who cashed those mystery checks from your charity's account," Law growled.

Kinley hated to believe that her sister could be capable of stealing from her. Cheating on her husband, yes. Becks had all but admitted it just before the ill-fated wedding. Sleeping with

Greg was crushing enough. But this… It felt like a poison-laced ice pick to the chest. But who else could it be? No one else knew where she kept the paperwork for Hope House. Becks was clever enough to forge her signature, too.

"Or I guess your dad could have taken the funds. After all, he has all those gambling debts to pay," Law said matter-of-factly.

"Gambling debts?"

Dominic dropped a series of photos of her father at the race track and at a poker table, smoking and drinking, his face grim. "Riley took those. He had a camera in his hoodie."

"Your father likes to play deep and he's horrible at the card table," Riley added. "He tugs on his ear or blinks a lot when he's bluffing. They're obvious tells."

Kinley didn't even know that her father liked playing cards. "Leave my dad out of this! He's got cancer."

Law knew that. She'd cried to "Mike" during a long conversation one night. She'd confessed how scared she was that she would lose her dad the way she'd lost her mom. She'd tearfully explained all the long nights she'd sat up with her mom and how she'd been forced to watch the woman who'd given birth to her waste away.

"Maybe this is a distraction for him," Kinley spit at them. "If he needs the diversion to escape a possibly terminal illness, I can't blame him. I'll talk to him about not playing in high-stakes games when I get home, but for now, he's off-limits."

"After you told me about his illness over the phone, I had Riley check it out," Law began. "He hacked into the patient records of the hospital your dad said he'd be going to. They have no record of him. Neither does a single oncologist on staff. Your dad doesn't have cancer. It's all a ruse to bilk you out of money."

"That can't possibly be true!" Of course it would be great news if her father wasn't dying, but she could hardly believe that he would scam her for money.

Law's face remained like granite, resolved and grim. She

had a sudden feeling that the bad news wasn't going to stop. She forced herself to meet his stare. "Please don't do this to me."

He gave her no mercy. "Your father has been coming to you for money so he can pay his bookies. He's also run up all his credit cards. Someone, probably your sister, forged your name on his new applications as his cosigner." He grabbed yet another of those seemingly never-ending photos and shoved it toward her.

Her father, Becks, and Greg were sitting in a swanky restaurant, looking like they were having a grand old time. There was a date and time stamp on the photograph.

"Kinley, this was taken four days ago. The night before you told me that your father had an oncology appointment at noon the next day. You confessed how worried you were that he wouldn't let you go with him."

"He said he didn't want this to be a repeat of Mom's illness. He said he couldn't stand the thought of putting me through it again." Had it all been a lie? "I begged him to let me go, but he convinced me to just write the check. Greg promised to help pay for Dad's treatments after we were married. It's why I agreed to bump the wedding up. Originally, I wanted to get married in the fall."

But that hadn't suited Greg's or Becks's plans. Kinley had been stubborn about it because she'd always dreamed of a fall wedding in New York. She had also wanted more time to get to know Greg…and to see if she could pull them out of their financial problems without being forced to marry.

And then her father had gotten sick. Supposedly. Now she didn't know what to think.

Kinley tried to channel her anger toward Law, Dominic, and Riley for spying on her family and trying to crush her illusions. But she couldn't quite get there. All the evidence pointed to her family and fiancé betraying her. Dominic, Law, and Riley were simply revealing it.

"Poor little rich girl," Dominic drawled.

That voice grated on her nerves. She grasped at whatever straws she could find. "How do I know you're not fabricating evidence?"

"Why would we do that?" Riley asked. "Think for two seconds. Give me one good reason we would."

"Because you want revenge on Greg."

"What kind of revenge would making evidence up give us, Kinley?" Dominic grilled her.

"You could release the pictures and cause a scandal. That would be a big story for a long time. He wants to make contacts with society people, businessmen who were close to my mother and grandparents. I have those contacts. If those people think of him as a cheating, swindling scumbag, or I publically malign Greg, they will have nothing to do with him. He won't make the connections he wants to."

"This is about far more than scandal, Kinley. I firmly believe he's using your charity as a front for some illegal venture. You should want to know if that's true yourself."

Her gaze strayed back to the pictures of her sister and her fiancé. Kinley's whole world was crashing around her. Everything she'd thought she believed about her family and her future was now being called into question. She whimpered.

Kinley wanted to hate Dominic, but didn't have the energy. Every bit of her strength right now went into keeping her chest from imploding and not crying in front of him and the other two.

"No one tells you the truth, do they?" Law said without any trace of the lover who had held her so tenderly just hours ago and given her a kiss she would dream of for the rest of her life.

He certainly hadn't been honest with her. Greg hadn't either. That rat bastard had told her that he thought she was lovely, that he couldn't wait for their honeymoon. The whole time he'd been sleeping with her sister. Even her own father had been lying to her. As much as she'd tried to bend for the people in her life, to please them…it had been one giant waste.

Apparently they saw her as a target to con.

All of her insecurities welled, a giant wave threatening to crash over her. Her father had always preferred Becks. Apparently, Greg did, too. Now that she really thought about it, all of the women he'd dated before had been slender and model-like. Had Greg been dreading the moment he had to touch her fat body? Had he put it off all this time until it was absolutely, positively necessary? But why marry her at all if he didn't want her?

Ten million dollars. And Becks must have known about the scheme. It seemed far too coincidental that she'd taken out a three-million-dollar policy on her husband at roughly the same time. Which meant Becks and Greg were probably in this scheme together.

Her sister wouldn't really let someone kill her…would she? She couldn't possibly be that cold. The way money wasn't mysteriously disappearing from her charity? The way Becks hadn't been sleeping with Greg? Oh dear god. Was it possible Dominic, Law, and Riley were right about everything?

"You need to start using your head, Kinley. Read over the accounting reports. Something is wrong at Hope House. Greg, Becks, and your dad have kept you too busy with the wedding for you to notice. Well, guess what, honey? We've made sure you have all the time in the world to figure it out now. So look at the fucking reports and tell me your fiancé is clean. Because either he's dirty or you are. One way or another, whoever's guilty is going to jail." Dominic stormed out of the room.

The bulldog stayed, his eyes on Gigi.

Riley set the accounting paperwork in front of her. "Don't bother trying to escape the kitchen. I'll be right outside the door. The other entrance is locked. The windows don't open in this room, and if I hear you trying to break one again, I'll put you over my knee. No one will stop me from smacking your ass red."

"I thought you were supposed to be the funny one," she

muttered under her breath.

Riley's eyes strayed back to Law. "Is that what he said? Well, there's nothing funny about this situation."

He sent his brother a long look and left.

She didn't understand what he meant at all. "Could you please leave, too? I'd like to be alone. I promise I'll look at this stuff."

"I'm staying in case you have some trick up your sleeve."

She was beyond tired. "What would I try, Law? Everything I try fails. I try to be a good sister, and Becks sleeps with my fiancé. I try to be a good bride, and my fiancé plans on killing me once I'm his wife. I try to do good in the world, and apparently everyone just uses me, including my father. In fact, everyone I've loved and trusted just might be plotting to kill me. Hell, I even tried to make a friend, but it turned out that even you lied to me."

"I didn't lie to you about anything except my name."

"You told me you cared." Why was she harping on this? She hurt so badly, and somehow the thought that Law had fabricated a bunch of crap to placate her only made her feel twenty times worse. Why?

His face softened for a moment. "Kinley, I…" His jaw firmed. Then he closed his eyes and pulled back, and she knew she'd lost him. "I did what I had to do."

"Then leave, and I'll get through this stuff faster. Like I said, I won't try anything. I would just fail."

He stopped, and for the briefest of moments she thought he would insist on staying with her. "Fine, but know that if you try, I will let Riley spank you. When he's done, I'll have you over my knee, too. And I won't let you up until we're on the same page."

"Brutalizing women. Very nice."

He stopped in front of her, his stare holding and drilling into hers. "I didn't say you wouldn't like it, baby. I just said we would be on the same page." He frowned. "How do you do this to me? How do you make me forget everything I planned?

Come on, Butch. She doesn't want you anymore than her owner wants me. Let's go."

Butch slowly padded toward the door, his doggy eyes lingering on Gigi.

Law left with the big animal, the door swinging behind them.

Kinley stared down at the photos and reports, the brutal proof that her whole life was a lie. Her tears began to flow in earnest.

* * * *

Law walked out of the kitchen feeling like the lowest fucking piece of shit on the planet. He crossed the hall and stalked into the office he, Dominic, and Riley were using as their base of operations. "I really hope you two are happy."

Had ruining Kinley's life been worth it? Maybe if he had tried again, he could have figured out a way to put Greg behind bars without wrecking all her illusions.

I would just fail. Her big brown eyes had been filled with tears. Pain had been etched onto her sweet face.

He'd caused that. Maybe he hadn't been the fucker cheating on her or planning to kill her, but he'd helped to expose it all. And he'd done it coldly because he knew his feelings for her were hopeless. Dominic was right. Hell, even Riley was probably right. Even if he hadn't abducted Kinley, how would a woman with her class and sweetness ever survive a relationship with him, a brooding Dominic, and a smartass Riley? It sounded impossible, and he was such a stupid ass for fighting that realization.

"No," Dominic said. "I'm not happy. And we have a problem. Annabelle is on the line. Riley, can Kinley hear us?"

Riley crossed the room and shut the door. "No, the doors are thick, and we're far enough away. I can see her through the panes if she tries to come out of the kitchen. I secured the other doors, and the windows won't break. We're good."

Law was happy about that because the last thing Kinley needed was to know that her best friend had been in on this plot from the beginning. One more betrayal, and Kinley might not survive, even if Annabelle had participated with good intentions.

Dominic pushed a button on the phone. "Annabelle, tell us what's going on."

"Greg is freaking out." Annabelle's voice was hushed. "He suspects you. I overheard him talking about it with that goon of his, Dargo. At first he thought that Kinley got cold feet. He was really upset about the luggage."

"Why would he want her luggage?" Law asked.

"It's designer," Riley explained. "You'll have to excuse my brother. He's not into designer anything. We're lucky he doesn't still wear his BDUs."

They wouldn't let him or he would. He'd spent so much time in uniform it felt weird to be in civvies, even years later. The Army had been simple. No need to pick out his clothes. No wondering if he looked like a douchebag. Kinley probably liked a man who knew how to dress.

Annabelle sounded thoughtful over the line. "I know a full set of Louis Vuitton is expensive, but her engagement ring cost far more, and he didn't give a damn about it. I overheard him talking to Becks, and he was pissed. He told her that she needed to find Kinley and get that luggage back or she would be the one in trouble."

They'd been through her luggage. Law hadn't found anything but her clothes, makeup, and an iPad. He'd put the tablet in airplane mode, and she didn't know the password for the Internet, so Riley had declared it harmless, but maybe he should look at it again. All he'd seen was a bunch of games, pictures, and her e-reader app, which was completely full of romance novels. Unless Greg liked cross-dressing in private or needed to catch up on his reading, Law wasn't sure why he would want anything she'd packed for her honeymoon.

"We'll go through it all again. Something's not right

there," Dominic said. "We're working on Kinley, but I can't tell if she simply doesn't know anything or she doesn't want to tell us."

Law was pretty fucking sure she didn't know. "Come on. You saw her face. They've kept her out of the loop, and we just crushed her with all that information. She's looking over everything we left her now. Maybe once she's convinced, she'll start thinking about what she knows. One thing about Kinley I'm sure of, it's that she has a good heart. She wants to do what's right."

Dominic sent him a sigh that was somewhere between thoughtful and contrite.

"Spare me." Riley rolled his eyes.

He got in his brother's face. "You spare me. Why don't you stop assuming she's just like Simone and fucking get to know her before you jump to all kinds of assumptions?"

Dominic cleared his throat. "Has anyone been able to find the accountant she uses?"

"Yes," Riley muttered. "Tate found Steve a few hours ago. I hadn't had a chance to tell you. He claims Greg fired him eight weeks ago. Since he worked from home, he rarely saw Kinley. Imagine Steve's surprise when he found out that he was supposedly still employed. Tate showed him the reports someone had filed on his behalf since he was fired. He claims none of the work is his. So we have to assume that Greg has been quietly putting his own people into position."

And isolating Kinley from anyone who could help her. "The bastard."

"There's no question about that," Annabelle replied, then her voice became even more grave. "We have another problem. When he couldn't find Kinley, he called the police. They found a surveillance tape."

"Seen it." Riley sounded long-suffering. "It's all over the news. Not our shining moment."

Law groaned. He was never going to live that shit down. "I'm sorry."

Annabelle ignored him. "The police identified Law as the man on the tape."

Law's chest tightened. Just as he feared, he would likely be going to prison. And that brought up more than one problem. "If I turn myself over, do you think they'll let Riley and Dominic off? I can say they had nothing to do with it, that I had a different crew."

"Don't you fucking dare." A male voice came over the line. He wasn't trying to be quiet at all. "This is Kellan, and I need to hear you verbally authorize Annabelle to pay me."

"What?" Law asked.

"Do it," Dominic ordered in that CO voice of his.

"Whatever. Pay the man, Annabelle," Law said.

"Law, I'm giving Kell a dollar as a retainer," she explained. "He's now your lawyer. As such, he can advise you, and everything he says is protected under attorney-client privilege. Everything you tell him is covered as well, with the exception of knowledge of crimes being currently committed. Do you understand?"

So he was supposed to lie. "Yep."

Kell's voice came back on the line. "I'm a very smart man. I can guess what happened if the police come to ask me about anything. Let's see if I have this straight. You and Kinley have been having a whirlwind affair. She didn't have the courage to face Greg, and you carried her away from her wedding because she had gotten very emotional and taken a sedative. She was so incapacitated that she couldn't walk. You knew she would be horribly embarrassed, so in an attempt to save your lover's peace of mind, you had your brother help you carry her out. You disguised yourself and hid her in the laundry cart because you were avoiding the paparazzi."

Kellan shouldn't be a lawyer. He should be a fiction writer. "Yeah, sure."

"You two will come home after all the chaos has died down. Can we get Kinley to support that story?"

"Not yet."

"Ah, she's still emotional and feeling the aftereffects of the medication designed to calm her nerves. Well, call me when she's better. With so much going on, I understand it could take a day or two. Whatever you do, I would advise you not to confess to crimes. How is the investigation going? Has Kinley explained where the invoices are coming from?"

If they could come up with evidence that would make the RICO charges stick, the feds would take up the case again. The whole idea had been that if Kinley saw how she was being used, she would forgive them for abducting her. He'd been so sure of that. He wasn't anymore. "She's not talking yet, but then we just hammered her with the fact that her fiancé, sister, and father have all betrayed her."

"Is she all right?" Annabelle asked, obviously concerned.

"How would you be if you found out your family was lying and planning to off you?" Law couldn't imagine it. Riley, for all his sarcasm, was such a part of Law, he couldn't fathom not having his brother around. For all of Kinley's privileged upbringing, other than Annabelle, she was utterly alone in the world.

Law wanted her to know that wasn't true, that someone was willing to fight for her. She needed a man who wasn't so self-absorbed or insecure, who would stand up for her, risk himself to keep her safe and happy. The woman Mike had met deserved that.

"Kinley's stronger than she knows. Let me talk to her. Maybe if she knew that I believe this is best for her, she would cooperate," Annabelle said. "She knows I don't have any motives other than saving her."

"That's a horrible idea," Kellan said. "If Kinley even once said where she was or explained that she wasn't, in fact, still recovering from her emotional bout, then Annabelle would become an accessory after the fact if she didn't go to the police."

"I can handle it, Kell," Annabelle insisted.

"Not on your life, baby. You're not doing this. You're

lucky we allowed you to be involved in this in the first place."

"Allowed?" Annabelle wasn't trying to keep her voice down now. She was practically screeching. "Allowed! You don't own me. She is my best friend. I brought this case to you."

"And now you're out of it. If you don't obey me, we're going to have a long talk."

"I am not one of your club subs, Kell. I will talk to my friend if I want to. And I will lie to the cops all day long if the mood strikes me."

"Gentleman, my assistant and I are going to go and have a brief discussion. I am so happy to hear that Law and Kinley are settling into their future as a couple. I will advise any law enforcement that comes my way to that effect. Unfortunately, I was not given the whereabouts of your love nest. And Annabelle isn't privy to any of that information, nor will she be. Oh, and unfortunately Annabelle has dropped her phone and stepped on it, rendering it utterly useless for finding the phone numbers of her most recent calls. So sad."

"No need," Riley explained. "This is a burner. We have about fifteen in our possession. No names are attached to the numbers, everything was paid for in cash, and they come from completely different parts of the country. We'll call in again. And we'll get rid of this line. Talk to you later."

As Riley pressed the *End Call* button, Law could hear Annabelle arguing. He wasn't sure what was going on at that law firm, but Annabelle was going to be in trouble. He'd seen Kell, Tate, and Eric watching their administrative assistant like she was a fluffy bunny and they were lions who had gone without a meal for far too long.

Rather like he watched Kinley.

"I'm going to go to the kitchen and talk to her again."

"I don't think that's a good idea," Dominic said. "She needs time to process all we've told her, and we're probably the last people she wants to see."

"I should at least check on her." He wasn't going to leave

her alone in there with all the evidence of betrayal around her and no shoulder to lean on. Law knew to his core that she was a good person whose only sin had been in trusting the people she should have been able to.

Law turned and walked back into the kitchen, ready to talk to her, to try to make her understand what was really going on. And he froze because she no longer sat in the chair in which he'd left her.

His heart nearly stopped, but then Gigi was at his heels, whining up at him. He looked around the kitchen and saw her. Her body was facing the large pantry door, her hands covering her face. Though she wasn't making a sound, her body shook with the force of her tears.

Law felt something break inside him.

Fuck this. He was done pretending he wasn't in love with her. He was done acting as if this scheme was just something he'd agreed to in order to help Dominic. He was done lying to himself that he didn't need her.

He'd spent a lifetime being the badass, being the guy who didn't feel a thing. He was fucking done with that, too.

Law stormed across the room and did what he'd been dying to since the moment he'd seen her. He wrapped his arms around her and offered her his strength. "Don't cry, baby. I can't stand it when you cry. I'm here for you. I'll make it better."

Chapter Seven

Kinley knew she should pull away, but Law was so warm, solid, and strong. She felt so in need of human comfort. The minute the door had closed behind them, she'd stared at the photos they'd stuck under her nose and seen her life laid out for her. Then the wedding, the abduction, the interrogation, the kiss, the mess her life had become—all crashed down on her.

The fact that she'd been alone and crying her eyes out only magnified her sense of loneliness. Until Law had arrived and given her someone to hold on to, an anchor so that she wouldn't continue drowning in shock and sorrow, confusion and hopelessness.

Sheer need propelled her into his open arms. She'd spent a solid week getting to know him. He might have used a different name, but she'd learned about the goodness of his heart. Yes, and his goodness deep down had her clinging in his embrace.

Then the memory of their kiss made her lift her face to him and silently beg for another.

Law's mouth descended, slanting across hers, claiming her lips and giving her blessed moments of respite. Kinley didn't have to think. She didn't have to worry. His kiss obliterated everything else. She only had to feel.

Her heart raced as she breathed him in—a hint of his aftershave, the mint on his breath, the masculine scents of leather and coffee and man that seemed uniquely Law. She ran her palms up the muscled slab of his torso, covered only by the thin material of his T-shirt. Everything about this man was hard with the exception of his lips.

And his words as he broke their kiss and cradled her face in his hands, his mouth just over hers. "You're so fucking sweet. You shouldn't ever have to cry. Jansen doesn't deserve to have you in his life."

Law sank his hands into her hair, sweeping it from the loose bun she'd created to keep it off her face. He tugged at it, lighting up her scalp. He forced her head to tilt up, and his mouth closed off any protest.

As his tongue traced the seam of her lips, she felt a tug in her womb. He held her still as he explored her mouth. She parted her lips wider for him, unwilling to let go of this heady, consuming feeling. She'd been kissed before, sloppy brushes of lips in awkward embraces that had made her shudder with discomfort. Kinley felt none of that with Law. Everything about being with him was completely different. Totally arousing. His gentle comfort and rough insistence created an intoxicating demand she fell into and hoped would never end. He held her as though she was precious, as if he savored her. His kiss made her feel hot and happy and restless for more.

Kinley wasn't about to end this embrace with the same regrets as the last. This time, she clutched him tight and slid her tongue along his. He growled into her mouth, and she felt the sound vibrate just under her skin.

Encouraged, Kinley moaned and opened wider for him to deepen the kiss. Law didn't hesitate to take advantage of her offering. For the first time, she felt her feminine power. Always, she'd waited, allowed life to come to her on its terms, never even asking for what she wanted. But as Law kissed her, she suddenly understood the "more" she'd been yearning for in the bridal suite. She ached to make him growl and moan. To sweat and burn. To make him hungry for her—like he was making her hungry for him. Kinley gloried in simply feeling.

She pressed her chest to his. Law stood so tall that he towered above her and nearly had to bend in half just to kiss her, and she loved feeling petite.

Then a kiss wasn't enough for him anymore. Law

surrounded her, pressing her against the pantry door with an indrawn breath and a groan. Again, he seized her mouth. Kinley's nipples sparked to life, and her head reeled as he took the kiss even deeper, leaving her dizzy and feeling out of control.

She'd always been the good girl. Her mother had taught her that she had to be the responsible one because her father and sister just didn't have it in them. After her mother's passing, the never-ending job had fallen to her. She'd taken care of her family because it was her nature.

But this wild gush of emotion felt natural, too. It felt right to be with Law.

It was probably stupid. She would likely regret the hell out of it because he would ultimately use her passion for him against her to coerce her to cooperate with Dominic's plans. But right now was for her. Kinley wasn't thinking about what anyone else would think or say. For the first time ever, she was living in the moment and refused to stop because she wanted to feel adored, like a beautiful, desirable woman just this once.

Suddenly, he lifted her like she weighed nothing. She gasped. No one had picked her up since she was a child.

"I need you higher, baby. Maybe you should always wear those heels of yours. Have I told you how fucking gorgeous you are? Have I told you that I've been hard for you since the minute I laid eyes on you? My cock has been in hell." He stopped, his eyes flaring. "Shit!" He let her slide down gently, making sure she was balanced. "I'm sorry. I shouldn't talk to you that way. I should be gentle."

No way was she ready to stop yet. She pulled on his shirt with a little whimper. Didn't he understand? She didn't want to think or talk or be gentle. "Don't you dare. You can't kiss me like that then ignore me again. Not yet."

She couldn't face that possibility or all the other crap on her plate now. She wanted to forget, at least for a while. Just a few kisses. Just for a few precious moments. Then she could return to the real world where no one wanted her and figure out how to cope as everything fell apart.

"I don't know how to be gentle with you, like I want to be." He smoothed her hair back, staring down at her. His eyes were so blue…

"Just be you. No more lies. No more pretending." She wanted that more than anything. She wished that she could simply be Kinley, without the everyday responsibilities that caused her to shove down her wants and needs for everyone else. She could be herself and Law could be the tenderly rough soldier who took her to a place where only they mattered. She wanted to be free, even if it was temporary. Even if it wasn't real.

"You don't care that I'm too rough?" He tugged on her hair, seeming to hold his breath as he waited for her answer.

"How would I know what's too rough for me?" Nothing he did felt overly forceful or physical. Every touch felt just right. Kinley peppered kisses up his neck, across his jaw, clutching his T-shirt in her fists. "Please…"

"Baby, you asked for it." His growl resonated in her ears low, sexy.

Then she was in the air again. He picked her up, wrapping his arms around her waist. She had to hang on to his shoulders as he turned and walked toward the huge island in the middle of the kitchen. He set her on the sleek black granite countertop and immediately stepped between her legs, making a place for himself there.

"I was a soldier. Special Forces. You can't imagine the things I've done. I didn't go to college. I don't deserve you, Kinley, but I fucking want you. So bad."

She had the urge to wrap her legs around his lean hips and get as close as she could. Her whole body felt like it was softening, warming up, aching to be even closer.

He pulled her in, aligning their hips, making it impossible to mistake just how hard Law was. His penis nearly pressed out of his pants, he was so erect. And big. Feeling just how much he wanted her made Kinley restless. She writhed to relieve the ache as her heart tried to beat out of her chest.

Law Anders truly, genuinely wanted to have sex with her. He wasn't paying her lip service. As far as she knew, men couldn't fake erections. He actually desired her.

And she wanted them.

Oh, god. She'd just thought the word "them." As soon as she had, a vision of herself in the middle of Law, Dominic, and Riley had seared into her brain. They would surround her, maybe even crowd her. They'd boss her around…but in her fantasy world, they would also adore her. Because they were all so big, she would feel small and feminine against them. Their hands would explore her body, caressing and stroking her. It might not be love, but she could hold onto the memories during the long and lonely days that were sure to follow her into her future.

What was she thinking? How could she have sex with three men? The notion was ridiculous. Scandalous. And so arousing that she could barely breathe.

Law captured her lips before she could think another word. His tongue surged in, and he made love to her mouth—deep, ferocious, lacking all restraint. Kinley was lost.

He slipped a hand down her neck and shoulders, curving his palm over her breast. His touch seared her. She melted into him, giving herself over to the delicious burn.

Law kissed her neck, nipped at her ear. "Do you know what you want? Where you like to be touched? What gets you hot? Just tell me, and I'll give it to you."

"I have no idea what I like besides your kisses." Beyond that, Kinley had no way of knowing. She'd spent her high school years studying and trying to be the perfect daughter. When college had come, her mother had fallen sick. As she'd slowly wasted away, years had passed. All she'd known then was duty—to her family, her schoolwork, her community, then her mother's legacy.

Never once had she ever simply let go and explored.

"Dear god, you're a virgin?"

They both pulled away, shocked at the low, masculine voice cutting through their thick passion.

Dominic Anthony stood not three feet away, watching. He'd taken off his jacket and now stood dressed in a button-down shirt, gray form-fitting slacks, and designer loafers. Open at the throat, the white dress shirt contrasted with his olive complexion. Dominic stood as tall as Law, but he was built leaner. With jet black hair, fathomless dark eyes, and a jaw that had been cut from granite, everything about him screamed savage.

She remembered what California Mike—no, Law—had told her about him. Dominic was the idealist. He'd left behind a pampered upbringing to protect and serve his country. He'd loved his sister and wallowed in guilt because he hadn't stopped her murder. Because Dominic was also a protector, he couldn't forgive himself for not saving Carrie. He wanted a woman he could share with his friends because he'd found a part of his family, and now they were all waiting for the woman who would complete them.

"I came to check on you, to say I'm sorry for bombarding you with so much at once," Dominic croaked out. "It's not your fault that Jansen is a murdering asshole. But I really need your help." He swallowed "I need…"

He watched her in Law's arms, and Kinley couldn't miss the loneliness and longing as they carved themselves into his face.

Without thinking, Kinley reached a hand out to him to help him…somehow. Immediately, horror flooded her. Dominic would likely reject her. He wanted a woman for them all, but not *her*. She had to stop remembering what "Mike" had said about the man and use her head. Dominic had orchestrated her abduction. She shouldn't care if he hurt.

She started to jerk her hand back, but Dominic grabbed her like a lifeline, his fingers threading through hers as he used the grip to drag himself closer.

"Goddamn, I shouldn't do this, but you're too sweet."

Dominic's feral snarl zipped right to the moist folds between her legs. And they curled around her heart. "Tell me to stop. Tell me to walk away. I need you to because I fucking can't. And if I stay, something is going to happen. The fact that you're a virgin won't matter at all. Knowing you're innocent just makes me want you more. It makes me want to stake a claim. That is not what I came here to do, damn it."

Right. Dominic had come here to smooth talk her into aiding his justice against Greg Jansen. He didn't really want to get close to her, not logically. But Kinley could also tell that he didn't have the strength to walk away from her. The knowledge made her swell with power and need. For whatever reason, he desired her. He needed her to ease the hurt he bore like a scar.

She pulled on their joined hands, and Dominic didn't hesitate. He wrapped his arms around her, pressing against her everywhere as his lips crashed over hers.

He dominated. Where Law cajoled, Dominic simply commanded. He took full control of her mouth, his tongue surging in. She melted. As he devoured her, Law's fingers moved from her waist to her hips to her thighs. Fingers tickled across her skin, dipped into her panties, then thrust inside her swollen, slick folds.

Every cell in her being nearly imploded. Nope. She didn't have a problem with rough—except that she wanted more. Could see herself coming to crave it.

Dominic's tongue surged as Law's fingers played. Fire licked along her skin. Her knees actually shivered. Pleasure threatened to overtake her. She felt dizzy and stunned and euphoric. She'd never known anything like this, never realized her body could tighten and quake from the inside.

"Make me stop," Dominic pleaded, his lips playing along hers.

"Don't, baby," Law said, kissing her temple. "Don't make us stop. Can't you feel how right this is? How much we want you?"

She could feel a number of things. From freedom to pride to a sense of herself as a woman for the very first time. She practically drowned in pleasure. Law's fingers still played in her pussy, and he could have no trouble discerning how wet she was. It would be embarrassing…except that the lubrication helped his fingers move against her. And it made him groan in her ear. Which made Dominic kiss her even more feverishly.

Hot. She was so hot. In fact, she'd never been this hot—not even close. Her skin sizzled. There was nothing gentle about Dominic, even the way he kissed. He took over. He ruled. She found her body arching toward him in offering and aching to give into his demands. Though he felt different than Law, he felt so very right, too.

"God, that's sexy." Law's deep voice conveyed his satisfaction. "You look good together."

She was kissing another man, and he was happy. Because she was enjoying it? Because it fulfilled her? Or because his "brother" was getting what he needed while he was a part of the experience? Probably all of the above. Their way of looking at the world might be completely different, but it was still desire, need…and maybe more.

All the while Law's clever fingers played inside her. He parted her labia, sliding through her folds, to find the little nubbin that suddenly seemed to control her whole being. Her clitoris was filling up with blood. Urgent desire spread through her. With every flick of his fingers, he lit her up until she panted and moaned in Dominic's mouth. The way they played her should embarrass her or make her feel uncomfortable. But no. Just a searing, soul-freeing desire filled her.

Dominic tugged her shirt free from her skirt, and she felt his warm palm against her skin. He released her lips, kissing her nose and cheeks. "Spread your legs for Law."

Vaguely, Kinley figured she should at least ask why, but her thighs seemed to have a mind of their own. They obeyed Dominic's command without question, spreading wide for Law until he stepped between them.

"She's wearing panties," Law said. "Those white cotton things. I don't like them."

"She's going to stop that. That's one of our rules, Kinley. No panties. Nothing covers your pussy except our hands, our mouths, and our bodies when we fuck you." Dominic's voice was a dark rumble. "Do you understand? If I find a pair, I'll throw them away. You'll get a spanking if you try to wear more."

Every word that came out of his mouth seemed to ratchet up the temperature—and her arousal—another notch. She ached and burned and needed. But his words confused her. Why did he have rules? And why did the idea of him or Law smacking her backside make her feel antsy and restless—and not in a bad way?

"You guys talk about spanking a lot," she managed to say in between kisses.

Riley had talked about putting her over his knee and not letting up until she understood, too. At the very thought of him, Kinley wished for his sharp wit and hard body. Then she shoved the thought away. Law and Dominic wanted her. Riley had cast her as a villainess. If he didn't want her, then she didn't need him. She'd played that game for too long to continue.

"These panties are in my way," Law groused.

Kinley frowned. How? He didn't seem to be having any trouble. He'd just pushed them to the side and shoved his fingers deep in her pussy to work magic on every one of her sensitive spots. Her blood heated, her heart raced, her pleasure swelled, her breath caught. He pressed one big finger inside, against some nerve-laden spot she'd only ever read about. Kinley gasped.

"Make her come, Law," he growled against her ear, his teeth nipping at her lobe in a sharp little bite that flared into something beyond pain. She shivered against him.

Dominic reached under her shirt and bra until he cupped her breast, plucked at her nipple. Heat flared. "You've never come, have you? Tell me, and don't you lie. I know you haven't had a man inside you. We're going to change that, but I want to know everything you've experienced so far. Have you ever brought yourself to orgasm with your fingers? Have you ever rubbed yourself until you screamed, until your eyes rolled back in your head and your whole body shook? Tell me. I want to know if this is your first."

Kinley could barely find her breath. Law's finger still caressed her insides, massaging that deep place, while his thumb rolled over her clit. She couldn't stop her hips from rolling against his hand. She wanted more friction, more of that heating, building sensation that was firing urgently between her legs. She wanted to figure out where this road led.

Dominic tweaked her nipple. The sharp pain brought her back from the brink of something new. She keened in protest and need.

"Answer me," Dominic demanded. "When you do, Law will use his hand to make you come for us. Do you understand?"

She managed to gasp. "Please…"

"What sweet begging. I'm going to watch you come and hear you scream. And I will watch your pussy clench around Law's fingers. But you answer me first. I'm the top here."

He wasn't on top. She was on top of the counter, but she didn't have time to wonder about his odd phrasing because he pinched her nipple again.

"Never," she panted. "I've never come before. I tried a couple of times, but I don't think my body works that way."

She'd touched herself in the middle of the night a couple of times, but found every incident both embarrassing and frustrating. More than once, she'd tried to find the magical spot that would send her soaring to sexual Shangri-La. If the whispers she'd heard were true, other women seemed to be able to get themselves there. Kinley had never even come close.

"Oh, it's gonna work. Your pussy is so wet, baby." Law

pressed in a second finger as he stared down at her. She felt helplessly impaled, stretched and wanting and poised on the edge of something she desperately needed.

She groaned low as he shoved those two fingers inside her as deep as he could. He packed her so full. She liked the slight burn of him stretching her.

Law's entire focus was right between her legs, watching his fingers disappear inside her before he pulled the slick digits nearly free, then shoved her full again. "I know who and what you are, Kinley. You just need something extra, and we can give it to you. Dominic, tell her to come. Order her to do it."

His words made her heart thump in her chest. Yes. She wanted to be told, to be commanded. She wouldn't have to think, just obey—and feel. That demand would compel her, remove the stress of wondering if she could and how she would from her mind.

"Fuck his fingers, pet. Hard. Move your hips against him. That's right." Dominic continued to toy with her nipples, twisting and pinching, sending crazy little beams of pleasure all through her system. His words clouded her brain. "Do it now."

Everything made sense then. Kinley gave herself over to his words and just obeyed. Every cell in her body responded to them, to their actions and words, to the sound of their deep voices. Something important lay just within her reach, hovering right before her… And now she had permission to take that pleasure for herself because pleasing her would please them.

She shoved aside any self-conscious thoughts and thrust against Law's hand. His thumb circled her clit, pressing down and around. Over and over. With a cry, she writhed, taking his fingers even deeper than before.

Dominic tangled his hands in her hair and jerked, snapping her gaze up to fall into the snare of his. "Beautiful, pet. That's exactly what we want from you." He looked back to where Law's fingers disappeared into her body. "Do you feel how wet your pretty pussy is? That's perfect. We want you sopping and desperate for our cocks. Then we'll fill you up."

His words made her whimper. She couldn't form a coherent reply.

Dominic's smile was both triumphant and wicked. "Listen to me and listen well. You're going to come for me and Law—all over his hand. Let it go, pet. Now. We'll catch you."

Law stroked her again, the sensation igniting inside her. His fingers pressed up, circling inside, his thumb scraping over her clitoris. Dominic drank from her lips.

And she fell over the edge with a smothered scream.

Pleasure bloomed across her flesh, a wild rush of energy and pounding sensation that had her gasping for breath and shaking, gyrating against Law and holding onto Dominic for dear life. Her body burst, her soul opened, and she surrendered to the moment completely.

As the sensations crested then slowly lulled from electric to tingling, then finally to lazy satisfaction, Dominic's hand softened at her breast. His kisses became sweet and gentle. "Beautiful, pet. So fucking gorgeous. That's what I wanted. Tell me how you feel."

She felt free. She felt open. She felt incredibly alive.

"Amazing." A happy little grin tried to stretch across her lips.

Law smiled back, his face more open than she'd ever seen it. His eyes were lit with something that looked a lot like joy, and Kinley warmed at the thought that she'd contributed to his pleasure.

"She's going to be so tight, Dom. I could barely fit two fingers inside. We need to prep her. As soon as possible. God, I can't wait to fuck her." Law withdrew his hand. The digits were soaking, and he didn't care. In fact, he licked his fingers, sucking the cream from them. He let loose a sexy groan. "Hmm, she tastes as sweet as she looks."

Her whole body throbbed with residual sensation and a

new flare of desire. Her heart still chugged, even as languid pleasure coursed through her. Time slowed.

Law's hands had been inside her body. Now he was tasting her essence and he seemed to love it. He'd known exactly how to please her. Both of them had, actually. Now just looking at them both amazed and aroused her. Though she'd been kidnapped, dragged away from her wedding—albeit one that she deeply suspected would have ended in her death—and she sat on a kitchen island with her legs spread for the men who had ripped her life apart, Kinley was happy.

What was wrong with her? What would people think? Magazines wrote about her family. Her kidnapping would be all over the news. If anyone learned what had just happened, the fact that she'd allowed her captors to touch her would be plastered all over America.

Horror flooded her system.

"D-don't."

Dominic jerked back, yanking his hands to his sides. His face closed down. Just seconds before he'd been flushed with desire. Now he looked stony cold again. Though they were still standing close together, there seemed to be miles between them.

"Changed your mind, huh, pet?"

She closed her legs and scrambled away from them, trying to regain some form of dignity. Her hands were shaking. What had she done?

"Kinley?" Law reached for her. "Baby…"

She couldn't listen or trust herself at the moment. She was too emotional to make any decisions now, much less one to surrender her virginity to two of the men who had whisked her across the country against her will.

No matter how sweet they had been to her. No matter how they were very likely saving her life. No matter how much pleasure they had given her.

No. No! She couldn't listen to those voices. She couldn't trust them. Like all of her female parts, they screamed that being with these men was right. That she would be safe with them.

Her clitoris had Stockholm syndrome.

"I need to be alone for a while." She had to think. Figure out how to put this embarrassing catastrophe behind her and never fall prey to the lust they roused in her again. What kind of woman fell for her captors?

If she stayed here, she would make a complete fool of herself. They wanted information, assistance. They didn't really want her. She was nowhere near their league. They were gorgeous and undoubtedly good in bed. She was plump, naïve, and inexperienced. If she slept with them, she would forever be the debutante who'd been dumb enough to spread her legs for her kidnappers.

"Kinley, let's talk about this, baby." Law stepped up, his big, masculine, oh-how-hot-would-he-look-naked body blocking her way to the door.

She shook her head. "Move. Please."

"Let her be, Law," Dominic warned. "You don't want to give her any reason to say we forced her. It's exactly why we should have stayed away. I lost my fucking head." Dominic gathered the papers from the table she'd sat at earlier, before Law carried her to the island and nearly seduced her.

And darn it, she'd liked being seduced.

"Study these. You have tonight. In the morning, we'll talk again. I hope you understand that what just happened here was consensual." Dominic thrust the papers at her, his voice so matter of fact. She missed the way he'd whispered passionately to her.

Everything had been consensual. He'd even begged her to stop it, and she hadn't. She'd wanted what they could give her and hadn't stopped to think about how she would feel afterward until it was too late. She couldn't be the woman who completed them. Fate had merely placed her in their way. They wanted someone, and she happened to be in their path. End of story.

She held the files to her chest. She really did need to review them, figure out if Greg was using her charity for criminal purposes. She needed to piece together the evidence and decide if her sister and her father were truly plotting to kill her. But mostly, she needed distance to figure out what had just happened to her body. Her will. Her heart. She'd nearly given everything to a couple of men she barely knew. She wasn't ever rash or irresponsible. Why them? Why now? And why did she want to put her arms around Law? Why did she want to brush against Dominic and see if she could arouse him again?

Why did she feel as if Riley was missing and ache to invite him in?

The conflicting thoughts and wants in her head were making her crazy, dizzy. She was exhausted.

"Gigi, come on." She turned to look for her dog, but her little Yorkie was gone.

"She took off with Butch. Sorry, but he's been nosing around her all day," Dominic supplied. "Is she in heat?"

Oh, god. Probably. She'd been intending to breed Gigi once before getting her fixed. After all, her puppy was a pure bred, and Kinley knew plenty of other AKC Yorkie owners whose pets could sire. But Gigi and Butch were totally off plan…just like her ill-fated tryst with Law and Dominic had been.

Damn it, her dog was likely in heat, and so was Kinley. She'd gone so long without sex that she'd been desperate to do it with anyone. Except that she'd never really wanted to before. And she definitely hadn't wanted Greg. In fact, she'd kind of decided she was asexual—until a few minutes ago. Now she couldn't get her mind off sex.

"If your dog forces himself on mine, I will hold you responsible for doggy rape." Even as she said the words, she realized just how silly and righteous they sounded. No court would uphold human laws for nonconsensual canine violation. It was irrational, but Kinley was irritated and hurt that her only comfort in life now was apparently off somewhere trying to become pregnant by some overgrown hound.

Just the way she'd narrowly missed the chance to be knocked up by a pair of Special Forces soldiers.

The thought was mortifying. She stomped toward the kitchen door. Riley stood in the hallway, a stark look on his angled face. He'd been leaning against the wall, his head down. He masked the expression quickly, his eyes narrowing on her. How much had he heard?

"You want to try me, cupcake? Now that you've had some of the big brothers, do you need more? Or is this your way of trying to gain the upper hand, disarm us all with pussy? If so, you played the virginal card with just the right amount of innocence. Bravo."

So he'd heard everything. Shame filled her. "I want to go to my room."

Riley stood in her way. "Are you planning to cry rape now?"

She shook her head. "I wasn't raped. Not in any way."

"We both know that, but you seem like the kind of woman who'll use every tool in her arsenal to get her way."

"You don't know me! And you're a jerk. Your brother is wrong about you. He told me how kind and funny and smart you are, but you're just a big bully. I'm away from home, I'm scared, and I'm totally out of my element. Yet you enjoy kicking me when I'm down. Get out of my way so I can go back to my cell. Then you can go to hell for all I care."

Law approached her from behind. "I'll take you to your room."

"I can find my way there."

"But I doubt you'll lock yourself in."

The quip made her fume, but she still marched off without another word, down the hall, ignoring the men behind her. She zipped into her room and slammed her door. Immediately, she heard them lock her in.

She was alone again. Alone with the evidence against her

family. Alone with a million questions. The fears and doubts started to sink in once again.

A moment later, Law opened the door, and Gigi padded in, her pink bow askew. He slammed it once more, locking her in with her furry little harlot.

Gigi stood at the door, whining a little, probably crying for her lover.

"Yeah, I kind of want to do that, too." But for now she would settle for taking a shower. Maybe when she was clean she wouldn't feel their hands on her, stroking her, making her want more of what she couldn't have.

She walked into the en suite bathroom and turned the shower to hot. All her favorite products had been placed there, from her razor to the shampoo she used every day. Greg probably didn't even know what color her eyes were, but one of these men knew that she preferred lavender soap.

What was her next move here? What should she do? What did she believe?

She looked up at the window beside the shower enclosure. It was high on the wall, but she could see that the glass in the bathroom wasn't nearly as thick as the panes in the bedroom.

Kinley climbed on the toilet and was able to just grasp the handle. Holding her breath, she inspected the window. It wasn't sealed shut and didn't have a lock. It should actually swing open and let her free.

She had to swallow her shout of surprise. She'd found a way out! In a few hours, she could have her bags repacked and a plan in motion. The sun would be coming up, and they'd probably still be sleeping. She could be long gone before they even knew she was missing.

All good news. But Kinley couldn't help but wonder if, now that she'd found a way to escape, should she take it?

Chapter Eight

Riley stretched and looked out over the vast expanse of green. From the wide front porch, he got an eyeful of mountains rising up like the sun.

Dawn had come, though it didn't really mean much this time of the year. Summer days in Alaska were seemingly endless. His system hadn't quite adjusted from East Coast time.

The smell of coffee filled his nostrils. He hadn't slept much. Whether that was because the sun barely dipped below the horizon or the fact that he couldn't shut his brain off didn't matter. It was all Kinley's fault in the end. He'd thought about her all damn night. Over and over during the long hours, his mind had played out the memories of Kinley as he'd stood outside the kitchen door and listened to her shudder and gasp and scream as she came. Under his brother's hand. And apparently for the first time.

How the hell had a woman who looked like that managed to stay a damn virgin? He hated Greg Jansen for various reasons, but he'd never thought the man was an idiot. Any straight male who could be engaged to Kinley Kohl and not keep her in bed for days and days was obviously a complete moron.

But then Riley knew he wasn't exactly smart either. None of them were if they believed she could really want them.

"So she turned away from you?" Riley asked, looking at his brother who sat in a rocking chair not five feet away.

"She got scared." Law sipped his coffee, not looking at him. "It's not so surprising. She has very little experience. We have to be careful with her, but she's coming along."

Had his brother lost his ever-loving mind? "She ran from you. She couldn't get out of the kitchen fast enough."

Law's face bunched up in consternation. "No, Kinley was afraid, not of me or Dominic. She enjoyed the way we touched her. A lot, in fact. What she felt scared her. Put yourself in her shoes. If her own family is willing to betray her, she's going to find trusting anyone, especially the guys who kidnapped her, really hard. But she wants what we're dying to give her. She won't be able to hold out for long."

Law sounded more confident than Riley had ever heard, assassinations excepting. His brother never worried that he wouldn't be able to take out a target, but when it came to women, he often seemed dead inside. Or maybe Law's attitude had stemmed from the fact that he hadn't cared about the females they'd shared in the past. Maybe he'd always just gone along with what Riley and Dominic wanted. After all, Law had never brought a potential female to them. Sure, he'd enjoyed the sex, but he'd never fought for a girl the way he was fighting for Kinley now.

"Did you ever care for Simone?" He'd never asked Law before. Now Riley realized that once he'd fallen for Simone, he'd assumed his brother would too…eventually.

Law shook his head. "I find it hard to really care about a woman who's completely cold. Now, as a beer cooler, she worked perfectly. I could set a brew down next to that woman and it was chilled in three point five seconds."

Where had the sense of humor come from? "Could you be serious?"

"All right. Here's the truth: Simone was interested in you because she liked having a Harvard-educated man on her arm. She wanted Dominic for his social connections and his millions. She put up with me because fucking me was the price of admission if she wanted to keep you two. And she never let me forget it."

Simone had said that to his brother? Why had Law never

told him? "When shit got serious, she didn't want me either."

Law sighed. "When she turned your proposal down, she claimed it was because she couldn't live an openly perverted lifestyle because everyone would call her a whore. I call bullshit. Everybody already knew she was a whore. I firmly believe she would have been more than happy to spend the rest of her life in bed with both you and Dominic. And she would have put up with me. Your trouble was the marriage proposal didn't come from the right person."

As soon as Law had spoken, Riley realized there was a lot of truth to his brother's words. God, he'd been so fucking dumb. "She wanted to be legally married to Dominic."

"Money wins over brains," Law said, sympathy in his voice.

"Fuck me." He felt like he'd been kicked in the gut all over again.

His brother shrugged. "Look on the bright side. Your brain still won out over my brawn."

Despite that, if Simone had said yes, Law would have sacrificed his heart to make him and Dominic happy. "Why did you let me propose to her, knowing what she was? Why would you have stayed in a relationship with a woman you didn't even like?"

"Beyond the extra freezer space?" Law took a sip of his coffee and sat back. "You were in love with her. Or you thought you were. I've never felt that way before and I thought at the time that I was incapable of it. So I played along. And, to be honest, I didn't think it would work in the long run anyway because I knew Dominic wasn't going to marry her."

"Finding and sharing one woman is never going to work, is it?" The family they had talked about didn't make sense in the real world. Legalities aside, no woman wanted to deal with three men. Not even if she realized it meant she'd never be alone, that she would always have someone to care for her. That she would never end up like his mother.

"I think it can, if we handle her in just the right way. Our strategy has to be stealth. We have to point out all the great things about having three guys around, reel her in with the sex, downplay the cooking and laundry, then maybe..."

"I'm serious, Law."

"So am I."

"You've got to stop imagining that Kinley is our dream girl."

"You weren't in there," Law argued. "You were outside listening. You didn't see how Kinley reached for Dominic. No hesitation. She saw him and she grabbed on. If you had walked in, she would have grabbed you, too."

The door opened, and Dominic joined them on the porch for the chilly morning, steaming mug in hand. "It was a mistake."

Law's eyes rolled. "God, when did you two turn so whiny? It wasn't a mistake. It was the first thing we've done right with her."

"Are you serious, Law? She was horrified. She pushed us away." Dominic looked fresh from a shower. He'd changed into sweatpants and an Army T-shirt. It was odd to see Dominic out of his usual suit, and made Riley realize that the last few years had been a never-ending series of jobs. None of them had actually relaxed in forever.

"Yeah, after she had her orgasm." Law's lips curled up again. "It was a perfectly natural time for her to run. She's a virgin, and I think she feared what came next. We have to put her at ease. And I think we can all agree she's a greedy girl who needs to learn her place."

"Her place? Law, we kidnapped her. We can't just tie her up and spank her ass. In a way, she holds our fate in her hands. If she tells the feds we raped her, we're going down even harder."

Dominic was right, and Riley knew damn well just how fast a woman could turn on them.

The tablet next to Law chirped, and all three heads snapped toward the device.

"Is that our security system?" Dominic asked.

"Stay calm." Law was always cool under pressure. "None of the locals know we're here. Riley, you deal with this thing."

He took the tablet from his brother's hand. Well, thankfully they still needed him for something.

Mind racing and fingers flying, Riley tapped in the passcode. He'd modified the tablet to meet their needs, connecting it to the wide band of security cameras he'd placed throughout the house. They all fed into Riley's computer, which then communicated with the tablet.

He moved swiftly through the protocols and discerned the issue. "Someone tripped one of my motion detectors on the west side of the house. Probably an animal."

There was always something walking around the grounds since the forest wasn't far away.

"Or Butch, I let him out a couple of minutes ago. He's been scratching at Kinley's door all morning." Dominic leaned in, looking at the screen. "Can you bring up the cameras? Kinley's room is on the west side. I just want to be sure…"

He quickly brought up the perimeter camera. "What the hell is that?"

Dominic squinted, his brow furrowing as he peered at an unfamiliar, out-of-place brown square on the grass, visible on the tablet screen. "I think that's one of her roller bags."

Another item dropped, hitting the roller bag, then listed to the side.

"Is that her purse? How is she getting out?" Law demanded.

Riley forced himself to remember every inch of the suite they'd put her in. He'd checked it over himself. And then he remembered… "Shit. The bathroom window!"

When the owners of the house, the James brothers, had given them a tour, their wife Hannah had mentioned they'd had the window specially placed there. It had come from her great grandmother's home. Hannah had wanted a piece of her history here, so her men had made it happen. Because it wasn't hurricane glass, it actually opened. And Kinley had figured that out.

"That window is supposed to be decorative. It's eight feet up," Riley said.

The biggest grin lit up Law's face. "Damn, she's resourceful. I appreciate that in a woman. How is she going to get the dog down?"

Gigi's body came into the frame, her eyes bugging out and those little paws shaking as she was lowered down.

"Did she tie a sheet around the rat thing?" Dominic asked.

"Don't talk bad about your dog's baby mama. Oh, look she's got her bow back on straight." Law didn't seem upset that their prisoner was attempting escape.

The minute the dog hit the ground, Butch came into view as though he'd been sitting just outside the camera's edge, waiting for his true love.

As Butch rather clumsily attempted to mount Gigi, Dominic cursed. "Goddamn it. I'm going to get his ass fixed."

"I don't think his ass needs fixing. His dick on the other hand seems really interested in Gigi. Aw, look. He's frustrated. He can't get it in there with that sheet wrapped around her."

"Well, aren't you a fucking comedian?" Dominic groused.

Law sent him a deprecating shrug, then shot to his feet with a frown. "Damn it, how is Kinley planning on getting out? That window is too high. She's going to break her neck. I've got to stop her."

"Wait." Dominic stayed Law with a tap on the arm. "Would you look at that? I've got to hand it to her."

"How did she manage to not only get herself through that window, but fashion a rope from the rest of the bed sheets?" Riley was stunned. "Shit! She's rappelling down the side of the house in heels."

She was trying to run away from her kidnappers in stilettos. Riley couldn't see their color on the black and white feed, but he imagined them as fire engine red. And damn, he couldn't focus on anything but those heels. They would make her legs look a million miles long as he spread her wide for his cock. Well, when someone else did all that. He wasn't touching her.

"Yeah, and look at that ass in those jeans. Damn." Law sighed and adjusted his fly.

His brother was right.

On the screen, Kinley hit the ground and immediately tried shooing Butch away from Gigi. She scooped her dog up, but Butch just barked happily like it was all a game. They could hear the commotion coming from around the side of the house.

"Be quiet," Kinley hissed in a whisper that he heard clear as a bell. "Nice dog. Hush. Go find your master."

Dominic groaned. "Does she know what that word does to my cock? Fuck, yeah, I could master her."

Riley had kind of thought the same. Except he refused to be led around by his dick like the dog and his brothers by some female destined to leave them. He was too smart for that. "Are either one of you going to stop her?"

Dominic and Law just stared at the tablet like it held all the secrets of the world.

"Soon. I want to see what she's going to do. I'm at a complete loss with this girl," Dominic admitted.

"She's going to get away," Riley pointed out.

"Dude, she can't even get rid of Butch. I doubt she's going to make it very far, especially in those heels. They're sexy but fucking impractical." Law pointed to the screen where she was shoving Gigi into her oversized purse and pulling at her roller bag as she pleaded with Butch to stay. "Do you see her trekking miles to civilization in those shoes?"

"And that's if she even knows where to go." Dominic started around the end of the porch. "But it looks like she's trying to head north. Why is she going toward the forest?"

Riley followed him with Law trailing after. "Maybe she just wants to find cover."

Law snorted. "She should want to find a road. I don't

think she really believes she's in Alaska. I bet she thinks she'll walk a mile or two and find a town."

"We're not going to let her get that far, right?" Riley prompted.

Kinley wouldn't do well out in the wilderness. She would be all alone, and he'd bet she had zero outdoor skills, like starting a fire or building shelter, much less knowing what plants were safe to eat. In fact, she might have negative skills since she seemed to think that her heels were proper footwear for mountainous terrain.

Law left the porch as she hobbled to the side of the house, giving them a clear line of sight. Kinley shoved her hair aside with one hand and tried to shoo Butch using her roller bag with the other.

"Nah, I just want to see how far she'll go before she runs back here," Law said finally. "She's being impulsive. She does this a lot. In the end, she's always sensible. Trust me."

Law was the subject matter expert when it came to Kinley Kohl. Just as he said the words, she stopped, and Riley watched as her shoulders rolled and she drew in a deep breath. She seemed to be having an argument with herself.

"See, Kinley is telling herself that she's being stubborn," Law explained. "She did the same thing when she went to the spa to get a bikini wax earlier this week. She stood outside that damn building for twenty minutes telling herself that she was being dumb and that most women didn't shape their pubic hair into a style. Finally, she made the right decision and got a full Brazilian."

"How the hell do you know that?"

"I listened in on her conversation with Annabelle," Law explained. "There's a coffee shop right next door. She sat down at one of the tables. I was beside her. At first, I was pissy that she waxed for that douchebag, but then I didn't care *why* her pussy was soft and ready to eat. I just appreciated that it was. She might have been thinking of him when she did it, but I'll be the one reaping the reward. Oh, look, she's not ready to make the right call yet."

She started walking again. Butch was still following along, but now Gigi had decided she wanted dick more than designer luggage since she was trying to climb free of her carrier.

Kinley's blonde hair bounced with every wobbling step she took. Heels in soft earth just didn't make a stride easy. She'd put on a sweater, but it didn't cover her ass. That luscious, gorgeous backside swayed, and Riley couldn't seem to pry his stare from her juicy cheeks. That was an ass made for a man's hands. The rhinestones all over her butt glittered in the sun, a veritable *Get It Here* sign right across her tush.

She turned slightly as though she felt eyes on her, but she didn't see them under the shadow of the porch.

God, she was an adorable bundle of chaos, Riley admitted. Definitely not someone who overthought everything, the way he tended to. Kinley lit up a room with just her smile. She fucking glowed. Okay, so she was naïve and didn't always make the most rational choices when she let her emotions rule. Because she used her heart far more than her head.

Riley stared with a thoughtful sigh. She needed a man. Or two. Or three.

Damn, but she was getting to him.

"Oh, shit." Dominic pointed to the edge of the tree line where the forest started ahead.

A massive moose lumbered along. Kinley focused on Butch barking behind her.

"Kinley! Baby, watch out!" Law yelled as he jogged toward her.

Butch started growling at the moose. Kinley finally turned around—and her whole body went rigid. She gasped.

"It won't hurt you!" Law yelled.

It wouldn't charge her, but it might kick her if she got too close.

"It's an herbivore!" Dominic promised, laughing. It had been months and months since Riley had seen Dominic even crack a smile. "Do you think the moose likes designer luggage?"

Kinley let out a little scream, then turned and staggered as fast as her heels would take her. She didn't just run from the moose. She darted straight toward Law, dumping everything on the ground except Gigi and her carrier, then practically jumped into his arms, wrapping her legs around him.

Law's whole body shook with the force of his laughter, but he held her like he meant to protect her, no matter what. He didn't even seem to mind that Gigi's head poked out of the purse and that she seemed intent on licking every inch of his arm.

"Law is in love with her," Riley muttered. "Fuck."

"Yeah." Dominic sobered. "And Law's only going to fall once. If this doesn't work out, he'll mourn her for the rest of his life. I can't fix it, man. If this was another time, another place, I would be all in. I like her. She's a little impractical and stubborn at times, but she's also loyal and so damn sweet that I almost can't help myself."

"But we have to help ourselves because this isn't going to end well." Riley couldn't stand the thought of his brothers being hurt. But unless Law changed course, it was inevitable. And if Dominic hopped on the bandwagon, too…shit.

And Riley hated the ache that split his chest as he watched Law turn and head back to the house, still carrying Kinley. His brother's face was completely open and happy. She said something, looking both terrified and animated. Law howled again, then leaned in to brush his lips against hers. She met him halfway. When the kiss was over, she didn't try to retreat, but simply buried her face in his neck and held on.

"You're right. It probably won't end well," Dominic admitted, his prior joy draining from his face. "But I think you should be ready to let Law make his own mistakes. If she wants him, then let him be happy for however long it lasts. Not every woman plays with a man like Simone," he reminded. "I'm going to go grab her bags before the moose decides to take a dump on them. We need to get a lock on that window."

"There's so much nature, Law. It's everywhere!" Kinley insisted as Law carried her to the porch. "Why is there so much of it?"

"It's Alaska, baby. Nature is a big selling point here. No one comes to this part of the world expecting a Neiman's around the corner." Law glanced his way. "I'm going to sit her down and feed her some breakfast. Do you want anything?"

Riley didn't want food. He was shocked to realize that, deep down, he wanted to feel the way Law felt now. Some dangerously yearning spot inside him railed that she didn't cling to him—or even look his way. He wanted to know her, feel like he had a place beside her.

He had to stop thinking this shit.

"No. I've got some work to do. Come on, Butch. Let's go look at that window."

The dog utterly ignored him, following Law, Kinley, and Gigi inside.

Everyone had a crush it seemed.

He watched through the window as Law sat Kinley at the table and poured her a cup of coffee. She peeked at Law from beneath her lashes and bit her lower lip, her eyes downcast until he handed her the mug. Then her brilliant smile damn near lit up the whole house.

Riley took a step back. He was not falling for a woman to try to share with his brothers again. He couldn't. She was Law's. Dominic could flirt with sharing a corner of their sheets or whatever. Not his problem, and Riley knew he had to let this go. If the other two didn't care about getting burned again, that was their call. They'd see the light when she used her charm to escape, this time for good. Kinley didn't really want them, and the fairy tale complete with the picket fence Law was envisioning would never happen. The sooner he and Dom figured that out, the better.

With a sigh, Riley went back to work.

* * * *

Kinley took a long swallow of her wine and stared at the accounting books spread across the table in front of her. Hours and hours had gone by since she'd escaped, only to turn around and run back into her captor's arms.

Moose shouldn't be that big. Like huge. Enormous. And slobbery. That thing could seriously put out the mucous.

"You all right?" Riley Anders stood in the doorway, leaning negligently against it.

He was heartbreakingly gorgeous, and it was so obvious that he wanted nothing to do with her. He was the only one who never invaded her space, who stayed as far from her as possible.

She knew these men considered themselves so close that they were all for one and one for all. If Riley didn't want her, she was screwed. Or not screwed.

"I'm okay." Except that she was dumber than dirt, and the evidence in front of her proved it. The last six weeks showed a series of payouts that she couldn't account for. And apparently her accountant wasn't doing his job anymore for whatever reason. Someone had been keeping the books, but nothing like meticulous Steve.

And she was a fool because she just knew she was falling for the men who had kidnapped her.

Nothing in the world had felt so right as running toward Law this morning. Even as she'd crawled out the window, something inside her kept insisting she was making a huge mistake. But logic told her that she should want to escape her abductors, so she'd kept walking. Very quickly, Kinley had realized that she knew absolutely nothing about surviving in the woods. And obviously, they hadn't lied about the whole Alaska thing. The sun didn't stay down for very long. She'd managed to sleep a little, but the lack of darkness threw off her whole system.

So did they.

Riley stood in the doorway, almost staring a hole through her. "How about the rat thing?"

She wasn't sure she liked them referring to her dog as a rat. "Gigi is fine now that's she's been fed."

Riley frowned. "Is that what all the barking was about? For such a little thing, she can be awfully loud."

Gigi was simply a dog who knew what she wanted. "She's used to a certain feeding schedule. The whole kidnapping thing threw us off. If she starts up again, she's likely hungry so if you want her to stop, feed her a little something. And she's smart. She knows where the food is. She'll come running into the kitchen at least twice a day barking up a storm now that she knows where the food bowls are kept."

"Good to know," Riley said. He looked back at the door as though he was contemplating walking back out, but then he seemed to come to a decision. That straight-line jaw of his firmed. "Are you going to run again?"

After the whole snot-nosed moose incident? "No. Now that I've seen what's out there, I feel much safer here. You're not going to murder me and leave my body in the woods, are you?"

"No." He took a single step toward her. "We really are trying to help you. Your boyfriend meant to kill you."

She'd just about accepted that fact. "He was never my boyfriend, just my fiancé. That may sound weird, but a boyfriend is someone who wants you. A fiancé can be bought. I should know."

She'd bought Greg with her name, her connections, and apparently her charity.

Riley stared at the floor. "I wouldn't know about that. I've never had enough money to buy one."

She heard the bitter tone of his voice. "Yeah, well, I would tell you to hold out for someone you love. The whole sacrifice thing tends to go wrong."

"Is that how you saw it? A sacrifice?"

She'd been sacrificing her whole life. She'd given up so

much time, energy, and love. She'd always thought that, while her sister and father meant well, they struggled with self-discipline and showing affection. But now she knew they simply didn't have any kind of a conscience.

"Yes. I was marrying Greg because I firmly believed my father had cancer and my charity was going under. The economy has been bad. Donations are way down. Hope House was the work of my mom's heart. I couldn't let it die. And the thought of my dad having cancer and no insurance nearly killed me. Mom was the one who worked. Dad, uhm…he didn't think about practicalities like paying bills and stuff."

"Or he was too busy gambling to send his check in."

She started to protest and stopped. Because it was true. "Yeah."

"So you were marrying Greg to save your dad and your charity?"

"And because I was lonely." Her heart ached, and she was too tired to lie. "I'm twenty-five and I've never had a lover. I was lonely, and I wanted a family before it was too late."

He was silent for a long moment. "You want a family? Like a husband and kids and a white picket fence?"

That had been the dream, but… "I think I would take love any way it came to me."

He laughed, but it was a bitter thing. "I've never known a woman like you to care about love."

"A woman like me?"

"Pampered. Rich."

"Money doesn't buy happiness, Riley. And we've already covered that it can't buy love. At the end of the day, I'm just a woman. I can't speak for all of them, but me? I just want to have a good life."

"What would a good life be?"

That idea hadn't changed in the years since she'd first understood what the word family meant. "Someone who loves me. Someone I could love back. Children. A purpose that's meaningful. I'm not talking about fame. I don't care if anyone knows who I am. I just want to make a difference. I want to make other people's lives better because I walked the earth. I want to make the people who love me proud. Is that too much to ask? I guess it is, because I don't seem to be able to do it."

He stared, a long moment passing before he spoke. "I hope you find it. I came in here for a reason. Uhm, Jansen is on TV right now. Look, Law doesn't want you to watch this, but I think you should. You're strong enough to handle the truth. Greg is holding press conferences and telling people you were taken. He's trying to make a case for you to return to him."

"Why?"

"Well, for starters, if you married Jansen, you wouldn't be compelled to testify against him."

"Show me." She wanted to see whatever Law sought to protect her from. It was sweet that he didn't want her hurt or upset, but she needed to know. She was quickly realizing that she wanted what these men could give her. Law offered utter devotion. He would try to shield her with every ounce of his being. Dominic challenged her. He wanted her to be smarter, better than she thought she could be.

And Riley was an equal, who supposedly appreciated life and humor and the people he shared them with. Which was why it hurt so much that he wasn't interested.

He turned on the TV hanging on the opposite wall and changed the channel to a twenty-four- hour news network. Greg's face immediately came up. He was wearing a perfectly pressed suit as he spoke to the camera. It didn't look like he'd missed any sleep.

"Someone took my fiancée. I can only pray they treat her well. She's my heart. She's the better half of me. I'm begging for Kinley's swift return."

A voice came from the audience. "How do you reply to Kellan Kent's assertion that Kinley Kohl is a runaway bride who fled your wedding with her lover?"

She had a lover? Oh, this story was way more interesting

than her actual life.

Greg frowned. "My bride isn't interested in lovers. This is pure libel. She's an innocent. Kinley is one of the world's most true and pure souls."

Meaning an idiot who couldn't get a guy—or see when the one in front of her was trying to profit from her death.

Greg droned on. "Kinley would never abandon her family without a word. She values her loved ones and knows that her sister misses her. That her father needs her. I pray she'll find a way to survive this because my everything depends on her coming home."

He stared into the camera, giving her that same look he'd given her when he'd offered to save her charity. It made her feel dirty and selfish because she had to choose between throwing caution to the wind for what she wanted and whoring herself for the people who needed her.

Becks was in the background, her face shining in the sunlight as she stood behind Greg. She had on her best suit, the one that showed off the ten grand she'd spent on her boobs. She kept her left side to the camera because she'd always told Kinley that was her good side. It was so comforting to know her sister was concerned with how hot she looked on camera.

Kinley loved her niece and nephew. She'd never understood how Becks could send them off to boarding school, especially so young, but it was all there in her sister's plastic face. The woman didn't feel anything. Something was deeply and profoundly wrong with Becks. She was missing her heart, possessed an empty soul. She didn't care about anyone but herself.

Same with her father.

Her mother had been so lovely, but she'd accepted less than she'd deserved. Would her mother have wanted her to do the same? What did Kinley want for herself? What was she willing to accept? How much was she willing to risk?

A plan started to germinate in her head. Law, Riley, and Dominic had kidnapped her…

"He sounds sympathetic." Riley frowned at the screen.

"I'm not going to press charges."

He turned his head. "What?"

She'd decided that before she made her one escape. When she'd been wrapped around Law's body, his arms holding her close, she'd known she didn't want freedom. Freedom had kind of sucked because it couldn't love you back. "I'm not going to press charges. I'll go along with what Kellan said. You were smart to involve him. He's Annabelle's employer. She cares about him. I'm not going to take him down any more than I would the three of you, so I'll go along with his cover story."

"You're going to tell the press that you took medication for your nerves and were sleeping it off while you let Law whisk you away to a secluded lovers' retreat?"

Why not? What did she have if she went home besides a life of taking care of people who would never thank her and always want more? And that was provided Greg didn't kill her first. Here was a totally different tale. Nice accommodations, good food, sure. Law had actually asked her for her preferences before they'd cooked dinner. Dominic had even asked what kind of wine she'd like. Before these guys, no one had ever given a damn what she wanted. And now that she thought about it, she was pretty sure Riley had been the one to pick her warm clothes.

"Sure, why not. I'm just a bride gone wild. This sweater is a little scratchy."

He narrowed his blue eyes. "It's one hundred percent pure cashmere. It can't be scratchy."

Yes, Riley had picked her clothes with care, like she was important to him. Law carried her around like she didn't weigh a thing. Dominic looked at her like he wanted to eat her up.

And her fiancé? The man she'd been ready to marry was sleeping with her sister and planning to murder her so he could take over her business.

She'd played by the rules for far too long. The rules

hadn't gotten her anywhere. These ridiculous ideals had left her a virgin, completely and utterly alone. They had placed her in a position where everyone lied to her. Getting kidnapped had brought her clarity, shown her a place where at least a couple of men wanted to bring her pleasure.

Pleasure was better than the nothing she'd had before.

"Could you call Law and Dominic in?" An idea had been brewing in her brain all day, a way for her to get something out of this. Determination had replaced mildness in the last several hours. She wanted something beyond just getting to live and keeping her charity. She wanted something for *her*.

"Why?" Riley asked.

"I want to talk to them." She didn't want to explain it to Riley. He wouldn't understand. He would probably be horrified. But she hoped that Dominic and Law would grasp her meaning immediately. They had kissed her, held her, brought her pleasure. Dominic had gone cold only after she'd pulled away. And Law had just been hurt.

Kinley supposed that some would argue that Law had hurt her by abducting her. But he hadn't. In his head—and heart—he'd really believed he was saving her. She kind of had to agree. Because of that, she didn't like hurting Law in any way. The idea that she had made her feel anxious inside.

She wanted more than that unfinished experience in the kitchen and she was willing to give in order to get. If Riley didn't want her, fine. She would go into the situation knowing that whatever passed between her, Dominic, and Law wouldn't be long term. But she would finally ask for what she wanted. If they turned her down… she had no idea what she would do.

Riley turned and exited, leaving her alone with the cable news channels who questioned everything from her whereabouts to her morality. There was a short story on Annabelle's law firm and how they were handling the case Greg was trying to build against the "unnamed suspect."

So Annabelle had a hand in this. Kinley wasn't sure of her exact role, but she smiled anyway. Of course some people would be deeply disturbed by a friend's involvement in a criminal act, but Kinley had looked at all the evidence now. Belle had done her damnedest to persuade her to not marry Greg…and Kinley hadn't listened. If she had been in Annabelle's shoes, she would have fought like hell to save her friend, too, including having her kidnapped.

So Law had a good lawyer who had floated the story that she was overwrought and medicated. Legally, it was a good play. The story wasn't totally implausible. It bought them all some time.

The doors opened, and her heart rate tripled as all three men strode into the room. Law was at least six and a half feet tall with stark blue eyes that pierced right through her. Dominic was so gorgeous and commanding, he made her heart stop. Slightly taller than Law, he was just as broad, his body lean and strong. And Riley's face could be on a movie poster. He was stunning, not to mention blazingly smart, which was a kind of sexy all its own. Three amazing men.

She could only really make a play for two.

"Baby, you want something?" Law asked.

He'd been so easy to connect with. She'd fallen for him so quickly. He'd held her when she was scared, when she felt alone. Law was the kind of man who did what it took to protect the people he cared about. Kinley couldn't deny she admired that.

"I have an idea and I'd appreciate you listening." Her heart was pounding out of her chest, and she was surprised she couldn't hear it. But she couldn't shy away. She was done being the good girl. She was done playing by anyone's rules but her own. She was more than ready to find out who Kinley Kohl really was and what she was capable of. "I want to trade."

Dominic stepped closer, scowling. "Trade?"

"You need my help with your case against Greg. Fine. I'm willing, but I want something in return."

Law's mouth turned down. "What is it?"

"Knowledge."

Dominic turned to both of his partners with a shrug, then back to her. "What kind of knowledge?"

Kinley bit her lip. Was this stupid? Maybe, but she was still going to do it because she wanted—needed—this. "About sex."

The words dropped inside the room like a bomb, and the silence that followed in the aftermath seemed to go on forever.

"Sex?" Riley finally asked, his tone intimating that she had to be kidding.

"Exactly." Kinley dragged in a rough breath. "I would like to trade information about my charity and Greg for information about sex."

"You want to watch a video?" Riley asked incredulously.

"No." Law shot his brother a dirty look. "She's not asking for a porn flick, idiot. She wants to talk about sex."

There was a bit more to it than that. Were they really going to make her say it? "I want to maybe, probably…a-almost certainly actually have sex."

Kinley resisted the urge to slam her eyes shut and pray they didn't laugh.

Instead, Dominic stared a hole through her. "Let me see if I've got this right. You want to trade information for a good fucking?"

God, when he put it that way, she felt two feet tall. And she was done feeling like crap about herself. "If I'm not putting you out too much or making you do something against your will, yes. I would like to exchange what little I understand about what's happening with Hope House for first-hand sexual knowledge."

"Why not just ask us if we want to go to bed?" Law asked, arms crossed over his chest.

"I want to have sex with men who know what they're doing. And I don't expect something for nothing. I know that everything comes with a price."

"You said *men*." Dominic emphasized the word with a

hard edge.

"Yes." She needed to make herself clear. "I don't know anything about sex. It seems to me that I wouldn't have been deceived by the people who are supposed to love me if I wasn't so naïve. Maybe if I'd been more worldly, I would have realized that my sister was sleeping with Greg. Maybe if I knew what good sex was, I would have admitted to myself sooner that I had no interest in him and stopped fooling myself that marriage between us would work. Maybe if I wasn't a naïve little virgin, I wouldn't be here."

Those weren't her only reasons, but the ones the guys needed to hear. Kinley ached to know what it felt like to be in their bed. God, she wanted that so badly. The days she'd been with them seemed surreal. She'd been terrified, then surprised. They'd confronted her with realities that had broken her heart. Before she could go back and deal with the real world—where she faced the likely loss of her family and her charity—she needed a few moments of pure fantasy.

"You read the evidence?" Dominic remained still as a statue, his eyes cold on her.

"Yes. I still don't know exactly what he's doing, but it's obvious that he's using Hope House for something nefarious. If you ask the right questions, we might be able to find answers. I suspect you don't want to go to the feds until you actually know what he plotted."

Dominic nodded. "I don't want to give him any wiggle room or loopholes to jump through."

"Though he's likely covering his ass right now," Riley explained. "He would have started the minute the police identified Law on that tape. I know the media is keeping his identity quiet because Kellan is handling it, but Greg knows who Dominic works with, so he knows who has you. It's another reason we moved your accountant. He's under watch at Black Oak Oil offices. We have some friends who can make sure he doesn't have a convenient accident or house fire."

"So you can see just how serious all of this is?" Dominic

asked.

"Yes. Of course."

He huffed, an oddly aristocratic sound. "And yet you want to negotiate for sex? You want to sell your body to us, like you tried to do with Greg? Is that all you know how to do?"

Shame flooded her. Somehow she'd expected them to jump on the offer. It was just sex, after all. Men were supposed to really enjoy it. Kinley didn't know what to say.

"I won't barter for sex, so I'm going to have to turn your offer down." Dominic scowled. "I happen to believe that you will cooperate because it's the right thing to do."

Kinley had always had the impression that he'd do anything to avenge his sister, so his refusal was a blow to the gut. "Are you saying no because I don't have any experience or because I don't arouse you?" Actually, she didn't need to hear them explain all the reasons they didn't want her. She could guess. "Forget I asked. In fact, forget I said anything at all."

Kinley closed her eyes in mortification. She wasn't experienced, and they were men who had likely taken a lot of women to bed…as well as on sofas, across tables, and against walls. She wasn't beautiful enough for them and knew next to nothing about being sexy. She lacked grace and height and the ability to look really good in a short skirt. Not that they were so shallow as to want only those traits. But Kinley knew that she often wore rose-colored glasses, wasn't a fan of adrenaline, and probably didn't seem level-headed enough. She was all the things men like them wouldn't want in a woman.

Kinley gathered up the folders and clutched them tight to her breasts. Time to retreat and not emerge from her room again until she'd figured out what Greg was doing. After that, hopefully she could go home. She might just go to Annabelle's and start over again. But she sure as hell wasn't going to beg these men for anything again. She needed to salvage whatever shards of her pride she could.

"Kinley," Law began. "Baby, why don't we all sit back down?"

Tears pricked at her eyes, but she was determined to not shed them now. "I think I'd rather go back to my room. I promise no more running. Dominic, you're right. I will do what I can to help you. It's the right thing to do. Please forgive me for what I said earlier. I was just joking, badly it seems. If you have any questions, of course I'll answer them."

She turned away from them, acutely aware of their silence, and walked to the door.

"Kinley!" Law finally called.

She didn't reply, simply fled to her room and closed the door as the tears began to fall.

Chapter Nine

A flaming fury kindled in Law's gut as he stared at Dominic. "What the hell is wrong with you?"

Dominic's whole body stood stiff, defensive. "I should be asking you that. Have you forgotten about Carrie? I guess so, since you're completely willing to toss this operation away for a couple of orgasms with a woman who wouldn't talk to you in the real world."

Law scoffed. "She talked to me just fine for a week, and you know what? Never once did she hang up on me because my bank account wasn't fat enough or because I wasn't 'good enough' for her. She always treated me like a human being worthy of concern. You're the one with the serious problem, *Master* Dominic."

Dominic's eyes flared. "What the fuck is that supposed to mean?"

Riley moved between them, his hands up as though he could stop them from fighting. "Let's take a breather, guys."

Law didn't want a breather. He wanted to have it out. "Get your head out of your ass. You introduced me to this lifestyle. And the first thing you told me was to treat submissives with the respect they deserve. All you've done is treat Kinley like shit."

"She's not my sub," he pointed out, tossing his hands in the air. "Hell, I doubt she even knows what the word means. If I'd taken her up on her offer, my need for her submission would probably send her running and screaming."

Dominic was being purposefully ignorant. "Maybe not. She is a sub, and you know it. You knew it the minute you saw her. Just like you know the way you're treating her now is wrong."

"I'm supposed to respect the fact that she wanted to trade sex for information that will bring down my sister's killer? Not going to happen. Besides, if I'd said yes, she just would have regretted it later."

Law glared at his friend. "When did you get so stupid? Or are you just lying to yourself so you don't have to face the fact that you want her? Kinley was asking for what she needs and hoping you would help me give it to her. She was willing to give you something in return. That was her way of negotiating with us. Why are you acting like this is something foreign? Insulting? We always negotiate our encounters with subs. You've never made a single one of them feel like a whore—until Kinley. Congratulations. How does it feel to be an asshole?"

Dominic sighed, then rubbed at the bridge of his nose. "She caught me off guard. Besides, this is a fling, at best. You have to know that."

"And you think we have meaningful relationships with the subs we pick up in clubs for a night?"

"No. It's just… Once we've put Jansen away, Kinley won't have anything more to do with us. You're kidding yourself if you think otherwise, Law. And I'm not sure if she can handle a short-term affair. Why give her another reason to hate us?"

"You don't know her like I do." He had Dominic on the ropes. "But you need to make up your mind. Is she a whore or an innocent we need to protect?"

"Back the fuck off and stop thinking with your dick for two seconds. We're close to nailing Jansen. I've worked for years to get Carrie justice, and I can't let Kinley stop me."

"Is your whole life about revenge, man? I'm not telling you to give up on bringing Jansen down. He deserves it. But isn't there more to life? Are you really such an empty shell that you can't see Kinley is everything we could possibly want. She offered herself to us on a platter, dumbass. Look me in the eye and tell me you don't want her."

Dominic stayed silent, his stare holding Law's.

"It doesn't matter if you're willing to admit it or not," Law grumbled. "Even if you don't want her, you should've let her down easy. Goddamn it, I've seen you handle women for years. You know how to treat them kindly even when they're rude. Kinley tried to play by your rules and negotiate because she didn't feel that she had the right to simply ask for what she needed. And you treated her like crap."

Dominic opened his mouth, then stopped. Sighed. "I didn't mean to make her feel bad."

"But you didn't hold back, did you?"

"I did what I thought I needed to do," he shot back between clenched teeth.

"To protect yourself, yeah. And you didn't care if you hurt her in the process." It wasn't a question. It was the truth.

Law was done He couldn't seem to get through Dominic's thick skull, and Riley had built up a fortress around himself that Law wasn't sure anyone would ever get through. Was he willing to give up Kinley because his brothers wouldn't give her a chance?

No one ever put her first. If he was going to be her man, Law knew he needed to think about her above all others.

"I'm done here," Law said. "I'm going to Kinley. I'm glad I'm not too dumb to see the future possibilities with her. I'll take care of her from now on. If she figures something out that will help you put Jansen behind bars, I'll let you two know. But starting now, she's mine. I make any decisions that concern her."

"What the hell, Law? You can't just take ownership of her like she's a stray."

"I'm taking *responsibility* for her. And I'm going to get a collar around her neck as soon as I can. Once I do, I expect you both to respect my rights. I was more than willing to share her, but I can see I'll have to do this on my own."

He turned and stalked out, frustration welling. He'd finally found the right woman and they were too stubborn to see it. How could something so right go so fucking wrong?

He stopped outside Kinley's door, hesitating for the first time. Would she even want to talk to him? Or would she put him in the same category as Dominic? Law could almost forgive his brother. Riley had been deeply hurt by Simone. But Dominic? He'd known the relationship with that bitch wouldn't work out, yet he still hadn't treated Simone half as badly as he'd just behaved toward Kinley.

That was past. Time to forge his future. Law took a deep breath and knocked on her door.

"Go away. I'm not trying to escape."

He turned the knob and walked in, standing over her as she stared out the window, attempting to hide the fact that she'd been crying. In fact, they'd made her cry far too much for his liking.

It was past time to take charge.

"I know you aren't," he assured.

"Good. I said I'll help you. And I'm not going to press charges when this is over. So you can leave me alone."

He could hear the tears in her voice, and they tore at him as he approached her. Damn, he wished he was better with words. "Baby, I won't do that. In fact, I won't ever leave you alone again."

Her shoulders shook, and she sniffled. "Don't say things like that."

"Why not?"

"It's not fair."

"Aww, baby…" Law pulled her into his arms, and she buried her face in his chest. "Don't cry. Dominic isn't usually so harsh with women. I think he's confused. He's caught between wanting you and avenging his sister. You have to understand that he's been trying to implicate Jansen for a very long time."

"I wasn't talking about what he said. I meant the whole

situation. I finally find a man who seems to really want me, but his two best friends don't. And that's a deal breaker for you."

Oh, he could solve that problem for her.

Law hooked a finger under her chin and nudged her head up. "Do you want me, Kinley? Do you want me to teach you about sex? Because I will. I don't need Dominic and Riley to do it."

She bit into her lower lip, and his cock ached. "Yes."

"Listen, what the other two want doesn't matter. *I* want you. I can't wait to teach you everything, but before we go any further, you should understand that I'm a rough man. I have certain…needs."

How did he explain to a virgin that he would want to tie her up until she was completely helpless and, oh yes, he was definitely going to want to fuck her ass well and often.

Sexy pillow talk. He wasn't good at it. Dominic was. Sometimes the man wouldn't shut up about how much he wanted a woman and what he intended to do to make her scream down the roof.

But Dominic wasn't here now. Neither was Riley to smooth things over. He'd made the choice to have Kinley on his own, so he had to try to make this right.

"What kind of needs?"

He could start out with the basics. "I need you to listen and obey me in the bedroom."

Though her eyes were shining with tears, a little smile curved her lips up. "Since I don't know anything, I think I can handle that. I'm really not completely idiotic, you know. I mean it's not like you have to teach me what sex is. I took the class in high school."

What he wanted to teach her, no classroom sex ed course would have covered. But thoughts of every wicked thing he intended to do to her ran through his imagination. His cock was already rock hard and straining against his jeans.

Law couldn't help himself. He had to kiss her. He talked

between sweet brushes of their lips. "Tell me what you know. You've been kissed before."

"Yes, but it didn't feel this good. It didn't make me…antsy." She caressed her way up his biceps, to his shoulders, then wrapped her arms around his neck.

Antsy. He liked making her feel that way. He could keep her on the edge for hours, licking and sucking and playing with her. In fact, he was dying to. "Before Dominic, has a man ever played with your breasts?"

"Once, but I didn't like it. In high school, my biology lab partner kissed me and grabbed my breasts. It kind of hurt."

"He was rough, and you weren't aroused, baby. Trust me, I'll make sure you're ready for some rough play eventually. You liked when Dominic touched you. He was gentle, right?"

"Not when he pinched my nipples." Her skin flushed a pretty pink. "I liked that, Law. It hurt at first. Then it felt good."

Because she was at least a bit of a masochist. A man like Jansen would use that against her, but Law wanted to set her free. The pain he intended to give her would only intensify her pleasure. If she didn't have it, if she forced herself to live a vanilla life, she would always be missing that deep surrender that only a Dom could coax and command from her.

"That's honest. I needed to know that. It's great that you need more bite to the sensations I give you. We'll go slow, though. I promise." He rubbed their noses together.

Law had never reveled in the physical. Sex had been a bodily function, pleasurable for sure, but he hadn't ever had the impulse to lose himself in a lover the way he did with Kinley.

He brushed his hand across her breast, and she shivered. "Going slow will make getting to the end so much more special. You deserve a lover who takes his time with you, Kinley. You need a man who will protect you and cherish you. One who worships you. I'm going to fulfill all your needs."

She looked both hopeful and a bit skeptical. "No ploys?

No front to help your buddy?"

"Nope. I'll still help Dominic. Losing Carrie nearly crushed him. But I won't let him hurt you to do it. You trusted me before. All that's really changed is my name and a few minor details. Everything else was real. I'm that same guy."

Kinley chewed on her lip, considering. "What you're describing—taking care of me—that wasn't how it worked in my family. My mother took care of my father, but he didn't give her much in return. I see that now."

"It won't be that way between us. Your men should adore you. Your men should think you're the sun in the sky." He closed his eyes briefly. *Man, not men.* It would take him a while to give up that fantasy. And he'd have to figure out how to ensure her safety and future in case something happened to him. But for Kinley, he would. "Your man, I mean. And I'm going to put you first. Do you understand me? Kinley, if you let me have you, you're going to be above everything else. When I make a decision, it will be with you in mind."

It struck him suddenly that he was being too open. He was putting everything out there—his heart, his pride, his soul—and maybe he shouldn't. Kinley had only asked for sex, not commitment. She might reject him.

He had no idea what the fuck he would do if she did. Or worse, if she laughed at his devotion.

"You can't take it back." She reached up and cupped his jaw. "I see you hesitating and… You can't say those things to me, then change your mind."

Kind of what Annabelle had told him, too. Kinley was a forever kind of girl. Law was ready to devour the cake.

Peace settled over him. This was the right woman. The timing might be shitty, but that didn't matter. He wasn't giving her up.

But damn it, even if his head had given up on Dominic and Riley, his gut refused to do the same. "Can we give the others some time? They might come around."

Maybe when they saw that Kinley wasn't going

anywhere, that being with her didn't have to mean the end of Dom's justice or be the start of another heartbreak for Riley, they would give her a fair chance.

"What if they don't want me?" she whispered. That clearly worried her.

"They do. Oh, baby, I know them. Dominic might not be blood, but he's my brother in all the ways that count. Trust me, he's practically dying from hunger. It's why he's acting like such an ass. Riley is just..." God, he didn't want to bring up Simone now during a time that was supposed to be about Kinley and her needs. "He's being a pussy. Sorry."

He had to stop cussing like a fucking sailor in front of her.

"Stop apologizing, Law. I like you the way you are. Will you...kiss me? Touch me?"

"Gladly." He covered her lips with his and got ready to teach her everything. She deserved all he could give her and more.

* * * *

Kinley really deserved better than him, Dominic decided. He stomped to the liquor cabinet and poured himself three fingers of Scotch. Thank god the James brothers had excellent taste in liquor.

He downed it without really tasting it and poured a second glass.

"What do we do now?" Riley asked, his voice tight.

Because the guy thought he'd just lost his brother. Dominic conceded that he might be right. "We do what Law asked. We respect his rights."

Law meant to claim Kinley and become her rightful Master. He would be the one to take her hand and her virginity, then lead her into the world of Dominance and submission they'd all come to crave.

God, once Law took her under his wing, even if he forgave Dominic, the woman would probably still drive a wedge between them. He hated that fact. And he saw only one way to avoid it. Give in.

Law also had damn fine instincts. Did he sense that Kinley could handle what they all needed? Dominic paced, his thoughts racing before he paused to pour more Scotch. Instead, he put the bottle down and stared out the door, toward Kinley's room. Had he made a mistake? Had he just thrown away something precious?

"Law is going to regret this, right?" Riley's stare, too, trailed to the hallway where Law had just disappeared.

"I don't know." Dominic wasn't sure what to think. He'd been so certain earlier what path to choose. Now, he was at a loss. All because he couldn't stop thinking about one blonde—who just happened to be the key to the revenge he'd made the cornerstone of his life for years. If he embraced one, did it necessarily mean he had to give up the other?

"You want to join them, don't you?" Riley's tone came out almost like an accusation.

"Don't you?" Dominic turned on him. He could see plainly that Riley was struggling as well. He'd seen how Riley looked at Kinley, the way his eyes kept straying to her mouth, her breasts, and that luscious ass of hers. He'd noticed how Riley hung on her every word.

"It's a bad idea."

"But what if Law's right?" Dominic argued. "Your brother is no fool. What if she's the one?"

"Get your head out of this fucking fairy tale. There's no such thing as 'the one.'"

Riley was probably right, but Dominic couldn't stop wondering. "What if Kinley could be happy at the center of a ménage, at least for a while? It's more than we have now." What if she really was strong enough to handle them and could hold them all together?

"Women don't want what we have to offer. Kinley might seem open at times, but only because she's too innocent to understand what a future with three men would be like. She's got a high profile. She's giving in now because she's scared and doesn't know how else to feel safe."

Dominic turned Riley's words over in his head. Kinley hadn't seemed scared when she'd bartered with him, almost boldly telling him what she wanted. That didn't seem like an innocent looking for shelter from a terrifying situation.

Shit, Law was right. Kinley had been negotiating, offering him something for what she wanted in return. He'd taken it as a play for control, a way to shut down the investigation into Carrie's murder—and he'd been dead wrong.

He'd spent years building a business with one thought in his head: avenging his sister's death. Nothing else had mattered. Law had followed him to freaking Afghanistan and nearly lost his legs. And Dominic wasn't willing to give it a shot with the girl his brother so obviously loved? A girl he couldn't get out of his head?

"She's just going to take what she wants and walk out in the end." Riley grabbed a glass. It looked like Dominic wasn't drinking alone tonight.

"Maybe." *But maybe not.* How would he know if he never took the chance?

Then a terrible truth hit him like a bolt of lightning. He'd never really intended on sharing a woman with them forever. Law and Riley had probably been searching for one, and Dominic had been utterly content to just have sex. Law was right. He made himself seem like a stand-up guy because he ensured all the subs he used got a few orgasms. He could be gracious with them, kind even, because nothing was at stake. For too long, the only abiding love of his life had been fucking up Greg Jansen's.

How proud would his sister be of that? Dominic grimaced as the question rolled through his head.

He glanced over at the bed he'd laid out for his dog. Butch was the only responsibility he'd really taken, and then only because the damn thing had shown up on his property half starved and refused to go away. He'd fed the poor mutt out of pure pity, and Butch had just kept following him around until Dominic got used to having him underfoot.

And now his dog was cuddled around the rat thing, his bigger body shielding Gigi from anything that might come their way. He was contentedly asleep, having given up the softest part of his bed to whatever the hell one called a damn dog's true love.

Even Butch knew how to care for a female. And Dominic had done nothing but kidnap Kinley and use her for his own ends, while offering her absolutely nothing in return. Oh, he'd paid lip service to protecting her, but he wasn't really offering protection. Once Jansen was behind bars, the press would eat Kinley alive. Dominic planned to be long gone.

That was a hell of a hand he'd dealt her.

He'd walked in and torn her life apart. When she'd asked for the one thing she needed, he'd repaid her with insults. Kinley was supposed to have had a wedding night. Wasn't it just good manners to offer her another replacement…or two?

"How are we going to deal with this when it's over?" Riley asked. "We live together. Is Law just going to move Kinley in?"

Riley wasn't thinking straight. He needed to get all his anxieties in order. "I thought she was leaving him."

"She probably will, but what if she doesn't?"

If she didn't, then they both would have missed out on what they claimed they'd been seeking. What he'd damn well knew he'd wanted before Carrie's murder.

How much was he willing to let Jansen take from him? He'd already snuffed out Carrie's life. Was Dominic willing to let Jansen rob his, too?

"If she doesn't, then you're going to have to listen to a whole lot of sex," Dominic pointed out.

Would Law and Kinley even stay? Or would Law move them out? Hell, maybe they'd even move to New York. That pissed Dominic off because it filled him with a vague panic. He'd lived with Law most of his adult life. He didn't want

Law to leave any more than he wanted to give Jansen his future.

Kinley was everything he looked for in a woman. He'd been hard since he'd first seen her, every photo making him fall just a little more in lust. And watching her in person had made him rethink his whole position. Hell, his whole life.

Since bringing her to Alaska, Dominic had seen how sweet and kind she could be. She'd stood up to him when she was scared. But she'd used her head when presented with the hard evidence. Kinley hadn't curled into a ball and cried when she realized she'd been abducted. She'd fought. Hell, she'd even dropped herself and half of her belongings out a window, trying to escape. Life with her would never be dull.

Dominic wanted her and her trust. And he hated the thought that she might fear him. Damn it, he wanted her to give him the information she knew because she trusted him, not because they'd made a deal. But how was she supposed to trust him when he'd put his own crap into her innocent plea for help and pleasure, then thrown it back in her face?

"I need to apologize."

"What?" Riley asked like he was out of his mind.

"I have to talk to Kinley."

He needed to be in that bedroom with her and Law. Or try to be. She might slam the door in his face, but he would take it with good grace as long as she allowed him to apologize first.

Without another word, he strode down the hall and found the door, unlocked now because Law was inside with her.

He wouldn't lock her in again. She'd said she would stay. If they had a shot at any sort of forgiveness or future with her, he had to learn to trust her, too. He knocked.

"Go away." Law's deep growl sounded through the walls.

He was cock blocking his best friend. Dominic winced, then he knocked again because he wasn't going away. "I want to talk to Kinley."

"Later."

"Now." *Damn it.*

Someone wrenched the door opened. Law. He'd already tossed his shirt off and was breathing heavily, scowling Dominic's way. "Can't it wait? Or has something happened?"

"Yeah, I decided I was wrong and I want to apologize."

Law's eyes narrowed. "You interrupted us to say that you're sorry?"

"Unless I can convince her to take more than just an apology. I'm sorry, Law. I don't know how to make this right. I don't know what any of this fucking means. I just don't want to miss out. I think you might be right. She might be important." He felt like an idiot. He'd never been in this position, on the outside, practically begging to be let in. It wasn't a feeling he liked.

Kinley stepped up behind Law, peering out from behind his back. "Are you sorry you kidnapped me?"

He had to be honest with her. "No. If I hadn't, you wouldn't be here. I'd be a lot sorrier about that. I think you would, too."

She pursed her lips. "Are you sorry that your dog raped mine?"

He wasn't about to take that. "No, your dog led mine into sin. He has a thing for bows. She used it against him."

He caught the faintest hint of a smile from her. "I'll admit, she's a flirty thing. So if you're not apologizing for kidnapping me or very likely turning my dog into a single mother, what are you sorry about?"

So many things. "For being rude to you."

She shrugged. "Well, it's probably rude to offer sex in exchange for putting away a dangerous criminal. I've already told Law that I'll help out. I'll give you everything I know."

Kinley curled her arms around his buddy's torso as though she found comfort in being close to him. They were already bonding as a Dom and sub should. And Dominic almost choked, wondering if he was too late.

It couldn't be. He wanted to worry about her, be responsible for her. Comfort and care for and pleasure her. He and Law should be a team when it came to Kinley. "I'm sorry I hurt you."

"You're forgiven."

Just like that? God, how good was this woman?

Law had a shit-eating grin on his face. "Baby, I think he's sorry about a whole lot of other things."

"I'm not going to make him beg. I forgive him and I hope we can be friends."

"I think that's what he's most sorry about," Law explained. "He's really fucking sorry he's on the wrong side of this door. He wants in and he's not sure how to ask since he's never had to."

Kinley stared at him, her eyes wide, her lips parted. He wanted to kiss her desperately. "Do you truly want to come in, Dominic?"

"Yes. I want to give you the knowledge you asked for. I want to teach you what it means to submit to a man, to trust him enough to place your body and your pleasure in his hands. I want to help show you just how high you can soar. And I want to share you with Law and Riley, though Riley might not come around. Even if he doesn't, I want to be a part of your training, Kinley. For as long as we're here, I want to be your Master."

"I hadn't exactly hit her with the kinky stuff yet, Dominic. Let's start with sex before we get to the spankings."

"Understood." He could wait until tomorrow to tie her up as long as he was in her bed tonight. "I want in, Kinley. Will you let me?"

She shared a glance with Law, then stepped back. For a second, he thought she would decline. Then she opened the door wider. "Come in."

Law eased away, allowing Dominic to enter the room. He stared at the woman he wanted more than his next breath.

"Call me 'Sir,' Kinley." With gnawing hunger and hope, he reached for her hand, ready to start her lesson and see where their future led.

Chapter Ten

Kinley took Dominic's hand, her heart thumping in her chest. "Sir?"

"It's a quirk of mine, pet." He stood over her, looking down into her eyes as he tangled his fingers in her hair. "You're so fucking soft."

Law moved in behind her, his chest brushing her back. The thick line of his erection pressed against her backside. "I'm glad you're here, man. You're better with the whole talking thing than I am. I was struggling with how to explain what we want."

Sex. They wanted sex, right? "What do you mean?"

Kinley knew what she wanted—to be right where she was, crowded by them. They took all the space surrounding her, as they enclosed her, protected her, covered every inch of her skin with theirs. She reveled in the sensation.

Dominic frowned. "Law?"

Law's hand cracked against her bottom. A sharp pain flared across Kinley's butt.

"Damn, those little rhinestones are hell on a man's hand," he complained.

She whipped her gaze over her shoulder and blinked at him. He'd spanked her. Actually spanked her. Then after he slapped her backside, he'd cupped and felt it.

And heat burst across her skin, making her tingle and aware.

Dominic cupped her chin and brought her attention back to him. "What do you call me in the bedroom?"

"Sir." She answered him readily because all she could

think about was how her bottom practically hummed. "If I forget to call you Sir, Law will spank me?"

"Now you're getting the gist." Dominic's eyes darkened, his skin flushing with desire. "You obey or there will be punishment. But understand, this is a game, pet. It's meant to be enjoyable for us all. If you're truly scared or if something hurts beyond what you find pleasurable, say the word 'red' and everything stops. If you get anxious and want to slow down, just say 'yellow.'"

"We want you to be happy, baby," Law said, still palming her butt. "We want you to crave this type of play."

"Exactly, but we take it as seriously as we take your pleasure. Yesterday in the kitchen we gave you your first real orgasm. But we intend to train your body to expect that pleasure every time we touch you. When we're done, we'll merely look at you, and you'll remember how it feels to have an orgasm overtake your whole body. You'll know what it means to be completely possessed. You should never accept less from a lover."

His words were making her antsy again. Hot. "Completely?"

Dominic's lips moved to her forehead, planting a sweet kiss there. "Yes, pet. I want you to understand what's going to happen. How do you expect to take more than one man into your bed?"

"You're not talking about taking turns, are you?" The realization stunned Kinley so deeply, she could barely breathe.

Of course she'd read some books, heard some friends talk about…that. Annabelle sometimes confessed her fantasies after a couple of glasses of wine. More than one man would require a certain amount of flexibility.

"No, we won't be taking turns. Tonight, we will because you're not ready for more, but we'll require that you allow us to prepare your body to accommodate us both at once." Law's hand slid around, cupping her intimately through her jeans. "One right here in your sweet little pussy."

Dominic's hand found her backside. "And one in your ass."

Heat flared everywhere they touched, everywhere they whispered along her skin. Every place they pressed their two hard erections against her. What would it feel like to have both of them deep inside her? She would be caught, immobile, with absolutely no escape. Not that she would want it. What would it be like to have these men moving in and out of her body as she took Riley in her mouth?

She forced herself to concentrate on the situation at hand. Riley wasn't with her, but Dominic and Law were. It might not be forever, but while she had them, she was going to explore a whole world she'd never dreamed of. She'd lost so much in the last few days. She'd lost her family and the future she'd thought would be hers, but maybe she could find a new version of Kinley Kohl in their arms. A better, more confident version. Maybe she'd meet the Kinley who didn't let fear keep her from trying something new or shrink away from pleasure.

"I'll do it." As much as she'd feared them in the beginning, she realized that she trusted them now. They'd risked prison time to remove her from a dangerous situation. Yes, they'd done it for Carrie, too. But they'd cared for her since bringing her to Alaska. Kinley was self-aware enough to know that she would have resisted believing anything if they had merely tried to talk to her. She would have gone straight to Greg and demanded answers. For that, he might have killed her then and there. Method of transport notwithstanding, they had treated her better than any other men in her life.

Her heart would probably break if this didn't work out, but she refused to be too scared to take a chance anymore. She would rather mourn the loss of them than never have them at all.

Dominic shook his head with a sigh. "Law?"

"Sir! I'll do it, Sir." She was going to have to get used to that.

It was too late. Law smacked her backside again as he

chuckled against her ear. “Keep it up, baby. I could do this all day. I enjoy spanking your ass.”

And she was starting to enjoy the feeling, too. It hurt…but then it didn’t. Then only heat licked through her.

Dominic stepped back. “Undress for us, Kinley.”

Just like that all her self-doubts pushed to the forefront. They were so magnificently masculine. Obviously, they worked hard to stay in peak physical condition. She’d been starving herself for weeks and had barely managed to lose one dress size. And she wasn’t sure that her boobs looked so great without the support of a bra.

“Is there a problem, pet?” Dominic settled into the wingchair on the far side of the room with a dark brow raised. Somehow he made the comfortable leather piece look like a throne. His black hair was slicked away from his angular face, and he was dressed casually, but there was no way a T-shirt and sweatpants could detract from his regal air of authority.

“Can we turn off the lights?”

Law turned her to face him. “Are you looking for a serious spanking? No, we are not going to turn off the lights. We are not going to huddle under the covers and fumble around so everyone’s modesty is preserved. There is zero place for that here. We’re going to fuck. It’s going to be dirty and nasty, and it’s going to feel so good. And when we’re done, I’m going to hold you all night long. But now you’re going to obey, and that means you’d better strip off every garment and show us what you’re offering.”

Tears threatened. She turned slightly so she could see them both. “What if you don’t want me after I’m naked?”

“That will not happen,” Law promised.

Dominic’s stare delved into her, his will apparent in the intensity. “Kinley, you wanted to trade your business information for knowledge about sex. I’m going to give you a little of that advice up front. Be brave in life. Accept that there’s always a chance you won’t get what you want. On the other hand, you’ll never have what you seek unless you ask for it. Sex is the same. If all you ask for is a man to climb on top of you and try to get you off, then that's likely what you'll get. But if you want more, if you want real intimacy and connection, then offer it. Offer yourself to us."

Offer herself? Hadn't she been doing that for years? She'd offered her love and devotion to her sister and father. She'd offered her future to Greg. She'd done it all without any thought to her own needs beyond being a dutiful daughter, of doing what was expected. In fact, she'd done everything society thought was proper and right. She'd sacrificed for her family because that was what a good woman was supposed to do.

Being good had gotten her nothing. She was alone and empty-handed. She would always be if she didn't change something.

Starting with being brave.

Kinley pulled at her sweater, dragging it over her head and handing it to Law. Dominic sat back, fingers steepled, an air of satisfaction humming around him. He said nothing, merely watched her with hot eyes that never strayed from her body.

"You're doing great, baby. Take off the jeans. I've been wanting to see your ass for months." Law stood behind her. His hands encircled her waist as he undid the snap on her jeans. Like all the jeans Greg had given her, it was encrusted with little rhinestones. "Let me help you."

He eased the zipper down and then his warm hands met her flesh. She nearly sighed at the sizzling connection.

He pushed the waistband down and helped her step out, leaving her in nothing but her plain white support bra and cotton undies.

"I don't like the underwear, pet. I thought I made myself clear." Dominic frowned.

He looked gorgeous when he frowned. And when he smiled. He was just entirely perfect.

"Yes, Sir. That was before I tried to escape. I thought it would be easier to get away with underwear on."

Dominic looked as if he repressed a smile. "I assure you it won't be any easier to get away because you've covered your pussy. If you try to leave us again, expect a spanking and some other punishments that will be…uncomfortable."

"Like I said, I've decided to stay. Especially once I found out you have a guard moose on the payroll." She'd known escaping into the wilderness was a stupid move, but she'd been trying to protect herself. Kinley didn't want that now. If the heartache was going to come, she wanted to have a damn good reason for it.

"It's for the best. We can protect you here while we figure out how to put Jansen in jail," Law said.

She held up a hand because she didn't want that to go any further. "Let's not talk about Greg now. I don't even want the thought of him to come between us."

This was their time to bond. Greg couldn't be allowed to ruin it.

"Then take off his rock," Dominic demanded with a firm jaw and uncompromising stare.

Rock? As Kinley brought her hand down, the light caught her engagement ring, the four-carat diamond glittering.

Kinley stared at it. How was she still wearing Greg's ring? For the last month, it had just become an extension of who she was: Greg's fiancée. Not anymore. The ring had to go. She didn't care that it was worth hundreds of thousands of dollars. She just wanted it off her finger. Though she pulled and yanked, it wouldn't budge. She hadn't taken it off since the day he'd placed it on her finger. Now it was stuck.

"Come here." Dominic held a hand out.

She went to him, trembling and wondering if she was about to get another spanking.

Gently, Dominic took her hand, his fingers sliding over the ring. "You want to be rid of this?"

"More than anything."

Very slowly he brought her hand to his mouth. He kissed the tips of her fingers, the sensation soft against her flesh. He sucked her finger into his mouth. Heat sizzled through her, all the way between her legs, as his tongue played against her skin. He enveloped her whole finger in the heat of his mouth. His teeth skimmed her flesh, the little bite sending a jolt of need through her body before he anchored them around the band. Then very slowly, he dragged the ring up her finger, freeing her.

He spit the bling from between his lips and placed it on the nightstand. “Better?”

Kinley nodded, eyes glued to him.

“Good. Now hand me your bra and panties. I want to see all of you.”

Her body was starting to hum. Despite the fact they were standing apart, his gaze felt like an allover caress.

Swallowing down her nerves, she pushed the bra straps off her shoulders, then reached behind and unhooked the band. As soon as the garment slid free, Law’s big hands cupped her. Kinley closed her eyes in pure pleasure.

He and Dominic had seen her naked breasts. And they weren’t turning away.

“Now the underwear, Law,” Dominic said, his voice low.

Law’s palms skimmed her body and settled on her hips. Then he slid his fingers under the elastic of her panties and dragged them down her legs.

Dominic sat back in his seat again, his eyes darkening as his stare drank her in. “You’re lovely, Kinley. You’re womanly and beautiful. Being naked doesn’t take away an ounce of your innocence.”

She blushed, but it had been the perfect thing to say. “Thank you, Sir.”

Dominic’s satisfied smile made her heart do little flip-flops before he turned to his friend. “Law, how is that backside of hers you’re so deeply interested in?”

Law groaned behind her. “So fucking perfect. Round and delicious.”

“Show me.”

Law turned her, and her heart softened as she looked up into his eyes. Dominic was dangerous and sexy, and Kinley was falling for him fast. But she'd already tumbled over with this man.

She rested her hands on Law's perfectly ripped chest and looked up at him, melting into him a bit.

"Now that is a luscious ass," Dominic said.

"And this is a sweet, smooth pussy." Law leaned out and stared down, grazing her nipples as he worked his way down her body. "Spread your legs. Don't hesitate. Just obey me."

Kinley moved her feet apart. Cold air brushed her sensitive folds, and she felt exposed with Law's eyes on her. But it wasn't an unwelcome feeling. In fact, she liked being on display and seeing the appreciation in his stare.

Suddenly, Law's hot fingers cupped her mound.

"That's right. This skin here is so fucking soft. And you're getting wet, baby."

She was. Kinley could feel how easily his fingers slid over her labia. It took everything she had to not moan and jump and plead for more.

"I want a taste. You've already had one." Suddenly, Dominic stood behind her. He turned her to face him, then his lips descended on hers.

She opened for him, giving him complete access to her mouth. As he groaned, his hand found her pussy, caressing her possessively. Law's ran over the curves of her ass. It was so decadent to be naked when they were still mostly dressed. The roughness of Law's denim gently chafed her skin, while the soft cotton of Dominic's shirt brushed her nipples almost like a feather. The distinct sensations made her tingle. She was so aware, so completely alive.

Dominic pulled back, his hand leaving her pussy and going straight to his lips. He sucked her cream off his flesh, his eyes closing in a pleasurable little smile. "She tastes so sweet."

"Yep," Law agreed, skimming his lips up her neck.

"Lie down on the bed and spread your legs, Kinley,"

Dominic commanded. He tugged at his T-shirt, pulling it over his head and revealing a gloriously cut chest. His sweatpants rode low on his lean hips. The longer she stared, the more the notches on the sides made her mouth water.

"Pet?" he asked sharply.

Law tugged on her hand, gesturing her toward the bed. "Lie down. It's time to get you ready. We're going to make sure you're so wet and soft that we'll slide right in."

They were going to take her body, her virginity. They were going to merge with her and give her an experience—a knowledge—she'd never had before.

Kinley climbed onto the bed and opened herself to them.

With eager fingers, Law tore at his jeans, shoving them down. His thick cock came into view. Kinley stared, wide-eyed, as she took in the sight. It wasn't that she'd never seen a penis before. She certainly had. Not in person, but she'd seen pictures. Law went so far beyond those flat, almost inanimate pictures. Thick and fully erect, his member stood against his belly, nearly touching his navel. His whole body looked like a work of art, every muscle lovingly chiseled and handcrafted.

He climbed on the bed beside her. "Don't just stare, Kinley. Touch me."

Law laid himself out for her, as open to her as she was to them. He offered himself to her. Kinley couldn't wait to take him.

With a shaking hand, she reached out to touch him, sighing as she wrapped her fingers around his velvety yet hard shaft. But more, she felt the connection between them with just that one touch.

With hot, hooded eyes, Dominic watched them.

And Kinley felt as if she'd finally found her place.

* * * *

Riley took a long swig of Scotch. Nothing was going to make him sleep tonight. Summer nights in Alaska were brutally short, but it wasn't the lack of darkness keeping him in the kitchen now. It was the fact that if he wanted to get to bed, he would have to walk right past Kinley's room where Law and Dominic were undoubtedly relieving her of her virginity right this freaking second.

No, he didn't want to walk by and overhear that…and know he could be in there. His brothers were claiming her, no doubt. They were going to fall in love. While it lasted, he'd be left out in the cold.

What the fuck was he going to do?

Sometimes he felt like Dominic was completely content to just wander through life, while Law was looking for the fantasy that didn't exist. Riley wasn't sure what to do, but he knew he wanted more than one casual fuck after another. He wanted a family. He wanted kids to shelter and protect, who never had to endure the poverty and desperation he had growing up. He wanted to make up for everything he'd lost out on by giving his own children a great life.

Riley flicked on his computer and turned to one of the news feeds. His system was fully set up to catch the news channels from Black Oak's satellite system. The feed wasn't as clear here as it would be inside the work compound, but it was enough to keep Riley in the loop.

But having the news drone on in the background didn't distract him. Why the hell couldn't he let go of the crushing, wretched feeling of rejection Simone had handed him years ago?

Until her, no one had ever hurt him. He'd never given anyone that power. But the first time he'd tried to open up and trust, the one time he'd come really close to getting what he wanted, she'd cruelly slammed the door in his face.

Simone had been well educated. She'd seemed so free and open. He'd decided it was time to take the next step, and she'd been right there. Dominic liked her, and since Law never really liked much of anyone, Riley was content that his brother seemed able to put up with her.

He'd even picked out a house for all of them to live in.

But she'd laughed as she'd said "no." Riley had figured out in that moment that no woman would willingly tackle society's opinions to be with them. Dominic had tried to let him go his own way with no fuss, and Riley knew he stood a better chance of having the future he sought if he took a woman of his own. Deep down, that wasn't what he wanted, but he'd been trying to resign himself anyway.

And then Kinley waltzed in with her damn chocolate-colored eyes and those bouncy honey curls he wanted to sink his fingers into. If he had a redo, he'd be in her room right now, fucking the living hell out of her…except for one small problem.

Kinley was the kind of woman men fought wars for and sang songs to. And there was no way that woman married three men.

No.

Fucking.

Way.

She was too good, too sweet, too kind. She'd made it her life mission to help the damn poor, for god's sake. He would fall for her in a way he'd never fallen for Simone, and inevitably she would either laugh in his face when he asked her to marry him or crumble the first time some society bitch or a tabloid called her a whore for having three men. Either way, she'd be gone.

At most, she would probably really want Dominic because they came from the same world. Or she would only want Law because he had that brooding quality that made a lot of women want to fix him. Why the hell would she want him?

A flash of color caught his eye, and he turned the sound up. *Shit.* There she was, on the news. A picture of Kinley dominated the screen with a headline underneath: *Runaway Bride or Victim?* He turned up the volume.

Socialite Kinley Kohl remains in the news as we enter the third day following her disappearance from her wedding in

New York to controversial shipping tycoon Greg Jansen. The entire scandal is made even more mysterious by lawyer Kellan Kent's claim that he is representing the man seen taking Ms. Kohl away with his unknown associate. This program has positively identified the man as Law Anders, a former Special Forces soldier who is being sought for questioning in the alleged kidnapping.

Riley groaned. Well, the cat was sure as fuck out of the bag now. And he was a little miffed that he'd been demoted to "unknown associate."

"Ms. Kohl is not a victim of anything but love." Kellan flashed a wry, likely practiced smile for the cameras. "My client rescued his lover from a marriage she didn't want. Kinley Kohl was afraid of telling Greg Jansen she refused to marry him, and I think there is ample evidence that she was right to do so. His first wife died under mysterious circumstances, and that is all I'll say about that. When Kinley is ready, she'll contact her family, but for now she is in seclusion. My client would appreciate it if you would respect their privacy at this time."

It was a good play, but without Kinley to support the story herself, it would only work for a day or two. Then, no matter how much they tried to hide her location, the authorities would hunt them down or Jansen would ferret it out. Then he would either try to kill her or take her back.

Speak of the devil. Jansen's face popped on screen. It was obviously a previously taped interview. He stared at the camera and poured out his staged plea. "Kinley, darling, if you're out there and you can hear me, your father, your sister, and I just want you home. If there's any way to escape, please do it. As to the men who took my wife—sorry, I think of her as my wife—I will pay any ransom. Just send me a sign of life. Send me back her luggage to prove you actually have her. Please. I'll give you money just for that one little sign."

Riley paused the feed. Luggage wasn't proof of life. Jansen knew the way this whole thing worked. So what the fuck was he talking about? Proof of life was actual physical evidence that the person was alive at a certain time. He should be asking for a tape of Kinley talking while holding up today's paper or a phone call that included actual vocal contact.

But no. Jansen wanted her luggage. Again.

Riley didn't understand. He'd been through all of her belongings at least ten times. She didn't have a laptop here, so he had no way to search that. The only things on her tablet were games and books and a ton of pictures.

What was he looking for? What was more important about that luggage than Kinley herself returning home? It had to be something if Jansen was willing to pay for her luggage.

Which meant that, more than likely, Kinley herself couldn't help them.

Time was running out. He needed connections.

Riley turned the news feed off and settled in. It was all there, hidden somewhere in the charity's files. He just had to find it.

Since he couldn't be in her bedroom, telling her how beautiful he found her or how much he wanted her, this was all he could do for her now.

* * * *

"More. Touch me again." Law wanted her hands on him more than anything he could remember.

Kinley rolled to her side, looking down the length of his body. Law held in a groan. He'd never been so fucking hard. He was practically shaking. He hoped he didn't blow the minute she started stroking him.

Dominic stood at the edge of the bed, and Law wondered if he was going to be a hard ass. The little light spanking they'd already given her had been flirty and playful—a good way to begin introducing Kinley to the lifestyle. But Law wanted tonight to be all about her.

"You should touch him, Kinley. He looks needy." A smile

played at Dominic's lips.

Thank god his brother understood. "I am. So fucking needy."

She touched his chest, her fingertips drifting down his skin. Law drew in a shuddering breath, trying to force himself to calm. He'd keep it together and take it slow and easy with her, even if it killed him.

She brushed her hand over his cock again, and it twitched with need. "The skin is so soft."

But he was fucking granite. "Grip me, baby. You won't hurt me. Wrap your fingers around me and stroke hard."

"Like this?" Kinley enclosed him in her palm. He couldn't hold onto his moan. It tore from his chest when he felt the heat of her touch.

"Tighter," he managed to grit out.

She did as he asked, and of their own volition, Law's hips pumped up. His whole focus shifted to his cock. No way to stop it.

He'd never made himself really vulnerable before. Sure, he'd had women give him hand jobs, but that wasn't the point of this exercise. He wanted Kinley to explore, so he opened himself to her as she'd done for him.

"Kiss me." Law wanted her to understand the power she had. Even though he planned to take her as their submissive, she should know that her lovers would give themselves to her, too.

Her hair fell like a waterfall around him, locking out the rest of the world until all he could see was her sweet face coming toward him. She closed her eyes. Closer, closer, her lips came until she pressed them down on his own. Her soft whisper of a kiss made him crazy. Her tongue skimmed along his bottom lip, light as the brush of a feather. The gesture was almost hesitant, but when he shuddered and groaned, she seemed to gain confidence. Her hand tightened around his cock, then she moved her lips more forcefully on his own.

Kinley needed this time to learn and grow. She was shy

and naturally a lady. But once she came into her own as a woman, she would be able to move mountains. He and Dominic could give her that.

Riley could, too, but he was being a chicken-shit pansy ass.

Law opened to Kinley and let her in, her tongue sliding sensuously against his own, so silky and smooth. He couldn't help but drag his fingers into her soft hair and draw her closer.

As he did, her nipples touched his chest, hard little pebbles that signaled her arousal. Soon, she would be ready. And he couldn't wait.

Though he didn't want to, Law broke off the kiss. If she kept up the intimate press of their lips, along with the slow grind of her hand, he was going to come. No way was he ready for that. "Now touch Dominic."

He looked up to find that his partner was more than ready. Dominic had shed his sweat pants and now stood at the end of the bed, watching and dragging his cock through his fist in long strokes.

With a little gasp, Kinley let go of him and turned her sultry gaze to Dominic, focusing on his rhythmic movements over his cock.

"How long have you guys done this?" Kinley asked, reaching toward him.

Dominic took her hand and helped her up, then dragged her closer. He hissed a little when her fingertips skated over the sensitive head of his dick. "For as long as I can remember."

Kinley was staring at the little bead of opaque liquid seeping from the slit of Dominic's cock. She swiped at it with the tip of one finger.

"We've done this since we were old enough to have sex," Law explained. "Actually we probably weren't really old enough. I was barely seventeen, and Dominic was sixteen. Mrs. Landers. We were both really hot for teacher."

Kinley's free hand drifted toward his cock. She flicked

him a little glance before she began stroking Dominic with her right hand and him with her left. She was a fucking natural. "You lost your virginity to the same woman?"

"Yes, pet." Dominic's voice had deepened with every brush of her palms. "I went first and I am deeply ashamed to say that Law went about two minutes after I started. I was young and very inexperienced. I will not have the same issues with you."

She giggled. "I'm sure you won't. When did you bring Riley in?"

"When he was ready, about a year later," Law replied.

Fuck, she gripped him like a pro, bringing him closer and closer to the edge with every sweeping caress. It was easy to see that Kinley was getting more comfortable with the intimacy of being naked in front of her men. Her earlier shyness had evaporated, and her natural curiosity had taken over.

"What happened?" she asked.

"Dominic and I were dating a woman. Jayne. Sweet little thing. Looked like a librarian, but she had the single filthiest mind I've ever known. She didn't even blink when I asked if we could invite my little brother in. She just smiled and said 'pool party.' She could do some crazy things underwater."

Dominic slapped him upside the head, and Law winced. Shit! He was talking about other women. What was he thinking? Oh, he wasn't. He needed to say something and fix the situation quick. He needed to bring up feelings and shit.

"But I didn't care about her the way I do you," Law swore.

"Smooth, Law. Very smooth." Dominic rolled his eyes, then brushed her hair from her face with a gentle hand. "Pet, what my partner is trying to explain very badly is that we had easy relationships with women we liked."

"This isn't an easy relationship?"

"Given that most of America thinks we kidnapped you, no," Dominic explained. "I should walk away but I can't. That should tell you something."

"His willpower is usually iron," Law added with a nod.

"But we want you to understand that our sharing you isn't going to stop. It's what we do. You could very likely make a play for one of us. Perhaps you could even take him, but he would always miss this."

"I would never—"

"Even after the people in your life start to tell you it's wrong?"

"Why is it wrong?" Kinley countered. "We aren't hurting anyone. If we want to make each other feel good and we share some affection and respect, I really don't see how our bedroom activities are anyone else's business."

Dominic gripped her wrist, stopped the stroke of her palm. Instead, he dragged it to his lips and laid a tender kiss in the center. "It isn't. Now, lie back. It's our turn to touch you."

Kinley practically floated back to the mattress. She looked so warm and feminine lying there. Law covered her breast with his hand, loving its round weight and lush curves.

"Baby, I'm sorry. I shouldn't have talked about other women."

She smiled. "I asked because I want to know you. You talk about those other women fondly. You didn't just use them and toss them away. You actually liked them."

"Mostly," he admitted. "Sometimes I went along because Dominic or Riley wanted someone, but that's not the case with you."

"And I'm certainly not with you simply because Law wants me here." Dominic settled on his knees. "I'm here because I can't fucking resist you. And I won't wait another second to get a real taste."

As Law kissed his way down her neck, he admitted that he was already completely addicted to her. And now it was Dominic's turn.

Chapter Eleven

Kinley was drowning in pure sensation. From the soft comforter at her back, to Law's warm hands on her body, then Dominic's fingers wrapped around her ankles—all of that combined to overload her senses.

Law kissed his way down to her breasts. She could feel her nipples engorging and beading, straining for his attention.

Dominic spread her legs wide. The cool air stroked her overheated pussy just before he did. "It seems you enjoyed touching us, pet. You're creamy and wet."

"I did, Sir." In fact, she'd loved touching them.

Kinley had been surprised at how silky the skin covering their cocks felt, but the flesh underneath had been rock hard, proof of their desire for her. It had seemed a bit unreal for these two beautiful men to stand still and allow her to explore their bodies. It had been the single most erotic experience of her life.

Until now.

Dominic breathed in her scent like it was an intoxicating perfume. With a firm grip, he lifted her thighs, spreading her open even more.

"And you smell delicious." His low voice rumbled with passion, with possession.

Kinley doubted that.

The thought had barely cleared her head when Dominic descended, his mouth covering her mound, his tongue delving past her slick folds to her most sensitive, nerve-rich spots. She bucked against the electric jolt of desire that seared her veins and screamed.

Law tightened his grasp on her immediately, holding her down and still. “Don’t move. Dominic is eating your pussy like you’re his favorite dessert, baby. Let him. Don’t interrupt a man who’s enjoying his sweets.”

She couldn’t imagine half the women she knew allowing this. They’d call it dirty. So why did it feel like heaven? Nothing in her life had ever felt as pleasurable as Dominic suckling her clitoris and laving her affectionately with his tongue.

“That’s it, baby,” Law murmured against her skin. “Just lie back and let us have you.”

She was giving herself over to the very men who had kidnapped her. Though that should seem terribly wrong, it felt so perfectly right.

What would people say if she gave her virginity to two of her captors? The press was covering this story. Who knew what they’d dig up and air in the name of journalism and truth?

Kinley forced herself to relax. There would be plenty of time later for self-recrimination, probably a lifetime of it. Now, she wanted pleasure, to feel like a woman, to make her own choices. She wanted to know why her friends blushed when their husbands or lovers entered the room, be able to share in their talk about passion. Because chances were, when her time with these men was over, she’d probably return home alone. There would be no more passion, and she would have to figure out how to be the same old Kinley again—the one who served those around her without much thought to her own wants and needs. What she did today wasn’t anyone’s business but hers.

She set all of her worries aside. For now, there was only the heat and joy of touching Law and Dominic.

Law’s mouth closed over her right nipple in a caress of wet heat while his hand covered her left breast. He licked and tongued her nipple, every now and then giving her a hard nip that sent her eyes rolling to the back of her head with a whimper.

Dominic gently pulled at her labia, parting her pussy for the long slide of his tongue. He licked her everywhere, sucking the petals of her sex into his mouth, then settled over her clit.

Nothing had ever filled her with this much euphoria, not rollercoasters, nor her favorite candy, not the funniest movie she'd ever seen. Not even family holidays when she was a child. This feeling was like pure, breathless happiness tingling through her veins.

Between Dominic's tongue spearing inside her and Law's sweet play at her breasts, the tension, the greedy need for more, built toward something, a bigger, more explosive version of what they had given her the day before in the kitchen. That moment had been a revelation, but now they were forcing her higher. She gripped the comforter in her fists, fighting to stay still, but it was so difficult. She wanted to buck against Dominic's mouth, force him to go faster, harder, deeper.

"Look at me." Law lifted away from her breast and stared into her eyes. "Tell me you like having Dominic eat your pussy."

"I like it, Law," she gasped. "I like it so much."

Helplessly, she looked down her body where Dominic's dark head was moving as he brought her such amazing pleasure. She arched, digging her heels into the mattress, and cried out.

"You want more?" Law demanded.

Couldn't he see the answer? Her every muscle had gone tense. She panted. Perspiration broke out across her body. Blood rushed just under her skin. He had to know that she did.

"Please…"

"Look at me, Kinley." Law pinched her nipple, and she moaned.

"You like that bite of pain?"

She should probably deny it. Lie. But Dominic's tongue driving her closer and closer to a climax that she so desperately needed didn't leave any room for coyness. "Yes."

"Good. I'm going to have your nipples pierced so I can play with them. A little flick here, a little suck there…"

His words made her burn hotter, shoved her closer to the edge of orgasm. She writhed and thrashed, on the brink of pleading for just that little something more.

"I'll run a chain through the rings," Law continued thickly. "When you misbehave, I'll tug on it and bring you back in line. But for now this will have to do. Hold still."

He twisted her nipple, the pain flaring, snapping her back to attention, hurtling her body into confusion. She sent Law a beseeching glance. His brilliant blue eyes were sharp, fixated on her as he stared with obvious desire. He didn't look like a man having casual sex. He was connecting with her, trying to build trust with her. This felt like far more than intercourse.

Not only that, Law had mentioned the future—again. He'd seen her naked and he still wanted to talk about sharing a tomorrow? Dominic hadn't said anything, but the way he ate her intently and kept at her didn't exactly signal his indifference.

She stared up at Law. God, she had a lover, and it gave her the oddest sense of strength. "I'm sorry. I will. I just…love what Dominic is doing."

"That's good to hear, baby."

"It means so much that you're here to share it with me." She fell into Law's blue eyes.

As Dominic nipped at her clit and another shard of pleasure scraped its way up her spine, Kinley realized that she wanted them all. She didn't care what that made her. Law, Dominic, and maybe someday Riley, if he would have her. She would do her best to make them happy—like they would undoubtedly make her. Who else's opinion really mattered except their own?

"I need…" She bunched the sheets in her fists again and tried to focus on staying still, but the lash of Dominic's tongue kept pushing her harder, higher.

"We know what you need, baby," Law assured. "I think you should give it to her, Dominic. I want to watch her come."

With a thick finger, Dominic circled the opening of her pussy, coating her folds. Another joined the first, stretching her wide before sliding inside.

"Hmm, that's sexy. He's fucking you with his fingers," Law said, his voice husky. "But in a minute or two, it will be my cock pressing deep inside you, Kinley. I'm going to take you like a man takes a woman. I'm going to make you scream. Are you ready for that? We'll go slow if you need."

Slow? She'd gone about as slow as a woman could go. "No. Now. I want it."

She couldn't stand another night passing without knowing how it felt to be taken by these men.

"Give it to her, Dominic, so we can get on with this. I'm fucking dying here."

Dominic's head came up briefly. He smiled slyly. "I'm more than ready, brother. So is she."

He speared his fingers deep inside her, rubbing at a spot that made her arch and shiver and want to climb the walls. Then he sucked her clitoris into his mouth gently.

Sensation rolled over her then crested, tossing her into the raging abyss of pleasure. Kinley merged her stare with Law's as she came, her body flying higher than before. His eyes darkened, heated, then he captured her mouth and swallowed her cries.

"That's what I wanted, baby. So gorgeous. But now it's my turn to make you scream." He rolled off the bed and walked to where he'd dropped his pants.

Dominic stood tall above Kinley as she tried to drag air into her lungs and recover. She couldn't stop staring at him in all his glory. Tight muscle roped his body all the way up his arms, across his broad shoulders, down his chiseled chest and that six-pack to die for. She swallowed.

He held out a hand to her. "Let me help you up."

Why was she leaving the bed? Before she could ask or

protest, Dominic gripped her hand and hauled her to her feet. Her whole body was so languid, her legs almost didn't support her.

Then he eased back on the bed, taking her down with him, her back against his chest. She could feel his hard cock prodding her backside.

She couldn't help but melt into Dominic's chest. She was so relaxed…yet she wanted to entice him more, tempt him to touch her. Kinley writhed against him.

It worked. Dominic cupped her breasts as he spoke in her ear. "Hold on to me. It won't hurt for long. You're ready, pet. We both want to fuck you. We can't take your delectable ass tonight, so we'll each have a turn at your pussy. But you can stop us at any time."

"I won't stop." She wanted them both. Hell, she wanted Riley, too. She yearned to revel in these sensations and share her love. What was so wrong with that?

"Just know that you can. We don't want you afraid." She'd never heard Dominic's voice sound so concerned, tender.

She smiled, then sent him a saucy stare over her shoulder. "That's not how you felt a couple of days ago."

His hands tightened on her, bringing her closer as if he was afraid she would run. "Forgive me. I thought I was doing the right thing, pet. I let vengeance blind me. I don't want you scared. I don't like knowing you thought I would kill you—even for a moment. You're precious, and I would never hurt you."

He might break her heart, but she believed him when he said that he'd never physically harm her. "I know, Sir. I won't hurt you either."

And she wouldn't. Not physically or emotionally. She feared she would fall in love with him and want him forever. But that was her problem, not his.

"You could, you know," he whispered in her ear. "Hurt me, I mean. I can't tell you how much that scares me. It's been a very long time since I've allowed myself to be vulnerable to a woman."

She believed him. Yes, he could be lying, but why? She'd already said that she would help his case against Greg. What else could he want? She'd already said yes to sex, too. Dominic seemed like the most self-possessed man on the planet. He wouldn't give her any power over him unless it meant something.

"Can we hurry?" Kinley wanted to feel them so badly.

Dominic scowled. "Law, have you forgotten how to roll a condom on?"

She turned to find Law stroking his cock, a small foil packet in his other hand. He ripped it open and held the tip of the condom as he shoved it down his massive cock. Once he completed the task, he looked up at her, his face softening as he climbed up on the bed.

Law spread her legs wide. "I'm so honored, baby."

"We both are." Dominic kissed her ear. "Your trust is not only imperative. It's everything. Do you know what it does to me? To us?"

With fierce blue eyes, Law drilled into her soul as he settled his body on top of her own. He eased his cock against her swollen opening. He felt very large, while she…did not. At least not there. Her breasts might be big and she was still a little overweight, but that didn't translate into anything else being more sizeable than average.

Kinley whimpered in both anxiety and anticipation.

"Shh." Dominic soothed her with his whisper and his touch. "It will all be fine. You were built to take your men. Relax and give yourself to us."

Law loomed above her, his stare fierce. "He's right, Kinley."

Pushing back apprehension, she reached for him. "I'm not hesitating. I want you, Law. And I want Dominic."

"Good." He held himself above her, body tense, as he carefully began probing his way inside her, a prod, a nudge, a shallow stroke. It all added up. Pressure climbed one slow inch at a time and threatened to overwhelm her.

When panic began to encroach, Dominic soothed her with a whisper. "You're beautiful, pet. We want you so much. Do you have any idea how happy we are that you waited for us?"

She gripped Law's shoulders and let Dominic's voice sink into her as Law began to penetrate. His hips held her legs wide so his flesh could stretch her own. He moved in and out of her slick folds, gaining ground with each thrust. Over and over, he entered and retreated, inch by inch probing her deeper until she felt him stop.

The pressure and the anxiety overwhelmed her. Law exercised all his restraint. It was obvious he wanted to shove himself inside her in one agonizing thrust. Instead, he shook and cursed under his breath, clearly holding back. Dominic kept soothing her, whispering that she was so sexy and lovely, he couldn't stand it. He played with her breasts, brushing and pinching her nipples.

With a shove of his hips, Law breached her barrier and groaned. Kinley felt something tear inside her. She gasped and froze, impaled and in pain for a moment. In the next, he held himself still, his cock buried completely inside her. Then he waited, giving her time to adjust to the feel of him. The pain evaporated.

Heaving a ragged sigh, Law touched his forehead to hers. "You're ours now, baby."

Kinley sank into the moment and gave herself over to them. Nothing had ever felt so right. They had treated her with more affection and kindness than anyone else. Besides being crazy about them, she was making love with them for the right reasons.

Law kissed her for the longest time, tangling their tongues together until she was utterly limp. "Are you ready for more?"

She wrapped her arms around him tightly as her legs encircled his waist. She was willing to give them everything. Yes, when he'd first pressed inside her, she'd felt a momentary flaring pain, but it paled next to the breathtaking intimacy of the connection they all shared with Dominic behind her and Law on top.

She belonged to them now. Maybe not for always, but for these moments, she was completely and utterly theirs. And they were hers.

Law began to thrust, gently at first, then gaining power and speed as she rocked with him. Dominic held her too, his big body acting as her pillow, though nothing about him was soft. He made her feel utterly safe, grounding her even as Law sent her flying. She could go as high as she wanted because Dominic was right behind her, hugging her tight.

"You feel so fucking good." Law's face was a mask of tension, every muscle tight as he used his whole body to push inside her before he pulled back again. Over and over, his big cock slid across a sensitive place high inside her passage. With each thrust, every bit of friction, she moaned and thrashed. Pleasure was right there. That ecstasy she'd felt before shimmered just out of reach.

Determined to have it, she tightened and arched up to meet Law's next stroke, then sank her nails into his back. Law thrust harder, his pelvis crashing against her clitoris. He growled and ground down, then thrust up hard until she couldn't take another second.

Orgasm flowed over her. Kinley cried out, screaming his name as she came.

Law's big body shuddered. He growled out in pleasure, holding himself tight against her. His arms shook as he pumped out his release. His excitement sent her into another frenzy, and she shook with him.

"I'm crazy about you," he managed to say through long breaths a moment later.

She nuzzled his cheek, caressing his hair as her body came down from the high. Sweet peace flowed through her.

* * * *

Dominic was so hard he could barely breathe, but he watched as Law nestled his face in Kinley's neck. She caressed his head, keeping him close, coveting him. The moment seemed almost sacred, as though they had both been washed clean of their past pain by their emotional joining.

God, this was far more than sex or a mere exchange of pleasure. Kinley was truly giving herself. Once she'd made the decision to surrender, she'd done it perfectly, without hesitation. She wasn't someone he would be able to forget once he hopped out of bed and had a shower. If he slid deep inside her body and claimed her, he would have a responsibility to her for the rest of his life.

Was Riley the smarter one here? Dominic wasn't sure he was ready to be this woman's Master. Her husband. That was the direction this was heading. Was embracing someone with such close ties to his sister's killer a betrayal of Carrie's memory?

Law sighed and looked down at Kinley. He smiled, an open expression of pure joy that Dominic had never seen his friend give to anyone but her. It made Law look younger, freer, than he'd ever seemed.

Maybe in her heart, she belonged to Law alone. Dominic wondered if he was making too much of taking Kinley to bed. The woman already had a forever sort of man that she was clearly half in love with. If Dominic really wanted to, he could just have sex with her. Law would take care of her and be her Master, leaving Dominic to be her occasional Sir. He could simply visit and spice up their sex life. No fuss. No muss. No worry if he was shitting on Carrie's memory. Just hot sex with a beautiful woman.

Kinley turned her face up to him, her smile both a glow from the inside and pure invitation. Dominic nearly stopped breathing.

He'd heard men describe their wives as the most beautiful women in the world. He'd never been able to see it or understand. But Kinley lit up from the inside, and it wasn't just for Law. She gave that to him, for him. No doubt in his mind that right now she was more beautiful than every other woman on the planet, at least in his eyes. When she was old and gray with a load of grandchildren around her, he would still see her like this, in a golden aura of passion he couldn't resist. For him, she would always be the sun.

Was he willing to walk away because the timing was terrible, because he worried what Carrie would have thought? She'd been the one who told him that love was all that mattered. She would weep at the thought of him choosing revenge over joy. She would be disappointed in him if he chose punishment over love.

Carrie would have wanted his happiness more than anything.

Was he willing for Kinley's grandchildren to belong exclusively to Law? Did he want to be the footnote in their relationship, the perverted little secret from their past?

"Kiss me," he commanded almost involuntarily, as though his body knew what he needed more than his mind. But he wouldn't take the words back.

Law chuckled and rolled off her. "Kiss Dominic, baby. He needs it."

She tilted her head back onto his chest and lifted her face up for his kiss. She reached over her head to cup his cheek with her palm, and he could have sworn a jolt of electricity charged his body the moment she touched him. Her lips were still warm from Law's, but that was fine with Dominic. That meant she'd been recently loved and by someone he considered a partner. A friend. Law backed him up. They shared a brotherly rapport. Law was his family.

He remembered that moment so long ago when Law had risked everything for him, protecting him, though they'd had nothing in common. Dominic had been afraid. He was the poor little rich boy who had no friends, and he'd realized even at a young age that caring about a person was a choice that required courage. They could leave him. They could stop caring about him. They could use his affection against him. They could trap him in something loveless and bland like his parents' marriage.

Or they could support him, give him roots yet set him free. They could make life richer. They could surround him in so much peace he would never want to leave.

Kinley could be family, too. She could add light and love to his life. If he just let her.

He didn't restrain his urge to kiss her again. Instead, he sank his fingers into her silky hair and tangled his tongue around hers.

Dominic was done questioning everything. The future wasn't certain. God, Carrie had taught him that. But the very thing he'd thought had wrecked his life had led him to Kinley. In one moment, he felt his sister's love, her caring spirit. She'd been snuffed out by a monster, but it had all led him here, to his salvation from a life of hatred and vengeance. Now, he had a shot at saving Kinley, the woman he was pretty sure was meant to be his. He would only dishonor Carrie by rejecting Kinley for stubborn reasons.

She separated from him, dragging in oxygen with a shuddering breath. "I should go and clean up."

Oh, she had so much to learn about the way this worked. He put his hand under her chin and pulled her up to his lips again. "You're not dirty, pet. I want you now."

He wanted her in every way. The fact that Law had just taken her didn't make her dirty. It made her theirs. It made her the center of their circle.

Kinley turned in his arms until they rested chest to chest. Her breasts were crushed against him. She lay between his legs and his cock surged with need. He'd barely managed not to come when he'd heard her cries, felt her move against him as Law had taken her virginity. But in so many ways, she was still innocent. No one could take that from her. She was simply one of those souls who would be innocent until the day she died.

And when he left this earth, he wanted to be holding Kinley's hand.

Why this woman?

He kissed her again and realized it was a combination of fate and his own needs. Everything about her seemed to align just right with him. With her sweetness, she balanced his cynicism. With her femininity, she tempered his sometimes too-aggressive nature. With her love, she would lift the darkness from his heart. She would always stand beside him.

Riley was wrong. This woman wouldn't falter. Nor would she refuse them. Kinley would take everything that came her way because she treasured love. And she could teach them all to love deeper and more unconditionally.

"I need you so badly, pet." God, that sounded selfish. He shook his head. "If you're too sore, tell me no. I'll understand." He could because he'd just realized that this woman's happiness and comfort meant everything to him.

"I'm fine, Dominic." Kinley's hands cupped his face, and suddenly he felt precious. It was probably dumb, but just for a moment, he was important to the one woman he held above all others. "I need you, too."

"Take me." He'd never had sex with a female on top. He'd always been the aggressor, climbing above a woman or fucking her from behind. But he wanted Kinley rising above him now like a goddess, taking him in as she took her pleasure.

He shifted, easing his legs close together so she could straddle him. His cock strained up, the pearly evidence of his desire surging from the tip.

Kinley gasped and her whole body moved, shivering around his. "What do you mean? You want me to be on top?"

Law was suddenly beside him, handing him a condom. They didn't have the right not to use one yet. But the three men had made a promise to each other. When they all agreed, they would toss out the birth control. That meant the woman with them was the one. Foregoing condoms would be a collective contract, a blood vow, to take care of any children that came from the union. Law and Riley had their reasons, of course. But Dominic had his, as well.

He wanted his kids to have at least one loving parent. His own childhood had been devoid of that. He'd considered Carrie, Law, and Riley his family, and he counted his blessings for them. But he wanted more for his own children. With Law and Riley beside him, he knew he could promise a child a good life.

And Kinley would die before she allowed her child to know a loveless existence. God, she'd given up nearly everything for people who didn't deserve her. What would she do for a baby she delivered? There would be no limits. She would never stop sharing her heart with her little ones.

"Yes," he answered her, his tone low, husky. He wanted her to take as much or as little as she could. There would be time enough later for her to service him. Tonight, he wanted to give to her. He wanted to be a part of her first night as a woman.

The Dom inside him chafed to mark her with some symbol of his ownership, but the man simply needed to feel her with him, around him. He needed to know that, good and bad, she wanted and accepted him.

Hell, he needed a wife. He hadn't realized it until the moment he'd held her. He'd been waiting for so long for the right woman to bring him closer to the brothers of his heart and make them all an official family.

He needed Kinley.

She moved over him, awkwardly at first. She spread her legs wide, straddling him, dropping her gaze to look at that place where she would take him inside her luscious body. Kinley took a long breath, then gripped his cock, holding it up.

"Hey, baby, condom first. Until we're ready." Law passed her the little foil wrapped package.

She took it with the faintest hint of a smile on her face.

"Yes, Law."

Dominic gritted his teeth as she opened the condom and placed it on his cock with a bit more finesse than expected.

"Where did you learn that, pet?" he rasped out.

"I was getting married, so I took a class." She pinched the tip and started to roll the rest down his length. "But we used bananas. You're bigger than my banana."

God, he hoped so. She was killing him. He had to close his eyes as she stroked him, rolling the rubber down his length. She was so careful, taking her time and easing it down his screaming flesh inch by torturous inch. He gritted his teeth to stop himself from coming in her hand like a damn teenager.

"I got it." She sounded so proud of herself, and all he wanted to do was force her down on his cock and pound every inch inside her.

It took everything he had not to move as she positioned herself over him. Her little hand caressed his cock again, ensuring the condom was in place. He tightened every muscle of his body to stave off the mind-blowing feel of her touch.

And then she was poised on top of him. She closed her eyes for a moment, then her lashes fluttered up, opening those vibrant eyes to him as she lowered herself. He looked right at her as he gripped her hips and began to surge up, a promise, a vow to always care for her.

Heat and pressure gripped him. He'd been right. Law hadn't taken her innocence, and he couldn't either. She was still as sweet as she'd always been. Anyone who tried to take that purity from her would find himself flattened by Dominic Anthony. He would defend her innocence to his dying day.

She took him in bit by delicious bit. He watched, not wanting to forget a moment of the experience. He memorized the tiny changes in her expression as she worked her way down his cock. He noticed how her breasts moved with every breath and gasp, the feel of her hips in his hands when she spread them wide to accept him. And he couldn't keep his eyes off her pussy. The sight was burned into his brain. Her pink flesh opened for him, sinking on to him as his cock disappeared inside her heat.

Tight. She was so fucking tight. He had to grit his teeth against the pleasure as she gripped him hard.

He would never last. Feeling Law take her virginity had nearly been enough to send him off. Actually being inside her was just about to kill him.

"He never does this, baby." Law was watching, his eyes slightly hooded with desire.

Kinley started to move in small slides. Up and down, going deeper each time. "I think he's probably done this a lot, Law."

His friend chuckled. "I mean, he's never given up control like this. Not once in all the years I've known him. You're special."

Kinley stared down at him, her eyes going soft. She caressed his cheek, her palm sliding across the bristle of his five o'clock shadow. "You're both special to me. I won't ever forget you."

She wouldn't have to. He'd be as slow as she needed, but Dominic intended to introduce her to an entirely different world. He would make sure she understood the joy of submission.

He reached down to toy with her clit, his fingers finding slick cream there. "I'll make sure you can't forget me, pet. And by tomorrow, you'll understand."

By then, he would be her Master. There was no going back now. He would have her collared and at his side before she realized what was happening. She would belong to him and Law. If Riley finally pried his head out of his ass, he would be welcome to join them.

Law had been right; she was the one.

Her eyes widened as he pressed down on her clit, working that sensitive nubbin of flesh. "I can't. Not again."

"Yes. Again. You'll come as many times as I tell you to. You'll take as much pleasure as we can give you, pet. Come for me now."

He pressed down hard even as he thrust up, forcing her onto his cock completely.

Kinley's mouth opened. Her eyes widened. She came on a keening cry, pulsing around him, her skin flushing magnificently. She was a sight to behold, and knowing that he'd given her this pleasure only ramped him up more.

And then Dominic couldn't stop himself. He flipped her over to her back, gripping her hips, and pistoning deeply over and over like a man possessed. Whatever soreness she experienced, he would make it up to her. But damn it, he needed to be inside her completely now. He needed to fuse himself to her.

Holding her close, he meshed their mouths together as he fucked her. He went as high as he could go, turning and twisting to find the right spot, then her nails sank into his back. Her breath hitched. Her whole body tensed.

She came again, her pussy clamping down on his cock, sending him straight over the edge into a drowning pool of pleasure he never wanted to be rescued from.

Dominic's spine tingled. His balls drew up close to his body and the heat swelled, overtaking him, finally firing off in a burst so supernova he'd never felt anything like it. His whole body coalesced, every cell alive in that moment.

He collapsed on top of her, his head in the crook of her neck, his cock still embedded deep in her pussy.

Dominic had decided; he was never going to let her go.

Chapter Twelve

After crawling over the foot of the bed so she didn't disturb either Law or Dominic, Kinley stretched and eased out of the bedroom door. The guys were still asleep and darkness had finally fallen, but she couldn't seem to drift off. Jet lag, the time zone change, and the sun's abbreviated absence each night had thrown her body into confusion.

She should be comatose—or at least at rest. After more orgasms than she could count, Dominic and Law had gotten her into a hot tub with Epsom salt to help ease her soreness. The warm water had relaxed her, but as they'd all fallen into the bed, sleep hadn't come for her. Instead, her stomach rumbled, sending her looking for a late night snack. All the vigorous activity had added to her appetite.

Despite the fact that no one was looking, she blushed as she walked down the hall wearing nothing but Dominic's T-shirt. As she rounded the hallway to the kitchen, Kinley caught sight of the faint glow of a monitor and the sound of a familiar voice talking.

My wife is missing. I don't have time to talk about something as ridiculous as that lawyer's claims. I'm going to sue him for defamation of character. If he really knew Kinley, he would know that she would never walk out on her family. She's too pure to be interested in torrid affairs.

"Of course I didn't have any interest in torrid affairs. I didn't know what I was missing. And I am not his wife," she grumbled to herself.

It turned her stomach that Greg preened for the cameras while pretending to care about her. And what the devil did he mean by "pure?" What century was he living in?

As she stepped into the room, Riley zipped his stare in her direction, his blue eyes raking her from head to toe. "Do you need something, Kinley?"

She turned on the light. "Looks like I'm not the only one who can't sleep. Sorry, I didn't mean to disturb you. I just came to make myself a sandwich and check on Gigi."

Riley stood, his face guarded. He'd taken a shower recently and now wore nothing but his low-slung jeans and a pair of socks, baring every muscle and corrugated ripple of his torso. His hair was still wet. He'd brushed it away from his face. It hung longer than Law's or Dominic's, curling around his ears. Riley was beyond masculine and so beautiful standing in shadow that Kinley had a hard time breathing.

"Uhm, I think they tired themselves out." He nodded toward a comfy-looking dog bed in the corner. Gigi's head was resting on Butch's shoulder and the bigger dog was wrapped around her.

Kinley herself had been a little like that, all cuddled up with Law and Dominic. Every time she'd turned, one of the men would wrap her up in his arms so she felt warm and safe. Until hunger and restlessness had sent her from the cozy bed.

"I guess I should get used to mutts. I can't imagine Gigi coming out of this without a litter." Butch and her Yorkie looked so cute together, she couldn't help but smile.

"Well, I guess you're used to mutts by now after a couple of hours with Law. Dominic's a thoroughbred, but you should know that my brother and I come from nothing." His handsome face was a complete blank, but he spoke the words like a taunt.

"Wow. That is a mighty big chip you have on your shoulder. Who was she?" Because no man got that cynical without a woman being involved.

He shrugged. "I'm just being honest."

Right.

The way Riley sneered at her got her back up. "Your

brother is one of the kindest men I've ever met. I won't let you call him that. Besides, there's nothing wrong with mutts. I'm going to love every pup from Gigi's litter."

"Sure you will, sweetheart."

She'd had just about enough of his attitude. "Don't call me that."

His brows rode up sharply. "Why not? Law calls you 'baby' and you don't mind."

In the past she would have just taken his crap. But having sex seemed to have had a positive effect on her self-confidence. Now, she refused to put up with his snide comments, especially because he was the one standing in the way of any sort of tomorrow with Law and Dominic. It couldn't work without Riley.

If she could convince him to tone down the douchebag routine, that would be a start. But if she wanted any shot at keeping her men, she was going to have to fight for it. What had Dominic told her? She couldn't get what she wanted if she never went for it.

"I am Law's baby. And apparently I'm Dominic's pet. I wouldn't have said that 'pet' could be a sexy endearment, but I love when he says it. You don't get to call me sweetheart because you don't mean it."

"Fair enough." He took a long breath and walked to the fridge. "So you really like my brother?"

She was pretty sure she was madly in love with his brother. "I do. I like Dominic, too."

"I knew you would like Dominic." He yanked open the refrigerator and looked in. "I'll make you a sandwich. We have ham and turkey."

"Turkey, please. With mustard if you have it. And why would you automatically assume that I'd like Dominic? He was kind of scary at first. But I'll confess that my affection for him has grown since he stopped threatening me." And started kissing her. And giving her crazy-good orgasms. Just the thought of his deep voice had her shivering again.

Riley grabbed the turkey, some mustard, and veggies, then walked back to the island. "I knew you would like Dominic because you come from the same world. He's got money and all."

She was getting a little sick of Riley's attitude. "I don't care about the money."

"Bullshit. You were marrying Jansen for his bank account. You might lie, but your actions don't, sweet…Kinley." He grabbed a loaf of whole wheat bread from the nearby pantry, then slammed the door.

Just like that, the glow from her lovemaking with Dominic and Law vanished and reality crashed back in. "Because I thought my father was sick. I thought he needed treatment. And my charity was going to go under. I couldn't stand the thought of Hope House being shut down after my mother worked so hard to build it up. The homeless community depends on it. I wasn't marrying Greg for shopping sprees and trips around the world. I was doing it to help my family."

Riley didn't look up as he started slicing tomatoes and spreading mustard. "I'm sure it makes you feel better to think about it that way."

She wasn't going to win with him. Not ever. There had been a moment when she'd felt like she could have it all, but she should have known it was just a fantasy. Riley wanted something else in a woman. Kinley didn't know what, but it wasn't anything she could offer. She wasn't the girl people loved. Even her own family had cared so little, they'd been willing to kill her off for a buck.

"You know, I'm not hungry anymore. I'll see you in the morning and maybe we can figure out what Greg is doing. And we need to call a press conference or something because I'm sick of Greg telling lies about me. I promise I'll clear everything up, then you won't have to see me anymore."

So he could move on with his life. And she could try to find a new one.

Kinley turned away, but he was suddenly beside her,

gripping her wrist. "Don't go. I'll stop being an asshole. Sit down and let me make you something to eat. Please. It's the least I can do."

For a moment, she considered stomping out of the room for effect, but she didn't really like fighting. Ducking out might only confirm her guilt in his head. Not that he had much doubt, but why make it easier for him to cast her as the villainess? Besides, she really was hungry.

"All right."

"We've talked about the press conference, Dominic, Law, and I. It's not a good idea. Right now, Jansen doesn't know if you're cooperating with us, so he's in a holding pattern. If he realizes that you're helping our case, he might destroy all the evidence or simply disappear. I don't think we'd ever convict him then. That would leave him roaming free…and he might come back for you. You don't want to be one of Jansen's loose ends."

Riley had some good points.

He towered over her, his eyes soft for once. "My brother is crazy about you. I…it would be better if we could be friends."

Friends. Law wanted more. Dominic wanted more. And Riley just didn't. That deep connection she wanted so desperately was a puzzle, and she only had two of the pieces.

"Sure," she said, hoping he couldn't hear the defeat in her tone. "Do we have any tea?"

He nodded and gestured to the cabinet over the sink. "All kinds. The James family keeps this place stocked. And the kettle is already on the burner."

He released her wrist. The momentary sense of intimacy between them ended when he broke physical connection. Now, Riley was so far from her in all the ways that counted. "Thanks."

As she went to study the collection of tea, he resumed fixing the sandwich. "I'm sorry. I really don't mean to hurt you. We've just tried this before and it didn't work."

She filled the kettle and set it on the burner, flicking the gas on. "Tried what?"

"The whole 'We-all-love-you-so-let's-get-married' thing."

They'd been engaged before? She staggered back. She knew she didn't have a right, but jealousy stabbed its way through her system.

Kinley tried to keep her tone casual. "Really? Why didn't it work?"

"She didn't want to marry me, not legally. She wanted Dominic's rock on her hand while she kept me and Law on the side. She had no intention of acknowledging the two of us in public."

That had to have hurt his pride. "She wanted to have her cake and eat it, too."

He shrugged. "She wanted a normal social life, I guess."

There was so much more to that small statement than his manner suggested. Kinley picked out a packet of chamomile tea and set up two mugs. She'd bet Riley needed some sleep, too. "Maybe, but having it at the expense of you and Law wasn't right. Besides, what's normal?"

He huffed incredulously. "You know what I'm talking about. Normal. One man. One woman. A couple of kids and a white picket fence."

She rolled her eyes. "I think that's overrated. I've known gay couples who stayed in love so much longer than straight ones. And all the 'normal' couples I used to admire are cheating or splitting up. I assumed I would have a normal marriage with Greg. He's one man and I'm one woman, right? Well, he turned out to be a criminal jerk who's screwing my sister and plotting to kill me. The two guys I have are wonderful. Our relationship might not be traditional, but they make me feel special."

"When you're done thinking about yourself, cupcake, consider Dominic and Law. If you stay with them, everyone will assume they're gay." His stare met hers, a challenge rife there.

Where was he going with this? "And we'll know they're straight."

"Huh. Well, okay. I guess it's not that bad, being considered gay and all." He focused on the sandwich again.

Something had rubbed him raw. Kinley knew she should probably let it go, but his words niggled at her, telling her that understanding Riley was too important to give up. Even if he never joined their relationship, he was an integral part of Law and Dominic. They had to get along.

"So…your fiancée was worried that it would seem like she was sleeping with gay guys?"

Riley let out a low chuckle, but it held no humor. "Not exactly. She was more concerned about what people would imagine went on if they knew she was sleeping with brothers."

It took Kinley a moment to process what Riley was saying. Once she did, her jaw dropped with shock at what this mystery woman had insinuated. "That's ridiculous! You and Law would never… She's a bitch."

Kinley never used that kind of language, but it seemed terribly appropriate now. How dare she?

Riley stared at her for a moment, his face impassive. "I share women with my brother. It's not the average, so a lot of people let their imaginations go wild. If I was also involved with you, we'd all get tainted by the whispers. How are you going to get people to donate to your charity when everyone calls you and the men you consort with perverts?"

"First off, not everyone would. A lot of people wouldn't think that at all or care about my personal life. The ones who want to presume that sort of crap behind my back, I don't care about." At least she didn't anymore. She'd wasted too much time trying to please other people.

"You say that now, but once we get back to the real world, you'll change your story."

"Riley, I've lived my whole life being worried about what people will think of me. I grew up in high society where a woman's reputation is everything. My sister has a sterling reputation. She's considered one of the finest women in the city. She's a selfish liar who cheats on her husband and thinks her babies are just a way to control him. She's planning on letting someone snuff out her only sister, and her parting shot to me was 'ta-ta.' She lives that so-called 'normal' life brilliantly, but I think she must be one of the most miserable human beings on this planet to behave the way she does. If that's normal, it's pretty crappy. And I want no part of that."

Riley shook his head. "You say that now, but wait until you don't have your stellar reputation anymore. You don't know what it's like to have the whole world look down on you."

He was completely missing the point of life. "Do you know what it's like to have one person lift you up? Because I might not have had the world look down on me, but I haven't had anyone really love me either. I think I would risk almost anything to have that in my life."

"You're awfully naïve."

"I've been told that before, but I think you're awfully cynical."

"That happens fast when you're the kid of the town whore."

"Don't you call her that." No matter who he was, Kinley wasn't about to let someone talk about Law's mother that way. When he'd talked to her as California Mike, Law had been completely open about his mother. Though she'd been flawed and damaged, he'd loved her.

Riley shrugged. "It's what she did."

"But it didn't define who she was," Kinley argued.

"I'm just being realistic, the same way Simone was. She wanted Dominic's connections to climb the social ladder, using my back and Law's as the rungs. Keeping him separate from us in public was the only way she could hope to achieve that because a woman who slept with two brothers and their friend…who knew what went on there? Speculation would always run rampant, and she'd always be a whore."

"You were in love with her." Nothing else explained his bitterness.

Riley hesitated, then shook his head. "I was in love with the idea of her. I was in love with the idea of having the relationship I wanted. Simone showed me the truth."

"No, Simone showed you what a horrible person she was."

"She wanted what all women want."

"What do you think that is? In my book, it's love and companionship. To be desired and needed."

He snorted. "Try money, respect, and a place in society."

"Wow. She did a number on you. I'm surprised. I wouldn't have expected you to just lie down like that and take it. You either loved her with every ounce of your soul or you're not the person I thought you were."

He frowned her way. "I didn't love her."

If that was true, he sure seemed willing to give up an awful lot for a woman who didn't have his heart. "But are you going to let her dictate the rest of your life?"

His cynical smile was back. "Oh, please. Are you going to try to tell me that you're not going to let what Greg Jansen did affect you? You already have. You just tossed out twenty-five years of saving yourself for marriage to give Greg a big old 'fuck you.' So I wouldn't say too much about not bowing to bitterness if I were you."

"You think I slept with Dominic and Law because I wanted to get back at Greg?"

"Of course. Greg was going to be your husband, and you saved yourself for him. Spreading your legs for my brother and Dominic probably made you feel powerful. Was revenge sweet?"

It had been, but not for the reasons he thought. "I didn't save myself. I just never cared enough about anyone to sleep with them."

"And yet you came to care for my brothers in the couple of days since we drugged and kidnapped you, then ripped your world apart? Yeah, I believe that."

But she had. And she was starting to think that maybe her love and future were worth fighting for.

"I don't care what you believe, Riley. I know who I am. I know what I've done and what I feel. I've absolutely come to care a great deal about your brother and Dominic. Sleeping with them had nothing to do with revenge and everything to do with moving on with life. You can't understand that because you're clinging to the past. Some woman hurt you, and now you won't let it go, so you'll take it out on me. Fine, but stop and think about the fact that I'm not you. Greg hurt me. Becks hurt me. My dad hurt me. Guess what? I won't let them ruin my life. I won't allow them to change me. I might be naïve and stupid, but I will keep trying to find love. I don't care how it comes to me. If it comes from one or two or three men, I'll take it. I don't care what the rest of the world thinks because no one there cared that my fiancé was going to kill me. You, Dominic, and Law cared. That's all that matters to me."

"We didn't care because of you." The words came out on a harsh rasp.

That hurt, but then he seemed determined to make her see his twisted truth. "They do now. I can't change how you feel."

And Riley didn't get to choose her reality either. From now on, no one ever got to decide who Kinley Kohl was or what she would do. No one got to change that deeply held part of herself that kept trying to fill her heart, despite all the evidence that it wouldn't work. She refused to believe that she would end up alone.

"Have you thought about the fact that we're just isolated here in Alaska and they're horny? Or that they feel sorry for you?"

Hurt flared again. It was time to leave. If Riley wanted to be mean, she needed to stay away from him. That woman had damaged him, and he didn't even want to recover.

But the question haunted her. Did Law feel sorry for her? When she thought about it…no. She'd felt his caring. It might not be love, but Law felt something for her. It wasn't strictly pity or desire. And Dominic Anthony would never sleep with someone because he felt sorry for her.

Riley was glaring down at her, challenging. Some beast trapped under his skin wanted her to fight with him. He just kept poking at her, then pulling her back when she tried to walk away. He behaved like a kid who didn't know how to emerge from the dark corner he'd put himself in.

Anger fled in a rush of sympathy. Riley had loved and lost, and he didn't know how to find his way back. It was sad, and railing at him wouldn't help.

His deep disconnect would likely cost her everything, but again, she wouldn't allow that to change who she'd become or what she believed.

Kinley didn't hesitate. She simply stepped closer and wrapped her arms around him, resting her cheek on his chest. "I'm so sorry."

He tensed around her. "What are you doing?"

"Offering you what Simone didn't. She didn't deserve the three of you. I know you miss her, but you need to let her go and find someone who will love you. The three of you deserve a woman who will stand at your side and proudly be wife to you all. Don't compromise or settle, Riley. This is your forever. You have to fight for it. I just learned that. Don't let anyone take it away from you."

Riley blinked at her in silence, his expression incredulous.

She eased back enough to look into his eyes. "Find someone who makes all of you happy. I know I'm not her because you're not interested in me, and when the time comes, I'll step away quietly. Just let me have a few days with them. Let me know what it means to have a lover. By the time we have to return to the real world, I know it will fall apart, but can't you and I be kind to one another until then?"

He held his hands up, shoving himself out of her embrace. "What are you doing? I've been horrible to you."

"I'm being true to myself. You're hurting, and I'm not the

kind of person to ignore that. So I'm offering you comfort."

She slid against him, her eyes downcast because she didn't think she could stand to see censure in his stare. To her shock, when she pressed closer to him, she discovered that his cock was stone hard.

A little voice inside her prodded her. If Dominic and Law were interested in dominating a woman and they usually all took her to bed together…maybe Riley wanted some control, too. "Sir."

"Fuck." Suddenly, he wrapped one arm around her, yanking her against him in a tight embrace. The other hand wound through her hair, his fist closing around the strands. When he tugged and forced her to meet his stare, she hissed. "You're insane, Kinley. It won't work. It can't."

She could feel his heart pounding against her, his cock hardening even more against her belly.

Her heart rate tripled as she met his gaze with beseeching eyes. "It can. Don't give up. The right woman, one you all can love, is out there."

"And what if that woman couldn't possibly love me? What if I'm the one who fucks everything up?"

"You won't. Just believe and give her a chance." She wanted to be that woman so badly. Her whole body was softening for him.

Riley said nothing for what seemed like an eternity. He just stared into her face, as if trying to read her heart and mind. The tension drew tight, thick. Her belly coiled up. Excitement throbbed inside her body. "Will she give me a chance?"

"If she's smart, she will." Kinley forced herself to close her eyes. He didn't mean her, and she needed to extricate herself from his embrace and step away or she was going to make a fool of herself.

He swallowed thickly. "Give me a chance, Kinley."

His mouth descended toward hers.

* * * *

Time seemed to stop just for a moment as Riley covered Kinley's lips with his and kissed her for the first time. It would probably end badly. He'd avoided the pull between them for as long as he could, but now he felt utterly helpless. He'd completely lost his resistance the moment she'd wrapped her arms around him and called him Sir.

She couldn't possibly know what that did to him, the place that sent him to. Dominic might have introduced Law to that world first, but Riley had come to crave it. As a kid, everything had happened *to* him. He'd had no say for so much of his life that being in control now was paramount. He could cede some decisions to his brother and Dominic, but he needed to feel like he was in charge of his own destiny.

And he hadn't liked the truths Kinley had pointed out.

Need raged inside him. He had to take charge of it. Of her. Conquer this desire so it didn't control him for another second.

Riley crushed his mouth against hers, his cock twitching the minute she softened underneath him, accepting him.

He'd been awake all fucking night, studying her. He'd read articles about her, watched the newscasts about her kidnapping, stared at pictures of her—anything to get his mind off the fact that she was in a bedroom with his brothers, making love.

When she'd walked in, he'd used all his restraint to keep himself from hauling her into his arms and taking his fair share. He'd tried to anger her, scare her away, but she'd seen right through the smoke screen, through to the core of him. Instead, she'd given him compassion.

How the fuck was he supposed to resist that?

He cupped her lush breasts. Damn, he loved these. She tried to hide them away in punishing bras held up by metal wires. Even so, they were achingly soft and weighty in his palms. Though she wore a cotton T-shirt, he couldn't escape how warm and luscious she felt through the fabric, how her feminine curves moved against him.

Riley delved beneath her shirt, desperate to get his hands on bare flesh. Now that she was in his arms, he couldn't make himself stop.

He found her breasts, palming them in turn as he crowded her against the kitchen table, plunging his tongue deep inside her mouth. Her nipples were hard little pebbles against his hands and her skin so damn soft that he groaned.

Kinley wasn't turning him away. In fact, she clutched him, filtering her fingers through his damp hair like she still wanted him. Like he still had a chance. Right now, he didn't even want to question whether he wanted that chance. It didn't matter. He just wanted *her*.

He skimmed his hands around her to find the cheeks of her perfect, round ass and dragged her up against his cock. He rocked against her, loving the way she gasped into his mouth. His whole body pounded with arousal. He couldn't even remember the last time he'd wanted a woman this way. But Kinley eclipsed everyone else in his memory. With Simone, there had been a desire for sex, a hope for something lasting—nothing more. With Kinley, he felt a pulsing lust he couldn't deny. And a pang in his chest he couldn't ignore. Riley didn't even bother trying.

"Get ready, sweetheart. I'm going to lay you out on the kitchen table and fuck you. If it breaks under both of us, I'll just fuck you on the floor."

Kinley pulled back, her lips swollen from his kisses, her chest heaving. "I can't."

He felt as if the floor dropped out from under him. She couldn't? Yeah. Not with him at least. What the hell had he been thinking?

Riley jerked out of her arms. The damn teapot started to whistle. She'd come here for a sandwich, not to be fucked again. He'd totally misinterpreted the situation and made a complete idiot of himself.

He forced himself not to look her way, to concentrate on the task at hand. As quickly as he could, he'd get her something to eat, then retreat to his own room, masturbate, and wonder if he would ever be able to look her in the eyes again.

After pouring her tea into her mug, Riley ignored the cup she'd prepped for him. He didn't need fucking tea. He needed a metric shit ton of Scotch.

Drawing in a shuddering breath, he steadied himself and turned. "Your tea is…"

Kinley knelt on the floor before him, minus the shirt she'd been wearing. Her creamy skin was on full display. In the low light of the kitchen, she practically glowed, a pearl that shone in the night. Her honey hair flowed around her shoulders, and her eyes were steady on him. "I don't want the tea. I want you, but I'm too sore for sex on the table. Your brothers really did a number on my, uhm…"

"Pussy?" The word slipped out without thought. In fact, all he could think of was her, naked, luminous, and presenting herself to him.

"Yes." She blushed. "I need a day or so before I take you there." She glanced at his fly, then licked her lips nervously. "I've never done this, but I want you to be my first."

Riley damn near dropped her cup. He had to steady his hands and put it down. Was she saying what he hoped? He didn't want to assume and make an ass out of himself again. Time to be smooth, romantic. "Are you talking about a blow job?"

Really fucking smooth, moron.

Her luscious lips curled up. "I believe that's what people call it. I might not have a ton of experience, but I know the words, Riley. Blow job. Fellatio. Hummer. I want to take you in my mouth and swallow you down."

Just like that, his cock got so hard it hurt. "Kinley, you don't have to do that."

Her eyes went wide. "You don't want me to?"

God, he hadn't meant that—at all. Actually, he hadn't meant a damn word he'd said all night. "Yes! I want you to. I want you to so bad I just might die if you don't."

She relaxed slightly, then bit her lip uncertainly. "I might not be good at it."

"I can teach you." The idea that she'd never had a cock in her mouth made his spine tingle. His brothers might have had her first, but they hadn't taken everything. This first of hers would be for him. "You'll be good at it, Kinley. You're good at everything."

"I don't know about that."

He'd just spent all night really studying her. "You are. When you want to do something, you do it. You feed and clothe the homeless. You've made my brothers smile. You arouse the hell out of me." He moved closer. "I want you to take my cock out."

Kinley blinked up at him, then her hands fluttered to the waistband of his jeans, those perfectly manicured fingers working on the button of his fly. She was awkward at first, but her earnestness was so sweet. Nothing about her was artificial. Every bit of apprehension and desire to please she felt was written all over her face.

So was her submission. She was offering him something that always aroused him, and not just physically. Something about watching a woman take him in her mouth brought out all of his dominant instincts. And with Kinley, he wanted nothing more than to tangle his fingers in her hair and feed her the hard length of his dick, inch by inch, and claim this part of her.

Slowly—so slowly he thought he would scream—Kinley unfastened the button and started to ease down the zipper. His cock pressed against his boxers as if trying to get closer to her.

"You're wearing underwear," Kinley said with a little frown. "I'm not allowed to wear underwear. I don't think you should either."

Little sub thought she got to make the rules? "You don't know it yet, but if you keep talking that way, there will be spankings in your future."

How would she handle a true spanking? The thought of her naked body over his lap made his groin tighten again.

Jesus, so much of the blood in his body had rushed south that he felt dizzy.

She wrinkled her nose and sent him a saucy stare as she pulled his boxers down his hips. "I can handle it. Law gave me a couple of swats earlier because I forgot to call Dominic 'Sir.'"

Dominic was insistent on protocol, but that wasn't Riley's thing. "I like to hear my name, Kinley. And I won't just give you a couple of swats to make your ass blush. I know this will surprise you, but Law is the soft one when it comes to this."

"It doesn't surprise me. He's very sweet."

Sweet? Law had killed more men than she could imagine. He'd done it in service to his country, but… "Has he talked to you about his military service? If not, you should know that he's only soft with you. Law is a trained killer."

"No," she protested. "He's a trained protector." She pulled his boxers down and wrapped her fingers around his cock—finally. The softness of her touch nearly undid him.

And he kind of loved that she saw them through different eyes. In fact, he liked being with her, just talking to her when no walls stood between them. "Maybe you're right, sweetheart. Maybe we should all take a second look at how we view the world, but you should understand that I'm more like Dominic than Law when it comes to sex. I'll get you over my knee. I won't let you up until you beg me to stop. Even then, I'll make you come before you're allowed to leave. You'll feel my hand on your ass all the next day. Just like you'll feel my cock in your pussy."

Eventually, yes. But for tonight, he would be satisfied with her mouth. And with being the man who taught her.

Her face had flushed, a sure sign that his words had either embarrassed or aroused her. Given the fact that she was still there and still staring at him with wide brown eyes, he was banking on the latter. But he had to be sure. "Touch yourself."

Her eyes flared with surprise. "What?"

"Touch yourself, Kinley. Drag those fingers down to your

pussy and touch yourself. Play with your clit until I tell you to stop. I want to watch you." She was so prim and proper, and Riley couldn't wait to strip that veneer right off her and get to the woman under the surface. "Or I could show you my version of a spanking."

He was okay either way. In the end, she would do what he wanted because she wouldn't be able to help herself any more than he could.

She was tentative at first, the tiniest bit awkward as she slid her hand down her body until her fingers found her clit. He stroked his cock as he watched her, running his hand from base to tip. She trained her stare on him as she touched herself, and his blood surged.

"Like this, Riley?"

A wave of approval surged over him. This was where he felt most comfortable. "Exactly like that, sweetheart. Rub your clit, then slide your fingers into your opening."

Her breath shuddered as she found her sweet spot, and he loved that she was a very obedient girl. After two strokes of her clit, she slid her fingers deep. When she withdrew them, the digits were coated in her cream.

She wanted him. His harsh words hadn't scared her off. And she wasn't doing this out of pity or because Law and Dominic had told her to.

He snagged her wrist in his grasp and pulled it to his lips. The sweet scent of her arousal flooded his nostrils. Kinley was creamy and ripe. He might not be able to feel that pussy around his cock tonight, but he sure as hell could learn her taste.

He sucked her fingers inside his mouth, reveling in her essence. Tangy and sweet and so very Kinley. He licked every ounce off and still wanted more.

"Why does watching you do that excite me?" Kinley's eyes were hot with desire. "It was the same when Law did it and when Dominic…"

He could guess what Dominic had done. "Did Dominic

shove his face in your pussy and not leave until he'd had his fill?"

There was that gorgeous blush again. He adored making her color rise. "He kissed me there. At first, I thought it should make me uncomfortable, but then I just loved it. It's more than the sheer pleasure. There's something very intimate about it."

"Your lover likes the way you taste, Kinley." He touched her chin and moved closer, his cock almost against her lips. "That's the way it should be. Your lover should want to eat you up twice a day and three times every night. I'm going to tongue you and love you and make a meal out of you when I can. But I need you right now."

She stared at his dick, then leaned closer, her hot breath on him. Then she swiped at his cock with her tongue, licking it up and tasting him. On a little moan, she closed her eyes as though she was cataloguing the sensations and flavors. "You're salty and rich. I like the way you taste."

And she had no idea what such innocent words did to him. His lovers in the past had all just talked dirty and told him what they would do to him. Not a one had just looked at him and told him they liked him—his body, his taste. They hadn't really cared about him or his happiness.

He was in deep and saw no path out. He wasn't even sure he wanted to find one. Regardless of what Dominic and Law thought, chances were high she would walk away in the end. Or he would be forced to leave her for her own good. Kinley might try to stay, despite all the bad things that would come to her for loving them. He might well have to protect her in the end.

But they had tonight and perhaps a few more after that. Maybe it made him a greedy son of a bitch, but he was going to take them.

"Let me give you more. Run your tongue all over me." He held his cock out, but soon her hand replaced his.

She explored him, her tongue like a darting hummingbird lighting him up everywhere she licked. She paid special attention to the sensitive *V* at the back of his shaft, and his eyes nearly rolled into the back of his head as she worked that spot over and over.

"God, sweetheart, you're a natural." She didn't need anyone to tell her what to do.

"Since you gave me permission to explore, I wanted to taste and know all of you." She sucked the head of his cock into her mouth, heat surrounding him.

"Yes, sweetheart. That feels good. *So* good." He closed his eyes and shoved his hands into her hair. "Take more."

She obliged, enveloping his cock in her hot mouth. Her tongue whirled around, a tease, a taunt. Then she sucked hard on him, thickening the sensations, drawing out the anticipation. He could feel his cock pulsing in time with his rapid heartbeat as she sucked him deep.

Over and over she worked his hard flesh, drawing on him, taking him fully into her mouth. She worked tirelessly as she moved herself up and down, taking a little more each time, her whole body swaying with effort.

She reached up and caressed his thighs through the denim of his jeans. Slowly, he felt her fingers journey up until she found flesh. As she sucked his cock, she cupped his hips and ran her palms over his abs, a lover's tribute, a silent expression of her desire. Finally, she caressed her way down to the base of his shaft and held him there as she raked his cock with the gentle edge of her teeth.

He looked down to find her cupping his balls with her free hand. All her shyness seemed to have evaporated the minute he'd given her permission to play with him, as though she'd just been waiting for the opportunity to indulge.

She rolled his balls in the palm of her hand, eliciting a deep groan from Riley. He was going to lose his fucking mind.

"I won't last long if you do that, sweetheart. Are you sure?" He didn't want to flood her mouth if she wasn't ready for that.

She hummed around his cock, the vibration charging

through his veins and making him shake. She'd worked him all the way in, almost to the base of his dick and now played with his balls. Holy hell, he could feel the back of her throat. Her tongue coated him, a consistent caress that drove him up, higher and higher.

Until Riley gave in.

"Swallow me." He growled the command as the orgasm took him, ecstasy pulsing deep inside him as the head of his cock exploded, spewing into her lovely, waiting mouth.

And she took every drop, swallowing all he had to give her. As her head bobbed over him, she licked him, laving up one side, then down the other, not leaving a drop behind.

Riley was floored by how giving she'd been, how open and honest. He smoothed her hair back as he withdrew slowly from her mouth. He drew her up to her feet, then dragged her against him until he could kiss her. He didn't give a shit that his jeans had fallen down around his knees. He just knew he wanted his mouth on hers, his arms around her body.

"Thank you, sweetheart. That was incredible." He'd never thanked a lover before. He'd bought them flowers, trinkets, but never just appreciated the gift they'd given him. He'd never thought of it that way until now.

Kinley was different.

"It was okay?"

He had to laugh because her fears were understandable but completely unfounded. Joy lit over him like a happiness sparking inside him. He held her close, not yet ready to let her go. "It was the best. And I'm not just saying that to make you feel better. I've never felt anyone's desire to please the way I felt yours."

He kissed her, fusing their mouths together, tasting the intimacy between them. For now, it was enough. Of course he wanted to get deep inside her. Tomorrow he would. Then he would revel in her and take mental pictures that would never fade, even after she was long gone. That way, he'd have something to hold back all the darkness that would encroach when everything fell apart. He wanted his memory to be full of her, like a computer that had been filled to capacity. He wanted to be full of her until he couldn't put anything else in. Like her tablet, even. Its memory had been full, as well. He'd noticed that when he'd disabled her Internet capabilities.

And it had bugged him.

"How many gigabytes of memory does your tablet come with?" An idea played in his brain. Riley began to suspect that what Jansen wanted from Kinley's luggage was tied to that tablet, and he doubted it was because the douche was dying to read the latest romance.

But he might want the photographs. Kinley had hundreds of pictures on her device. If he was right, the pictures would take up the majority of the storage capacity—though they shouldn't. That tablet had been designed to hold thousands of pictures. Yet it was oddly full.

Kinley looked up, met his stare. "What?"

He shook his head. "It doesn't matter, sweetheart. I need to look at your tablet again. I need it now." He kissed her again, trying to soften the quick jump in subject. "I'm sorry. Sometimes my brain has to think about things for a little while and I need something to jar me before I figure out a puzzle. Or maybe I just need the best hummer of all time to make me a genius." He grinned. "But I think I figured out what Jansen is desperately trying to get his hands on. Wake up Dominic and Law, then bring me that tablet."

She reached down and grabbed the shirt.

Riley snatched it away. "You don't need clothes to wake them up."

Her face contorted in the sweetest little frown. "I thought we were switching to business mode."

She was under some mistaken impressions. "Business mode does not mean clothes for you, sweetheart." He grabbed the shirt. "I think better when you're naked. Look at what playing around did. Hell, if you're naked all the time, I might solve world hunger."

She giggled. “Solve mine, at least. I’ll do everything you ask if you just finish making that sandwich. I’ll be back, but I can’t say I won’t be dressed. It’s Alaska. If you want me walking around in my birthday suit, next time kidnap me and take me to Hawaii.”

She turned away, and he watched the hottest ass on earth sway out of the room. His cock leapt right back to attention, but he tucked himself into his jeans because he had a job to do.

As she turned down the hall, it hit him that if he was right, though his time with her had just started, it was almost over. He would have to go back to the real world. And he would lose her there.

Sometimes it wasn’t so great to be smart.

Chapter Thirteen

Law looked down at the tablet. There was a perfectly sweet photograph of Kinley and Annabelle. They were standing in a gazebo, each smiling and holding wine glasses together as if toasting one other. Kinley was in a yellow sundress, and Law couldn't take his eyes off her.

How was this photograph on Kinley's tablet the key to nailing Jansen?

"Who took this, sweetheart?" Riley asked her.

Law looked between the two of them and wanted to ask some questions of his own. When Kinley had come into the bedroom to wake him, she'd been completely naked. He'd reached for her, intent on drawing her back to bed, but she'd explained that Riley wanted to talk to them because his righteously geeky brother had figured out some computer stuff.

He was pretty damn sure she hadn't gotten dressed, talked to Riley, and then taken off her clothes just to wake them up. His brother might like technology, but he also liked their women naked. Something had happened between Riley and Kinley, and Law wanted to celebrate.

But now he had to deal with a bunch of techno crap he didn't really understand.

On the bright side, Kinley was naked. His brother had totally called that right.

"Are you sure I shouldn't wear a robe or something?" Kinley asked, crossing her arms over her breasts.

Dominic sat at the kitchen table, crossing one leg over the other as he looked at her with approval. He, like Law, had put on a pair of sweatpants. "You don't need clothes. I turned the heater up. If you need someone to warm you, you're welcome to sit on my lap while Riley gives us his very likely to be long and technological explanation. It will be boring. We need something to liven up the discussion. Your breasts will do nicely."

A surprised little grin brightened her face. "Those will enliven the discussion?"

Hell, yes. "Baby, your everything livens up the discussion. Now answer Riley and stop hiding your breasts. When you put your hands over them, we just look at your pussy and that fabulous ass of yours."

Kinley gave an embarrassed laugh and rolled her gorgeous brown eyes. But it worked. She visibly relaxed as she leaned over and glanced at the picture on the tablet. "Greg took that one. What's evil about that picture?" She frowned. "Huh. I don't remember adding that one, actually. Can you scroll through them all? I didn't load this tablet."

Riley gave her a little "gotcha" smile. "Jansen did, didn't he?"

"Yes," she murmured. "It was a gift from him. I'm kind of technologically idiotic. I can use my phone to make calls and text, but other than that, I'm lost. Greg bought my phone, too. Do you think my emoticons are evil?"

Law stifled a laugh. When he'd been California Mike, Kinley had texted him many times. She ended every single message with a flurry of smiley faces and thumbs-up symbols. He'd kept every single one.

"Since that's a readily available app, your emoticons should be safe. So Jansen loaded the photos?" Riley asked.

"He loaded everything. I gave him a list of the books I wanted. After I'd read those, I figured out how to buy more, but the last time I tried, the device gave me a message that I didn't have room, so I had someone in my office teach me how to archive my books. Do I have a virus?"

Law sent his brother a long look. He had a feeling Riley

was on the right track. He wasn't the technophile Riley was, but even he knew that it was damn hard to fill up a tablet with nothing but forty books, a couple of games, and some photos. There should be tons of space left. She didn't have any video on the system to eat up her memory. No audio, either.

"You don't have a virus, but you do have a rat fink bastard," Law growled. He hated Jansen more and more every single minute.

Riley nodded at him, then turned to Kinley, reaching out for her. She took his hand, and he tugged lightly, pulling her into his lap.

Yeah, something had definitely happened. Kinley seemed awfully comfortable naked in Riley's lap, and he wrapped his arms around their bare bundle of femininity with an air of familiarity. Law might not have to worry about losing his brother after all.

He glanced over at Dominic, who looked both as surprised and pleased as he was.

"Pet, you amaze me."

She shrugged. "I didn't do anything."

Dominic nodded at her perched on Riley's lap. "Are you sure?"

Kinley blushed, and Riley utterly ignored him, though he tightened his arm around Kinley's waist, pulling her closer.

Then Riley was all business again, pointing at the screen with his free hand. "It's all about these photographs. Everything we need is in here. It's called steganography."

Kinley frowned. "Like stegosaurus?"

Dominic shook his head, his affection for Kinley visible. "No, pet, it's not a dinosaur. Quite the contrary, this is on the cutting edge of criminal practices."

"I'm going to kill that fucker," Law snarled.

Jansen was willing to let Kinley carry his fucking criminal banking information? He was going to die and slowly. Technology might be Riley's forte. Dominic might be the money behind their operation. But Law was the muscle, and that meant he got to kill Greg Jansen. He knew just how he'd do it, too. He was going to eviscerate the son of a bitch, but not so much that he died immediately. Oh, no. He wanted to make sure Jansen suffered for a nice long time.

"Killing aside," Riley interrupted Law's vivid fantasy, "steganography is the act of hiding secret messages in seemingly innocent data. You see this picture as a whole, but the computer sees it as a series of data bytes. What criminals do is imbed their information in the very fabric of whatever they're corrupting. In this instance, Jansen is hiding his financials in these photos."

Kinley frowned at Riley. "All I see is a picture."

Riley clicked a few keys and an entirely different screen came up. "That's because you have to know how to extract the code. And there it is."

Kinley gasped. "That looks like an accounting report. Like one of *my* accounting reports."

Dominic cursed. "Well, now we know where he put the second set of books to Kinley's charity. What does it say, Riley?"

"That Hope House is doing just fine. He's had a mole in your organization for about a year as far as I can tell. He's the one who made you think your charity was going under. You have an employee named Fred Buck who sent through these records." Riley scrolled through the files with a scowl.

"Yes. He was in charge of my donations. Are you saying I have more than I thought I had?" Kinley put a hand to her mouth. "I feel so stupid."

Law reached for her. "You aren't stupid. Baby, they played you. You couldn't have known. He sent this guy in before you had even met him. He selected you as his target, and you didn't have a chance. I bet Jansen swept you off your feet, then arranged one distraction after another from the charity."

He knew how Jansen worked. He'd seen a ploy like that before. The last thing he wanted was for Kinley to beat herself up with guilt.

"He absolutely swept me off my feet. Two days after I met him, he took me on a date to Paris. We spent a week there. In separate rooms, but I'd never been. I'd never taken the time before. It was so different."

"He knew how to dazzle you," Dominic said. "I understand that Alaska isn't Paris, but we brought you with us for the right reasons. I want you to think about that when the tabloids start gossiping about us."

Law followed Dominic's line of thinking, and he was in complete agreement. "Yes. We didn't play you properly at all."

Kinley smiled slightly. "You didn't have to. You took off your shirts."

Dominic and Riley laughed.

Law couldn't. He couldn't stand the thought of losing her now. "I'm just saying that we've been real with you because what we wanted from you in return is real."

Panic had flooded his system when Riley had shown him the crap Jansen had put on her computer. Everyone else had seemed happy to find some concrete evidence, but Law had known it was the beginning of the end. He'd thought he would have more time with her. He'd thought he could take a week or two to bind her to them, so that when Jansen was behind bars, she'd stay.

Now… Well, fuck. He didn't see how it was going to work.

She leaned over the table, her breasts swaying enticingly. She reached out and cupped his face. "Is it real? I don't know what's real anymore. I thought those were just harmless pictures. Now I have to question every one of them. Everything. Annabelle tried to tell me, didn't she? I was stubborn, and I didn't want to listen."

Law knew that story. "She tried to explain her suspicions about him to you, and you nearly walked out on her. She was terrified of losing you."

Tears pooled in Kinley's eyes. "I was afraid of everything and everyone falling apart around me. She sent you to save me, didn't she? I know it sounds dumb, but if I can keep Annabelle, I think I might be all right."

"Baby, she loves you. And we approached her. She wanted us to talk to you, but we couldn't tell how you would react. If we had, and you'd confronted Greg… We were worried for you. And given that you'd been a bit upset when Annabelle tried to talk to you—"

"I was a raging bitch," Kinley acknowledged. "But I felt wretched for marrying a man I didn't love and didn't want to admit it because I thought I didn't have a choice. I thought my family would collapse if I didn't."

"Given all that, we decided to take a 'wait-and-see' approach," Law explained.

"Until Jansen took out that policy on you two weeks before your wedding," Dominic continued. "Then all bets were off. We couldn't allow you to marry him and we didn't exactly have the proof we needed."

"It was a desperation play." Riley admitted, cuddling her against him and stroking her hair. "Although I didn't think Law would let your marriage to Jansen happen. When we decided to kidnap you, he practically did his happy dance."

"I don't dance," Law retorted. "But I was happy. Kinley, I know the way we saved you was unorthodox, but we really were thinking of you. I truly believe he planned to kill you on your honeymoon. And I think that tablet proves it."

"He was using me to take his information to his contact?" Kinley frowned.

"That's my guess." Riley tapped on a few more keys. "And it looks like he's using your charity to smuggle something into the country. I can't tell what. It's in a numeric code. Stock 2445. That's all the description I've got. Damn, that is some expensive shit if I'm reading this right."

"But what is it?" Kinley looked totally puzzled.

"It could be anything," Dominic explained. "It could be

cash, bonds, drugs…anything, but he's moving it through your charity. I suspect it has something to do with the new manufacturers he found for you. They're shipping him something in those boxes. Not a lot of people look through charity donation shipments."

"That bastard." Kinley looked ready to spit nails.

Riley soothed her with a caress. "We're getting closer to nailing him. This strongly suggests that he's using your U.S. based nonprofit to move funds offshore so the mafia can use it for their purposes. I think this is what we've been looking for so we can get him on RICO charges. A forensic accountant should be able to take him down."

Dominic sighed. "I would love to know what kind of product he's moving. Please let it be drugs."

Because that might up the time the fucker spent in the can. Except Law wanted to make sure Jansen never saw the inside of a jail cell. A morgue was a better place for scum like him. "Let's see what the feds say. We can call them in the morning."

Dominic nodded and turned to Kinley. "We have some inside contacts at the FBI and the Department of Justice. We'll get them out here. I'm hesitant to send them the information. I would rather talk to them in person. Explain."

Kinley reached for Dominic's hand. Already she was looking to them for comfort, seeking out her men. He just hoped her burgeoning trust was enough to make her stay after the dust settled.

"Shouldn't we go to Washington?"

"Where I can't control the meeting? Where Jansen has hired scumbags who might try to pick us off and take you back?" Law asked. "Not on your life—and that's what's at stake. No. The feds will come here and look over the evidence. We'll call our lawyers in the morning and set up a meeting. Until then, we stay put."

And after everything had gone down? Law didn't know. There would be a ton of questions, of course. From reporters, from the feds, from freaking society. It would come at them from all sides. They would be tested.

He wasn't sure they were strong enough yet.

Could he handle it if Kinley walked away?

He needed more time to bind her to all three of them, to make her understand exactly what they could offer her.

But time had just run out.

* * * *

"Did you make the call?"

Dominic turned to Riley, who had just asked the question. Sunlight filtered into the office, showing off the deep, rich hues of the mahogany and leather furnishings. "Yes. I talked to Kellan. He and Eric will call their contact at the DOJ. Someone from the FBI will call us soon about arranging a meeting. It could take a day or two before anyone can get here. Kinley signed an affidavit for the feds stating that she was never a hostage. Kellan is making sure the FBI sees that before he proceeds. Hopefully, that will keep them from arresting us."

Kinley was sitting on top of the large desk and had been for some time. She stared over her shoulder at one of the computers Riley was working on, her hand on his shoulder as he typed. It seemed she always had a hand on one of them now. She was an affectionate woman, showing her caring with frequent hugs and handholding. She'd curled against them most of the night. Dominic smiled fondly at the memory of her in his lap this morning, eating breakfast from his plate.

"Do you think that will satisfy the feds?" Kinley asked, straightening to look at him.

Law left his place on the couch and walked to her. "I don't know, baby. I suppose they could assume that we forced you to sign it, but I'm counting on Kellan to smooth it all over. There's no way to know until we actually meet with the FBI."

Dominic hoped it was enough. He'd been playing through the scenarios and he didn't like a few of them.

"But all that information was on my tablet. How can I prove Greg loaded it on there?" Kinley asked, neatly summing up at least one of the ways they could get fucked.

"I'm working on that." Riley looked up briefly from his place behind the massive desk that dominated the room. He'd spent most of the morning with computers around him, all cluttering the top of the desk. "Thankfully, the last two of these photos were sent in e-mail. I'm almost sure I can trace them straight back to Jansen's computer."

"I got busy with the wedding. He insisted that he needed to update the tablet's software before we went on our honeymoon, but I couldn't find the time to figure out how since I'd never done it. But I didn't give him the tablet to update until the last minute. Maybe that's why he had to e-mail them," Kinley explained.

"Whatever the reason, he got caught in his own trap." Riley never looked up. "He tried to keep you so busy with the wedding that you couldn't see straight."

"The wedding planner had me on this crazy schedule." She closed her eyes. "Damn it. I'm an idiot. The wedding planner was in on it, too. Greg insisted we use her. Becks said she was the best. Becks was in charge of the charity for most of the last couple of months because I was dealing with wedding details. I just walked right into their trap, didn't I?"

Law wrapped an arm around her. "Don't blame yourself. Jansen is very good at what he does. And he had a lot of help."

She frowned. "And I turned into a bridezilla who wouldn't even listen when my best friend tried to save me."

"She's going to get spanked for that," Dominic said.

"Annabelle? Why on earth would you spank her?" Kinley asked. "She meant well. Besides, I don't think Eric, Kellan, and Tate would like that."

"It's not Annabelle I'm planning to spank. But to your point, we went to visit her on the job because we thought her help would be valuable. Having lawyers on our side was a perk, too. You wouldn't believe what those three put us through before we were even allowed to sit down and talk to Annabelle." Dominic shook his head.

"Why didn't you just go straight to her?"

Law scowled. "Because we honor the rights of other Doms, and it was obvious they're planning to stake their claim on her."

"Doms?"

Riley finally looked up. "Dominants. BDSM. You know."

"BS what?" Kinley asked, wearing a look of pure confusion on her face.

Dominic raised a dark brow, almost amused. "I thought you read romances. Doesn't every female walking the face of the earth have a deeply romantic vision of BDSM by now? It's a catch-all term for bondage, dominance, submission, and masochism. It's what we started teaching you yesterday."

"I'm the submissive. And you three are the Dominants. And Annabelle is a submissive, too? Does she know that? Because I think she would have told me. I *know* she would have told me if she had three Doms. She tells me everything. She called the other day to let me know she was out of sugar. I was three states over so there was nothing I could do, but she told me anyway. She would have mentioned if there was some backside slapping going on."

"Oh, something's going on there," Law swore. "They haven't claimed her yet, but they're definitely watching over her. In our world, that means they have certain rights. One of those is the right to protect her. After we took you, they completely forbade her from doing or saying anything that might give the appearance that she was an accomplice. Annabelle was allowed to talk to us shortly after we arrived here only because she was beyond worried about you and about to lose her mind. Other than that, the lawyers made sure to leave everything to us. Her men don't know you well enough to trust that you wouldn't want a little revenge and throw Annabelle to the wolves if everything went bad."

"She's my best friend. God, she's just about the only

person in my life I can trust now." She sniffled. "After everything that's happened, she's my only family. I would never hurt her. And if those three lawyers think they can take all kinds of rights and stuff without giving her anything back, then they should know that I have a shotgun. I don't know how to use it, but I can take a class. In fact, I just might shoot my sister first. I'll need a little practice."

"Whoa, there, warrior princess," Law said with a laugh. "If we do this right, your sister is going to jail. You're going to have to be satisfied with seeing her in an orange jumpsuit. Is your sister bisexual by any chance?"

Kinley threw up her hands. "I have no idea. I wouldn't put anything past her at this point."

"Well, she should think about shifting her orientation if she's not because I suspect she won't be lonely in prison."

Dominic watched Kinley, studying her. She looked so young and innocent without a hint of makeup on her face. She was wearing a light sweater and a pair of those blinged out jeans she'd brought with her. She'd obviously foregone the bra, and since Law had been supervising her all morning, Dominic assumed she'd followed the no-underwear rule. Otherwise, they were going to spank her and hard because he had no notion how else to defuse the tension clogging the room.

The anxiety blended with the light hum of sexuality and hung over all of them. The hard truth was they would soon have to leave this place and reenter the real world—where Kinley had a completely different life and they worked all over the globe. Dominic had no idea how—or if—their relationship could work, and he was pretty sure that neither Kinley nor Riley did, either. Law, he suspected, would tender his resignation before leaving her, but he wasn't thinking of the long term. Kinley was actually about to be out of money. Her charity's funds would be tied up in court for years most likely, and she would be involved in a whole lot of legalities. Law couldn't take care of her and all those expenses if he was working as a mall cop.

They had to convince her to come with them.

Starting now.

"The other day, you asked me for an exchange, pet. Are you still interested?"

Kinley turned to him, frowning. "What?"

"An exchange. You offered information for sexual knowledge. I want to teach you about our lifestyle and what it can offer you."

"I don't think this is the time, Dominic."

"We don't have anything else to do while we wait on the feds, unless you want to watch Riley play with his keyboard all day."

Riley's middle finger shot up. "I'm doing more than playing with my keyboard."

"All right," Dominic conceded. "Tell me, what can you really accomplish by examining all these files now?"

Riley groaned. "Not as much as I'd like. I need to get into Jansen's systems, but he's protected himself. They're shut down right now. I hope to fuck he's not destroying them as we speak."

"We can't do anything about that until the feds get back to us. So we need *some* way to occupy our time," Law drawled. "Any ideas?"

He thrust his hands in Kinley's hair and lowered his lips to her, kissing her hard. He winked at her as he came back up for air.

"I'm not sure I can figure out what he was transporting with the information in front of me." Riley sounded really disappointed about that.

Dominic understood. "But we're not leaving here until we've pieced everything together with the feds and we think the case is pretty tight. Until then, we're holed up, pet, and I can't think of anything I would rather do than take you up on your offer."

Law rubbed her arm, his whole body relaxing. "You gave

us the information we need."

"Not exactly. Riley found it," she pointed out.

"On *your* tablet. So now it's our turn." Dominic had some very specific things he wanted to teach her. "Unless you're still sore. If that's the case, we can simply talk for a while."

"I'm fine." Her voice was a soft, breathy tone. Instinctively, her gaze dropped to the floor. "Are you a Dominant, Sir?"

"Yes." A smile played at his lips. Hearing her call him that would never get old.

"And I'm a submissive?"

"Absolutely," Law whispered in her ear. "You're the sweetest little sub I've ever seen."

A grin curled her mouth up. "So I call you my Doms?"

"Yes, pet."

Her smile widened until she looked as if she was trying to keep a straight face. "You're Dominic, the Dom."

He sighed. "Yes, pet. I think I was aptly named."

"You're Dom Dominic."

"While true, that's not exactly how you should phrase it." He frowned.

"You're Dom Dom." The smile zipped across her face. "I get to call you Dom Dom."

Kinley burst out laughing. Law and Riley joined in.

Dominic was not about to spend the rest of his life being called Dom Dom. "Pet, every time you call me that, I'll give you twenty swats. They will not be for pleasure. You may call me Sir for now. If you accepted a collar from me, you would call me Master. I am your Dom. It's a status, not a title."

She pouted. "But Dom Dom is so much fun."

The girl was begging for it. "So is reddening your ass. Off with the clothes, pet. That's twenty over my knee."

She turned to Law, and Dominic couldn't miss the high-pitched squeaking sound as she wiggled that fabulous backside on the glass top of the desk. Everyone in the room winced at the noise.

"He has no sense of humor," Kinley complained.

Law shook his head. "Not a lot, but I think this time he really just wants to smack your ass. Have I told you how good those jeans look on you?"

"I have a great sense of humor," Dominic insisted. "But I will not allow my submissive to call me Dom Dom, even if she does look like sex on two legs in those jeans. I confess, the fuzzy pink socks distract a bit from the vision."

She wrinkled her nose adorably, obviously happy with the compliments. "If you want bare feet, don't take me to Alaska."

Law moved between her legs, dragging those pink clad feet up around his waist as Kinley laughed. "I don't know. I think the socks are easier on my back than a pair of stilettos."

"I'm not leaving my socks on when we're in bed." Kinley held on to Law for balance, looking breathless, flushed, and excited.

"We're not going to bed, pet," Dominic explained.

"But I kind of thought by 'explaining,' you meant you were going to teach me some naughty bedroom things." She was blushing again and obviously hoping she was right.

"This relationship will not be relegated solely to the bedroom. Your first rule is that we will take you anywhere, anytime, and in any way we wish. I want to see you in the sunshine."

"But—"

"Ah, ah, ah. Don't protest. There's no one out here, except perhaps the moose. And we'll protect you from him."

Riley chuckled. "I can think of so many places to play with you, sweetheart. We're going to have fun walking you through a dungeon."

"A dungeon? Like a medieval torture chamber?"

Law sent his brother a dirty look. "No, baby. It's not scary like that. A dungeon is just what we call a play space. We have a nice big one back home. It's got all kinds of toys. We have plenty here, too. The James brothers are…well, we know them from a private club."

"So they're all Dommy, too?"

Law groaned. "Oh, baby, we're going to have to teach you a little respect. Hand over the sweater. I think Dominic's just about at the end of his rope after the Dom Dom crack. If he doesn't get you over his knee soon, he'll pull out the big guns. Delayed gratification."

"That sounds horrible," she grumbled as she pulled the sweater over her head. "We have to work on his sense of humor. I hope Annabelle's men aren't so stuffy."

"You might not think I have a sense of humor, but I assure you, I possess a fine sense of decorum, pet. I expect that what happens between us stays between us. There is a very big difference between Annabelle running out of sugar and you treating our relationship like fodder for the gossip rags."

Kinley stood naked from the waist up. Now, she didn't try to hide, but merely placed her hands on her hips and stared him down. She seemed more comfortable with her own body now than she had last night, and that pleased him immensely.

"If you think I am not going to talk to my very dearest friend in the world about the fact that I finally made love, you really don't understand women," she insisted.

Dominic had to school his expression to something properly masterful because all he wanted to do was grin. She was utterly adorable. And fuckable. Though he would probably have to correct her sassy tone, he loved the fact that she felt safe enough to try using it with him. She wouldn't have two days ago. "I would think women, especially a woman raised the way you were, would be a bit circumspect."

She shook her head and looked to Law. "Does he watch TV? He has to know that if Annabelle was actually sleeping with those men—which she isn't because I would know—but if by some miracle she is, then we will be comparing notes, if you know what I mean. So if that's one of the rules, then you should just start spanking me now. This is the most interesting thing that has ever happened to me. All of my life, all I've had to contribute to the conversation was things like, 'Hey, I got a great deal on a ton of used clothes and after I finish washing them, I'm going to hand them out.' Once I get home, it's possible that everyone will just want to talk about how pathetic I am because my family and fiancé wanted to kill me. So I will totally be switching topics to talk about my suddenly crazy sex life with three hot guys."

"I think she has a point," Riley commented. He suddenly wasn't so interested in his computer. In fact, Dominic didn't think he could get his friend's stare off Kinley's breasts even with a crowbar. "Though she's crazy if she thinks no one will talk about her sex life."

Kinley giggled. Dominic's hand started to itch.

"I don't care what the tabloids write anymore. They've never been kind, so I don't think they'll start now. And I didn't say I would talk to the press about what happens in freaky dungeons, just Annabelle. But I might lay it on thick with a couple of Becks's friends who have never been nice to me, the ones who used to say that I couldn't snag a man to save my life. Maybe the three of you could show up at the country club without your shirts on. That'll drop some jaws and make some ladies faint." Kinley grinned.

Riley had wrung his hands about Kinley accepting them? Dominic shook his head incredulously. Hell, she was ready to parade them around. And that wasn't happening.

"The pants, pet," he barked.

She unbuttoned the fly of her jeans and stood. Riley was right there to help her pull them down. He made sure to cup her every curve as he dragged them off her body.

"I probably won't go back to the country club," she admitted as she pulled off her socks. "I won't be able to afford it. I didn't like it, anyway. Maybe I'll just move to Chicago and live with Annabelle."

Not if he had anything to say about it. "Come here. There will be time to decide all that later, but at first I think it's best if we either stay here for a while or hole up at my place. It's gated, and we'll want to keep the reporters out."

Kinley sent him a cautious stare. "I thought you would just send me home."

Understandable assumption since they hadn't worked anything out yet, but she definitely wasn't going home or in any way leaving them. "No, pet. You still won't be safe. You'll need one of us with you at all times until Jansen is permanently in jail."

Or dead.

"I could hire a bodyguard." She frowned. "Maybe I couldn't."

"You can obey your Masters and everything will be fine. I know there's an awful lot to think about and discuss—later. Now is for us. Do you understand?"

Dominic didn't want her to worry. It would be easy for her to do, and she had every right, but he'd rather have her here in the moment with all of them together…just in case their meeting with the feds didn't go as he hoped. He wanted to forge a bond that would be difficult to break.

She squirmed a bit, looking pensive. Then she relented. "Yes, Sir."

"Excellent. Law, would you see if the James brothers have a few essentials in their playroom while I take care of our sub's discipline?"

Law hesitated for a moment then nodded decisively, as if he'd just reached the same conclusions Dominic had. "On it."

"Is she ready?" Riley asked.

"I just want to be equipped in case she is. And there's always prep work to be done. We might as well begin opening her to us in all ways now. Unless you were planning on taking turns forever."

"We don't have to rush her," Riley argued.

Dominic disagreed. Riley had spent less time with Kinley, so he didn't know her capabilities yet. Hopefully, today would rectify that. It was vital that they all begin functioning as a unit—as a family—in case their tomorrow was put on hold by the feds, the press, her family…whomever.

"I don't want to wait," Kinley protested. "I've waited all my life. I've been careful, and the one time I did something crazy, well…that was the happiest night of my life. Too many things can happen, Riley. I want all my men."

Riley nodded and brushed a gentle kiss across her lips. Law beamed a proud smile her way, then strode out the door.

Dominic patted his lap. "I think we're up to forty now, pet."

"Forty? What the—"

"I don't recommend finishing that question unless you want sixty instead." He was going to love disciplining her.

Kinley shook her head mutely.

"I knew you were a smart girl. Remember how fun you thought it was to call me Dom Dom? Well, now I get to show you my version of fun. Then we'll move on to the orgasm-denial portion of the afternoon."

Kinley stifled the argument he saw on her face and practically jumped across his lap. They would have to work on her form, but he appreciated the enthusiasm. "I'm ready, Sir."

"I bet you are. Riley, are you joining me? I suspect that despite your attempts to be standoffish, you've already given in."

He'd looked too satisfied the night before, and it hadn't been merely because he'd figured out Jansen's secrets. The other big clue had been the easy way Riley had been touching her.

"I did, and let me tell you, she is a natural at oral." Riley sauntered over to Kinley and palmed the fleshiest part of her ass. "Best blow job I've ever had."

"Shouldn't I get points for that?" Kinley twisted around and asked Dominic hopefully.

Riley knew what to do. He brought his hand down on her ass with a sharp smack. "You get my eternal affection, but rules are rules, sweetheart."

"Precisely," Dominic agreed. "If anything scares you, Kinley, all you have to do is say stop." They would find a more appropriate safe word when they had adequate time to establish the dynamics between them, but for now he wanted her to know that any negative word would work.

"What scares me is that Riley hits like a girl."

Dominic sucked in a sharp breath. Oh, god, he was in love with her.

And Riley was at least in lust. He smacked her ass with a stinging crack three more times. The sound pinged through the air, mingling with her little gasps.

She shuddered across his lap but didn't try to move off. "That was better."

"She's going to top from the bottom," Riley said, shaking his head.

She would try. And he would allow it from time to time, when it suited him. But not today. "That was four. Where are we, Kinley?"

"I'm getting antsy, Sir."

Her word for aroused. He liked it when she was antsy. "Let's see if we can move this along, then. I prefer aroused begging."

They took turns smacking her gorgeous ass, each carefully spreading out the slaps. Over and over, keeping careful count, they turned her backside pink and hot.

Kinley moaned and cried out. She flailed a bit, her legs moving restlessly, but made no move to get away. She strained for breath, her chest sawing up and down with effort. Her skin turned a delicious rosy red.

Dominic ran a hand down her heated backside. "You're doing quite well, pet."

"Why do I like this?" She wrapped her hands around his calf, holding on to him, her voice thick with both bewilderment and arousal.

How should he explain? He'd never had to before, as they tended to play with experienced submissives.

"What do you feel right now?" he asked.

"Pain. Excitement. A weird sense of pride. Pleasure. I

don't know. It feels like…everything."

He bounced a glance up at Riley. "And you were worried she wouldn't be able to handle our needs."

"She really does like it." Riley sounded almost astounded as he knelt down to her. "Sweetheart, what you're feeling, besides arousal, is the connection between a Dom and a sub. You could get it with a lover in other ways, but this is how we find it. We play. We grow together. We share these parts of ourselves."

"It's about honesty." Dominic ran his hands over her ass. "I want to know how you feel. I want to know what you like and what you don't. So many people don't talk about their sex lives—or anything else important. We're going to talk, pet. We're going to communicate often. We take this seriously."

"I want it to be serious," she gasped out.

"Good to hear." They hadn't been quite so serious with any of their other subs, but everything was damn serious with her. Kinley was a woman who needed sex to mean something. He'd enjoyed the women who didn't, but everything was different with her.

Law walked back in the room carrying a large leather case. He stopped and stared down at Kinley's ass. "How many?"

Dominic smiled with a deep satisfaction. She'd been magnificent. "Forty. And she could take more."

"Not right now," Kinley shouted. "I need something else. Can someone touch my pussy?"

He smiled. She was so damn open. There wasn't a bit of artifice about her. She simply said what she meant and didn't embellish. Dominic repressed a grin but sent her a fond glance. Her honesty made him feel…safe, like she would always be exactly who she was with them. Riley, especially, should be relieved. No more nasty Simone-like surprises.

Though Kinley's ass was a beautiful flushed shade, he had a deep instinct to push her. Law's thumbs-up told him that he'd brought all the instruments to further their intimacy.

When Dominic tried to gesture back, he found Law's stare was glued to her ass.

"Pass me a plug and some lube," Dominic requested.

Kinley gave a little moan, a singular sign that he was in tune with her body and her wishes. Pleasure surged through him. Dominic realized how far gone he was for this woman.

She gave him pleasure by the simple act of agreeing with him. They were in sync. He could call himself the Dom, but he'd spent his life looking for the woman who could move him and make him want to surrender his heart.

Kinley was that woman, and there wouldn't be another after her. He and Law were similar in that respect. He would love once, and it was brilliant kismet that he and Law loved the same female. She wasn't at all what he'd imagined when he'd thought of his ideal. She wasn't always easy to handle. She wasn't always controllable. Then again, she embraced Law, reassured Riley, and made him laugh. Who else would call him Dom Dom while pushing him to be a better man?

"I have everything." Law dropped the bag on the desk and stood over Kinley's prone body. "Fuck, that's beautiful. She's so rosy." He traced the line of her ass with gentle fingers.

Law was right, and Dominic wasn't sure how to keep her with them—to bind her to them—completely. He needed more time to draw her in. More time to bring them together.

But their time might end once the FBI arrived. They would likely separate them all and interrogate each of them while they studied the evidence. Once that was behind them—and who knew how long it would take—then the media circus would begin. Kinley might well want privacy and some time to herself. Here in Alaska, the concept of her father's betrayal and her sister's possible jail time were almost theoretical. But once home, she would be confronted with those realities. They would hit her hard. She might find trust difficult then. If she couldn't count on the people who shared her blood, how could he, Law, and Riley expect her to cleave to them after only a few days? Without reality pounding on their door, the rapport and sex had been relatively easy. But it wouldn't be long before all of that could change…

For the first time, Dominic hoped Jansen stayed out of jail long enough to win her trust, her love. Maybe if they proved how good they could all be together, she would stay.

"Touch her pussy. Give her a taste." He was in charge now.

Law dropped to his knees, obviously willing to give her what she needed. He moved between her legs, shoving them wide and spreading her cheeks. "Want me to prep her now?"

"Yes." There was no reason to wait. They needed to move on her as quickly as they could. Kinley was an affectionate woman. The sooner they had taken her in every way possible, the sooner she would feel surrounded by their devotion. The sooner she would give them her heart.

"It's time to prep her. It's time to take her," Dominic insisted. "Now."

Chapter Fourteen

Kinley stayed perfectly still as she tried to figure out exactly what Dominic meant by "prepping her now." She was pretty sure it had something to do with her backside, because they'd been paying special attention to that.

After her spanking, the cheeks of her ass were throbbing, and she kind of liked it. But that wasn't the only thing she enjoyed about being with them.

Connection. Riley had used that term, and Kinley understood immediately. She needed the connection that came from this kind of sex. They said it was serious, and she felt the gravity as they surrounded her and communicated with her through pleasure. Dominic had assured her that they would talk about sex precisely because it was important. Kinley was beginning to understand why.

"What are you going to do?" Most likely, she would have been silent in the past and simply accepted whatever they gave her. Perversely, despite the fact that they intended to dominate her, Kinley wanted to know their plans because being the one to accept them would make her feel more powerful.

"Bluntly put, I'm going to open your asshole up for our cocks," Dominic explained. He held up a small, oddly shaped piece of plastic. It was tapered at the end, then flared out to form a bulb that rounded into a graceful oval. There was a long flat piece at the end that seemed to be some kind of handle. "I'm going to take this plug that Law sterilized and sink it deep inside your ass. If it acquiesces, then we can take you now. If you have a stubborn little anus, it could take a week or two."

She wanted them today, not later. A lot was happening very quickly, but she understood clearly that she might not have a week or two with them. She only hoped her body would cooperate with her wishes.

How did one convince their sphincter to open up and get with the program? "I'll try."

Because Kinley wanted more than the sex. She wanted the connection with all of them. She wanted to know what it meant to be the center of Dominic, Law, and Riley's universe. She wanted to be the sun in their sky—even if just for a while.

Her backside pulsed with tingling anticipation. Every single one of those forty smacks had impacted her, showing her exactly what she needed, revealing the part of her she'd denied for twenty-five years.

This was the truest Kinley she'd ever known, the most comfortable she'd ever been in her own skin. Heavens, she never wanted this exultant feeling to end.

She relaxed, giving them her trust, allowing them the control. Oddly, Kinley felt not only a freedom, but a certain power in giving herself over. She had only to tell them that she didn't like something and they would stop. That made relaxing and allowing things to happen so very easy.

Because she trusted them.

It occurred to her that she'd never really trusted anyone this deeply. Not boyfriends or family. Not even Annabelle. She'd never just allowed herself to relax and wait for whatever came because she knew it would be pleasurable.

Now, she could.

Collectively, they stroked her, both soothing and arousing her as they explained what would happen.

"We'll start with the small plug," Law suggested.

Dominic grunted. "No, the medium one. She can handle it."

"Just use your fingers," Riley added to the argument.

Strong fingers pulled her cheeks apart, cool air hitting her opening. She'd never been touched like this. Never been parted and inspected.

"Look at that." Law whistled.

"Fucking gorgeous." Dominic sounded like he really meant it.

Riley sighed happily. "She's going to be so damn tight."

For long minutes, they fondled her, told her how gorgeous she was and how much they couldn't wait to sink their cocks into this one untried hole she'd never imagined a man using, except in her wildest dreams. Maybe it should have been odd or off-putting, but she just felt utterly wanted, as if they couldn't wait to feel every part of her. The thought made her shiver.

Their hands roamed every inch of her skin until she couldn't tell who was touching her where. Kinley only knew that they all had a hand on her. The experience felt both intimate and thrilling. Her men. Touching her. All at the same time.

How many women had to choose the sort of lover they wanted? How many had to give up pieces of their heart that completed them in order to receive affection?

Gruff Law could be so gentle. He understood her wholly, gave her affection without asking for anything in return. Perversely, it made her want to give him every bit of herself. She also found comfort in knowing he would protect her without question or fail.

Dominic, whom she would always call Dom Dom in her head, challenged her. He held her hand as he stripped away the veneer of the girl she used to know and showed her the woman beneath, all the while giving himself fully in return. He offered her trust and honesty.

And Riley…he had been so scarred emotionally. But once she'd reached him, he'd simply asked her to give him a chance. He was so smart, so capable, so interesting…but less sure. She could see herself learning from him each and every day. She could see them growing together.

She was taking a chance with them now, and the terrified

part of her that had been betrayed before knew it. That part shouted at her to walk away. Kinley silenced the insidious voice. After a lifetime spent avoiding risk, she was now throwing herself in their path, at their mercy. She didn't want to go through life suspicious or cynical. Of course she could get hurt again. But her past proved that life without risk was also a life without rewards.

A finger slipped between her cheeks, and something cold coated that intimate, previously untouched entry, jolting her from her ruminations. She shivered at the chilly, foreign sensations.

"It's lubricant, Kinley," Riley explained. "It's going to help with insertion."

Of the plug. Right.

Then once her body was ready, they would insert themselves in her ass. She couldn't imagine how that would feel—or how she would feel about opening herself up this way.

Sex was intimate, yes. But it was also sometimes awkward and sweet, often blisteringly hot…and yet oddly pure.

A weird, jangly feeling took over as something warm made its way through the lubrication and began to penetrate her.

"That's my finger, pet," Dominic said as he circled her, pressing in a bit more. "Relax. I know that's difficult. Just think about breathing out and letting me in."

She drew in a long breath and released it, then felt Dominic's finger sink deeper. It didn't hurt at all. It was different. She felt pleasantly filled. Most of all, the nerves he awakened there with just a touch aroused her. Kinley let herself go completely limp and trusting in his arms.

"That's right." Law was kneeling at her side, his big hand stroking her back. "So pretty, baby. Your trust is gorgeous. Let us take care of you."

They had been taking very good care of her. She'd never

had anyone care so much about her feelings and experience as these three men. They made sure she had what she needed, from clothes to food to affection, then they gave her more. Understanding, safety, concern, guidance. They thought of her first.

Relationships should be like this, Kinley realized. Her mother had been so in love with her charming father. He'd been good at making her mother love him, but he hadn't shared his heart in return. She saw now that her father had simply taken everything her mother had, as if she owed him, and never given anything back in return. Becks was like that. Her husband loved her, and she cheated on Brian as if he didn't matter.

But what Kinley shared with Law, Dominic, and Riley—this was the way it should be. They put her first. For as long as it lasted, she would do the same with them.

Dominic submerged his finger completely inside her, and Kinley clenched around him.

That earned her a smack that made the already tender skin of her ass tingle. "Don't try to push me out."

"Let him have his way, baby," Law advised.

"You'll be so full, sweetheart," Riley vowed. "You'll enjoy it."

A second finger joined the first, stretching even wider little by little. She hissed at the slight burn, but then let loose another breath, relaxing her muscles. Dominic's second finger penetrated her completely.

"You're tight, pet, but I think we'll fit just fine." A wealth of satisfaction resounded in Dominic's voice.

Anticipation filled her.

Gently, he pulled his fingers free, and Kinley felt the loss—but not for long. Almost instantly, something harder filled the empty space. "This is a training plug. While we play a bit more, I'm going to leave this inside you to stretch you for us. Don't lose this plug or we will have to start all over again and I'll do so with another spanking."

She'd loved the forty slaps they'd given her, the primal heat that it churned inside her, but was more than ready to move the experience along.

She dragged a breath in as the plug began to breach her. "Are you sure that's only the starter size? Because it feels really big."

Pressure, insistent and unrelenting, jammed her as the plug scraped her nerve endings. Kinley forced herself not to clench, but to simply let Dominic press the plug in farther. Finally, it popped past a tight band of muscle inside her and slid in all the way. Kinley felt no pain, just a fullness that made her gasp and writhe with a shocking curl of want. That plug filling her made her ache and perspire and need. A little thrill of pride lit her up, too. She'd taken everything they'd given her so far. Now she couldn't wait to give back.

"I assure you, it's smaller than me," Dominic said as he worked the plug in and out, simulating the way they would take her ass for their own.

"Good, sweetheart. Now hold that plug in, Kinley," Riley said as he helped her to her feet.

She clenched and had to concentrate on not letting the bit of silicone slip free.

Dominic stared down at her, obviously already in that mental place he found when he spanked and commanded her. It made him stand taller, made his voice deepen. It was so sexy, she could hardly stand it. "I'll be back after I clean up. I think it's time to torture our little submissive a bit. Law, Riley, you can handle that, right?"

"Absolutely." Law had taken off his clothes when she wasn't looking. His cock thrust out, reaching up nearly to his navel.

Riley just smiled in a way she didn't find comforting, but it was sexy as hell.

Once Dominic had left her alone with Law and Riley, they circled her like two predators sizing up particularly juicy prey.

"You did so well, baby." Law's stare roved hot all over

her body. "Your ass looks beautiful all pink and hot, *and* you're getting ready for us."

Kinley was aware of her body like never before—the rushing of her blood, the goose bumps breaking out across her skin, her shortness of breath, the fullness deep inside her, and the tingles dive-bombing her from every direction. She'd never felt more awake or vibrantly alive.

Riley shrugged out of his shirt and stepped close to her, caressing his way down her body and making her nipples tighten. "Clench your cheeks together, sweetheart."

She did as he asked, and he dropped to his knees.

"Yes, that's exactly what I want." Riley nuzzled his face to her belly. "You see, when you clench like that, it makes this little jewel stand out. I really like to play with this."

He barely touched her clitoris, which was pulsing now. A shiver wound through her. She wasn't completely sure what he was planning next, and Kinley found a deep excitement in not knowing. In being at his mercy. She didn't know if he would give her the bliss of pleasure or a sweet bite of pain—or both.

Riley dragged a finger through her labia then slid it back up, rounding her clitoris but not quite touching it. Taunting her.

Then Law was at her back, moving her hair aside and placing little kisses on her nape that made her shiver. His hands brushed around her torso and molded to her breasts, lifting them as he pinched her nipples. Kinley gasped as her whole body clenched.

Riley finally slid the pad of his thumb over her clitoris, just as Law pressed down on her nipples. Their timing was perfectly in sync. Pleasure mingled with a bite of pain, bringing her nerves into a crazy harmony she couldn't understand or deny.

"We like this game, baby," Law whispered in her ear. "We like to figure out exactly what trips your trigger then parse it out slowly."

"But only when you're good," Riley added. "Only when

you beg sweetly."

"Exactly," Law agreed, laving his way up her neck, bestowing on her a warm, fuzzy sensation that made her shiver and writhe. She adored it.

Riley's nose was suddenly buried in her labia, his head moving back and forth. And then Law nipped her, just a little bite as Riley's tongue bathed her pussy in pleasure.

Pain and pleasure, each one complementing the other.

"I brought something fun." Dominic returned carrying a small silver bucket in his hands. There was a bottle of champagne chilling there, but he ignored it. His fingers slid into the bucket and came back with a small cube of ice. "Allow me."

As he slid the ice down her spine, she shivered again, the chill of the cube blending with the heat of their flesh to make something new and intoxicating.

"This is sensation play, pet. It's meant to arouse you, to engage you." Dominic trailed the ice around her body and slipped it over her nipple. She sucked in a breath against the freeze, but then Law bent to take that same nipple into his mouth, heating her up again. Dominic played with the second nipple before they exchanged positions, chilling and heating her over and over. She gripped their shoulders as her knees seemed to melt underneath her.

Riley pulled away from bathing her clit with his tongue while Dominic selected another cube and touched it to that very spot. Kinley groaned and dug her nails into them.

"Our ice won't last long." Dominic chuckled.

"No. She'll melt it very quickly. And I'll help her. God, I love the way she tastes." Riley buried his head between her legs again as if he couldn't stay away.

As Dominic's ice trailed all over her skin, settling on her nipples again, Law pulled on them, sucking and defrosting them and making them ache all at once. Kinley's senses felt so overloaded, her blood sizzling with need, that she thought she might scream.

Riley pulled her clitoris into his mouth again and began to suckle, the tip of his tongue raking her bud just where she needed it most. Just as her clit swelled and need began to coalesce between her legs, he pulled back. Dominic slid the ice over her sensitive pearl again. Her head reeled with sensation.

"Your orgasms belong to us, pet," Dominic explained. "We want you so used to coming for us that you can do so on command. And we don't want polite little orgasms. We want to make you scream."

"I'm ready to scream now," she panted out.

They were killing her. She was so close to the edge, but they kept pulling her back. It was torture of the sweetest kind. She felt beloved and worshiped and adored…but denied what she needed most.

Dominic took her nipple between his fingers and twisted. "Do you want to come, pet?"

She wanted it more than she wanted her next breath. "Yes! Yes, please. I need it…"

He tightened his hold. "Ask me. Or rather ask Riley since he's the one currently in charge of your pussy. And when you ask, be very polite, pet. Maybe he'll oblige."

She could do polite. "Please give me an orgasm, Sir. I would be so grateful."

A sexy, sinful smile slid across Riley's face. "Well, now, I do aim to please, sweetheart. And since you asked so sweetly."

He put his face to her pussy, then licked and suckled before he slipped a finger between her slick folds, reaching for her sweet spot. She was still clenching tightly to keep the plug in place, so that finger felt huge in her pussy. He foraged deep while he sucked on her clit, and Kinley lost it.

Screaming, she went over the edge, all the previous play making her ripe and ready to give her entire being over to it. She let the wave of ecstasy sweep her away, gratefully taking what Riley was so generously giving her.

"Very good, pet." Dominic's silky voice played along her ear. "You're soft and wet and you held the plug well. But I think you need to prepare your men to fuck you. On your hands and knees."

Law and Dominic helped her down to the soft carpet. She nearly melted into it, her body was so languid after the orgasm, but they had rewarded her. Now, they were counting on her. They'd given her such pleasure, and she wanted to give it back.

Dominic remained behind her, forcing her knees wide. She could hear the soft shuffle of him removing his clothes. He settled himself between, placing his hand on her back.

After shucking off his pants, Riley scrambled in front of her. On his knees now, he aligned his cock with her mouth. "You know how to do this, sweetheart. Get me hard enough to fuck you. I want inside your pussy. I want it so fucking bad I can't stand it."

He looked really hard, but Kinley was more than game. She loved the way he'd tasted the night before, how he'd shaken and moaned as she'd sucked him down. Now, she licked at his cock, laving the head with affection, moaning around his flesh.

Law knelt at her side and she felt his hand slip under her body, finding her clit again. "Be good, baby."

She got the idea. As long as she sucked Riley attentively, Law would play with her. And she loved Law's touch. Despite the fact that she'd just come, her body was already building again.

She drew the head of Riley's cock into her mouth, laving her tongue all around. She loved the power she felt when his whole body went still, as though he didn't want to do anything to take himself out of the moment.

"Keep sucking, pet. I'm going to play, too." Dominic laid a hand on the cheek of her ass.

And then she was moaning again. He spread her cheeks apart, and Kinley felt him press at the plug. Pressure filled her pelvis.

"Oh, fuck that feels good, Kinley." Riley's hands tangled

in her hair, drawing her closer. "Whatever you did, Dominic, do it again. It feels so fucking good when she moans around my cock."

Dominic tugged and prodded the plug again, and Kinley couldn't stop the helpless sounds escaping her.

"She's taken this plug quite nicely," Dominic assured the others.

That plug was threatening her sanity. He moved it in and out of her, starting in small jaunts—a tiny bit out, then back in—before he withdrew it further, only to press in harder. He was penetrating her ass with the plug the same way he would soon take her with his cock. If just the idea and this much sensation was overwhelming her, she could hardly wait for the real thing.

Kinley tried to concentrate on sucking Riley, but blocking out the pleasure Dominic and Law were giving her proved impossible.

Law's hand stilled as he stopped toying with her clit. "Keep sucking, baby."

She whimpered but complied. As soon as she did and Riley emitted a long, low groan once more, Law continued swiping that relentless caress over her clit.

"It's my turn next," he murmured low and intimate in her ear. "Do you know how we're going to work this? How we're going to take you? Because we are definitely going to take you. Here and now. In the light of day. All together."

She listened, Law's words arousing her as much as their touches.

"I'm going to shove my cock past those sweet lips of yours," he swore, his voice husky. "I'm going to fuck your pretty mouth and make you take me until there's no place to go except down your throat. I'm going to watch your lips as you devour me. And when I come, I'm going to fill your mouth, then you're going to suck me down."

"And I'm finally going to get inside your pussy," Riley groaned as he shoved his cock into her mouth another inch. "I know you're going to be so wet and soft around me. And you're going to take every inch. I'm going to fill you up. I'm going to make you come."

"And I'm going to take your virgin ass," Dominic said with a tug on her plug.

He eased it nearly free of her body, the pressure letting up. Kinley held her breath, waiting, suspended, dying. Then Dominic ruthlessly fucked it back into her. She cried out in pleasure.

"Good, pet. But even though you've done well with the plug, I'll have to fight my way in back here. Carefully, of course. But every inch I take is going to be pure pleasure. You're going to be so tight around my cock. I intend to teach you to love this, pet. I want you to crave it. By the time we're done, you won't feel full and happy unless you have all your men. I promise you."

She already felt incomplete when they weren't all touching her.

Riley pulled out of her mouth abruptly, his face contorted with effort. "Fuck, I can't last much longer like that. I don't want to come until I get inside your pussy, sweetheart."

"She's ready." Dominic removed the plug.

Again, Kinley felt empty without the fullness and pressure back there, and she couldn't wait for Dominic to take his rightful place inside her, filling her up once more.

The men moved quickly, Law lifting her and carrying her toward the sofa. Riley threw himself down on the cushions first, his cock straining up. He covered it in a condom in record time and reached for her. "Come on, sweetheart. Ride me."

Law eased her over Riley's prone form. He was so beautifully masculine and he was all hers. For now, they all belonged to her.

She straddled him, taking his cock in her hand to guide him home. She sank onto his waiting inches and threw her head back with a groan. The feel of him inside her was pure pleasure.

"Don't forget me, baby." Law stood in front of her, stroking that massive cock of his with a rough fist. Even the sight of it turned her on.

All she had to do was lean forward to take him in her mouth, his length filling her as he worked his way in. She ran her tongue across his cock, reveling in the masculine taste even as Riley pumped his way into her pussy without restraint.

Then Dominic took his place behind her. "Stay still, just for a moment, pet. Tilt your hips back and push down. I'm bigger than the plug, but you can take me."

He dribbled more lube on her, then began to probe her ass. She felt her eyes widening because Dominic was right. He was much bigger than the plug. His cock began to breach her hole. She whimpered, the pressure was so great.

Law stroked her hair. "You can take him. Don't fight him. Baby, it's going to feel so good once he gets inside."

She concentrated on Law's cock. She sucked hard, drawing back until he almost popped out of her mouth. She kept him there, whirling her tongue around the head, playing with the little slit there, eliciting a curse and a groan from him.

Riley ran his hands across her skin, soothing her. "Just relax. I know that's hard, but it will be worth it. I promise. Do exactly as Dominic said. Let him in."

She wanted so much to give back to these men. Kinley tilted back a bit. Dominic sank a little deeper, and she took a long breath. She could handle the pressure. It wasn't real pain.

"She's so tight," he hissed. "Kinley, pet, you have to tell us now if you want this to stop." Dominic's voice shook with desire. His hands tightened around her.

"I don't."

"Then do as I say. Push down on me."

After a few seconds, she drew back and dislodged Riley halfway. Then she managed to tilt higher and pushed down. Dominic tunneled inside her until she felt every inch of him filling her ass. He pressed against her, holding her tight.

"Oh, fuck me. You feel so good." Dominic ground against her.

Heat threatened to overwhelm Kinley. She was packed full of them all, stretched to the limit. But she never wanted to escape.

Riley shoved his way back in, and Kinley gasped. Pleasure raked across her every nerve, screaming with tingling need. The ecstasy was robbing her breath, her mind. All the pain and heartache it had taken her to reach this place was suddenly worth it because she didn't just feel amazing bliss with these men. She felt warmed and surrounded and loved.

"Take me." Law pulled her close again, his cock against her lips. "None of us is going to last very long. Suck me hard, baby. Take all your men."

She did as Law demanded while Riley and Dominic started to move in perfect harmony. Riley filled her pussy as Dominic pulled out of her ass, exciting every cell, every nerve. As they settled into a pounding rhythm, she moved with them, still sucking hard on Law. He swelled against her tongue. His flavor turned salty.

"Get ready, baby. I'm going to come." Law's pace quickened as he dragged in deep, heaving breaths and anchored his hands in her hair. "Fuck! I need you, baby. Take me."

As she nodded, his cock pulsed then burst. He covered her tongue with his seed. Kinley drank from him, sucking gently as his essence coated her throat. Then she swallowed.

Dominic gripped her hips tighter and dragged her back on his cock. "Law, help us out."

He did, kneeling beside them and working a hand in between her and Riley. He pressed on her clitoris as Riley thrust up and hit a spot inside her that had her wailing. Orgasm swept her away, engulfing her. She thrashed between Dominic and Riley, mindless in her pleasure, seeking nothing less than everything from her men.

Riley joined her in ecstasy next, pumping his hips

frantically as he called her name, prolonging the stunning pleasure still rolling through her. Kinley thought it couldn't get better until Dominic ground against her and his cock pulsed deep inside her. He dug his fingers into her hips and howled.

As their movements slowed, then stilled, she dropped onto Riley's chest. Dominic carefully balanced himself over her, whispering soothing kisses along her nape.

Peace. She felt complete blessed peace now, so thick she imagined that absolutely nothing could touch her. Her men surrounded and engulfed her. She hoarded this moment in her memory, just in case the future ripped these three out of her grasp.

Law kissed her cheek. "Baby, I'm going to start up the hot tub. We can all relax in there while we wait for the feds to call."

She felt a little smile cross her face. "Okay."

As Law stood, Kinley nuzzled against Riley's chest once more.

"Shit. I just figured out what Jansen is moving." Law's voice broke through her languor. She looked up to find him staring at the desk in the middle of the office.

Kinley frowned, panic beginning to penetrate her perfect peace.

Chapter Fifteen

Law hated to break up the moment. Three minutes ago, he'd felt like the fucking king of the world. Now he jumped into his sweat pants because they had a job to do.

And it had just gotten harder.

Dominic helped Kinley to her feet, pulling her in for a hug as though he needed to protect her from the truths he knew were coming. "This can't wait until we take care of our sub?"

Riley was on his feet, getting dressed, and there was no way to mistake just how irritated he was. "I told you there's no way to know unless I can break whatever code he's using. It's all in numbers. I know it sounds simple, but it's actually quite difficult without some form of reference. Let's get Kinley settled, and I'll explain cryptography to you."

God, his brother could be a smartass prick at times. "I don't need cryptography. I have eyes. And we're not leaving her out of this discussion."

Kinley shook her head as she shrugged into Riley's oversized T-shirt. It practically hung to her knees. "No, we're not leaving me out. If Law figured out how my ex is using Hope House, then I want to hear it. Could someone pass me my jeans?"

Those jeans were the problem. Law picked them up, but held the denim in his hand. "How many pairs of these did Jansen give you?"

She frowned. "At least ten I think, all with slightly different designs."

"Why were you taking ten pairs of jeans to a tropical island in the summer?"

"Greg said he wanted a fashion show… What a load of crap. Greg never gave a crap about seeing me in anything. I should have known. What's weird about the jeans?" She walked over to him as though to inspect the pants, but her eyes caught on the desk. "Oh, no. Did I do that by sitting on the glass? It wasn't scratched before."

Dominic hustled across the room and stared down at the desk. The massive mahogany desktop was covered in a thick layer of glass, a precaution against damaging the wood. The glass could be replaced. Normally, it would protect against ink stains, heavy machinery, and someone being too rough on the wood.

This time it had taken the cutting brunt of the stones sewn onto Kinley's pockets.

"Holy shit." Dominic touched the grooves etched into the glass. "The feds suspected Jansen was transporting blood diamonds, but no one could prove it. It looks like he found someone to cut them."

"Diamonds?" Kinley asked. "Those are just rhinestones. Most women are wearing a little bling on their pockets these days."

Riley held out his hand, and Law passed him the jeans. As Riley held the pockets up to the light, they sparkled, creating a glorious little light show. "A little bling? This must be a hundred thousand dollars right here. He was going to have Kinley walk right out of the country with a million dollars worth of blood diamonds in her suitcase."

"How can you be sure?" Kinley asked. "Don't you have to study them? Have a gemologist—"

"Baby, rhinestones can't cut glass. The proof is right there on the desk." Law pointed to the scratches she'd left when she'd sat on the desk. He'd kissed her while there, then dragged her toward him, leaving the scratches behind.

"Conflict diamonds come from war-torn countries right?"

"Yes, usually from rebel-held territories in either Liberia or Côte d'Ivoire in West Africa. Reputable buyers won't touch them because of the brutal methods of their mining. So men like Jansen act as intermediaries. He would have smuggled them out and had them cut somewhere, maybe even in Africa. Somehow, he got them here. I'll bet every dime I've got that Jansen has a buyer he planned to meet in Bermuda on your honeymoon," Dominic explained.

"He was going to have you walk them right across the border. No one would question jeans. Airports look for guns and explosives and drugs. They don't look for diamonds, so they would very likely see what Jansen wanted them to see—a girl who likes bling on her pockets," Riley said.

"And if he got caught, he would just say it was all mine." Kinley sat down. "I was the one with all the cryptic stuff on my tablet. I was the one with conflict diamonds on my ass. Hell, I'm a regular criminal mastermind. I guess he was using shipments of new clothing from Africa, supposedly for Hope House, to smuggle his diamonds in."

Law put a hand on her shoulder. "Very likely. That's why he pushed you to start using Third World manufacturers."

"Oh, it wasn't because I was helping out emerging economies, huh?" Her face had gone a deep pink, and she closed herself off.

"Baby, you can't think this is your fault."

Her eyes came up, and a hardness lurked there he hadn't seen before. "Oh, I think I can safely blame myself. I was so naïve. I'm sure he laughed. He probably sat around cackling about what an idiot I was. I really believed him. He said he had contacts with clothing manufacturers who were hiring women at a decent wage, but a decent wage in Africa is different than here. He played me, knowing I wanted to help everyone. I believed every lie he told me because I was too busy getting ready for the wedding to do the research myself. Oh, and worrying about my father, too. Who apparently wasn't wracked with cancer, just busy at the track. God, you must all think I'm a moron."

He tried to reach for her, but she stepped away. "Kinley?"

She shook her head. “Don’t. Just give me a couple of minutes. I’m going to go take a shower.”

Dominic got in her way. “Kinley, pet, no one thinks you’re stupid.”

“I do.” She refused to meet his eyes. “Please, can I just have a minute to myself?”

Riley frowned her way. “The security system is on and I’ll be monitoring the outside cameras. I’ll know if you try to crawl out the window again.”

She sighed. “I’m not trying to run, but I can see where you would think that. I obviously make very poor decisions. Now, can I go to my room for a while? And I’m putting the rest of those jeans in the hallway. Please do something with them. I never want to see them again. I’ll keep this pair, but only until I can get a new one.”

“Yes, we’ll buy you new jeans, pet,” Dominic said. “As soon as we can. Go and take a couple of minutes for yourself, but we’ll have lunch in an hour, and I expect you to be there.”

She didn’t say a word, simply walked out without another glance.

Law started to follow her, but Dominic gripped his arm, staying him. “Give her some time.”

“She’s crying.” Law couldn’t stand it.

“Yes, and it kills me, too, but she wants to be alone. Her pride is aching, and you seeing her in tears won’t help that. She was already on emotional overload, and this pushed her farther.”

“None of us meant to hurt her with the truth,” Riley defended, looking to the door Kinley had just darted through.

True, but Law wished he’d kept his damn mouth closed. He’d never imagined she would react that way.

“Of course not, but all we can do now is give her a little time and space, then let her know she’s not allowed to pull away from us now,” Dominic said.

“I’m not going to let that fucker win.” Law clenched his fists in fury at the thought. “I’m not going to let him take our woman away from us."

"Kinley belongs with us, whether she knows it or not," Dominic said firmly. "And Jansen is an idiot if he actually thought anyone would believe that she was behind this. I think he was counting on not getting caught, then sliding her skinny bitch sister into the role after Kinley's 'untimely accident.'"

"Greg and Becks would have control of Hope House. They would install all their own people and start smuggling anything they wanted. Son of a bitch."

"And those island nations are the perfect place to commit a little murder. Jansen probably already had it staged. He'd probably bribed an official to call it an accident. She would have drowned on her honeymoon." Riley banged his fist on the desk. "We have to kill him."

"Absolutely, but I'm a little worried." Since the moment Law figured Jansen's scheme out, a thousand scenarios had played through his head, all of them crappy. "He had a buyer for these stones. It wasn't like he planned to transport them to the islands and set up a storefront."

Dominic shook his head. "You're right. He's had this planned for a while, which means he probably has a buyer all lined up. He has to get Kinley and the jeans back. He's probably already taken at least a portion of the money. Now he has to deliver the goods. If he's laundering money this way, then he's probably doing it for the mob. They won't like him missing his appointment."

"He must be desperate by now." Riley moved to his computer. "Since he can't go through with the transaction without Kinley and the jeans, maybe we should just wait it out here and let his mob connections take him down."

"He'll go to ground first. Then we'll spend the rest of Kinley's life waiting for him to show." Dominic summed up their problems neatly. "No. I won't have her looking over her shoulder. We have to be sure he's in jail. Or I want to see his body for myself. It's the only way to protect her. Otherwise, he'll come after her because he'll want revenge."

"Why haven't we gotten that call from the feds to make arrangements so we can turn over our evidence?" Law asked, feeling itchy. He didn't like this. "Is there any way Kellan hasn't called the feds yet?"

Riley sat down in front of his keyboard. "No. He swore he'd do it as soon as he and Dominic hung up. Kellan only knows about the encrypted files I found, but still… You're right, Law. I thought we would hear something by now." Riley frowned. "I've got a couple of burner phones left if you want me to make some calls."

Law had a bad feeling—and it was only growing. He'd learned over the years to trust his instincts, and every single one of them was telling him to regroup. "No. We need to move her."

"Where?" Riley asked.

Dominic grabbed his shirt. "Anywhere. Law's right. We grab her luggage and the dogs and we take off. We'll get in touch with some of our friends when we're in the air. Some of our friends who live in Bezakistan are in the country. Perhaps it's time we visited again. If we can get Kinley on a plane with Princess Alea, we can be sure she's safe. Not even Jansen has men inside the royal palace. But I'm beginning to suspect he has a few at the FBI. It's the only explanation for why we haven't at least received a call. They should be all over this."

Adrenaline started pumping through Law's system. "I'll go to the hanger and get the plane ready. Riley, contact Dane Mitchell. See where he, Landon, and Cooper are visiting with Alea. We're going to need help finding a place to land."

"I'll get the dogs." Dominic grimaced. "God, I hope the rat thing cooperates. It's time for her walk and her feeding. You know how much she'll bark if she doesn't get her food on time. I'll take her and Butch out after I move the jeans out of the way. I don't want them to upset her again."

Dominic set off to complete his task.

Riley was already pushing away his keyboard and jumping to his feet. "I just sent Dane a note. He has my cell.

Let's hope he calls before we take off. Otherwise, I'm calling Dex James, and we can head for Dallas to wait for Dane there."

Getting Kinley out of the country seemed like a damn fine plan.

"Tell Kinley what's going on and to get her cute butt in gear because I want to take off in the next hour." The silence from the feds was not a good thing. The quicker they took off, the safer he would feel.

He passed a harried Dominic who was carrying a stack of jeans in one hand and a very excited Gigi in the other. Butch lumbered along behind them. "I'm going to put these in the office before I take the dogs out. I swear Kinley's turned me into her butler."

Despite the adrenaline coursing through his body, he couldn't help but laugh a little. Dominic growled at Gigi, who no longer seemed afraid of the big bad Dom.

Law jogged through the house, disarming and rearming the security system—and grabbing his SIG as he left. The small private landing strip was two hundred yards away from the house, and he wasn't about to run out in the open with no way to defend himself, just in case.

He settled into his preflight checks after gassing up the small jet. Minutes passed in perfect silence.

That's when he heard the gunshots.

* * * *

Kinley turned on the shower and shrugged out of Riley's T-shirt.

What was she doing? She should probably still be with her men, but she'd walked away to lick her wounds. She didn't want them to see her cry or to watch them reevaluate their relationship. They all had to be wondering whether they really wanted a woman who could cause so much trouble.

Greg had used her and he'd done it with a smile on his

face. And why shouldn't he smile? She hadn't given him any trouble at all. He'd just walked in and offered to solve her problems, so she'd stopped asking questions. Brilliant.

When he'd told her to pack ten pairs of jeans for a vacation she normally wouldn't even pack one pair for, what had she done? Exactly as he'd asked because Greg had told her he wanted to see her in them. Like he'd ever stared at her butt before. She snorted.

Now Law, he stared at her butt. She caught him all the time. At this moment, her butt was sore after the spanking and even more thorough fucking. Why did she love the soreness? Why did every little ache remind her of Dominic and the gently forceful way in which he'd taken her?

What was he thinking at this point, that she didn't have a brain in her head?

They would dump her as soon as the feds had Greg in custody. And she couldn't blame them. How much had her actions already cost people? She was transporting diamonds that had been mined by slaves. She was working with factories that probably used child labor.

A sharp knock on the door brought her out of her thoughts. She didn't need anyone to see her like this. "I'm in the shower."

"Kinley, let me in." Riley's voice sounded through the door.

He was the last one she needed. He was so smart. Riley had resisted his physical attraction to her. Now he probably wished he hadn't given in. "I'll be out in ten minutes."

Maybe she could compose herself by then.

There was a slight rustling sound, then the door popped open. Riley had his driver's license in his hand. "Interior doors are a breeze. And you lied. You are not in the shower."

But she was naked. She grabbed a towel. "Privacy please."

He frowned, his eyes on the towel. "Why? You didn't want privacy before. You were perfectly happy to be naked in front of me. Or is it only Dominic and Law you're comfortable around? What happened, Kinley? You decide you didn't really like three men?"

"God, you are so damaged. That's where you go? Everything has to be about you?" She was just about done with his attitude. "It can't be that I just figured out how much of a fool I am? No, we have to go back to your problems and your issues. Go away, Riley. I'll be out when I'm ready."

She turned away from him, brutally aware she'd just been a complete bitch.

Riley's arms wound around her waist and pulled her back. "I'm sorry. It didn't occur to me because I don't think you were a fool. I think you're sweet and loving, and had no way to see this coming. You're far too good for the likes of Jansen…and me. But I'm going to ask you to overlook that little flaw because I'm crazy about you."

Tears filled her eyes. "That's not fair."

She wanted to be alone. She wanted to wail and blame herself for everything and Riley wasn't going to let her.

"It's all right, sweetheart." He said the word like he really meant it, his hand smoothing back her hair as he cuddled her close. "It's okay. You made a mistake, but it was an honest one. You did it because you were hopeful. He took advantage of your giving nature."

"Just like it happened to you." If she could get him to understand that what Simone did wasn't his fault, maybe all the pain would be worth it. "There was nothing wrong with you or Law or what the three of you want. Simone had the problem."

He stared down at her. "All right, Mary Sunshine. I'll go with it, but only if you promise me one thing."

"What?"

"Don't let this change you. Stay as sweet and hopeful as you've always been, and I'll try to find the positive guy inside me." He grimaced. "I'm warning you, though. He's buried deep. It might take me a while."

She could wait. "Okay. It's a deal."

Kinley tilted her head back, looking up at Riley as he kissed her, sealing their deal.

Reluctantly, he pulled back. He reached into the shower, turning the water off. "We need you to skip the shower. No cause for alarm, but we're thinking it might be a good idea to change locations. You know, stay safe, just in case."

"What about the FBI? Aren't they coming to see us?"

Regret skipped across Riley's face. Then the lights flickered and died.

His whole body stilled. When she began to ask about a generator, he shoved a hand over her mouth. His eyes bored into her as he whispered. "No talking. Give it a second."

The lights came back on. And died seconds later. A loud buzzing followed, an alarm signaling something.

"Fuck." Riley paled. "Listen to me very carefully. The security system is offline because someone cut the power to it. The generator is top of the line, and so is the backup. We have to assume someone took both of them out."

Shockwaves pinged through her system. "Do you think it's FBI agents working some sort of sting? They've been looking for me." She'd signed the affidavit that she wasn't a hostage, but who knew if they'd believe that or assume she'd been made to sign under duress.

"The feds would announce themselves, and the feds know what we're doing. I'm starting to think that Jansen has someone on the inside, and we're screwed. Here's what's going to happen. Jansen wants the diamonds. I have to hide them. If he gets his hands on them, he'll kill us all. My gun—Damn it, my gun is back in the office. Law is out at the hangar, and Dominic should be rounding up the dogs."

"Greg is here?" Oh, god, if he was in this house, he was coming after her. And he wouldn't come alone.

Suddenly, she heard an odd popping sound.

"Gunfire. Shit. Sweetheart, I need you to hide. I'm not sure where that gunfire came from, maybe the back of the house."

Kinley grabbed the clothes she'd brought in with her. She'd picked them up without thinking. She was holding a pair of jeans covered in blood diamonds. She never wanted to see another pair of jeans again.

An idea struck her. She quickly opened the medicine cabinet. There was a nail file, the metal kind with a nice pointed end. She went to work on the stitching in the back pocket. After a couple of good twists, it was easy to pull the heavy scrap of fabric apart from the rest of the pants. "We need to hide the diamonds, but the actual jeans are bulky and it would take too much time to pry each stone off individually." She reached for the bottle of her favorite shampoo. She dumped half of it into the shower and then stuffed the pockets in one at a time.

Riley kissed the top of her head. "I will spank you if ever call yourself dumb again. You're brilliant. He needs them all. Every single diamond."

She nodded. "All right, but I think Dominic took the rest of them. I don't know where they are."

"I do. He took them to the office. He was going to put them in a bag or something so you didn't have to look at them." Riley's face tightened. "I need to get to those jeans."

Riley hesitated, but Kinley knew his brothers could be out there dying right now. Her men were in danger, and she would do anything she could to stop it. "Go. I'll stay and be exactly what Greg expects me to be—a hostage. He won't kill me."

"You don't know that, Kinley."

No, but… "You have to leave. Greg and his goons could be here any minute." Her hands were shaking as she pushed him away. "Go. If you can find a way to get to the jeans, hide more of the diamonds. Hurry. We're running out of time. He won't kill me until he has them all. Can you get out the bathroom window?"

Riley drew her close, kissing her hard. "I can get out of it. You stay alive. Do you understand me?"

With a nod, she dashed into her room, the damaged jeans in her hand. She folded the jeans neatly, so the damage didn't show. Her heart pounding, she retreated to the bathroom where Riley was just disappearing through the high window.

She was alone.

"Kinley!" Greg's voice floated from down the hallway, inciting a sharp pang of terror. She bit her lip. Being brave didn't come naturally to her, but she had to find that within her now. "Come out, you bastards. There's no place to hide!"

He was getting close. She had seconds to decide how to play this.

Hide in plain sight. Like the diamonds.

She turned the shower on again. There was really only one thing to do. God, she didn't want to do it, but she pulled his shirt over her head and stepped into the shower. Cold water sluiced down her skin. She shook but forced herself to soap her hair.

The door shook as it came open.

"What do you want, you assholes? Are you going to rape me now? Trust me, the cold shower is working just fine to soften me up. I swear when my fiancé gets ahold of you, you're going to be sorry."

"Kinley?"

She hated the very sound of Greg's voice, but she forced herself to gasp in surprise and poke her head out of the shower. "Greg?" She asked the question tentatively as though utterly hopeful. "Oh, my god. Is it really you?"

He was standing there wearing dark pants and a black turtleneck. It was elegant, but now Kinley saw why he'd chosen it—black wouldn't show the blood he intended to spill. He was a well-dressed viper, waiting to strike.

He was also a damn fine actor. His face softened. "Oh, my sweetheart. I thought they had killed you."

He reached out his hand. With her stomach in knots, Kinley took it.

Chapter Sixteen

Dominic hid behind the west wall of the house, moving as silently as he could across the deck. The key was to stay close to the wall. He edged along, stopping every few seconds to listen and ensure that no one was sneaking up behind him.

Surely someone had heard the gunshots. One of Jansen's men would walk out any minute now and see the dead body on the lawn, but Dominic didn't have time to hide it. He needed to get into the house and get Kinley out. Unless Riley had already done it. He'd been the only one in the house with her. Dominic prayed that his brother had heard the gunshot and spirited her out to the hangar with Law. They had weapons there—and a radio. With any luck, Riley, Law, and Kinley were holed up and formulating a plan, just waiting for him to reach them.

Or his brother could be dead, and Kinley could be at the mercy of a man who had none.

What the fuck had gone wrong? This was all his fault. He should have moved her once a day, but no. He'd been so sure that no one would find them in the wilderness. Breaking Kinley down had been more important than protecting her from the monster she'd nearly married.

Dominic cursed under his breath. Guilt threatened to overwhelm him. He should have thought of her first. He should have put his revenge on hold and simply helped an innocent woman.

But then he would never have known what it was like to hold her, to watch her laugh, to love her.

God, he was in love with her, and now she might die.

Gigi yipped as though barking at him to move him along.

He looked down at the two dogs following at his heels. If he hadn't been in the woods while they ran around and did their business, he might have heard Jansen's SUV coming up the road himself.

"Hush," he hissed as quietly as he could.

Butch sat back on his haunches, looking up. He was a good little soldier, the mutt. But Gigi was one high-strung rat thing. It was probably getting close to meal time for her. And she was going to get him killed if she didn't shut up.

"Handle your woman," he muttered to Butch as he continued his slow, creeping steps toward the back door.

"How did you find me?" Kinley's voice was soft, but he could hear her through the thick pane of glass. He was standing right beside the window to her bedroom. His heart threatened to leap out of his chest when he realized who was in there with her.

"I have my ways, darling. I'm just so glad that I got here in time. You have no idea what the last few days have been like." Jansen's voice was deep with emotion. Dominic would hand it to him for that Oscar-worthy performance. "Tell me, Kinley, did they hurt you?"

He heard her sniffle a little. "Yes."

What game was she playing?

"How?"

"They scared me, Greg. They drugged me. They threatened my dog. They kept me awake for long periods of time. They tied me up. And then, just when I thought they were letting up because they allowed me a shower, they made it ice cold. They were going to make me as uncomfortable as possible. I don't know why. Why does that man hate you?"

Oh, he was so going to smack her ass for ever calling herself stupid.

Law was in the hangar. Kinley was with the enemy. Where was Riley? God, he had to pray his brother wasn't in there with Kinley.

"If it's who I think it is, darling, then he hates me because I was married to his sister," Greg said. "You know how I felt about Carrie. I loved her. It took me years to find another wife I felt I could care for as much. She was just…well, she was broken. I've kept this secret for far too long, but she told me her brother sexually abused her. He's insane, Kinley. Which is precisely why I need you to gather all of your things so we get you out of here. He could hurt you. He would do it because he knows it would kill me."

Dominic's vision nearly went red. He wanted to throttle that fucker. How *dare* he?

"You mean, he isn't in custody?" Kinley asked. "Didn't you come with the police?"

Dominic calmed slightly because he could hear the worry in her voice. Greg would think she was worried for herself, but Dominic knew the truth. His brave and smart sub was worried for her Master. She was doing such a good job. He couldn't let his temper get them all killed. For the first time in years, he'd found something he needed more than revenge. He'd found Kinley Kohl.

Greg hesitated. "Darling, I have some men looking for him now, but the police wouldn't come and arrest him because you signed that affidavit."

The one Greg could only know about because he had a source inside the FBI, just as Dominic had suspected.

"They made me sign," she said quickly, putting just the right amount of tears in her voice. "I think they were trying to buy time. Surely, the police are still looking for me. I-I was worried they would kill me if I didn't sign. I was so afraid."

Dominic needed to figure out how many men Jansen had brought with him. He'd killed one, but there were surely more. He'd caught the one coming out of the building that housed the generator. He'd seen the SUV as soon as he emerged from the woods. It could likely hold up to eight people.

One down, potentially seven to go.

And he still didn't know where his brothers were.

Looking up and down the deck, Dominic tried to decide which direction to go. The front would surely be guarded, but the house was rambling and massive. He probably had the best shot at getting in around the back.

Dominic started easing in that direction. Leaving Kinley was hell, but he couldn't shoot the fucker through the windows. The James brothers were paranoid about their wife and kids. The glass was damn near bulletproof.

He started to work his way down the porch.

And then he heard the creak that told him someone else was walking on the wooden structure as well. He stilled, holding himself perfectly quiet.

Gigi ran forward, yipping like a maniac.

The minute Gigi pranced off, Butch darted after her. They ran toward the back, barking all the way.

A gunshot split through the air.

Gigi yipped, and Butch growled. Then the motherfucker showed himself.

Dominic took the shot. The man in black went down.

Two down, possibly six to go. But, fuck, he was going to invest in a silencer or he would get caught because it was so damn quiet out here. If they were in New York, no one would notice him defending himself.

But they were in the fucking wilds of Alaska, and the sounds of birds chirping did nothing to muffle the sound of a gun going off.

"Hold it!" A voice called out.

Dominic heard another shot, felt a bullet whiz by his left arm.

"I got him, too!" A voice from behind him yelled.

He could shoot one, but then the other would take him out, no problem. He could try to fight but he would lose. Once upon a time, that wouldn't have bothered him. He would have died simply to avenge Carrie.

But then he'd met Kinley. He'd held her and loved her. He'd dreamed of a future with her and his brothers. She'd accepted him for the good and the bad and the kinky. She'd taken everything he had to give her.

He could fight and die. But that's not what Carrie would have wanted. She would have expected him to live for Kinley.

Now he just might die for her, too.

Dominic let the gun drop. "You won't find the diamonds without me."

He would take the beating, the humiliation that was sure to come, in order to give his brothers and their woman some time to escape.

He dropped his gun, opening himself to simply being killed on the spot. Thirty-one years into his life, and he'd finally found his true weakness: A sweet submissive with honey blonde hair and a smile like the sun. His love. His wife.

He would die so she could have a chance to live.

But he wouldn't die without a fight. "I know where the diamonds are. You need those, don't you? Your boss will be very upset if you kill the only man who can lead you to them."

"Fuck. Don't shoot him yet. Jansen needs to hear this." The one on his right kicked the gun out of the way.

The one on his left moved in. "Put your hands over your head."

Dominic held his hands up, though it pained him. In the distance, he saw movement by the hanger. A single figure shifted, as though taking in the danger before hiding himself again.

Law had seen him. Law knew what had happened. Law would do what it took.

Even if he died, Law would come for Kinley. If both he and Riley died, Law would kill them all and then take care of Kinley.

As lousy as the situation was, this was exactly why he'd sought a ménage. No one had been there for Carrie. When Greg had seen her as a paycheck, she'd been all alone. Three men were fighting for Kinley. She had three chances to live because every single one of them would die for her. He could relax because his brothers had his back.

"Where the fuck are the diamonds?" The man on his right shoved the barrel of his gun to his temple, jarring his head.

"I'm not saying anything to you. I'll only talk to Jansen." He needed to give Law time to do his thing. There was no doubt that Law was taking in everything, his brilliant battle mind deciding how to kill these assholes most efficiently and lethally. Law knew how to take down the enemy. He only needed time.

A foot kicked the middle of his back, and Dominic fell to his knees. Jansen's goon tucked the barrel of his gun between Dominic's neck and brain stem. One shot and he was done. "Tell me now or I shoot."

A vision of Kinley reaching for him wafted across his brain. She'd smiled slightly, like a beneficent goddess. She'd drawn them together, accepting them all. Happiness might have been short lived, but while it lasted, it had been glorious.

"No. I'm only talking to Jansen." Dominic closed his eyes and waited for whatever happened. It was so far from his usual behavior that he laughed.

"Get up, then." Someone roughly grabbed him and jerked him to his feet. "You want to talk to the boss, fine. But we're tying your hands first. I have some zip ties in my bag. We cuff him then take him to the boss."

As soon as they had bound his wrists behind him, Dominic began the long walk to the back door, every step bringing him closer to Kinley. At least he would get to see her one last time.

* * * *

Law watched as two assholes hauled Dominic along, forcing him to walk to the back of the house.

He didn't have a shot. If he'd had a sniper rifle on him, he could blow them away, but he didn't. He had his SIG Sauer and two hundred yards between him and two moving targets.

And whichever one he didn't nail first would run and warn the rest of his crew, no doubt.

He had one chance to get back in that house.

Where was Riley? God, where was Kinley? He hoped they were together. He prayed Riley had holed up with her and hidden them well.

A thousand questions ran through his head, but in the end he didn't care who had come or why. He only cared that he killed every fucker who had walked into that house, threatening his family. He would kill and kill and kill until he got to their woman. That was his job now.

He moved from the right to the left, hugging the hanger, keeping his body low as they walked Dominic along the west wall of the house to the back door. All their attention was on Dominic. He disappeared inside with a gun poking the back of his neck.

And someone was moving from the east side of the house, his body close to the walls.

Riley. His brother was alive.

Law moved along the building, trying to reach the shortest distance between him and that back porch. Two hundred yards. He had to get there without taking a bullet.

Adrenaline rushed through his system.

Riley looked out over the space between them. He stilled, his body going utterly motionless.

Law's prayers were answered as Riley saw him. He glanced behind him, before motioning Law on.

Law took off, his feet darting across the ground in utter silence. All his years of training rushed back to him, making his every move a graceful leap of faith. He stalked the distance between him and Jansen's thugs. He'd marked them for death. He would find them.

"Where the hell is Kinley?" Law asked between gritted teeth as he caught up to his brother.

Their backs were against the wall, each looking in the opposite direction, waiting for the threat.

"She's with Jansen."

Law was going to kill his brother. "You were supposed to stay with her."

"Jansen isn't going to kill her," Riley quietly explained. "He wants his diamonds too badly, so he's letting her think that he's rescuing her for now. This gives her time and a chance. I heard some of their conversation, and she's pretending that she's still afraid of us. If I had stayed, Jansen and his goons would probably have threatened to kill me. The truth would have come out, and they would have used me as leverage against Kinley."

"Yes, but now he'll take off with her." God, Jansen was probably getting ready to do that right now.

Panic threatened to overwhelm Law. He was an ice man, always cool under pressure, but the thought of his wife being taken hostage was just about enough to give him a heart attack and to send him running straight into that house like a madman.

Wife. She was their wife. It didn't matter that they hadn't taken vows. It didn't matter that he'd never told her he loved her. She was theirs, and he refused to let her go.

"He won't go anywhere without these." Riley pulled a piece of denim out of his pocket. "With the security system off, I managed to sneak in the side door before that asswipe put a guard on it. I snagged a pair of scissors and pulled the pockets off seven pairs before I heard them coming. I had to leave the rest there. I just managed to creep out. Between what I have and what Kinley hid, we've managed to tuck away about eighty percent of those diamonds. He's not going anywhere without them."

So they had some kind of leverage. But so did Jansen. "He has Dominic."

Riley's eyes flared. "Are you kidding me?"

Law shook his head. "No. We're all off our game, and we need to get the fuck back on it. Do you know how many men Jansen brought with him?"

"I know there's a dead body near the front lawn. I'm pretty sure that was Dominic's work. Inside, there's Jansen, Dargo, whom we saw in the elevator in New York, and at least one guy on all three of the doors."

"I think one left his post to bring Dominic in, maybe two." They needed to get in the house. He pulled his spare piece and handed it to his brother. "Take an extra clip."

Riley flipped the safety off his handgun and slid the extra clip into his pocket. "Let's head to the side door."

"If we can take them down quietly, let's do it."

Jansen might be able to guess that Dominic had two accomplices since he and Riley had kidnapped Kinley. And because Jansen was Dominic's former brother-in-law, the asswipe probably knew a thing or two about who Dominic shared a sex life with. Given that, Jansen probably knew how much manpower Dominic had. So taking these fuckers by surprise would be tough but critical.

"What the hell do we do if they threaten Kinley?"

Eventually, they would do just that to force her to tell them what she knew. When she refused, they would kill her. "We have to take them out first."

Or die trying.

There was a high-pitched yipping from the other side of the house. Gigi ran around the corner, her tiny body darting through the grass. She yipped and howled and jumped as though trying to get their attention.

They didn't need that.

Gigi ran onto the porch and right to the back door, clawing at it in an attempt to get in.

Someone would come to investigate. Shit. He had mere seconds.

Law crossed the space and put his back to the outer wall.

The door swung open. A man leaned out, his whole focus on Kinley's little dog.

"What the fuck?" the suited-up criminal asked.

Suddenly, Butch gave a low growl as he made his

appearance. Jansen's tool stepped onto the deck and stared at the dogs. It was just enough of a distraction for Law to slide behind the man. Before Jansen's guard could lift his gun or fight back, Law had his head in his hands. With a vicious twist, a neat crunch filled the air as he broke his opponent's neck and released him. The goon slid to the ground.

The dogs both stepped around the body as they trotted into the house. Thank god the rat thing was an inside princess.

"Gigi, stay." He kept his voice down. Butch obeyed, so Gigi sat beside him. It wasn't exactly obedience, but at least she wasn't interested in biting the males in her mistress's life anymore.

And she was a creature of habit. Once they'd settled in here in Alaska, he'd noticed that. Kinley had that dog on a schedule. It was past her damn feeding time and Gigi would run through the house barking until someone fed or killed her.

Law looked down the hall. No one. He looked back and gave his brother the go sign.

"Remind me to be more polite to you in the future," Riley whispered.

"Put the dogs outside." Kinley would kill them if some prick shot her dog.

His brother stepped over the dead body and entered the house, shaking his head. "I have a better plan. It's about time that thing earned her keep. Follow me."

Law followed, praying they were in time.

* * * *

Kinley tried to give Greg her best blank expression. "Why would they do that to my gorgeous jeans? I loved them."

She sniffled a little. The tears were real. She was scared out of her mind, but she wasn't about to show him that. She would let him think that her eyes were watery because she couldn't stand the thought of her clothes being damaged.

Greg had turned red as he held the jeans up. He seemed to

visibly take control of his reactions. “Darling, I need you to tell me where the men who held you are. And where they’ve stashed the rest of your luggage.”

She shook her head. He’d allowed her to get dressed in pajama bottoms and a tank top, but she’d felt utterly humiliated at being naked in front of him. It wasn’t right. Her body was meant for Law, Riley, and Dominic. She’d felt dirty with Greg’s eyes on her. “I don’t know. This was all they left me.”

“And where did they go?”

She didn’t like the way his tone kept dropping. “I have no idea. They told me I had ten minutes to shower, and then they closed the door and left me in the bathroom.”

His eyes narrowed. “Kinley, the door was unlocked when I opened it. Why wouldn’t your kidnappers lock you in?”

They had, at first, but since she’d started sleeping with them, the trust had built. But she wasn’t about to tell Greg that. “I thought it was locked. I guess they just think I’m too dumb to run.” She took a shaky breath. “I’m really just too afraid. There are wild animals out there.”

There was a brief knock on the door, then Greg’s right-hand, Vincent Dargo, opened it. “Bad news, boss. I just found Benny on the front lawn. He wasn’t the shooter, but the one getting his ass shot. Alan isn’t responding to my radio calls. We got trouble and we should move out.”

“You haven’t found Anthony? He probably has those two fuckheads with him. Make sure there’s a guard on every door. You check through every room of this house. I want that luggage.”

Vincent grimaced. “Already found it. Uhm, some of the jeans are there, but I only found two pairs with the dia…pockets attached.”

Greg held up the ones in his hand. “The rest are like this?”

Vincent nodded. “Yeah. Anthony and whoever he’s with probably got away with them. I think they took the product and ran. They could be in the fucking woods by now.”

Greg turned his focus on her, but the sweet act was gone. His voice became darker. "What do you think, darling? Do you think they're in the woods?"

What had she forgotten? Kinley's mind raced with possibilities. Because he was obviously not buying her act anymore. "I don't know."

"I'm going to give you one more chance, Kinley. First, explain the red handprints on your ass. You told me they simply scared you so I have to assume the spanking was consensual. Do you think I'm an idiot? Do you think I don't know what that fucker Anthony and his perverted friends are into? I might have been able to believe you if I hadn't seen the proof of it myself. So try again, you fucking whore."

There was a certain freedom in being able to let go of her ruse. "So I take it you're willing to admit that Dominic didn't abuse his sister. You killed her. The same way you planned to kill me."

Greg's whole demeanor changed, the concern sliding off his face and revealing the snake that resided under his skin. "Oh, my darling girl, I'm going to be so much rougher with you. I let Vince put Carrie down easy, but then she wasn't a whore. She simply heard too much one night and was going to tell her brother everything. Now, tell me where my diamonds are."

If she told him, she was dead. He very likely had a plan in place to frame Dominic for her murder and call it his sadistic revenge. So she couldn't tell Greg what she'd done. She had to hope that Riley had gotten away and found Law and Dominic, and that they wouldn't leave her.

"I really don't know."

Greg slapped her right across the face. Kinley was shocked at the pain that lashed through her system. Within seconds, her skin began to swell, her flesh aching.

He tossed the jeans aside. "You stupid whore. Do you know what you've done?"

"Found out how good sex with three real men can be?"

He wound his hand in her hair, pulling it until her scalp screamed. "Your sister told me you were cold as ice. I believed her. I should have known that a woman always thinks with her cunt. Now, I can beat the holy fuck out of you all day long and everyone will blame your kidnappers. I have friends in the FBI. How do you think I got out of the first RICO charge? They managed to intercept your little lawyer friends' messages. They also found Anthony's ties to a company called Black Oak Oil. I thought it interesting that Black Oak had a company jet leave from New York the same day you were taken with a flight plan filed for Alaska. And that they also own this compound. It didn't take much to put two and two together when you can get a federal wiretap going. So you should know that I intend to visit your little friend Annabelle after I take care of you. I'll pay that bitch back and make sure the lawyers who helped Anthony never work again."

The thought of Greg taking revenge on Annabelle and her employers chilled Kinley, strengthened her resolve. She just had to survive, to take whatever he dished out. "No, I don't think so because I think whoever we were meeting in Bermuda will get to you first. I think that person is going to want their diamonds, and, oh, how sad, you seem to have lost them."

She braced herself, but he merely tightened his grip in her hair and started to drag her along.

Pain exploded along her scalp as he walked toward the center of the house.

"Vince, I think it's time we showed little Kinley here what we're capable of. She got herself kidnapped, but those dipshits haven't really hurt her. I think we should make up for that. I wouldn't want her to miss out on the full hostage experience."

Vincent was behind her, pushing her along when she stumbled. "I agree. And though I know you like your women a little less chunky, I never minded fucking one with some meat on her bones. I can handle the rape portion of her experience."

Nausea welled. The thought of anyone else touching her made her stomach turn.

"Thank you for that. I definitely preferred fucking her sister." He turned to face Kinley. "Did you know your sister is the one who offered you up to me? She's going to be my wife after you're dead. She'll be thrilled to know that I had one of my employees fuck you. Or you can tell us where the diamonds are and we can kill you quickly." Greg shoved her toward the couch in the main living room. To her left was the kitchen, in front of her the hallway that led to the office, and to the right were the massive bay windows that showed Kinley just how isolated they were.

No sign of anyone except Greg's hired muscle.

She was all alone. The feds weren't coming because the corrupt officers would stop them. Annabelle's bosses were thousands of miles away, and Kinley had no idea where her men were.

Vincent reached into his boot and brought out a wicked looking knife. It was black, and she had little doubt what it had been made for—killing. "I like playing games, too, you little whore."

Greg stared down at her. "If I had known you were into the kinky shit, I would have let Vince fuck you before the wedding. You're nothing but a piece of ass to a man, including the ones who kidnapped you. Do you really think Dominic Anthony gives a shit about you?"

She didn't reply, simply stared out that window, praying for a glimpse of them.

"Anthony just wants revenge," Greg said. "He wants me. He'll go to any lengths for it, including fucking my fiancée. Hell, I bet he enjoyed that since I screwed his sister. You were just a payback for him. Nothing more."

Maybe they had run. Maybe they were trying to get help.

"Why would you think you could even get a man? You're twenty-five and the only man who ever asked you to marry him did it because you're a naïve little idiot. If you honestly think those men wanted to fuck you, you're dumber than I thought."

She hated him. God, she hated him because he was really good at bringing out that nasty voice in her head, the one that told her she wasn't good enough for Law, Dominic, and Riley, that she wasn't smart enough or pretty enough. It was his true talent. He likely got a lot of women to hate themselves. Then they gave in to him.

But she could still feel Dominic's arms around her. His embrace hadn't felt like revenge. It had felt like what she'd imagined love should be. Law hadn't been tricking her. Riley had fought the whole way…and still ended up wanting her.

The door from the kitchen swung open and her worst nightmare came through. Dominic's hands were bound behind his back, and it looked like they'd already worked him over a bit. His eye was swollen and there was a trickle of blood on his chin.

She couldn't hold back the little gasp that fell from her mouth. Fear seized her.

"Ah, Mr. Anthony, it's so nice to see you again." That reptilian smile crossed Greg's face as he looked over the prisoner.

"Sorry I can't say the same." Dominic didn't look her way, just kept his eyes on Greg, not sparing her a glance.

Greg turned to his cohorts. "Did it really take two of you to bring him in? Is Ross the only one still at his station? Vince, take charge of Mr. Anthony. You two get back to your posts. There are still two of them potentially out there. I'm going to have a little talk with my bride and Mr. Anthony. Then we'll see what happens."

The two thugs left, and Vincent took Dominic by the arm, forcing him to his knees.

Seeing him that way hurt Kinley's heart. He was always in charge, always in control. How humiliating it must be for him to be on his knees, at the mercy of his enemy.

"I'll help you look," Kinley offered. "Just don't hurt him."

Dominic's head came up. "What are you doing?"

Greg laughed, a nasty little sound. "She's being her true,

idiotic self, Anthony. You fucked her, and now she thinks it's love. How about it? Do you love her? Is she your little sweetheart?"

Dominic's eyes slid away from hers. "Of course I don't love her. I barely know her."

The words hurt, but she knew what he was doing. He was trying to save her, right? He had to be. He couldn't exactly declare himself here and now.

"It doesn't matter. I'll still help you if you leave Dominic alone." She had to get the focus off Dominic.

"Kinley, you will not go anywhere with him." Dominic seemed to think he was still in charge of her at least.

"Ah, so you do have some feelings for the girl." Greg hauled her up again. "Tell me where the diamonds are or I might decide that I'm bored." He ran a hand up to her breast. "I might have to find a way to amuse myself. I like it when they scream, don't you, Anthony?"

Now Dominic was looking straight at her with murder in his eyes. "Get your fucking hands off her."

She caught sight of something moving in the background. Gigi ran into the room, heading toward the kitchen door. She barked as Butch loped into the room behind her.

It was feeding time. Gigi always reminded her it was dinnertime by standing at her bowl and barking incessantly. Her bowl was in the kitchen where the tiny dog was headed.

For the merest moment both Vincent and Greg had their eyes on the chaos that had just run in.

She heard a gunshot, then saw Dominic rear back, catching Vincent in the gut with the back of his head.

Kinley took advantage of the distraction by pulling her elbow and bringing it straight to Greg's chest. He cursed and stepped back.

"Kinley, get down!" Law yelled as he entered the room, his gun drawn. He popped off a quick shot, hitting Vincent Dargo before the man could recover.

"Drop the weapon, Jansen. I took out everyone you

brought along," Law said, his eyes on Greg.

"And I arranged the distraction with the dog," Riley said, holding his gun up. "That little bitch is getting a treat. So you really should drop the gun. The game is over."

Greg had never lost his footing. He stood tall. "Don't you two realize? The game is never over. I'm not going to be taken in."

Time seemed to slow down. Greg raised his gun and aimed, and Kinley could see exactly where the bullet would hit. Dominic scrambled to his feet, but his hands were bound behind his back.

He was helpless.

Without thinking of anything but saving Dominic, Kinley jumped just as Greg fired the gun.

She heard the sound of more gunfire splitting the air. It seemed to come from everywhere all at once.

And then she felt fire in her chest, an agony unlike anything she felt before. The air left her lungs. She gasped as she hit the floor.

Dominic's panicked face suddenly loomed over her. "Oh, god. She's hit. Get me out of these fucking ties."

Hit. It didn't feel like she'd been hit. This was so much worse, like her chest had imploded. Fire scorched her lungs, taking away all the oxygen and leaving her gasping for the tiniest bit of breath.

But Dominic was alive and unharmed.

She held on to that thought as the world went dark.

Chapter Seventeen

The nurse took the tray from her bedside table. “You didn’t eat anything, hon. You have to eat to get your strength back or they won’t ever let you out of here.”

Kinley looked over at the nurse. She was the nicest one Kinley had found since she’d been admitted to the hospital in Anchorage two days before. “I don’t know why the doctor won’t release me now. The surgery went fine.” The bullet had merely nicked her lung.

She was ready to go home. Well, to whatever home she had left. And it appeared she would be going alone.

Two days and no visitors. No phones calls. Nothing.

She was alone again.

“Well, you need time to rest. You’ve been through a lot. And the press figured out where you are. The hospital is surrounded by news vans. Doctor Craig is keeping them all away with some help from the police, too.”

Ah, the police. “I’m sure they want to talk to me. I should just get it over with.”

The nurse patted her hand. “I’ll tell the doctor you said you were ready. He’s been holding them off because he’s worried about you. You’ve been…withdrawn. Do you think you’re up for a visitor? There’s a young woman out there who’s very insistent on seeing you. We’ve checked her out, and she isn’t a member of the press. This woman says her name is Annabelle Wright. Would you like to see her?”

Belle had come all the way to Anchorage? At least Kinley had one person she could count on through thick and thin. She nodded at the nurse. “Please.”

Two minutes later, Annabelle rushed in, heels clicking on the cheap linoleum tiles, carrying a massive bouquet of flowers. "Oh, girl, you are going to be the death of me. Thank God you're all right."

Tears welled in Annabelle's dark eyes as she set the flowers down and reached for Kinley's hand.

"Hey, I'm okay." She felt better with Annabelle here. A sense of comfort eased through her. It didn't stop the pain of Dominic, Law, and Riley's absence, but settled over the wound like a bandage. If she could stop the bleeding, maybe healing would follow. "You didn't have to come all this way."

Annabelle shook her head. "Of course, I did. God, Kinley, I got you into this. I agreed to help. I didn't imagine it would go so wrong."

"If anyone is to blame, it's me. I wouldn't listen to you about Greg being an obnoxious douchebag killer." Kinley took a long breath. "Speaking of, I need to hire a lawyer. Can your guys recommend someone for me? I have to sue my sister."

Annabelle's eyes grew wide. "They haven't let you watch TV?"

"I didn't want to." The last thing she wanted was to see the press interviewing Law, Riley, and Dominic, all alive and happy without her.

"Your sister has been arrested for embezzlement. The files on your iPad showed plainly that she was the one who moved the money around. Then pictures of her with Greg Jansen doing the nasty surfaced. Your brother-in-law has already filed for divorce and is bringing the kids back from boarding school."

So those sweet kids would finally get the life they deserved. "I'm glad. So the FBI is investigating?"

Annabelle huffed. "You have no idea. They've impounded the diamonds, including the ones they found in the shampoo bottles. Nice job there, Kin. They're investigating everything. They realized they have an internal leak."

One that had sent Greg Jansen straight to their hideout,

where he'd almost killed Dominic. Instead, he'd shot her.

She could still hear Greg's voice telling her all the things that were wrong with her. He'd preferred her sister. He'd wanted someone thinner, someone blonder. Someone more devious. "I hope they find the leak."

"My bosses are going to force them to. They were wiretapping us. You do not do that to lawyers without expecting some backlash." She sighed a little.

"Well, thank them for me, please. You saved me from a tropical death, so it seems. You were the only one willing to step up and do it."

No one in her family loved her. She would have to be grateful that Dominic had loved his sister enough to spend years bringing her killer to justice. Kinley had to be satisfied that she'd helped with that effort. But the men themselves…they were obviously gone. She'd probably been a total fool—again—to trust them, but she'd always think of those few days at the James compound as some of her happiest.

Annabelle squeezed her hand. "Gosh, Kinley, I'm so sorry they hurt you. I always knew Becks was a nasty bitch, but I can't believe she'd actually steal from you and plot to kill you. And your dad is being investigated for his participation. If I had to guess, I think he's going down, too."

So everyone was getting what they deserved. Somehow it didn't make her feel better. It just depressed her more. The one bright spot was her niece and nephew coming home. Kinley had to be happy for that. She only hoped that Brian would allow her into the kids' lives.

"It's okay. I'll survive." Kinley tried to shrug, but the wound in her chest was stiff and sore. "I guess I need to find a job."

Her charity was surely in limbo until the investigation was over, but she worried that with all the scandal it would go under anyway. She needed to be able to feed herself and buy kibble for her dog—and any puppies that came from her illicit union.

Annabelle stared at her blankly, blinking in confusion. "Why would you do that? I mean, you need to wait until you've settled into your new place in Dallas. Once the feds clear Hope House, you can start up again or find different work, if you want. I personally think you should sell your engagement ring to fund the reopening of Hope House, but I don't think those guys are going to let you get too far away."

"Guys? Dallas?" She'd never actually been to Dallas. Why would Annabelle think she was moving to Dallas? Though she would definitely sell the ring. She liked the idea of hundreds of children being clothed by Greg's ring. "I've really been thinking about coming to Chicago. Hopefully, I can find a job there."

Annabelle was the only person on the planet that Kinley knew loved her. She trusted Belle more than anyone. It made sense to move closer to her best friend.

"Oh, no." Annabelle squeezed her hand. "Sweetie, where do you think your men are?"

She shrugged, not wanting to have this particular conversation. "I don't know. The job was over. Mission accomplished. I'm sure they moved on." Kinley looked away. "They aren't mine."

"Who do you think these flowers are from? If I'd bought it, you would have two daisies, honey. But this is a really expensive arrangement. Those men gave me very specific instructions about what to buy you."

She glanced at the bouquet. They were high end, beautiful and expensive. The vase looked to be crystal. So at least they had wanted to send her something. They hadn't come in person…but she supposed she would have to mean something to them for that. "I'll send them a thank you note."

It would be polite and formal. *Dear Dominic, Riley, and Law, Thank you so much for the lovely floral arrangement and for saving my life. It was a kind thing to do. And I truly appreciated the lessons in sexuality and ménage. I will never forget the spankings. They meant so much to me. Sincerely, Kinley Kohl. P.S., you owe me for puppy support.*

Annabelle's phone chirped. She fished it out of her purse, then looked down at the screen. Her face lit up. "They made it inside. You have no idea how crazy it is out there. They've been trying to make their way in here for hours. Wait a second."

She turned to the door and opened it. A man walked through wearing scrubs and carrying a clipboard. Two more men in scrubs followed him.

Her heart seized when she realized that under the bland clothes and masks, it was Riley, Law, and Dominic.

Law tore his mask away and stepped up to her side, his eyes wide. His expression softened as he took her in. "Baby, tell us everything. We've been dying. Are you all right?"

They were here. Why? "Uhm, I've been here for days. I'm alive. Don't worry about me."

Dominic took her hand. "And we've been in a forty-eight-hour hold. The FBI has been questioning the hell out of us. They didn't have to give us a phone call or any rights. And the hospital is in virtual lockdown because of the media frenzy out there. Annabelle only got in because Tate threatened to sue the hospital. We had to sneak in to see you, Kinley."

Riley moved around to her opposite side and cupped her cheek. "Are you okay? They wouldn't tell us anything. They said we weren't husbands or family, so we didn't have rights to your information. God, I hated every moment they kept us away from you. We need to fix that."

He tried to pull her gently into an embrace.

What the hell were they talking about? She held herself stiffly until Riley eased back with a frown. "Who kept you away?"

She still didn't quite understand why Law, Dominic, and Riley had come. When she'd awakened alone, that had felt like a statement—one full of finality. She'd heard all those voices in her head that told her she wasn't good enough or pretty enough. That she would never be what three incredible men wanted. No one had been there to hold her hand or talk to her or reassure her that everything would be all right. Because no one cared.

"We've been saying that we were held for questioning, pet." Dominic reached for her other hand. "Do you understand? They held us the full forty-eight hours because your doctors wouldn't allow you to answer questions. And our lawyers took their damn time getting here."

Tears threatened. She couldn't deny how much she loved seeing them, even if she wasn't sure why they'd come. Guilt? "No one said anything. They wouldn't even tell me what happened to Gigi."

"We hired a dog sitter," Law said quickly. "We flew them out on a private plane. She's fine. She and Butch are going to be here tomorrow so we can all fly out together."

So they planned to take her home. That was nicer than making her find her own way back. She supposed that was the polite thing to do, given that they weren't really in the kidnapping business. "It will be good to get back to New York."

"You're not going to New York." Law crossed his arms over his chest in a deeply forbidding gesture. "You're going to Dallas."

Riley's jaw firmed stubbornly. "You're not going anywhere but home with us, Kinley. I know you'll have things to clear up there, but not until the press's interest dies down. We're going to hole up at Dominic's."

"It's our place, not just mine anymore. It's our home, and we want to take you there with us." Dominic took her hand.

Why? The question floated through Kinley's head, but she didn't speak it. What was the purpose? To put them in the position where they had to explain the duty they felt to her, the responsibility to make sure she was safe from the media, the feds, and whoever else wanted a chunk of her?

"Kinley, we're going about this all wrong." Dominic

raked a hand through his hair.

Annabelle rolled her eyes. "You sure are."

Dominic ignored her. "Kinley, pet, we want you to marry us and live with us. We'll take care of you in every way. Is that understood?"

Annabelle rolled her eyes. "Doms. What is wrong with you?"

Hope lit up a corner of Kinley's heart, but she refused to settle for less than everything. She wouldn't be the girl who took less than she deserved ever again. "I won't live with men who see me as just a responsibility to be taken care of. I won't marry men who don't love me."

Dominic's eyes flared. "You haven't said the words either, pet."

He had a point, just not a good one. "I got shot saving you. That should speak very clearly about my feelings. After all, I'll bear the scars of loving you for the rest of my life."

Dominic turned stark white. He looked somewhere between horrified and tongue tied, and suddenly Kinley believed what they were trying to say. It took everything she had not to giggle. She loved teasing her Dom Dom.

"You will never do that again." He pointed a finger at her. "I swear to god, pet, if you ever throw yourself bodily in front of a bullet again, we will give you the spanking of a lifetime. You won't be able to sit down for a week. A month. And there will be no orgasms. Ever again."

Law moved in, wearing a grin on his rugged face. She loved seeing him smile. "Forgive him, baby. We're all still in a little bit of shock. We thought you were going to die, that we'd lost you. I love you, Kinley. And if you don't come home with us and be our wife, I'll do everything I can to persuade you. No, I suck at that. I'll pester you." He sighed. "Fuck that. I'll just kidnap you again until you say 'I do.'"

Riley glared at his brother. "Smooth, bro. Thanks." Then Riley focused all his attention on her. "I love you, Kinley. Will you please marry us?"

Tears filled her eyes, happy ones. After Simone, she knew how much it took for Riley to be the one to ask. "Yes, and I love you so much. You, too, my stubborn and humorless Master. I love you, Dom Dom."

Dominic laughed, the sound booming through the room and filling her with joy. "I love you, pet. And once you're healthy again, you'll see just how much."

They all surrounded her, crowding her as they began to talk about what had happened. They held her and kissed her and promised to never be apart.

Kinley sat back and relaxed because she was with her men. Her loves. Her future. Her forever.

###

Read on for excerpts from Lexi Blake, Shayla Black, and M.J. Rose.

Their Virgin Secretary
Masters of Ménage, Book 6
By Shayla Black and Lexi Blake
Coming April 15, 2014!

Three determined bosses…

Tate Baxter, Eric Cohen, and Kellan Kent are partners for one of the most respected law practices in Chicago. But these three masters of the courtroom also share a partnership in the bedroom, fulfilling the darkest needs of their female submissives night after night. Everything was fine—until they hired Annabelle Wright as their administrative assistant.

One beautiful secretary…

Belle felt sure she'd hit the jackpot with her job, but in the last year, the three gorgeous attorneys have become far more than her bosses. They're her friends, her protectors, and in Belle's dreams, they're her lovers, too. But she's given her heart to them all, so how can she choose just one?

An unforgettable night…

When her bosses escort her to a wedding, drinks and dancing turn into foreplay and fantasy. Between heated kisses, Belle admits her innocence. Surprise becomes contention and tempers flare. Heartbroken and unwilling to drive them apart, Belle leaves the firm and flees to New Orleans.

That leads to danger.

Resolved to restore her late grandmother's home, she hopes she can move on without the men. Then Kellan, Tate, and Eric show up at her doorstep, seeking another chance. But something sinister is at work in the Crescent City and its sights are set on her. Before the trio can claim Annabelle for good, they just might have to save her life.

* * * *

Excerpt:

One year, two months, and four days. Four hundred thirty days all totaled, but Tate hated to calculate their time together that way. It depressed him. Ten thousand three hundred twenty hours wasn't much better, considering that was how long he'd gone without sex. Because that was how long it had been since he'd first laid eyes on Annabelle Wright. She'd walked into his office with her resume in hand, and he'd just stared, dumbstruck. He didn't believe in love at first sight, but he'd found lust in that single glance. Oh, yeah. He'd taken one look at the goddess applying for a job and known exactly why he'd gone to the gym five times a week since he'd turned seventeen.

But love? He'd taken a whole week of consideration before deciding that he had fallen in love with Belle. After all, he was a careful man. He liked to think things out.

"Indulgence leads to chaos. Dominic is going to rue the day he let his sub run wild." Kellan frowned at Kinley, then swiveled his gaze toward the dance floor. "Who is that?"

Tate followed Kellan's line of sight and scowled. Belle danced with some overgrown ape whose smile seemed way too friendly. She looked gorgeous in her emerald cocktail dress. Its V-neck and body-fitting lines showed off her every curve. She wasn't a tall woman, but those crazy-sexy black shoes she wore made her legs look deliciously long. Tate had no idea how women maintained their balance while walking on those high, thin heels. He was pretty sure, however, they would look great wrapped around his neck.

The only thing he didn't like about the way Belle looked was the animated expression she turned up at the lug hanging on her. Then she laughed—a sound that always did strange things to his insides.

Eric slapped a big hand across his back. "Chill, buddy. That's Cole Lennox. He's a PI here in Dallas. We've used his company before. He's happily married. I don't think he's trying to mack on our girl."

Tate still didn't like it. "Why isn't he dancing with his wife?"

He was rational enough to know that jealousy was a completely illogical response in this situation. Technically, Belle wasn't his. She'd never even gone on a real date with him. They'd had lunch exactly fifty-two times over the last year, but they'd mostly talked about work. He'd taken her to happy hour fifteen times, where she always ordered vodka tonics, Cîroc, or Grey Goose, with a half a twist of lime. They'd still talked about work. And the weather. None of that counted, though, because she'd treated him like a colleague, not a boyfriend. He hadn't kissed her yet or made his intentions clear, so he had no right to be jealous that Belle danced with another man. For once, he didn't care if he made less than perfect sense.

Kellan pointed to the other end of the floor. "He can't. His brother is dancing with her. They're twins and I've heard they share."

"Really?" Tate sat up and sent a challenging glance to Kell and Eric. "I'm seeing a picture here. The Lennox twins married the same girl. Those three oil tycoons over there have one wife, and we all saw the three royal princes walk in with their bride. Hell, the whole board of Anthony Anders decided to marry the same woman. But it can't work for us? Explain that."

That was the argument Tate had heard from Eric and especially Kellan for the past year, ever since the night they'd sat around the office and each admitted they were crazy about their new secretary. Administrative Assistant. Office Manager. Belle changed her title more than once. She took exception to the term secretary, but Tate thought it was kind of hot.

Kellan sighed, turning toward him. "Just because it works for some other people doesn't mean it would work for the two of you."

"The two of us? Really? You're still going to play it that way?" Eric challenged. "Tell me you don't want her, too."

Kellan's eyes hooded. Tate had made almost a scientific study of his friends in an attempt to really understand them. Kellan had four major expressions that he used like masks. This particular one Tate had named "stubborn asshole." Kellan used it a lot.

"Of course I want her. I've never denied that. She's a beautiful woman, not to mention lovely, kind, and very smart. If I was interested in getting married again, I would be all over her. But I'm not, and I doubt she's the type of woman to have no-strings-attached sex."

"I want strings." Tate needed to make that brutally clear because his partners seemed to constantly forget. They should take notes during their conversations the way he often did. But again, no one asked his opinion. "I want to be tangled up in all her strings. She's the one. I get that what we want is unusual, though it really doesn't seem that way today. I swear the two dogs are the only non-ménage relationship here. Belle might be surprised that we all want her, but she's not going to be shocked. She's fine with Kinley's marriage."

Eric sighed. "Maybe, but we need to be careful. She hasn't dated anyone since she started working with us."

Tate knew that very well since he'd been keeping an eye on her. Hopefully she never knew the extent of his observation because what he'd done was illegal. And possibly a little stalkerish.

"There's some reason for that," Eric went on.

Didn't they get it? "Because she's waiting for us to make a move."

"Or she's just working hard and isn't ready to settle down," Kellan pointed out. "She's young, man."

"It's not like we're old."

Tate didn't feel old. He was thirty-two. Given that the average life expectancy of an American male was seventy-six, that didn't sound old. Then he did the math and realized that he was forty-two percent of the way through his accepted life expectancy. Forty-two percent—closing in on half. When he looked at it that way, he did feel old. He refused to waste another second.

"That's it." Tate stood and straightened his tie. "I'm going in."

God, he hoped he looked halfway decent because he often got rumpled and didn't notice. He would probably still be wearing pocket protectors if he hadn't become good friends with Eric in tenth grade.

He'd tutored Eric through rudimentary algebra, and Eric had taught him that jeans weren't supposed to hit above the ankles. They'd been a weird duo, the jock and the nerd. But their relationship meant more to him than any other. His parents were cold intellectuals who told him he'd failed by not going into academic pursuits—because yeah, Harvard law had been a breeze. His brothers cared more about their experiments than their family. So Tate and Eric had stuck together like blood, and Kellan had joined them after college.

But Tate realized in that moment that he needed more. He needed Belle. So did they, but she had to come first. "I'm going to do it. I'm going to offer her my penis."

Eric's head hit the table and he groaned. "Dude, how do you ever get laid?"

So he wasn't smooth. At least he was honest. "She already has my heart. I would like for her to take my penis, too. Is that so much to ask?"

"If you ask her like that, she'll just smack you," Kellan pointed out.

Frustration welled. He sat back down. "Damn it, that's why we need to go after her as a pack. I'm not good at the smooth stuff."

"By smooth stuff, he means any type of actual

communication with a woman." Eric rolled his eyes.

They were totally missing the point. "I communicate fine. She'll know what I want and how I want it."

"Which is precisely why she'll know where she wants to slap you next." Kellan shook his head. "This might be a bad idea, but it couldn't hurt for you to dance with her. Can you do that without asking her to take your penis in marriage?"

He wasn't completely sure. His cock had a mind of its own. "I think I can handle it."

"Good. Go on, then. I'll talk to Eric." Kell sighed. "I guess we really do need to figure out how to handle her. I can't stand the thought of another uncomfortable plane trip back. She didn't talk to me the whole flight down. Taking the hands-off approach isn't working. I get the feeling she's just about ready to throw in the towel and leave all of us." Kellan's eyes narrowed suddenly. "And that asshole isn't married. Go. Make sure he doesn't get his hands on Belle."

Tate's stare zipped to her. Sure enough, a guy was cutting in on Lennox. He leered down at Annabelle, then peered straight at her boobs.

Those boobs were his, damn it. At least he fully intended for those boobs to belong to him. Well, a third of them anyway. "You two work it out because I'm making a move by the end of the night…"

Theirs To Cherish

Wicked Lovers, Book 8
By Shayla Black
Now Available!

The perfect place for a woman on the run to disappear…

Accused of a horrific murder she didn't commit, former heiress Callie Ward has been a fugitive since she was sixteen—until she found the perfect hideout, Club Dominion. The only problem is she's fallen for the club's Master, Mitchell Thorpe, who keeps her at arm's length. Little does she know that his reasons for not getting involved have everything to do with his wounded heart…and his consuming desire for her.

To live out her wildest fantasies…

Enter Sean Kirkpatrick, a Dom who's recently come to Dominion and taken a pointed interest in Callie. Hoping to make Thorpe jealous, she submits to Sean one shuddering sigh at a time. It isn't long before she realizes she's falling for him too. But the tender lover who's slowly seducing her body and earning her trust isn't who he claims…

And to fall in love.

When emotions collide and truths are exposed, Sean is willing to risk all to keep Callie from slipping through his fingers. But he's not the only man looking to stake a claim. Now Callie is torn between Sean and Thorpe, and though she's unsure whom she can trust, she'll have to surrender her body and soul to both—if she wants to elude a killer…

* * * *

Callie trembled as she lay back on the padded table and Sean Kirkpatrick's strong fingers wrapped around her cuffed wrist, guiding it back to the bindings above her head.

"I don't know if I can do this," she murmured.

He paused, then drew in a breath as if he sought patience. "Breathe, lovely."

That gentle, deep brogue of his native Scotland brought her peace. His voice both aroused and soothed her, and she tried to let those feelings wash through her. "Can you do that for me?" he asked.

His fingers uncurled from her wrist, and he grazed the inside of her outstretched arm with his knuckles. As always, his touch was full of quiet strength. He made her ache. She shivered again, this time for an entirely different reason.

"I'll try."

Sean shook his head, his deep blue eyes seeming to see everything she tried to hide inside. That penetrating stare scared the hell out of her. What did he see when he looked at her? How much about the real her had he pieced together?

The thought made her panic. No one could know her secret. No one. She'd kept it from everyone, even Thorpe, during her four years at Dominion. She'd finally found a place where she felt safe, comfortable. Of course she'd have to give it up someday, probably soon. She always did. But please, not yet.

Deep breath. Don't panic. Sean wants your submission, not your secrets.

"You'll need to do better than try. You've been 'trying' for over six months," he reminded her gently. "Do you think I'd truly hurt you?"

No. Sean didn't seem to have a violent bone in his body. He wasn't a sadist. He never gripped her harshly. He never even raised his voice. She'd jokingly thought of him as the sub whisperer because he pushed her boundaries with a gentleness she found both irresistible and insidious. Certainly, he'd dragged far more out of her than any other man had. Tirelessly, he'd worked to earn her trust. Callie felt terrible that she could never give it, not when doing so could be fatal.

Guilt battered her. She should stop wasting his time.

"I know you wouldn't," she assured, blinking up at him, willing him to understand.

"Of course not." He pressed his chest over hers, leaning closer to delve into her eyes.

Callie couldn't resist lowering her lids, shutting out the rest of the world. Even knowing she shouldn't, she sank into the soft reassurance of his kiss. Each brush of his lips over hers soothed and aroused. Every time he touched her, her heart raced. Her skin grew tight. Her nipples hardened. Her pussy moistened and swelled. Her heart ached. Sean Kirkpatrick would be so easy to love.

As his fingers filtered into her hair, cradling her scalp, she exhaled and melted into his kiss—just for a sweet moment. It was the only one she could afford.

A fierce yearning filled her. She longed for him to peel off his clothes, kiss her with that determination she oft en saw stamped into his eyes, and take her with the single-minded fervor she knew he was capable of. But in the months since he'd collared her, he'd done nothing more than stroke her body, tease her, and grant her orgasms when he thought she'd earned them. She hadn't let him fully restrain her. And he hadn't yet taken her to bed.

Not knowing the feel of him deep inside her, of waiting and wanting until her body throbbed relentlessly, was making her buckets full of crazy.

After another skillful brush of his lips, Sean ended the kiss and lifted his head, breathing hard. She clung, not ready to let him go. How had he gotten under her skin so quickly? His tenderness filled her veins like a drug. The way he had addicted Callie terrified her.

"I want you. Sean, please . . ." She damn near wept.

With a broad hand, he swept the stray hair from her face.

Regret softened his blue eyes before he ever said a word. “If you’re not ready to trust me as your Dom, do you think you’re ready for me as a lover? I want you completely open to me before we take that step. All you have to do is trust me, lovely.”

Callie slammed her eyes shut. This was so fucking pointless. She wanted to trust Sean, yearned to give him everything—devotion, honesty, faith. Her past ensured that she’d never give any of those to anyone. But he had feelings for her. About that, she had no doubt. They’d grown just as hers had, unexpectedly, over time, a fledgling limb morphing into a sturdy vine that eventually created a bud just waiting to blossom . . . or die.

She knew which. They could never have more than this faltering Dom/sub relationship, destined to perish in a premature winter.

She should never have accepted his collar, not when she should be trying to keep her distance from everyone. The responsible choice now would be to call her safe word, walk out, quit him. Release them both from this hell. Never look back.

For the first time in nearly a decade, Callie worried that she might not have the strength to say good-bye.

What was wrong with her tonight? She was too emotional. She needed to pull up her big-girl panties and snap on her bratty attitude, pretend that nothing mattered. It was how she’d coped for years. But she couldn’t seem to manage that with Sean.

“You’re up in your head, instead of here with me,” he gently rebuked her.

Another dose of guilt blistered her. “Sorry, Sir.”

Sean sighed heavily, stood straight, then held out his hand to her. “Come with me.”

Callie winced. If he intended to stop the scene, that could only mean he wanted to talk. These sessions where he tried to dig through her psyche became more painful than the sexless nights she spent in unfulfilled longing under his sensual torture.

Swallowing down her frustration, she dredged up her courage, then put her hand in his.

Holding her in a steady grip, Sean led her to the far side of Dominion's dungeon, to a bench in a shadowed corner. As soon as she could see the rest of the room, Callie felt eyes on her, searing her skin. With a nonchalant glance, she looked at the others scening around them, but they seemed lost in their own world of pleasure, pain, groans, sweat, and need. A lingering sweep of the room revealed another sight that had the power to drop her to her knees. Thorpe in the shadows. Staring. At her with Sean. His expression wasn't one of disapproval exactly . . . but he wasn't pleased.

Dungeon Royale
Masters and Mercenaries, Book 6
By Lexi Blake
Now Available!

An agent broken

MI6 agent Damon Knight prided himself on always being in control. His missions were executed with cold, calculating precision. His club, The Garden, was run with an equally ordered and detached decadence. But his perfect world was shattered by one bullet, fired from the gun of his former partner. That betrayal almost cost him his life and ruined his career. His handlers want him to retire, threatening to revoke his license to kill if he doesn't drop his obsession with a shadowy organization called The Collective. To earn their trust, he has to prove himself on a unique assignment with an equally unusual partner.

A woman tempted

Penelope Cash has spent her whole life wanting more. More passion. More adventure. But duty has forced her to live a quiet life. Her only excitement is watching the agents of MI6 as they save England and the world. Despite her training, she's only an analyst. The closest she is allowed to danger and intrigue is in her dreams, which are often filled with one Damon Knight. But everything changes when the woman assigned to pose as Damon's submissive on his latest mission is incapacitated. Penny is suddenly faced with a decision. Stay in her safe little world or risk her life, and her heart, for Queen and country.

An enemy revealed

With the McKay-Taggart team at their side, Damon and Penny hunt an international terrorist across the great cities of Northern Europe. Playing the part of her Master, Damon begins to learn that under Penny's mousy exterior is a passionate submissive, one who just might lay claim to his cold heart. But when Damon's true enemy is brought out of the shadows, it might be Penny who pays the ultimate price.

* * * *

"I'm going to kiss you now, Penelope."

"What?"

"You seem to have an enormously hard time understanding me today. We're going to have to work on our communication skills." Damon moved right between her legs, spreading her knees and making a place for himself there. One minute she was utterly gobsmacked by the chaos he'd brought into her life in a couple of hours' time, and the next, she couldn't manage to breathe. He invaded her space, looming over her. Despite the fact that she was sitting on the counter, he still looked down at her. "You said yes. That means you're mine, Penelope. You're my partner and my submissive. I take care of what's mine."

She swallowed, forcing herself to look into those stormy eyes of his. He was so close, she could smell the scent of his aftershave, feel the heat his big body gave off. "For the mission."

"I don't know about that," he returned, his voice deepening. "If this goes well, I get to go back out in the field. It's always good to have a cover. Men are less threatening when they have a woman with them. If you like fieldwork, there's no reason you can't come with me. Especially if you're properly trained. Tell me how much your siblings know."

She shook her head before finally realizing what he was

asking. His fingers worked their way into her hair, smoothing it back, forcing her to keep eye contact with him. "Oh, about work, you mean. Everyone in my family thinks I work for Reeding Corporation in their publishing arm. They think I translate books."

The Reeding Corporation was one of several companies that fronted for SIS. When she'd hired on, she'd signed documentation that stated she would never expose who she truly worked for.

"Excellent. If they research me, they'll discover I'm an executive at Reeding. We've been having an affair for the last three months. You were worried about your position at the company and the fact that I'm your superior, but I transferred to another department and now we're free to be open about our relationship."

"I don't know that they'll believe we're lovers."

"Of course, they will. I'm very persuasive, love. Now, I'm going to kiss you and I'm going to put my hand in your knickers. You are wearing knickers, aren't you?"

"Of course."

He shuddered. "Not anymore. Knickers are strictly forbidden. I told you I would likely get into your knickers, but what I really meant was I can't tolerate them and you're not to wear them at all anymore. I've done you the enormous service of making it easy on you and tossing out the ones you had in the house."

His right hand brushed against her breast. The nipple responded by peaking immediately, as if it were a magnet drawn to Damon's skin.

"You can't toss my knickers out, Damon. And you can't put your hand there. We're in the ladies' room for heaven's sake."

"Here's the first rule, love. Don't tell me what I can't do." His mouth closed over hers, heat flashing through her system.

His mouth was sweet on hers, not an outright assault at first. This was persuasion. Seduction. His lips teased at hers, playing and coaxing.

And his hand made its way down, skimming across her waist to her thigh.

"Let me in, Penelope." He whispered the words against her mouth.

Drugged. This was what it felt like to be drugged. She'd been tipsy before, but no wine had ever made her feel as out of control as Damon's kiss.

Out of control and yet oddly safe. Safe enough to take a chance.

On his next pass, she opened for him, allowing him in, and the kiss morphed in a heartbeat from sweet to overpowering.

She could practically feel the change in him. He surged in, a marauder gaining territory. His tongue commanded hers, sliding over and around, his left hand tangling in her hair and getting her at the angle he wanted. Captured. She felt the moment he turned from seduction to Dominance, and now she understood completely why they capitalized the word. Damon didn't merely kiss her. She'd been kissed before, little brushes of lips to hers, fumblings that ended in embarrassment, long attempts at bringing up desire. This wasn't a kiss. This was possession.

He'd said she belonged to him for the course of the mission, and now she understood what he meant. He meant to invade every inch of her life, putting his stamp on her. If she proceeded, he would take over. He would run her life and she would be forced to fight him for every inch of freedom she might have.

"That's right, love. You touch me. I want you to touch me. If you belong to me, then my body is yours, too."

She hadn't realized her hands were moving. She'd cupped his bum even as his fingers slid along the band of her knickers, under and over, sliding along her female flesh.

He'd said exactly the right thing. He hadn't made her self-conscious. He'd told her he would give as good as he got. It wasn't some declaration of love, but she'd had that before and it proved false. Damon Knight was offering her something different. He was offering her the chance to explore without shame.

Seduction: A Novel of Suspense

by M.J. Rose

Available Now!

A gothic tale about Victor Hugo's long-buried secrets and the power of a love that never dies . . . In 1843, novelist Victor Hugo's beloved nineteen-year-old daughter drowned. Ten years later, still grieving, Hugo initiated hundreds of séances from his home on the Isle of Jersey in order to reestablish contact with her. In the process, he claimed to have communed with Plato, Galileo, Shakespeare, Dante, Jesus and even the devil himself. Hugo's transcriptions of these conversations have all been published.

Or so it has been believed . . .

Recovering from a great loss, mythologist Jac L'Etoile thinks that throwing herself into work will distract her from her grief. In the hopes of uncovering a secret about the islands mysterious Celtic roots, she arrives on Jersey and is greeted by ghostly Neolithic monuments, medieval castles and hidden caves. But the man who has invited her there, a troubled soul named Theo Gaspard, hopes she'll help him discover something quite different—transcripts of Hugo's lost conversations with someone he called the Shadow of the Sepulcher. Central to his heritage, these are the papers his grandfather died trying to find. Neither Jac nor Theo anticipate that the mystery surrounding Victor Hugo will threaten their sanity and put their very lives at stake.

Seduction is a historically evocative and atmospheric tale of suspense with a spellbinding ghost story at its heart, written by one of Americas most gifted and imaginative novelists. Awakening a mystery that spans centuries, this multi-layered gothic tale brings a time, a place and a cast of desperate characters brilliantly to life.

* * * *

I remembered Juliette saying she would tell her maidservant to be on alert in case I needed anything.

"*Bonsoir*, Monsieur Hugo."

I nodded. "*Bonsoir*, Fantine."

"Madame said you might be hungry. Can I make you something more substantial?"

"No, I'm fine with this." I gestured at the plate.

"Everyone in town is talking about you finding that girl. It's quite wonderful."

"We all found her."

"But they are saying it was you. Yes?"

"Well, yes, but only because I went down the stairs first."

"Finding a lost child is a very worthy day's worth."

The melancholy expression in your eyes spoke more than your words. I knew what you were thinking. And as I looked, I admit I noticed more than the expression in your eyes. The sweep of your hair, your sweet scent, the swell of your breast under your chemise, I took them all in.

"Would you like some wine?" I asked.

You hesitated for a moment, then something flared in your eyes and replaced the sadness. Bravery? Rebellion?

Taking a glass from the cupboard, you sat down beside me. Poured some wine and then drank.

"The child was unharmed?"

I finished chewing the bread and swallowed. "She had a nasty cut on her arm, but that will heal."

"How did she get to the basement of the castle in the first place?"

"She said that she followed a dog who'd been playing outside her window."

"But there's more to it than that, isn't there? I hear it in your voice."

I shrugged, not ready to talk about the stranger events that I'd witnessed. Or thought I had. At that juncture, I hadn't even accepted what I'd seen. I was troubled by the possibility that my mind was touched and I'd manufactured a vision.

"What have you been doing this evening?" I asked, anxious to change the conversation.

"Sitting by the window, watching the sea. You would have thought that by now I would have stopped waiting. I know he is not coming. That he will never come."

"Why won't he?"

"His family. They didn't approve of me. I was working-class, he was aristocracy. They threatened him with his inheritance. After I'd been here for a few months I realized his having me come ahead and saying that he'd meet me was all an elaborate lie. It was just a ruse to get rid of me and the child he had no intention of legitimizing. And yet I watch the sea. I know there's no reason to hope, and yet sometimes when I hear a ship's horn coming into port, I still think..."

"Hope is the most difficult emotion to give up."

"What do you hope for, Monsieur Hugo?"

"That you will let me seduce you." I ran my thumb back and forth across your palm. The soft skin not hardened yet by housework. Juliette employed a laundress. I was glad of that. It would have been a shame to ruin that silkiness.

I waited for your reaction. When you neither resisted nor responded to my touch, I lifted your hand to my mouth and pressed my lips against your palm. I smelled a sophisticated and delicious scent. Lust surged inside me, which was a welcome distraction from the disturbing events of the last twenty-four hours.

"Is the perfume I smell one your father created?"

"No, it's one that I made. I have a small laboratory in an unused bedroom."

"Could I see it?"

"Of course."

"Your blush makes me desire you that much more. Your innocence is a delight," I said.

Following you upstairs, I watched your skirts move and caught sight of your ankles. I imagined putting my hand up that dress and searching out the warm wet spot between your legs. I wondered if you perfumed yourself there the way some Frenchwomen did.

At the landing, instead of turning left toward Juliette's room, we turned right. I'd never explored this end of the house as there'd been no reason to before. I smelled which way to go. Led like a dog by the nose to the far end of the hall.

As you opened the door a cacophony of scents reached out and embraced me. I'd never smelled such a rich, complicated aroma. For a second I closed my eyes and just inhaled. I was transported to a lush flower field, a spice market, a citrus grove, the forest and the sea all at once.

When I opened my eyes again I was surprised at how bare and unadorned the room actually was. The smells were so decorative and elaborate. The furniture consisted of a long table, a single chair and a tall glass-fronted cabinet. There were two frosted glass wall sconces and a fairly simple two-tiered crystal chandelier already lit. Noticing that, I surmised you'd been working.

There was a bay window. And it faced the sea.

But the room was full of your utensils and supplies. Everywhere were gleaming glass jars, canisters, small bottles and large beakers. Around me, the smell evolved. I found myself thinking I was inside a library, then a church, then a bedroom smelling a lover's body, hot with want.

The whole world of scents resided in this one single room. How was it possible?

"This is amazing. You are a true alchemist," I said.

"No, just a perfumer."

"Certainly that. Certainly that. Tell me, Fantine, why are you working as a lady's maid if you have all this talent?"

"I'm a woman, monsieur. You of all men know that. No establishment in Paris would have me except to wait on customers and fill bottles. Women are not noses. We do not create."

"Would you like to open a store in Jersey?"

Your shrug saddened me. There was so little energy in the

movement of your shoulders.

"No. It's enough for me to mix up scents for Madame Juliette and her friends. I do it to please her and because I miss my father and my home. While I work, I can pretend I'm back there for a little while."

"But I might be able to help you set up a thriving concern and sell your perfumes in the village. Perhaps you'd find some joy in it that you can't anticipate. Madame Juliette is an independent woman. Can't you use her as role model?"

I knew when you didn't answer it was because you were too well bred to argue with me. What I'd said wasn't true any longer. Juliette had been independent when I'd met her. But she'd since given up acting to accompany me, and now she was as dependent as my wife was.

"Do you have all the materials you need? All the utensils?"

"That's very kind, but I have everything. Madame Juliette orders what I need from Paris."

"Will you at least show me how you mix a scent? Make one for me?"

Finally you gifted me with a smile.

I settled in the chair and watched your performance, fascinated with the change in you as you worked. You were animated in a way you hadn't been before. The haunted look in your eyes was replaced by a determined concentration as you picked up one vial and then another, sniffing and searching and then settling on which one to use. Every movement was assured and knowledgeable, and I found myself as entertained as if I were at one of Juliette's plays. Drop by drop the formula in the tube filled up. Every so often you would dip a small length of ribbon in the liquid, wave it in the air, then close your eyes and inhale its essence.

I imagined you were dreaming your own dream, oblivious that I was even there. And that increased my desire for you. Often the wanting is more satisfying than the fulfillment. I have come to prefer anticipation to satiation. Longing can make one feel alive in a more profound way. You see everything through champagne bubbles. Your senses are alert. You imagine how your lover's lips will feel, how her skin will taste. What it will be like to unbutton her chemise, slip it off her shoulders, press your mouth to her skin, cup her breasts in your palms and feel her excitement harden her nipples. You picture her leaning into you, showing you just enough of her want that it ignites yours.

That knowing is all. You forget your enemies, your fears and your nightmares.

To live in the moment of desire is to be yourself in the most pure and painful way possible, because beneath every touch is the knowledge of how fleeting the pleasure is. How elusive the passion. How impossible it is to contain it for long.

"I think you might like this." You held out a small container filled with topaz liquid.

I held it up to my nose.

"No."

I was pleased to hear your laugh as you shook your head.

"Never smell directly from the bottle. Scent needs to breathe and interact with your skin. You have to put some on."

I held the vial out. "Would you please put it on me?"

A moment's hesitation. Your uncertainty was charming and seductive. The moment was a river to cross. On one side was the past, on the other side the future. I wondered what you were thinking. Then you tipped the bottle, wet your forefinger and gently ran your fingertip down the inside of my right wrist and then my left. I shuddered at your touch.

The scent wafted up and filled the air. You'd captured the scent of a primitive forest. Mysterious and woody. I visualized deep grottoes and mossy glens. I traveled a whole journey in just one inhalation.

"So is this how you see me?" I asked.

"My father taught me to paint portraits in perfume."

"Perfume portraits," I repeated, never having heard the expression before and enchanted by it. "Can you put on more?" I was teasing, testing, and was delighted when you obliged and touched your wet finger to small space behind my left ear.

"There are other places too," I said.

"I know." A whisper of a laugh. Was it excitement or just nervousness?

I took the perfume and put my finger over the top of the bottle. "Would you let me do the same to you?"

"If it would please you."

"What about its pleasing you, Fantine?"

That shrug, again without enthusiasm. I wanted to make you feel, push you to enjoy. I unbuttoned your top blouse button. When you didn't resist, I worked on another button. I might as well have been buttering toast. You didn't care at all, one way or the other.

"What are you thinking? Why do you look so sad?" I asked.

"You are making me remember that I used to care about a man touching me."

"Do you want me to stop?"

"No, it's all right. If you want to . . . please . . ."

I finished unbuttoning your chemise and pulled it down off your shoulders. Your skin glowed in the candlelight. It was the color of the inside of a nautilus shell. Your breasts were small but perfect. I wet my finger with perfume and painted circles around each nipple. Then I leaned forward and got drunk on the scent of the flowers on your skin.

My ministrations were not unpleasant to you. I knew that. I'd been with enough women. You didn't pull back in repulsion. But neither did you arch or purr. You simply didn't care what I did. My efforts to reach you were failing.

And yet you were willing to let me pleasure myself with you. That was something of a conundrum.

Then you slipped off your chemise and stood facing me, naked to the waist. God forgive me but I thought of nothing but burying myself inside you and forgetting everything else. I smelled skin, scented flowers and thought this must be what Eden smelled like, and then I slipped into an embracing wholeness that gave me shelter and soothed my soul while at the same time inflamed me.

I'd never made love to someone so dispassionate who was not a professional. I didn't understand. Why were you allowing this? Why were you willing to give yourself to me this way? What was wrong with you that I couldn't move you—not with my fingers or my words? But as I put my lips to your lips, I determined to discover your mystery, not thinking that learning about it might mean our very destruction.

About Shayla Black

Shayla Black (aka Shelley Bradley) is the New York Times and USA Today bestselling author of over 40 sizzling contemporary, erotic, paranormal, and historical romances produced via traditional, small press, independent, and audio publishing. She lives in Texas with her husband, munchkin, and one very spoiled cat. In her "free" time, she enjoys reality TV, reading and listening to an eclectic blend of music.

Shayla's books have been translated in about a dozen languages. RT Bookclub has nominated her for a Career Achievement award in erotic romance, twice nominated her for Best Erotic Romance of the year, as well as awarded her several Top Picks, and a KISS Hero Award. She has also received or been nominated for The Passionate Plume, The Holt Medallion, Colorado Romance Writers Award of Excellence, and the National Reader's Choice Awards.

A writing risk-taker, Shayla enjoys tackling writing challenges with every new book.

Connect with Shayla online:

Facebook: www.facebook.com/ShaylaBlackAuthor
Twitter: www.twitter.com/@shayla_black
Website: www.shaylablack.com

About Lexi Blake

Lexi Blake lives in North Texas with her husband, three kids, and the laziest rescue dog in the world. She began writing at a young age, concentrating on plays and journalism. It wasn't until she started writing romance that she found success. She likes to find humor in the strangest places. Lexi believes in happy endings no matter how odd the couple, threesome or foursome may seem. She also writes contemporary Western ménage as Sophie Oak.

Connect with Lexi online:

Facebook: Lexi Blake
Twitter: twitter.com/authorlexiblake
Website: www.LexiBlake.net

Sign up for Lexi's free newsletter at www.LexiBlake.net.

Also from Shayla Black and Lexi Blake

Masters Of Ménage
Their Virgin Captive
Their Virgin's Secret
Their Virgin Concubine
Their Virgin Princess
Their Virgin Hostage
Their Virgin Secretary, Coming April 15, 2014

Also from Shayla Black/Shelley Bradley

EROTIC ROMANCE
THE WICKED LOVERS
Wicked Ties
Decadent
Delicious
Surrender To Me
Belong To Me
"Wicked to Love" (e-novella)
Mine To Hold
"Wicked All The Way" (e-novella)
Ours To Love
Wicked and Dangerous
Forever Wicked
Theirs To Cherish

SEXY CAPERS
Bound And Determined
Strip Search
"Arresting Desire" – Hot In Handcuffs Anthology

DOMS OF HER LIFE
One Dom To Love
The Young And The Submissive

STAND ALONE
Naughty Little Secret (as Shelley Bradley)
"Watch Me" – Sneak Peek Anthology (as Shelley Bradley)
Dangerous Boys And Their Toy
"Her Fantasy Men" – Four Play Anthology

PARANORMAL ROMANCE
THE DOOMSDAY BRETHREN
Tempt Me With Darkness
"Fated" (e-novella)

Seduce Me In Shadow
Possess Me At Midnight
"Mated" – Haunted By Your Touch Anthology
Entice Me At Twilight
Embrace Me At Dawn

HISTORICAL ROMANCE (as Shelley Bradley)
The Lady And The Dragon
One Wicked Night
Strictly Seduction
Strictly Forbidden

CONTEMPORARY ROMANCE (as Shelley Bradley)
A Perfect Match

Also from Lexi Blake

EROTIC ROMANCE

Masters And Mercenaries
The Dom Who Loved Me
The Men With The Golden Cuffs
A Dom Is Forever
On Her Master's Secret Service
Sanctum: A Masters and Mercenaries Novella
Love and Let Die
Unconditional: A Masters and Mercenaries Novella
Dungeon Royale
Dungeon Games: A Masters and Mercenaries Novella, *Coming May 13, 2014*
A View to a Thrill, *Coming August 19, 2014*

CONTEMPORARY WESTERN ROMANCE

Wild Western Nights
Leaving Camelot, *Coming Soon*

URBAN FANTASY

Thieves
Steal the Light
Steal the Day
Steal the Moon
Steal the Sun
Steal the Night, *Coming June 10, 2014*

Made in the USA
San Bernardino, CA
02 May 2014